MERIT-HUNTERS SERIES

Crowned Worthy

MERIT-HUNTERS SERIES

Crowned Worthy

L.G. Jenkins

malcolm down

PUBLISHING

First published 2021 by Malcolm Down Publishing Ltd
www.malcolmdown.co.uk

24 23 22 21 20   7 6 5 4 3 2 1

British Library Cataloguing in Publication Data

A catalogue record for this book is available from the British Library.

ISBN 978-1-912863-70-9

Cover design by Esther Kotecha
Art direction by Sarah Grace
Printed in the UK

Dedication

To you, the reader.

Chapter One

It wasn't often that Ajay Ambers felt this alive. He kept telling himself it was a good thing. Healthy. Refreshing. It would give him that extra edge, as he'd be more alert than his colleagues. Yet there was still the nauseating reality that they'd all been there hours before him. He inhaled and closed his eyes, allowing the stale air to fill his lungs; he listened to the subtle hum of the sky train as it glided above the City below.

Opening his eyes again, Ajay suddenly noticed that he recognised no one in this carriage. Of course, living in a city of millions, this shouldn't have surprised him, but it did. Usually, when he wasn't painfully late, he managed to see the same people. There was the young girl who always tied her hair up in buns and wore a bright coloured anorak, even when storms weren't forecast, over some short skirt. She always stood by the doors, scrolling through her Watch.

Today, her place was taken by an older lady whose face was hidden from him by the black screen projecting from her wrist. Ajay admired her royal blue dress and golden earrings. He assumed she must be someone important. He glanced down to make sure his tie was still straight, and his shirt was still tucked in. Another common appearance on his usual commute was Ugly Briefcase Man, as he called him. This guy would sit down on one of the few seats with his briefcase on his lap, scowling at the world behind his thick, dark eyebrows and constantly tapping his clown feet impatiently until the train arrived at his station. Ajay often considered 'accidentally' stepping on his feet so the annoyance would stop. He never did. That would be rude, and no merit was available for rudeness. But he *had* been tempted to steal the briefcase, just to know what was in it. Wasn't everything he needed on his Watch? So, he supposed, there was a positive reason to be late: no annoying foot tapping.

Ajay did miss the other guy a little bit. His train mate. Well, they weren't friends. They didn't even know each other, but Ajay wondered if they might become acquainted one day. It was strange how seeing the same person every day made him believe he knew them. For example, Ajay knew that he lived in his neighbourhood on the Outer-Inner-Ring, as they boarded at the same stop. He also knew that the guy must be well off credit-wise, as he often wore the latest brands of office wear and also, without fail, had varying Watch strap designs. They didn't come cheap. One week this guy had blue lightning bolts, which Ajay thought was cool. The next, his wrist was wrapped in emoji smiley faces. Ajay wasn't so keen on that one. He also knew that his train mate must have had Glorified connections or at least worked there, because Ajay's stop was the one before the Quarters and they never departed together. Ajay often wondered what it would be like to have a permanent job in the Quarters, rather than just to volunteer there.

Maybe one day his train mate would tell him.

Genni often told him he was a creep for thinking so much about a guy he didn't know. Over the years, he had exhausted the tactic of passing time by Watch scrolling or clicking on personalised adverts for merit-making bonuses and educational movies, so what else would he do? This time, without his usual commute gang with him, he opted to look out the window, something he and others rarely did.

With this unusual moment of reflection, Ajay felt a strange sense of gratitude. It must be the natural sleep making him soppy, he thought. But he just marvelled for a second over the place in which he lived. A thriving metropolis that never stopped sparkling. Skyscraper windows glinting in the white sunlight, driverless cars gracefully sliding past each other, drones moving peacefully like a flock of birds in flight, and thousands of billboard adverts flickering with colour. It was a masterpiece, and he loved to be part of it.

The moment of reflection was gone as the advert for a new line of 0.5% beer caught Ajay's eye. As the train pulled into its next stop, Ajay lifted his wrist so his projected screen was in line with the billboard. He just managed to scan it before the train moved away again with its fast yet silent simplicity. Looking down at his Watch, Ajay ordered a crate of the beers. He'd pick them up later. As he went to shut down his screen, he saw an email pop through. He didn't fully digest its contents, something about a meeting today, but it did send his mind back to work and how late he was. A pang of anxiety crept across his chest.

He and Genni had overslept this morning. Or rather, they'd absolutely indulged in sleep. Eight straight hours of solid shut-eye. They'd both been a bit frantic when they woke up.

"I can't believe this . . ." Genni had been ranting and flapping her arms about, as if she was trying to dance but failing badly. Nothing was attractive to Ajay in that moment. She had tossed her red dress on and begun to throw stuff into her handbag with enough speed and frustration that each item had landed with a sharp clunk. Ajay barely acknowledged her at first, as he'd rushed from the shower with a towel wrapped around his waist. Genni sat down at her dressing table.

"*Morning, Genni.*"

A soft, mechanical female voice sounded from behind the mirrored screen. It had informed her that her facial pores had improved by 14% but recommended increasing her moisturiser routine. Ajay could tell Genni was frustrated by it with the way she'd smacked her make-up brushes back into their containers.

"Is that thing seriously telling you to put more products on your face? If anything, your skin is looking drier," Ajay had said.

That was his mistake. That comment. After that, Genni had slouched her shoulders and started to mumble words that Ajay presumed were profanities. He didn't really know why he'd said it. It was a slip of the tongue, or maybe somehow he thought sharing her frustration might make her feel better. Usually he was very good at keeping his thoughts to himself. He preferred to judge silently without the consequences. This morning, though, it was as if his filter had fallen out his mouth for a moment. Then again, he told himself, he was gracious enough not to highlight the rip he'd noticed in the armpit of her red dress. He had just let her go without burdening her with the weight of another imperfection. Ajay felt the train tip slightly, as it took one of its spiral route's sharp curves. He and others around him grabbed quickly at the yellow handrails. It felt cold on Ajay's skin, a nice relief from the clammy desert air. Once they were around the bend, it was Ajay's stop.

He stepped out onto the platform and didn't hesitate to advance towards the steps down to the lower street level. Marching past the all too familiar line of the station's digital displays, he hesitated slightly as he noticed that one of them had changed. It was once an advert for a line of very provocative female swimsuits, now replaced with a message about safe credit investments. A massive change in vibe, Ajay thought, as he moved quickly into the hustle and bustle. He always took a small, discreet breath before he was engulfed by the crowds. It was the street sellers that bothered him the most. He closed his nostrils from the smell of Standard Meat and ducked for escape from those displaying products on floating monitors. Today, he noticed one sweaty man trying to flog a few knock-off necklaces. The thought did occur to Ajay to get one for Genni. *Come on, she's worth more than that.* He corrected himself and pressed on towards the Prosper building.

"Fella." Ajay heard a gruff voice scramble after him. He ignored it and kept walking. "Fella, hey. You at Prosper? I got books and movies to help your merit."

The man was mid-20s, probably around Ajay's age, and was wearing a tattered, dark green vest. Small wisps of black chest hair protruded out from its neckline. So indecent, Ajay thought. The man got closer to him and walked alongside Ajay's march. Ajay wondered about punching him as a clear message, but as usual, he opted for the deadpan expression and silence. Still feeling reflective, Ajay thought about how he used to treat them. In his early days on the job, he would be very polite to them, using words and phrases such as 'sorry' and 'I'll come back later', thinking they deserved his kindness. As a result, it would take him a long time to get into the office. He no longer had time for that, especially not today.

"Back off mate, alright?" he said slyly to the seller, who stopped dead in his tracks. Ajay looked back. The seller was already onto his next victim.

Ajay marched quickly up the glass steps, but he groaned as he was interrupted by a familiar chirpy voice.

"What time do you call this, lover boy?"

Ajay turned around to see Ace behind him, wearing a sarcastic beaming smile. He approached Ajay, taking the steps two at a time, the fabric of his navy suit tightening around his stocky legs. It was a new suit, Ajay noticed. Nicely complemented by a maroon tie, fastened to perfection beneath broad shoulders and a square jawline. It must have been tailored, as Ajay admired how it made Ace's legs look longer. Ajay knew Ace wasn't just arriving at work. One, because he'd never be as stupid as him, but also because of his lack of headwear. Ace claimed that he was particularly susceptible to sunstroke, and so never spent extended amounts of time outside without his cap.

"Genni and I slept for eight last night." Ajay paused for a moment as the words fell from his mouth. That lost filter again. What was he doing? *Get a grip,* he told himself. He clearly wasn't quite over his lack of punctuality, beginning to feel more anxious to get up to his desk.

"Eight? That's rough." Ace rubbed the smooth skin of his chin beneath his fingers.

The two of them walked through the doors into the lobby as Ajay scratched his own chin, feeling its rough surface. He'd get that sorted later.

"I can't remember when I last slept that long. Maybe I'll see you selling on the street soon." Ace sarcastically nudged Ajay with his elbow, sending a sharp force through Ajay's arm. Ajay knew he should take the joke lightly, so he laughed back and rolled his eyes, but the comment did feel heavy to him. He wiggled his tie to loosen it slightly, but not enough to ruin his appearance. They reached the elevator and Ajay tuned himself to complete his usual office greetings to those from other departments; disingenuous honourable nods and smiles.

Ace turned to the book he was carrying. "Just got this new one from outside. The seller will get a handy bit of merit if I'm educated on this one." Ajay looked down at Ace's purchase entitled *Spending Credit Right: The Relationship between Credit and Personal Growth.* Ajay couldn't help but laugh, almost spluttering saliva over the other employees in the elevator.

"What?" Ace asked with a shove on Ajay's arm. The elevator stopped at floor fifty and a slender woman with blonde hair stepped on board. Her small lips formed a lascivious smile and her eyes were only looking at Ace, who gifted her with a wink. Ajay smirked and subtly shook his head. Did Ace have any other sort of behaviour towards women?

"It's just you don't need to worry about credit. Why waste your time with that?" Ajay said bluntly. He knew that this would spark an amusing reaction.

Ace stared at Ajay. "You dick. I don't waste time." Ajay sniggered.

"Honestly, you'll ruin my M-470 reputation." Ace's voice was slightly raised. Ajay assumed that Ace's latest female acquaintance was listening. Work, exercise and girls. That was Ace's life. Ajay sometimes envied it; it was a much simpler way of living. Less complicated, no strings attached.

Despite this elevator's state-of-the-art speed technology, Ajay was becoming aware of how slow it felt. His breath was quickening. Ace was still talking, but his voice was lost behind Ajay's thoughts. He began to wonder how many others, like Ace, had noticed he was late. He imagined the disapproving glances that awaited him. It felt a little like his first ever day. The sweating. The apprehension. The unknown. That realisation that for the rest of his days, he'd be battling to have one-up on his equally capable colleagues, just for the next promotion, credit-rise, or merit-bonus. He'd let go of his A-game. He convinced himself that it was okay as it was just one day, one slip up he could make up for. Mr Hollday was impressed enough with him as it was, so no need to worry. He began to impatiently tap his forefinger against his trouser leg. *No,* he thought. *I'm like Ugly Briefcase Man. What has become of me?*

Eventually, the elevator glided to a smooth, noiseless stop and the doors slid seamlessly open to the one hundred and fifty-sixth floor. He and Ace stepped out into the bright, open space encased in repeated diamond glass windows. Not bothering to say goodbye to Ace as they parted ways, Ajay discreetly moved through the office, past the usual whirlwind of others storming between meeting rooms and desks and throwing information from screen to screen. It was going well. No one seemed to notice him. Except for Dana. Ajay usually tolerated her poor attempts to flirt with him, but after this morning's stress, he anticipated he would have to force himself not to shout at her. That certainly wouldn't look good in his performance metrics.

Dana rose from her desk and skipped over in Ajay's direction, but not without disturbing the determined path of another worker. He watched them with one eye as they both jumped from side to side awkwardly and politely smiled through their mutual frustration. She spoke with smooth articulation. "Morning!"

Ajay sat down, willing her to go away. "Wow Ajay, you look great. New moisturiser or something?" She started to faff with her long hair to get it all sitting nicely over her right shoulder. He had to hand it to her; it did make her look prettier.

Ajay responded curtly. "Something like that. Sorry, Dana, I've got to get on." Ajay placed his Watch over the small oval of his desk's activation pad; it opened three transparent monitor screens.

"Yes, you are in later. I've been here since 4am." Dana persisted. *How is she still talking?* Ajay closed his eyes briefly to control his frustration. Ajay didn't look up but imagined she was looking smug by the tone of her voice. "Anyway, I just wanted to say hello. I'm just about to do a drone order actually, want in on anything?"

Ajay shook his head. He never understood that question. If he wanted something, it would be quicker for another drone to come straight to his desk rather than Dana having to trot over to him after her delivery. Any excuse to flirt, he supposed.

"Suit yourself." Dana lingered for a moment. What did she want from him? She knew Genni. They'd met before. Was she just wanting to be friends? Ajay didn't have many friends at work. Ace was an exception. His focus was on impressing Mr Hollday and anyone above him, which Dana wasn't. She was just an account manager, whose main job was to look after customers. Sure, Ajay knew that was important, but it was easily replaceable. Ajay started interacting with his screens, calmly swinging his arms to bring up the algorithm he had started yesterday. His silence finally gave Dana the message and she returned to her desk.

Ajay felt his wrist vibrate. *Hi Ajay, I detect you have begun your working day. Do you give me permission to record your progress?* Ajay selected 'Yes', like every day, allowing his Watch to record his activity. *Have a happy Merit-making day, Ajay,* the Watch encouraged. Ajay activated the earpiece in his right ear and felt the smooth tickle as it extended slickly over his head, through his black hair, to form a completed set of headphones. Music invaded and the office became a moving blur, his mind focusing on the task before him.

Chapter Two

The tips of her fingers felt delicate against the nib of the pencil. It danced around the small page stylishly, leaving the path of its beautifully crafted mark. In some places dark as night, in others light and soft, altogether becoming a grayscale picture of someone Genni didn't know . . .

"Genni, that toxicology report . . ." Genni slapped the cover of her black notebook down fast. She stared into her screen as Mafi's patronising tone was accompanied by the heavy tap of her heels. "My desk. By the end of the day. Maybe make it earlier, as you need the extra merit after 8 hours off last night."

Genni's manager brushed past her desk wearing a tight and stylish blue pant suit. She didn't even look at her. *Ouch,* Genni thought. That one hurt. She had stupidly convinced herself that they were back on good terms following their earlier discussion in her office. Clearly not. She probably deserved it, as Mafi had reminded her.

"I haven't had an employee log that many inactive hours in months. You've disappointed me, Genni." Mafi's small, tight lips had curled and strong, pencilled eyebrows had risen. Genni had somehow not reacted appropriately. She knew that Mafi had probably expected her to cry or respond with some sort of 'Yes, ma'am!' army shout, but Genni had just stayed silent. She had actually been trying to decipher why Mafi had decided to draw her eyebrows a solid black when actually her hair, which stuck unnaturally tight to her head, was a light brown colour. It made her look more masculine, Genni thought, and she wondered whether that was her aim. Once she'd pulled herself back to reality, she had been very gracious, explaining to Mafi that it wouldn't happen again. It ended well, but now Mafi was cold with her once again. Genni was exhausted trying to get her boss to like her. It was too hard, but it would be harder to stop trying.

"Of course, I'll get it done," Genni shouted after her, almost jumping up from her chair. *You idiot,* she thought. *Now you look like a right suck up.* She smiled slightly to her neighbouring colleagues. Ignoring the nausea stewing in her stomach and slipping her sketchbook into her bag, Genni ruffled her hair back into a small, neat bun. She checked the front-facing video on her screen and padded her cheeks. Ajay was right: her skin was drier. Pulling her skin back to get a closer look, the emails and messages popping up on screen were fuzzy to her. Her mind was elsewhere. *The chin.* She thought back to the picture of the stranger she'd drawn. *The chin is too thin.* She sat back in her chair. *It's out of proportion to the top of the head. Wrong angle, perhaps?* More messages, more tasks came bouncing in. Genni didn't register them. *More definition needed?* She'd always been better at painting landscapes, ones she'd seen in movies; there were only so many times you could draw the desert and City you grew up in. *Perhaps if . . .* Genni felt like slapping herself. *Get back to work. Stop daydreaming.*

Her thoughts turned to her father, which made her legs go floppy; they tingled with her rising frustration. They were to have lunch today. Another annoyance.

After inputting the report deadline into her Watch, she knew her head needed clearing. The office felt quiet to her today. It was almost numb, despite its usual activity: the deafening noise of chatter, the beeps and bleeps of computers, and many drones delivering mid-morning low-fat snacks. The subtle pink walls of the Beauty Dome felt grey, its usual glittering not feeling quite as sharp. Genni craned her neck. She spent a mindless moment watching people walk one way or another on the suspended walkways above, all nipping into a meeting room or office. She could paint a great canvas of the place – all the pinks, purples and blues disguised its internal greyness. Slowly pulling her cumbersome body up, she walked to the water dispenser. She placed her glass inside and iced water quickly fell from above. Maybe she was just being ungrateful. Working in the beauty industry did have some advantages – she experienced working long hours with the top scientists in the field, soaking up all their knowledge and the merit that came with it. Not to mention the great fashion advice, beauty tips and complimentary products. It was this department change that had really knocked her. Mafi said moving from Dressing Tables to Fat Reduction was a promotion. Genni had forced herself not to scoff in her manager's face. A promotion? She didn't call a drop in short-term merit a promotion. As the water was getting dangerously close to the rim of her glass, she stood still, resisting the turning of her stomach, musing over the lack of determination and passion she had for the project.

"I just don't care as much. It's not as sustainable or impactful for business. The health risks will mean less investment and therefore less merit," she'd confessed to Ajay one night, as they were walking to the library under the swoop of night drones and motivational adverts.

"Well, isn't that why they're building a team to test it?" he'd asked sensibly as he bit into a carrot stick.

"I guess. But will people *really* make more significant societal contributions after it? There aren't many significant people that are even overweight." They'd entered through the library doors, moving in sync with hundreds of others at two in the morning.

"I know a lot who need more body confidence, actually. Anyway, people will be healthier too. More time and energy for merit stuff. Look, your job is to make it work. Then you'll get your reward." Ajay had stopped her and swooped down to kiss her cheek. After three years of cheek kissing, Genni never knew if this was love or just a custom. He was so vague in his romanticism, only whispering the words 'I love you' late at night, as if others would judge him if they heard it.

As she walked back to her desk, she tried desperately to remember Ajay's reassurance and not his rudeness of that morning. Their oversleeping had set her mind spinning. One minute, she was thinking about the stranger in her sketch. The next, a beautiful waterfall. Then, Mafi and the report, to the loss of merit-making time, or how she wasn't invited to that planning meeting when Josia was. Then, finally, she screamed inside her head. This was common. She usually couldn't focus without some help. She always told herself she didn't need *it* and could get by, just like everyone else, but then that sneaky voice in her head whispered: *you're just not good enough*. Battling through her emotions, she felt relieved to see no merit had been deducted for her idle water break. Which was stupid, as she knew merit was never deducted for little things like that. Command was always banging on about the freedom it gave each citizen. *It's a citizen's choice how they use their time, though if no merit is recorded after 48 hours, we will do some routine checks and merit may be deducted for time-wasting.* It was the same guff at every annual announcement, Genni had noticed. Beginning to throw together statistics, she grimaced once more at the painful pang in her belly, gave her Watch permission to record and struggled through her report ahead of lunch with her father.

* * *

Lunch came too soon.

"Angel! So lovely to see you." Her father embraced her just as she emerged from the spinning of the turnstile door. She felt the warmth of his large-built body as she fell into his chest, and his bearlike arms clasped around her. Genni felt so dizzy, and ashamed that it had driven her to hug him in a clingier, needier way that she would have liked. She quickly pulled away, appreciating the smell of fresh garlic and other tantalising spices. Genni felt herself start to salivate. She was starving, despite feeling like she could throw up.

"Hi, Dad." She forced herself to smile, as always. Her father stood leaning on the welcome counter, with one hand in the pocket of his dark-green tweed trousers and his other holding a glass flute of sparkling water. Genni noticed the silver flicks in his hair had increased and the small wrinkles around his eyes had grown deeper. He smiled at her softly.

"Come on. I got us our usual spot." Genni obeyed as they brushed past other diners indulging into splendidly crafted gourmet dishes within the restaurant, which rivalled the decadence of a ballroom. Genni liked it here, though it was let down by a few grubby marks and blemishes across its white walls. This was the most upper-merit venue outside of The Glorified Quarters, so it was slightly down-market compared with what her father, and the child in her, was used to.

At home, she remembered, there would be real plants whose floral smell would lift the room. There'd be a peaceful, tranquil view of the desert mountains – not the riff-raff of the working district streets. Genni and her father approached their usual place, a secluded booth away from the window. Her father didn't like seeing street sellers or any Unworthies whilst he ate. Their dinner dates often included a smug reminder to Genni that *you don't get any of this nonsense in the Quarters'*. She never understood why he'd come to lunch with her, if everything was so beneath him. He could just wait to see her when she visited. Which was, Genni admitted, never.

They sat down and, of course, her father spoke first.

"So, tell me. What's new at The Beauty Dome? The drama of the explosive robo-stylists dying down?" he laughed. It wasn't an inclusive laugh but a condescending one. Genni took a deep breath, listing reasons in her head why she loved her father. It was short: *he's your father.* However, it always managed to help her keep her cool.

"Not quite, but there's been lots of positivity with its development despite the loss of staff, and those with the lost hair got good credit compensation. You know, they're thinking of approaching you to put them in your spas?" She was trying to drive the conversation from her side. A business opportunity might avoid any discussion of her job, her credit situation, or her merit score.

"Well, there's a long way to go to be worthy of a Mansald Spa." She watched his aging, wise eyes move from herself to the menu on his screen. He quickly dismissed it with an over-exaggerated tap. "I'm having the kale."

Genni didn't know what she wanted. Her head was beginning to sting a little, to meet nicely with the strange flipping of her stomach. *Just have the kale, too. But camel looks so good. Camel does real damage to the hips and waist.*

What she really wanted was a glass of water. Had a drone not realised they were here? He was Boris Mansald, for Tulo's sake. His privilege and status were another advantage of being his daughter, yet here they clearly hadn't programmed the drones to recognise him. *Wouldn't have this nonsense in the Quarters.* She eventually settled for the kale.

"So, how are the dressing tables? Now, there's an interesting thing. People love them in my changing rooms." He looked at her almost as if he was proud. Genni felt sick. She'd have to tell him. It would eventually come out, especially if her average daily merit went down, which he probably already checked. A man of his calibre probably had the connections, so he could see everything: her current location, activities, merit count, acquaintances. It wouldn't surprise her in the slightest. He probably even knew about her painting and all the sleep she had last night.

Those thoughts made her feel even more unwell. She just had to say it. Just say it. Quickly. "I've been moved to Fat Reduction." Her nerves skyrocketed.

Her father paused for a moment before speaking bluntly, laughter brewing in his tone. "That computerised fat removal thing? The one with all the bad press?" Genni curled her tongue within her mouth, held her father's eye contact and nodded her head. She could feel the clamminess of her hands between her fingers, wiping them on the seat. Her father exploded into laughter. Genni rolled her eyes, but not enough for him to see. She didn't want to lose face and let him know that she was embarrassed by it. Reaching in his pocket, her father found a handkerchief to dab his increasingly wet eyes. Genni spotted the curly calligraphic 'BM' on its corner. So pretentious, Genni thought, but she did like its familiarity: she was reminded of all the tears it had once wiped away.

"You're joking?" he asked.

"Not joking." Genni felt calmer. She needed to defend herself, if not for anything but her pride, even though the stabs of that headache were now forcefully making their way across her forehead.

"What merit will that give you?" Her father was no longer laughing, and his eyes were no longer joyful. He stared at her with a terrifying persistence. "Credit will be enough, I'm sure, but you're not even at M-450 yet. I was back in The Glorified Quarters by the time I was your age. Come on, girl."

Breathe. Remember the list: *he's your father.* Genni spoke calmly again. "Yes, at first I was sad to leave the tables, but that started out small. Remember, everyone thought they'd flop?" Genni thought back to all the bad press around having tech assistance to highlight your imperfections. "If we get this right, people losing weight in a fast but safe way will give them the confidence to become their more effective self. Their contribution could be higher than ever." Genni was surprised that she could recite the marketing pitch and do it well. Perhaps she had paid enough attention in the briefing meetings. "Plus, it will decrease the sales of weight loss drugs Downtown," she finished, smiling slightly and swallowing hard to moisten her increasingly dry throat.

Her father shrugged his shoulders and straightened his purple tie below his collar. "It's just a shame you're not home yet, like your brother is." He coughed through his solemn words and started bitterly swiping at his Watch. Genni had been waiting for it. The Rod drop. Her father never failed to remind her of what a disappointment she was in comparison to her overachieving big brother. She was a worthless worker next to that merit-making marvel.

"Where is this drone?" The volume of his voice took Genni slightly by surprise. She felt her body jolt uncomfortably as it made her jump. Her father sighed as he saw a drone heading in their direction. "You wouldn't have this nonsense in the Quarters," he mumbled. Genni literally wanted to laugh out loud; instead, she just strategically lifted a hand to her face to conceal her smirk behind it.

Her father looked at her again, but this time with a strange gaze that was almost like love. Stretching his arms across the table, he held out his hands. Genni shifted uneasily in her seat but complied and reached her hands into his, which felt dry. She considered offering him some moisturiser, but he wouldn't want it. It wouldn't be good enough for him.

"Genni, dear. I apologise. Maybe I spoke too harshly. You're still young . . ." He paused. Something had to be bothering him if he'd actually stopped talking. Genni noticed that his eyes were narrowing as he looked towards Genni's right armpit.

Following his eyeline, Genni really felt sick, both physically and emotionally. Was she nervous? In shock? Anxious about work? That wave of nausea surely wasn't caused by the small rip her father had noticed in the armpit of her dress. It had ruined her father's rare attempt at apology. She blamed herself for not noticing, not checking herself before she left this morning. A drone arrived and set down glasses around their arms, which were still connected. Her father let go and smiled at her without showing his teeth. Genni could tell he was holding himself back about the rip. It must be painful for him, she thought, not to pass comment. Genni wanted to go, as her brain was now pounding against her skull. She needed the water that arrived in front of her; she was thankful for it as it cut like sharp ice down her throat.

Chapter Three

Two hours had passed, but Ajay had barely noticed. Nothing unusual there. He often got so invested that it felt like seconds had passed by, not hours. His brain had stretched itself from encryption, to environments, to code, to all those other bugs, until finally came the beautiful moment when the test passed seamlessly. He'd solved the problem, like he always did. In those moments, Ajay always felt like punching the air and crying 'Yes!' out loud. Of course, he never did, even though most people in this office would understand his celebration. There was nothing better for a programmer than to finally get something working. This particular bug had been affecting the personal banking platform for months. Prosper didn't take client complaints lightly, and this little niggle had caused a whole raft of them.

Understandably so – the Watch screen freezing when a client wanted to transfer credit wasn't ideal. It was just a blip and only happened once in ten thousand times, but strangely no one had managed to fix it yet. The job had circled around the team at least twice and Ajay had been disappointed the first time he hadn't managed to crack it. Now that he had, he wondered if he'd be the talk of the office, and whether it would get him even more points with Mr Hollday.

Although, maybe this would just cancel out his eight hours of inactivity. Mr Hollday wasn't too upset, only popping up on Ajay's screen to remind him not to miss merit-making opportunities. It was frustrating that management was alerted in this way, but Ajay accepted it was necessary when working a job that required M-300 and above.

Ajay took a moment to slouch back and admire his merit-clock on his right-hand screen. It must be some sort of personal record, he thought. Maybe he should ask for the niggly little bugs no one else wanted more often. Sighing, he leant forward and pressed the coffee symbol on his middle screen. It was okay to have one today, given he hadn't had a *SkipSleep* boost in the last twelve hours. He inputted the consumption on his Watch to ensure he maintained his diet for the day and, moments after submitting his order, a drone appeared within Ajay's cocoon of floating screens to place the coffee down on his desk. The ding of the transaction rang from the drone as Ajay swiped his Watch across it. As Ajay took his first sip and tasted the sweetness of the chocolate sprinkles melting within the froth of milk, he was disturbed by Patt's arrival. Ajay had been so focussed that he hadn't even registered the desk beside him being empty again.

"Ajay!" Patt whispered, breathing heavily. Ajay unclipped his headphones quickly, swallowing his coffee and partially burning his throat, and observed as Patt staggered over to his desk. His hands were shaking as he started to unload the contents of his bag. As he did so, gadgets and snacks were getting tangled up with torn bits of paper to form one messy mountain on the surface of the pristine glass desk. Ajay grimaced, thinking over how disgusting it all was; he could actually see some mouldy biscuits within the mound. Patt frantically cleared away the paper and food until only his headphones, Watch and crumbs remained.

"What . . . Patt . . . where have you been? Mr Hollday is . . ." Ajay said, astonished to see him. He figured he wasn't coming back. Patt hadn't been in the office for days; no one had seen him nor knew where he was. The two of them kept their voices low, not oblivious to the sea of judging eyes staring in their direction.

"There's been some stuff going on," Patt said as he clipped his Watch back onto his wrist. He scrambled to tuck in his un-ironed shirt and flatten down the flicked-up edges of his hair. The purple around his eyes looked angered and his beard was a forest. He wasn't just missing work then, Ajay thought, self-care had been neglected too. Ajay watched as Patt lowered his Watch to his activation pad, thinking he could jump up to stop him.

A warning sound cut through the office, inspiring excited gasps of shock from the other workers. Screens flew from Patt's desk, covered in a red mist and displaying bold words flashing persistently. GROSS MISCONDUCT. Neither Ajay nor Patt moved. Ajay didn't know why he was thinking about trying to stop it. He knew Patt couldn't just sit at his desk and not get caught.

He'd always have to pay the consequences for not turning up for work. Right on cue, Mr Hollday's office door swung open.

Dressed in a cream tailored suit, Mr Hollday's presence alone earnt him everyone's attention. His deep brown eyes and defined cheekbones would surely allow him any modelling contact in Tulo. Well, that's what Dana had told Ajay once in her ramblings. Instead, Hollday had done the sensible thing and used his business intelligence to gain a score of M-590 before he was 40. Ajay, forgetting the situation for a moment, was pleased to see that Mr Hollday was wearing a mustard tie. His wardrobe had been right: mustard was in fashion. He looked down to his own and felt slightly jealous that his was just plain mustard, not overlaid with a floral pattern like Mr Hollday's.

"Mr Mull, let's have a chat." Hollday's hard, grinding voice carried weight across the office floor. Patt gulped as he walked swiftly through the rows of condemning looks. Ajay slowly returned to his seat, watching as the office door closed and the floor returned to its former activity. Ajay rolled his eyes then as he saw the screen belonging to the girl in front of him. It displayed immediate updates of the recent drama to her social groups. He hoped the conversation became so enthralling that her point count would fall. Ajay didn't make his worry over Patt obvious, simply clipping his headphones back in and getting back to work whilst remembering the technical conversations he and Patt had in the early days. Ajay had earnt significant merit from their friendship, one that he knew would now end. He shouldn't be seen with him, really. It wouldn't be good for his personal branding.

* * *

As early evening drew in, waves of colleagues returned from afternoon boosts. They may have noticed that Ajay hadn't left. He straightened his tie and acted as if he hadn't registered their return. Ajay often wondered where Tulo would be without the invention of *SkipSleep*. Back when people used to sleep more, progress was much slower. Then, after *SkipSleep,* the City just flew. Quite literally, with the building of the sky train. State-of the-art drones certainly wouldn't have existed for every household chore and delivery service; it had been confirmed that the Robotics industry historically had the highest number of employees going over the legal boost limit. Ajay's fingers still rattled furiously on the surface of his desk and lines of his code ran horizontally across his retinas. His flow was interrupted again by a clan of drones, this time not just carrying coffee cups.

They were hovering together outside Hollday's office, increasing in number. What were they doing? His screen flashed and wrist vibrated. Apparently, his heart rate was rising. Ajay leant over his desk to Dana who had a better view from her seat. He hoped that initiating conversation wouldn't make her think he was interested. "Psst, Dana. What are those drones doing?" Dana took out her earpiece, looked slightly confused, then followed Ajay's eyeline towards the swarm calibrating at the other side of the office.

"Wow," Dana responded, whispering, "the only time I've seen drones together like that is when they're from the TPD." Ajay went pale. She was right. Standard drones were always on the move, delivering a product or service. They didn't tend to hover.

"Are you alright, Ajay? You've gone whiter than a Glorified walkway."

"Yeah . . . I'm fine."

Ajay retreated slowly back into his seat. Should he move? Discreetly need the toilet? Surely they'd still find him. He told himself there was nothing in the situation that meant he should panic. Nothing at all. They could just be there for an inspection. Nothing to do with him.

Then his heart rate skyrocketed. The hum of the drones all taking off at speed was almost thunderous to him. He looked. They were heading straight for him. He'd seen this before in his nightmares; a villainous gang of TPD drones hurtling towards him, ready with their red-hot probes and sparking tasers. Ajay's only thought was to move. He jumped up and headed swiftly towards the toilet, not exactly knowing the next part of his plan. As he reached the toilet door, he briefly glanced back to see his hunters.

Then he stopped and observed the drones cleaning out Patt's desk from top to bottom. He let out a quiet sigh of relief. *You. Idiot.* He cursed himself.

Vulnerability hit him. His mad flurry hadn't gone unnoticed. Scanning the room, eyes were briefly assessing him before returning to their screens. They were judging him, thinking he was weird. Well, he had just sprinted to the toilet in a blind panic, away from a bunch of drones. It was hardly normal behaviour. It didn't matter if they judged him, he told himself. He could hold his head high; he was wearing a mustard tie. Ajay simply scanned his Watch along the wall and advanced into the toilet. He leant against the sink and swiped one hand over his face, as if to wipe off his embarrassment, and ignored the mirror's suggestion of a product for puffy eyes.

Moments later, he proudly strutted back across the office floor and no one was looking at him, not obviously anyway. Except for Ace, who seemed to be laughing, which Ajay ignored. He'd boast about his bug fix later, he decided. That would shut up his mocking.

As he arrived back at his desk, he saw how any former presence of Patt had been masked by disinfectant. It had never happened before, Ajay was sure of it. Something about it felt sinister and uncomfortable. It was about to get worse. A sound chimed from the staff photo board that was projected high above the office floor. Ajay looked at his photo on the second row daily. That was a good photo day. His medium length, black hair shone with just the right touch of wax, and his smile was perfect: teeth perfectly straight and glowing against his tanned skin. He couldn't wait for his score to increase. Then that face would be on the top row. It wouldn't matter so much if he embarrassed himself then.

The chime had been an update to Patt's record on the bottom row. His score dropped to M-290 and his picture faded into a blank space. A collective sigh of disapproval filled the air. Ajay felt unnerved. Whilst he knew this was deserved, he couldn't help but sympathise with Patt. Part of him wanted to find out what had been happening at home to facilitate his downfall. He had learnt over the years to quench sympathy and its paralysis. It had always stopped him from moving forward. Not anymore. Patt wasn't strong enough; that was the way it was.

Ajay noticed his screen had been invaded by a torrent of messages from Ace:

Ace: *That was intense. You alright mate?*

Ajay assumed he was referring to his toilet trip.

Ace: *Where do you think Patt is?*

Ace: *You don't think they've sent him packing to the Side, do you?*

Ace: *Should we try and contact him?*

Ajay looked behind him towards Ace's desk. His middle screen was down so Ajay had a full view of his friend. He wasn't working but chatting to the girl next to him. How that guy managed to get any work done, Ajay would never know. He replied to the messages:

Ajay: *Don't be dim. They wouldn't send him to the Side. Don't worry about it.*

Ajay paused.

Ajay: *And I was just desperate.*

Ajay: *For the toilet, I mean.*

At that moment, Mr Hollday came from his office and every ear stood to attention again. Ajay straightened himself up and bid his middle screen to shut down. Hollday scratched his chest and cleared his throat.

"I'm sure you've noticed that Mr Mull is no longer with us." Mr Hollday looked up to the staff board, looking emotionless. "Whilst this saddens me, I'm sure you understand we have to have the right people to make the contribution that is required of us." Mr Hollday paused as he swung his arms behind his back and casually walked towards the centre of the office floor. Ajay subtly looked down his own chest to make sure his tie was straight. It was.

"In better news, I'm happy to announce we can now reveal our plans for Liberation Day and how you can get involved." He smiled across the room, almost like a proud parent would look at a well-merited child. Mr Hollday joyfully sighed and clapped his hands together.

"The auditorium. 9pm tonight." He spun on his feet and disappeared back into his office, leaving his audience to explode into excitable chatter and Patt to evaporate into nothing but a memory.

Ajay read another message on his screen:

Ace: *Make sure you go to the toilet before the meeting. ;)*

He rolled his eyes and smirked. Tapping back at his desk, he buried his head into his work, but not without first giving the middle finger jovially in the direction of his friend's desk.

Chapter Four

It was a sharp pinch. Quick and keen. Ajay edged himself forward as the hand moved away from his backside. It was obvious whom the hand belonged to; Ace was always the joker and sometimes, when Ajay was in one of his sour moods, it got to him. He'd want to throttle Ace and throw him up a wall. Not that he ever would. For one thing, his measly biceps would instantly buckle under the weight of Ace's meticulously toned physique. It didn't stop Ajay considering swinging around to give Ace a pinch back, but he decided against it. Being surrounded by the entirety of the Prosper workforce was probably not the best place for a childish game. Though, clearly, that didn't stop Ace. It came again. The sharp, quick pinch.

"Would you . . . cut . . . that . . . out?" Ajay turned to his left. Ace sniggered as they continued walking closely alongside their other colleagues.

"Just thought I'd give you some action, seeing as you and Genni are sleeping so much."

Ajay sighed, hoping no one around took note of Ace's comment. It was these types of comments that he rarely responded to, mostly because he wasn't quick enough to come up with a witty or offensive comeback. His own silence made him wonder what Ace was thinking. Did he think he was weak? Not able to hold his own? Ajay knew Ace wouldn't have thought anything of it, but this didn't stop his own mind making a nuisance of itself. They all edged forward again, like products on a conveyor belt, down the corridor digitally decorated with the events of Prosper's timeline.

"Do you think this will take long?" Ace asked.

"I don't know. It was about an hour last year." Ajay could hear the familiar beeping sound as people scanned their Watches on the door one by one.

"I'm heading to The Tower after," Ace said.

"Oh, I was going to ask if you wanted a drink."

"Where at?"

"Just Skyhouse."

"I'll meet you after," Ace said as there was a slight pause in the line's movement. Ace leant against the wall behind him. It displayed a half-constructed Prosper building, surrounded by scaffolding and drone-controlled cranes. Ajay noticed a whitening spot on Ace's chin, illuminated by the screen's light.

"What are you training tonight?" Ajay asked.

"I dunno. Maybe get on the bikes . . ." Ace lifted himself back off the wall as the people in front moved again. "Unless you fancy tennis?"

"I was gonna work late before the bar. Blake and Jaxs are meeting me," Ajay responded. They arrived at the entrance to the auditorium, so he lifted his Watch to the scanner and felt his wrist vibrate as its screen turned green. Ace did the same after him. They walked into the familiar conference space, where thousands of seats descended down into a pit towards a central stage.

"Come on. Just ask them to push back an hour. The merit's better with tennis," Ace encouraged.

Ajay considered this to be selfish of Ace. Tennis might be better than bikes, but Ajay's overtime would be better than tennis. But, of course, Ace gets what Ace wants.

"Alright, alright. But you buy me an ale?" The timid side of Ajay regretted such a presumptuous question, but he reminded himself that he had a right to ask it. Friends owe one another when they sacrifice merit. Ace nodded, no questions asked.

The two of them walked further down the marble steps to find some vacant seats. Ajay never got tired of the atmosphere of these things. He even enjoyed the corporate cheesiness, the soft pounding of motivational techno music, and the swirling spotlights moving and falling over each section of the crowd. As they squeezed down their row, Ajay observed two ladies in front.

One wore a very simple, yet overly tight cream business suit, and the other mirrored the same style but in a bright purple. The purple wasn't as sophisticated. The two of them were cackling with laughter. He knew they were from different departments, so he decided their joviality was probably all fake, just a cover up as they assessed what they could offer one another. Ajay drew his mind away from them when Ace spoke again.

"It gives me an excuse not to go to Mum's as well," Ace said, as he wiped some imaginary crumbs off the folded seat he was about to sit on. Ajay had never heard much about Ace's family. Maybe it was because he never asked any questions about anyone's family, really. It worked well to avoid being quizzed on his own. He did know that like Genni, Ace was a Glorified kid, now distanced from his parents. Ajay often thought they were both ungrateful. They can't have ever been left wanting, growing up in The Quarters, yet they both managed to find ways to grumble, which was frustrating to him. A frustration he never expressed out loud.

The mechanical murmur of a drone came from behind. Ajay tilted his head to spot it flying about a metre above them. Everyone, including himself, was always slightly cautious after the malfunction a couple of years ago – termed the 'Drone Dumps'. Some bug in the drone's internal code had thrown their spatial awareness capability off completely. The Robotics industry had a lot to answer for. His best memory of the whole thing was seeing an Unworthy dumped on by one carrying a craft of takeaway food; they were covered head to toe in noodles and slimy, sticky sauce. Ajay had managed to avoid such an embarrassment. He was cleverer than most, more aware of his surroundings, so he'd rather enjoyed the whole situation. Disappointingly, it only lasted about a day. This particular drone was heading up above the stands and Ajay watched as it produced a projection out into the middle of the room. The Prosper logo, a three-layered flame, spun on its axis against a lilac gradient background.

The music subsided, chatter stopped, and a booming voice filled the room.

"Greetings, treasured colleagues and associates." Mr. Bancorp's voice sent ripples through the stands.

"Oh, here is he, the big man," Ace smirked.

Ajay smiled, his eyes focussed on Bancorp's face. He'd never met him in person. This was always the closest he'd ever been to him: Ajay sat in a faraway seat and Bancorp down on the stage below, looking like a small silhouetted person. He often looked at him on stage rather than the magnified version of him on the screens. It reminded Ajay that they were actually in the same room. Bancorp had become an idol to him. Tall, well-dressed, winner of prestigious business awards, CEO to a top Tulo corporation, and of course, Glorified. Plus, Genni always said that Bancorp's handsomeness hadn't diminished despite his hair going white. In fact, she mentioned it every time he was on a news update. He was just *it*. The type that everyone wanted to be like. Accomplished, good-looking, and respected, with a solid score on his wrist.

His voice also carried this weight with it. A kind of powerful husk that made people listen. "As you are all aware, another Liberation Day is fast approaching. Those in HR and Senior Management have been working diligently to ensure that our celebrations this year reflect the appreciation we have for your hard work and your dedication to our objectives here at Prosper. Before we get started, let's remind ourselves of the importance of this treasured holiday."

Ajay heard Ace sigh. He understood. They'd seen this video so many times that they could probably recite the entire thing word perfect if they bothered trying. It began with a birds-eye view of the old city, an area now known as the Side. Whirring, resonant sounds were repeatedly blasted from the speakers. Grey boxed homes and miniature skyscrapers were distorted by some strange, brown filter effect. Ajay hated the next part. Actors and actresses dressed in over-exaggerated rags began to walk slowly across the shot, scrounging around on the floor for scraps of food and cowering over empty water buckets. He wondered why Command hadn't bothered paying for better production. Despite not knowing what it was like before, Ajay was convinced this was all some hyperbolic performance. Here comes the victory story, he thought. A narrator began to speak.

Generations ago, Tulo was nothing more than buildings in the desert – defined by poverty. The working citizen was starving, and water was rationed. But only for them.

It then faded into flashes of regally dressed men surrounded by treasured possessions and exuberant food, unwelcomed by the crowd, who booed. The scene always made Ajay hungry and set him thinking about what to eat later. A salad tonight, he thought.

The government watched from above, towering over the dying city. They were gluttonous. All the resources that others had worked for, they took for themselves. The commoners, the contributors – people like us – didn't stand a chance.

Triumphant music began to accompany close-up angles of tattered but sturdy boots marching forcefully and flicking sand into the camera.

Our ancestors joined together in defiance against the injustice they were living in. Despite the obstacles and the challenges they faced, they fought valiantly and sacrificed everything for those who came after.

Images of laser bullets, fire, and smoke overlaid each other seamlessly. Ajay actually enjoyed this part. It reminded him of Revolution Combat, one of his favourite Watch games. He and Ace used to challenge each other for hours. That was before merit was such a big deal, when they were younger and had the whole 'we've got time' attitude. Then, when promotions, exclusive venues and A-list networks became a potential reality, anything unproductive fell off the agenda. The video continued.

Even though not all joined our new way of life . . . The Side as it was today came back onto the screen. It hadn't changed. *These war heroes gave us our reality. A society based on equality and justice. One where individuals can choose what they contribute but only reap the benefits of that contribution. Our constitution allows each individual to be fairly rewarded, according to the time they dedicate to moving society forward through technological reform, personal development and community spirit. Merit has become a statement of status: one earnt, not simply given.*

Drone footage of the beauty and grandeur of Tulo City reflected brightly across all sides of the conference hall. *We press forward, but never forget their bravery.* The narrator's final line was made even more powerful by Mr Bancorp joining him in chorus. *Progress is Strength. For a Greater Tulo.* Ajay mouthed the words too.

The video ended and, like every year, the auditorium erupted into applause. Ajay and Ace were both on their feet to contribute; it was like some ingrained, automatic response. Mr Bancorp returned to the podium and the screen, smiling and gesturing for the crowd to calm down.

"Liberation Day is not just about a week or so of partying and holidaying. It's a time to remember." He held a dramatic pause. "To remember that we didn't get here alone." He banged his fist on the podium in time with the rhythm of his speech. "That in unity, there is progress. In progress, there is strength. Every single one of you has the required skills and capabilities needed here at Prosper to move the Tulo economy forward." Ajay couldn't help himself. He was mesmerised by the man. He leant forward as an attempt to get closer. "To create more efficient personal banking, to design seamless transaction technology, to provide more security for the credit of businesses, and, indirectly, to improve the efficiency and well-being of working individuals in our society. That is what we remember on Liberation Day. Together, at Prosper, we can create more." The crowd clapped again, the applause shorter and more subtle. Bancorp raised his hands again, clearly keen to continue. Ajay noticed that his Watch clasp was a solid gold colour with, he assumed, engravings of phrases or names. He wondered what they said and decided that he'd look it up later. Ajay looked down to his own wrist and turned it over. His strap was the same as the day he got it – black and dull. Bancorp spoke again.

"Of course, like every year, you have the day itself to enjoy with your families and loved ones and to attend the celebrations in the Glorified Quarters. But as a treat for this year, we are giving you the day before Liberation Day as a networking event here at Prosper." Ajay watched as people's heads flicked rapidly to one another, bursting into excitable conversation. Bancorp paused for a moment, smiling proudly and scratching his round stumbled chin where wrinkles had started to form. Ajay remembered how Genni had said even those wrinkles were sexy.

"This will be an exceptional merit-making opportunity, one that won't come around often." He was right – it was rare to take a whole day out for networking, an easy and effective way to rack up the merit. Ajay once read the entire Command Guide on how to make the most of networking, also known as others helping you learn valuable skills that could improve your contribution. Despite his research, he'd never been very good at it. It wasn't that he had a problem with small talk, it was his little enthusiasm to listen to insignificant others drone on. He remembered one particular woman who swore by the religion of having a protocol for everything. Apparently, he should have a document for all his work, cooking, showering, and eating; he had lost the plot when she started hammering on about her document for how to put shoes on more efficiently. The merit also wasn't that good when being educated. Rather, the real bonus was in educating others, or meeting high scorers with Worthy connections. If the benefits weren't there for him, Ajay tended to lose interest fast.

To finish up, Bancorp stared sternly and deeply into the drone's camera lens, indirectly looking into the eyes of every Prosper employee who felt the chill of his final words, as if spoken just for them.

"Don't waste it."

Chapter Five

Genni's day had picked up. She'd had a lunchtime boost and then she was flying. That toxicology report was handed in three hours early and in her manager's words was 'surprisingly insightful'. Genni decided to not take the 'surprisingly' as a personal insult. Regardless, it was extra merit earnt very cleanly. Plus, she'd managed to order a needle and thread and sew the armpit of her dress back together. It was a bit of a half-job. She'd rushed it, having felt too vulnerable sitting on the toilet in just her bra and knickers to take her time, but everything seemed to be holding together for now.

As evening drew in, she needed a break, her eyes feeling tired as she stared at the screen. Just a quick breather to renew her mind and then she'd be more productive. She knew if anyone could hear inside her head, they'd laugh. There's no way what she wanted to do would in any way be seen as productive. She didn't care, she fell into the temptation and pulled out her notebook. The chin is definitely too thin, she thought, as she gazed over the stranger crafted in pencil. She began tracing an outline underneath his cheekbones faintly and softly. Time ticked by. Whenever she was drawing or painting, she felt as if she were on a cloud or in another world where time was insignificant, where she could do this all day, every day. It had become her sanctuary. A release.

Then came the all too familiar feeling as an hour had passed. Guilt. Shame. Frustration. Genni's screen alerted her to the lack of merit earnt and she dropped her pencil. Looking around her, she was relieved that the office was still buzzing, and no one seemed to notice her warning message. As if they'd take any notice of her anyway, she scoffed as she scraped her fingers through her hair and looked over her drawing once more. A waste of time. Always a waste of time. Her brain felt scrambled; she couldn't focus on work, on anything. She needed help, so she decided she would make a quick trip Downtown.

Bleeping out of the dome and walking across the Retail district's fountained plaza, she was graced by the sharp ringing of her Watch: *Pearl & Mila calling.* As Genni accepted the video chat, she was tempted to sit down on a bench, but she determinedly continued towards the station. Two smiling faces sprang up from her wrist.

"Hey, gorgeous," Pearl shouted in her obtrusive voice. Genni observed the shine of her lustrous black locks and skin tone, perfect even through cyberspace. She looked at her own face: dry, bland and undistinctive. She replied and then greeted Mila, who was leaning over a table in her work lab, dressed in her white coat with a thick elastic headband keeping her hair from her eyes. Her sweet voice travelled through the speakers.

"Hey beautiful. Good day today?" Mila asked.

Genni huffed as the approaching sky train blew the ends of her brown hair back. "Not that great but I did submit a really good report an-"

"Gen. Not being rude but I haven't got a lot of time," Pearl said proudly before continuing. "I'm actually ringing you for a little business proposition of mine." Genni was inspired by Pearl and the impact her job made, most of the time. Her social recommendations of clothing brands, beauty and fitness products had instilled positivity and efficiency into thousands of her followers. Despite her ability to empower others and improve their well-being, Pearl could suffer from not being a very nice person. Pearl flicked her long, black hair back to reveal the hooped earrings underneath, accompanied beautifully by her delicately crafted eye make-up. Slightly conscious about what Pearl would say next, Genni made herself small in the corner of the sky train carriage. She doubted the commuters of Tulo wanted to hear Pearl's bright idea.

"So, it was actually Mila's idea. Why don't you explain it, hun?" Pearl gave Mila permission to speak.

Mila's face was closer to the camera now. "Pearl was telling me she was hoping to widen her audience to people of greater merit scores than her current audience, who are ... average, low M-400ish. I was at work and was thinking, what do many of my bosses in healthcare really care about? Merit and contribution, of course. But credit is also big." Mila paused as she lightly scratched underneath her eye, being careful to avoid smudging her eyeliner. Genni looked up momentarily from the screen to see the train passing the stop for home. Her journey continued at speed.

"So, I wondered whether Pearl should start to deviate her content from beauty and fashion to different, more pressing concerns, so she's accepted by the big shots. Like credit management, or updates about the latest economic developments. She could interview those who work in the industry. And then I thought, who works for the top company in the Financial District?"

"Ajay!" They both screamed energetically and moved their faces closer to the camera simultaneously. Genni was taken aback by the sudden outburst and had to move her wrist and screen further away. A woman beside her grimaced with polite disgust. Genni turned her back to her and looked out the window as they descended into the outer rings of the City.

"You want Ajay to feature on your channel?"

Pearl nodded her head dramatically.

"You know he's awful in front of a camera? He hates being judged by others. He might act as if he's cool with it, but he doesn-" Pearl interrupted her again.

"Oh, don't worry. I have producers and stylists to make him look good." Pearl pursed her lips and looked inquisitive. Genni watched as the buildings transformed into cream sided cuboids that held simple bay windows instead of wall-to-ceiling glass. Adverts for cheaper and less exclusive products hung on their walls, tainted with specks of sand and dust. Maintenance and delivery drones following the line of the train started to drop off until only a dozen remained. She needed to sign off. "I've got to get off now. I'll mention it to him, but Ace might be the better choice. Okay?"

"Sure thing. But push him, Gen, he's got a clearer voice than Ace," Pearl said. All three girls blew kisses to their screens, and Genni felt a loose ache in her legs and a sharp pain in her stomach as she staggered out into the night's pressing humidity.

Genni heard the familiar squelch of the sticky pavements beneath her feet as she walked over the bridge into Downtown. She marched through the row of market stalls selling fresh produce and raw building materials; a Command-worthy disguise for what really went on. It wasn't long until she encountered the usual things she ignored: the indulgence of salty, fatty, highly saturated foods, illegal product trading between stall workers, people who wore sunglasses and covered their Watches with their sleeves. Unworthies were also hunched up asleep in doorways beneath the flicker of cheap, neon lighting. All of it was even more harrowing at night, but Genni had learnt to blur it all out. She was here for one thing. Always was. She held her bag strap tightly to her shoulder with both hands and, by some miracle, managed to step back and avoid being flattened by two men in some sort of brawl. She stopped still as a market worker smashed a rugged man into a wall. "You steal from my stash again, I'll kill you, you disgusting Unworthy." The market worker had a rough voice that grated against Genni. As he held the throat of the Unworthy tighter, he noticed Genni beside him and firmly loosened his grip. His voice became lighter, but was almost predatory. "Sorry, darling. We gotta teach them we only get what we work for, right?" He smirked, and Genni managed to master a sweet smile to hide her apprehension.

"He's in there. See you around." He winked at Genni and locked his gaze on her body, and the nausea she had felt mulling over all day threatened to manifest itself. She managed to hold it down. Quickly, and without looking back at the Unworthy who had rolled into a ball by her feet, she walked through the grey door behind them. She saw the familiar face and let the door slide swiftly shut.

Chapter Six

"In!" boomed the synthesised, masculine voice as the ball hit the ground.

Ajay wailed, straightening himself back up after stretching for the return. Another one missed.

"Oh, what a shot!" Ace roared from the other side of the net. Ajay had to hand it to Ace, he'd improved. A year ago he could never have made a shot like that, sitting so tightly on the line that the naked eye could call it *out.* Unfortunately, technology never allowed that privilege, with every bounce of the ball accurately recorded. Ajay steadied himself and referred to the screen. He was still holding Ace 3 games to 1. Nothing to worry about.

"Remember I'm going easy on you," Ajay called out whilst getting ready to serve. He bounced the ball up and down, up and down. Watching as it yo-yoed from the ground into his hand, his eyes felt blurry. He was tired. Not surprisingly, of course – it was 10.32pm and he hadn't had one boost today. As the ball continued to bounce, he took a deep breath as if to energise himself with air. He couldn't have Ace beat him. He wouldn't hear the end of it, and he wouldn't be able to blame it on tiredness; fatigue was a weakness. Ajay threw the ball high, and the sound system projected a smashing sound as the ball touched the racket. The same sound came as Ace returned the serve. Ajay had wanted to turn the sound system off, as well as the interactive LED court that glowed with colour on every bounce. He found it tacky and distracting, but Ace enjoyed it, so they kept it on.

Out!

"There was no way that was out!" Ace groaned with frustration.

Ajay walked towards the ball to retrieve it, smirked, and shouted loudly, "The technology never lies."

"So, what did you think about your boyfriend's speech?" Ace called out across the court, bent down low, spinning his racket between his legs as he readied for another of Ajay's serves. Ajay wasn't embarrassed about his fan-boy crush on Mr Bancorp. Almost everyone in the office had one.

"Good, yeah. Nice reminder of what we're working for. I wish they'd redo the promo though."

Ace nodded. "I know. I swear they're trying to con us. There's no way people wore rags like that." Ajay was tempted to remind Ace he should be careful saying stuff like that. Command could be listening somehow.

"What do you think about the networking event?" Ace asked. As he spoke, Ajay finally served, but batted the ball into the net. *Darn.* He hung his head and walked sluggish towards the rolling ball, the floor erupting in small specks of light on his every step.

Ace laughed loudly. "What is going on here? The great Ajay Ambers hitting the net?!"

"I'm just . . ." Ajay almost said the word. ". . . ready for a drink."

"Alright, let's just finish the game before you cry on me." Ace got ready again. He fluttered his hands for the serve to be taken, from which he won a point instantly. *Advantage Ace,* roared the sound system. Play continued without conversation for a few rallies. Ajay's body felt done; he was exhausted. His insides felt like gears jarring against each other, producing painful sparking and frayed wires. He could feel his unbeaten reputation slipping away from him. Tightening the grip around his racket, his knuckles were straining under his skin. The ball's return span fast towards him, rattling over the net, flying to his right. Ajay swung back his arm and, almost without thinking, walloped it with all the strength he had. It hurtled its way back towards Ace, knocking him sideways awkwardly and catching his wrist, shaking the arteries beneath through the ball's speed and momentum. Ace moaned as the system roared Ajay's name.

Ajay was exhaling deeply and Ace's softening cackle filled the court. "What a blinder!"

From then on, Ajay got every point and won the game.

Close call, he thought, as he and Ace shook hands and gathered their stuff. They made their way off the court and Ajay got to the exit screen first. He scanned his Watch against it and felt his wrist vibrate as the exercise merit added to his score. Ace did the same, and as the sliding door opened, Ajay briefly glanced at the lines of the tennis court disappearing from the glass floor, ready to transform for whatever sport was selected next. He walked next to Ace, his gym bag bouncing off the back of his legs as he did so. He'd get changed before going to The Skyhouse, he thought, remembering the embarrassing incident when he wasn't admitted wearing sweaty shorts and a vest.

Ajay didn't visit The Sports Tower half as much as Ace. When he did, he enjoyed people watching as they walked past other rooms. People cycled, ran, danced, circuit trained. They walked past an old man working on boxing with a personal trainer wearing a branded polo shirt. Ajay saw the wobble of the man's degraded limb fat as he jived to hit and kick the pads on the trainer's hands. It was painfully slow, and a bit gross. Ace was a few steps in front of Ajay, obviously not as enthralled by what others were doing. Then there was a couple ballroom dancing, rather elegantly, then a bunch of girls in a spin class, then a group of men playing football. Ajay stopped for a moment in front of the door, watching the ball pass quickly between the men's feet. It wasn't often he saw football being played; like most people, he opted to play sports that were more merit efficient – more people meant less activity. Though he remembered the one time he did play, and it instinctively brought a small smile to his face.

It was Tara's birthday, and she'd been wearing that denim pinafore with the luminous red and yellow t-shirt. She was so excited. Their mother had arranged a street party to celebrate. When they'd got outside, they had seen colourful bunting hanging from building to building above a long wooden table that stretched the length of the street. Their neighbours had all come out to see his little sister and had greeted her with contagious smiles. Ajay had thought it was all a bit of a show, but he didn't complain; the food looked good, and Callum was there to keep him company. He was his best friend back then, before he met Ace. He didn't think of him much now. It was irrelevant. Yet that day, he played football for the first time.

It was their neighbour, Joye, who brought the ball. It was bright yellow, with a few black marks on it. Ajay remembered it vividly. Neon, almost painful to look at. Joye got them all playing behind the street, across the sand. Many people stopped to watch as the yellow ball flew, bounced, and tumbled through goals outlined by piled-up t-shirts and jackets.

"What are you looking at?" Ace asked, pulling Ajay away from the memory, who was still standing in front of the door, watching the men kick the ball about.

"Nothing. Just thinking about playing sometime."

"Football? Fair enough. Come on, I thought you wanted that drink."

"Yeah, I do." Ajay followed Ace, just as a man with legs like tree trunks smashed the ball into the net.

Chapter Seven

As they walked down the street, Ajay was frantically straightening his tie and shirt again. Their conversation jumped from work to Ace enlightening Ajay about his latest M-500 hook up. It was a long story, it seemed, seeing as it lasted from street level all the way up to the bar at the top of a 500-story skyscraper. It was the same old thing. Ace met a Glorified girl, spent time with her once, twice if she was pretty, three times if her parents were influential, and then they stopped when they each got bored. It was sleazy, Ajay knew that, and something told him it was probably the part of Ace's personality he should despise. He didn't, though; Ace had gained strong merit from the connections it gave him, so Ajay saw the appeal. He often wondered about ending things with Genni to follow his friend's footsteps. The more he talked about it, the more Ajay's thoughts ran away. To his relief, Ace shut up as they walked past the familiar sign that read 'M-400 and above', beeped in, and the fluttering of instrumental music pleased Ajay's ears. The smell of Tulo Cyder, sweet fruits and moderately salted chips permeated the air as people were waited on by drones around glistening tables. Constantly moving spotlights on the small, delicately used dancefloor rivalled the twinkle and glitter of the glorious lights of the City. Tulo at night was breathtaking from any height, but at the five hundredth floor, it still stunned Ajay to a momentary silence.

The Skyhouse was much classier than the likes of City Tree or The Barbican further Downtown. Ajay often felt like its service and standard gave him a taste of life in The Glorified Quarters. Places like this gave him the motivation to earn M-500 and get there.

He lifted his wrist and messaged Genni. He needed to see her; they hadn't spoken since their stressful morning.

Across the venue, he spotted his friends. The two of them were sitting around a tall, rounded table. Jaxson was dressed smartly, but had removed his striped red and blue tie, which was curled up like a sleeping snake on the tabletop. He slouched slightly on his stool and flicked his long brown fringe away from his face. Blake was sitting with him, laughing with his large rectangular glasses falling over his nose; his pink and blue tinted hair was tied back slickly and sharply contrasted with his neon green suit. It was a daring colour combination, Ajay thought, even for Blake.

Sauntering through the bar, Ajay noticed how there were more people shopping than usual. They were all crowded by the windows, lifting their Watches up to the billboards outside, strategically placed within the city's shimmering skeleton. As Ace and Ajay reached the table, Blake jumped up in excitement, displaying the bright purple shirt beneath his suit. Another colour in the mix; Ajay couldn't believe it.

"Greetings." He embraced Ace first and kissed him on both cheeks. Ace pulled away and observed the length of Blake's outfit.

"Blimey, Blake, you're matching the flipping billboards!"

You're telling me, Ajay thought. Blake thanked Ace whilst slightly opening both sides of his jacket and twirling round on one foot. Ace reacted with a wide smile and a wolf whistle. Ajay laughed as he too received kisses from Blake, whose cologne was strong. It smelt good, but its aftermath was overpowering. Ajay stopped himself from coughing.

He overheard the conversation Ace was having with Jaxson as he and Blake joined them at the table.

"I've seen you're heading towards the M-460 mark. How are you finding things?" Ace had put an arm around Jaxson. Two drones arrived with Tulo Ales, ordered automatically due to the men's statistical preferences. Ajay watched Jaxson nod considerately and start fiddling with his beer bottle, moving it from side to side.

"I'm not doing bad, just trying to support Blake with his score. You've been struggling a bit, haven't you?" He looked at Blake, who suddenly looked sheepish. Ajay wasn't surprised. Jaxson had made Blake suddenly vulnerable to opening up about his problems. Ajay didn't think he had a right. He knew Blake had been finding things difficult, and he was there to support him when he needed it – on a one on one basis, not as a group.

"Yeah . . . err . . ." Blake spluttered, before smiling. "You just can't help talking about me, can you, Jaxs?" His calm, friendly response smoothed over the slight awkwardness. Ajay was relieved. He sat down on the vacant bar stool and its golden legs toppled beneath him. He managed to stabilise himself by slamming his hands down to grip the rim of the table. Ajay was expecting the others to stare at him or ridicule him, but pleasingly, they merely continued chatting. He tried to get comfortable on the rose gold padded seat, still very aware of the wobble in the chair's legs. What was this? He looked down at the left-hand legs, which he noticed were slightly bent. This wasn't the standard he was used to, so he would have to submit a complaint later, make sure they get that sorted out.

"Make your order, Ajay. None of the pricey stuff though," Ace demanded, taking a swig. Ajay had forgotten Ace owed him a drink. It was a great feeling, like whenever he found slightly more credit in his account than he remembered was there. A drone flew over. He initially opted against his preference Ale, feeling a bit fed up with the same bittersweet taste. As he tapped at its menu screen, he was reminded of the gorgeous *CodeBite* beer that came out the previous year. It was smooth on the tongue; the buttery flavours of cocoa and caramel was a taste sensation, absolute gold dust compared to the blandness of Tulo Ale. It never would have survived. All Command-owned 'Tulo' brands dominated the market; a little bit of the money went back into the City's fund, so merit was earnt for investing in the brands that mattered. Ajay longed for a *CodeBite* but just settled with the taste of Ale and jumped back into the already flowing conversation.

"He's got it in his head that I'm playing copycat. A bit vain of him, don't you think?" Blake said as he shot a cheeky wink in Jaxson's direction, who shook his head and sneered.

"What's this?" Ajay asked.

"Oh, I'm moving closer to Jaxson's flat," Blake beamed.

"Don't you need M-450 for that neighbourhood?" Ajay toned the question in a way that he hoped didn't sound condescending. Jaxson's flat was in the Inner-Inner-Ring, not far from Ajay's own apartment, which was on the border. Blake was only at M-430, so it seemed very ambitious.

"Yes, you're right. I know I've got to work hard. It's just the motivation I need so I don't get left behind whilst you guys climb the ranks." He flurried his right hand up an imaginary ladder in the air.

"We could get you some merit now if you like?" Ace asked whilst pointing to his Watch.

"What? No!" Ajay contested impulsively. There it was again. Words flying out his mouth without permission. "Sorry Blake, it's been a long day."

Ace looked at him with the look of a mother bitterly disappointed in her child. Ajay felt judged, and then ashamed, and then willing. As always, he relented to the peer pressure.

"Fine. What have you got for us?"

"Well . . ." Blake said. "I could teach you to samba." He projected his voice, adjusted his glasses and slipped off his chair onto the dancefloor, shaking his hips seamlessly from side to side. Ajay wondered if Blake realised how little people enjoyed dancing. It had become one of the least merit-worthy forms of exercise anyone could do. That was part of Blake's problem, Ajay thought. In some ways, he admired that Blake spent so much time doing what he loved, but ultimately, it was stupid of him. His current marketing job wasn't too bad, but he needed to spend his free time doing something more valuable. Yet here he was again, trying to dance.

Ace and Ajay looked at each other and smirked.

"You first," Ace demanded, as he gave Ajay a light push off his chair towards the dancefloor. The golden stool lost its foundation and tipped over onto its side, taking Ajay with it.

His side stung as he hit the floor and made an almighty crash. It wasn't happening, he thought. *What a dick.* What did he do that for? How many eyes are watching? *It's okay, just compose yourself.* He gathered himself up off the white marble floor. Feeling the pang of uneasiness, he couldn't bring himself to count the watching eyes. Was he a greater spectacle than other conversations and the moving life of the metropolis outside?

Ace stood up, slightly sniggering. "Sorry, mate. I didn't touch you that hard."

"It's the chair legs," Ajay said, knowing Ace deserved something, so he punched him square on the arm as Ace took a swig. Liquid splashed up from the bottle over Ace's chin. That'll do, Ajay thought. He turned back to Blake, who was clearly ready to begin his dance class.

"Sorry, Blake . . . but this isn't really a samba type of place. Maybe in a few nights' time at a Middle-Ring bar?" Blake nodded his head as if he agreed, but his disappointment was reflected in the lines across his forehead. Ajay wasn't sympathetic, as his suggestion would be better for him anyway.

"What can you teach us here, around the table?" Ajay asked.

It didn't take long for Blake to get over his disappointment and arrive at something new with the same vibrancy and enthusiasm. Ajay wondered how exhausting that must be.

"I could talk you through my tips for organising your home life! I've been writing about it in my memoirs. You really need it Ajay, darling," Blake chuckled. Ajay nodded his head gracefully despite his internal irritation. Really? Blake was judging *his* organisational habits?

Ajay saw the Watch's list of merit activities reflected in Blake's glasses; the list included everything from being at work to educating a child. Ajay always thought there should be an option for 'cooking a five-course dinner for an Unworthy', just to see how many people would actually bring themselves to do it. *For a greater Tulo.* Usually, the Watch would automatically detect an activity through the scanning of an activation pad but for merit-making conversations, it had to be set up manually; a real inconvenience in their world of immediacy. Following his input, Blake's Watch asked: *Who are you teaching today Blake?* Blake looked to Ajay, who brought his own Watch to bleep against Blake's.

Excellent. Do you give me permission to record your conversation today? Ajay saw Blake select 'yes', allowing the Watch to do its job.

Chapter Eight

It was like she was painting the most beautiful landscape. On a cloud. Floating freely. Drifting dreamfully. She felt free with the extra energy. It didn't always feel like this, but the highs had been getting more intense and more addictive. Genni's excitability hit a peak when she received a message from Ajay that they had gone to The Skyhouse and he wanted her there. She had let out a gleeful squeal at her Watch and tapped her feet joyfully as she'd boarded the sky train. She knew she was acting like an annoying, peppy teenager but she didn't care. It was as if nothing could bring her down from her mental paradise. A few blocks from the bar and slightly dazzled by the intensity of the bright lights, she reminded herself not to stay long. Hours couldn't be wasted after her trips to Downtown. *I was back in the Quarters by the time I was your age.* Her father's words spinning inside her head started to lower the high. *Stop thinking. Just go for one drink, then the library.* The lights seemed to get brighter and more painful. She suddenly felt vulnerable on her own. Briefly looking up to the yellow moon, she felt humbled by its magnificence, and began swinging her arms softly with the motion of a paintbrush stroke.

Then she felt it. A dark presence behind her that was getting closer. She stumbled forward due to the strong force inflicted upon her shoulders. Her legs managed to stop her from falling flat on her face and she spun around in fright to see her attacker, adrenaline pumping through her veins, her mind spinning but ready to fight.

Genni lowered her shoulders and relaxed, yet she was still angry.

"What do you think you're doing?!" Genni screamed at her older brother. Trust him to turn up and almost knock her out of her utopic high.

"Nice to see you too, Gen," Rod smiled.

Genni looked at him, his perfectly shaped face tinted red as he stood beneath a soda advert. She always wondered how he managed to get all of their parents' best features; Mum's perfect eyes and teeth, Dad's hair and height. Genni was convinced some overpriced genetic manipulation had gone on and they just didn't bother when she came along.

"What did you do that for? And why are you even here?" Genni asked. Surely, he had some prissy venue in The Quarters to go to.

"Well, there's something enlightening about hanging out in the peasant's dwellings sometimes," Rod winked. Genni stayed silent, not giving him the satisfaction of laughing at his so-called joke.

"Sorry, I didn't mean to scare you." He leant in closer to her, examining her face with his green, piercing eyes shining through the night. "Are you alright? You look a bit pale."

Genni answered quickly. "Yeah. Fine. You just startled me is all." She gulped through her rising dehydration and the heat that was running across her head. "I'm just off to meet Ajay at The Skyhouse. You can join us if you like?" She spoke with composure, but she couldn't believe what she was saying. What was she doing inviting him? *Say no, say no*, Genni pleaded in her head.

"Yeah, why not?" Rod said.

Crap, Genni thought.

Chapter Nine

Ajay gave an internal sigh of relief as he spotted Genni handing over her coat for the cloakroom. He was already exhausted, and if he had to listen to any more talk about how to colour code his socks, he knew he'd conk out right on the table.

Blake's words became background noise as he watched Genni move from the other side of the bar. She was subtly hunching her back as if she was squeezing her stomach into herself. Under the ambient lighting, she looked a bit sick; her face was riddled with the pale curse of fatigue but then blushing red with fever. Another make-up disaster. Ajay always told her not to slap so much on or she'd look less like her beautiful self. Those moments when she was just natural were the ones that softened Ajay. He thought back to that morning after she'd woken up. The morning sun had crept through the window and fallen over the dotted freckles on her cheeks. The rich blue of her eyes, not burdened by the heavy weight of mascara or eyeliner, had calmed him in his rush. That was before he had a shower, made that stupid comment about her skin, and she'd left in a justified strop. It was actually very rare that he saw her like that. She just covered everything up, until he could barely see the real her anymore.

". . . and if you double-up on your hangers . . . Genni!" Blake's words came back to Ajay as he too spotted Genni's arrival. He watched Blake skip towards her, and Genni let out an excitable shriek as Blake embraced her in a bear hug and swung her around off her feet. She looked to the floor, pressing her blue nailed fingers into her head. Then, there was that smile. Bright. Infectious. She dashed over to greet Ace and Jaxson with hugs and kisses.

She eventually came over to him.

"Hi," she said. Where was his girlish shriek? He sometimes wondered about the connection between Genni and Blake, and why she wasn't always that excitable and flirtatious towards him, the person who probably should be lifting her off her feet on a dancefloor. He didn't worry about it, really. Though, the thought occasionally crossed his mind in a fleeting sort of way, picturing them together, before he reminded himself that Blake's score would never pass the Mr Mansald test, so he wasn't really a threat. It was more likely that Ace could whisk her away. That thought was almost unbearable and, by the same token, completely ridiculous. These were his friends, and Genni was faithful – he just had to keep her.

"Hi." Ajay told himself to stop pratting around and swallow his pride. He grabbed her playfully into a hug and whispered lightly in her ear, "I'm sorry about this morning."

Genni smiled, scrunched up her face in the endearing way she always did, and placed a hand on Ajay's knee as she sat down beside him and a Tulo Tia arrived by drone. Ajay hated that stuff, basically watered-down juice with a drop of ethanol. He felt a further warmth radiate through him from her touch, and he moved his legs closer to her.

Someone else sat next to Genni. Oh no, why was he here?

As soon as Rod sat down and the two of them exchanged small smiles of tolerance, Jaxson immediately wanted to shake Rod's hand. Ajay had noticed that Jaxson had always been enthralled and fascinated by Rod's boastful explanations of what it was like working closely with Tulo

Command, especially on the frontline of Liberation Day. He watched Jaxson's conscious movements as he scooped his tie up from the table and proceeded to put it back on. For about five minutes that followed, unfortunately, Rod's life was the topic of discussion . . .

". . . and they cook up some fantastic food," Rod said as he placed a *SkipSleep Pro* into his mouth, a relief to the others and a space for them to talk. Ajay was jealous of the *SkipSleep Pro;* he was in serious need of some energy. However, only M-500s or above could purchase the small e-devices that allowed someone to top up on *SkipSleep* on the go.

"How's the dancing, Blake?" Genni asked, with quite a hefty cough following her words.

"Oh it's great," Blake said. "I can't imagine not doing it. I've been utilising my boosts to do it even more. Did I tell you I'm hoping to move to an Inner-Ring place? By Jaxson's?" He tapped his Watch to order a drone.

Genni had opened her mouth but Rod jumped in there first. "You'll have to do more than dancing to meet that standard," Rod said, very matter of fact.

He was right, Ajay thought. Rod often said exactly what Ajay was thinking, which meant they had a strange relationship. Ajay understood Rod's principles, but the way he voiced them out loud just made him a prick. And Genni disliked him, so Ajay, of course, was outwardly on her side.

Silence fell over the group, until Genni bluntly responded, "Well not everything has to be about technological progress, some merit can be about making people happy and more motivated."

Ajay felt the tension rise like a mounting inferno. It's awkward, he thought. It's so awkward. *Stop it, Genni. Don't give him the satisfaction.* He looked to them both; she was staring hard into his eyes.

Rod laughed as he placed his *SkipSleep Pro* back into the pocket of his smart lightweight jacket.

"Very little, though. No-one makes it to M-500 by dancing," Rod said. Ajay saw Blake was embarrassed; his shoulders slumped, his eyes looked down and his smile slowly flattened like the painful deflating of a lively helium balloon. Jaxson patted Blake's back as some sort of brotherly gesture, though it did little to lift Blake's head.

No one said anything, and just the muffled vibration of classical music disturbed the silence. People sipped at drinks and avoided eye contact with Rod. Except for Genni, still. Was this it? The moment when she'd actually have it out with him? Ajay hoped not. It wouldn't end well for her. He sympathised that she'd always been expected to follow in his golden footsteps, but his status meant he deserved her respect. *Move on, Genni, move on.* Ajay's hands felt clammy and fidgety. How could he distract her? Talk about something, anything, he thought.

He spoke impulsively. "How was lunch today?" He cursed himself. *Great one, another conversation about her family. Nice work, Ajay.*

Genni sighed and, understandably, rolled her eyes in Rod's direction, who was Watch scrolling. Ajay then remembered that she didn't talk about her Dad problems in front of Rod, because to him, to put it in Genni's words, their Dad was "some ethereal power that could do no wrong".

"You saw Dad today?" Rod jumped in. Ajay forgot he was always listening. "Did he tell you about Number Two?"

Genni's mouth was full of drink, but she widened her eyes, puffed out her cheeks, nodded her head and placed a hand on Rod's shoulder, who was laughing. Suddenly, any anger she previously had for him disappeared. As quick as that.

"What's going on?" Ajay asked.

Rod snarled. "Just one of Mum and Dad's Side servants asked for a reference for their Purification."

Genni giggled as she finally managed to swallow, and her laughter could be heard out loud. Despite the joy in her face, Ajay noticed a dullness in her eyes. She also kept touching her stomach. Probably ate something she shouldn't have, Ajay thought.

"You're joking?" Ace joined the conversation. He had both an interested and amused look on his face.

"Yeah, she said she was ready to make her contribution to society. Though apparently she's great at folding sheets." Genni ordered a drone to stop in the air next to her. "Another drink, anyone?"

Rod ordered another Ale but the others refused, having already been in the bar too long. Ajay wondered whether she should be having another one. Clearly, she wasn't feeling good. He wouldn't ask though. The others could think he was stifling her, and he didn't want her to be embarrassed.

"Yeah, I heard that folding sheets is a one-way ticket to M-500," Ace mocked. There were grunts of amusement around the table.

"Dad said he wasn't giving her the reference; he can't lose her, as the others are completely useless." Rod ordered the drone to wipe the apparently unclean tabletop. "It's not surprising, given their upbringing with the low-life Guiding Light rubbi-"

"Right lads, our half an hour is up," Ajay proclaimed. He had a sudden urge to leave and wanted to remind the others that they'd been inactive for too long. He rose from his golden chair, which wobbled slightly on his departure. He noticed Rod's expression, who clearly didn't care much for being interrupted. Ajay felt a little anxious. An apology almost fell from his lips, but that wouldn't have gone down well with Genni. She would never apologise to Rod. Anyway, they were close to breaking the suggested rest regulations, and he didn't want to have to make it up, so his sudden departure was justified.

"Come on, Ace," he said as he moved around the table and tapped Ace on the back, the contact of his hand on the suit jacket making a clapping sound.

"Fair enough. Let's go," Ace waved goodbye and walked from the table, where Blake and Jaxson were also preparing to leave.

Ajay embraced Genni. He wouldn't ask if she was okay. She'd tell him if she needed him. Instead, he opted for the obvious question. "What are you doing tonight?"

"Just going back to mine. I have work to do. Oh, I've been thinking I want a new Watch strap, will you come with me in the morning?"

Ajay nodded. She kissed him on the cheek. She seemed fine, so she probably was fine.

"Bye everyone." Ajay waved to the others. He skipped quickly to join Ace at the exit, but not without noticing Rod's eyes, still looking at him with some sort of disgust. Or was it suspicion? No, it couldn't be. Yet Ajay almost felt the strength of those eyes piercing through his skin and electrifying his entire body with anxiety as he walked away.

Chapter Ten

Ajay swiped into his apartment building following his short walk from the sky train. It was hot. Claustrophobically so. He loosened the knot of his mustard tie. As the door slid behind him, shutting out the chaotic streets, he looked at his Watch. 01.33am. Pretty average day, Ajay thought. He staggered into the elevator, untucking his shirt and feeling a very slight cool breeze making its way up his torso as the air conditioning kicked in. Once over the pleasure of it, he briefly glanced down the rim of his left trouser leg. Stupid fox, he thought as he saw a small scruff of dirt there. Ajay didn't normally notice anyone in the streets at night, as he was often mindless, desperate for a boost. People tended to filter past him like ghosts. On tonight's walk, however, this woman's fox had snapped and growled at his feet and his first instinct had been to kick it square in the jaw. In the end, a scolding look to his owner sufficed. She was a middle-aged woman whose cheap, polka-dot shorts, muddied trainers and muffin-topped waist suggested she was someone from the outer rings. A bit far from home, Ajay thought.

She'd apologised, and the dirt on the trousers was no big deal, so they parted ways graciously. He'd nearly told her to have better control over her pet. It had looked to be walking her rather than the other way around; it bounded down the sidewalk whilst she got dragged behind by the lead. He imagined that's how Genni would look walking a fox. That could be another one for the list of why they weren't getting one when they moved in together. A lynx would be much more manageable. Not that they had an actual plan to live together. It was something they'd talked about, and Ajay had decided he wouldn't be the one to initiate it into a reality. The longer they could go concentrating on their own merit and careers before any of the other 'stuff', the better. He did miss her when she wasn't around, though. Just her company made him feel more peaceful, even when they were working or watching some educational movie neither of them wanted to watch.

The lights came on as he scanned himself into his apartment. It was an open-plan studio with high ceilings, grey walls, and a tendency to get messy.

Ajay went about his evening routine. Walk around the bed, pick up dirty clothes, put them on top of the wash basket; walk around the bathroom, pick up dirty clothes, put them on top of the wash basket; look at the wash basket, tell himself he'd do the washing tomorrow; collect the dirty glasses scattered around the living room, put them in the dishwasher; tell himself to get a cleaning drone, remind himself he wanted no drones in his home; finally, drop himself down on the sofa.

Tonight, though, all of that was overlaid with his whirring thoughts about Rod. Why had he looked at him so angrily? Would he bad mouth him to other Glorified people? Just to know what he was thinking, that would stop Ajay over analysing everything. He'd decided a long time ago that if he could ever be given a supernatural power, he'd choose mind-reading. An ability he could turn on and off whenever he felt like it. So that if he heard old Mrs Kollideman from the apartment across from him humming some health advertisement tune, he'd turn that right off. Then, when he needed to know what someone was thinking about him, he could be enlightened. Like that woman with the fox. When he read her mind, he'd hope to hear her feeling ashamed and embarrassed. He could know whether or not Mr Hollday was considering him for the next promotion, or he could know how Ace really felt about women, or why Genni was looking so wiped out tonight, and if she really did love him like she said she did. And he would know if Rod looked at him in that distasteful way for a reason, and what that reason was, or that Ajay was making a thing out of nothing. That would be good, and then he could concentrate more time on merit-making and not agonising over his own stupid mind.

He also knew he was tired. His eyes felt like they were going to fall from their sockets. With that sensation, he sat up with motivation. Come on, he thought. He tucked his black hair behind his ears and swiped the activation pad embedded within the glass coffee table in front of him. The *SkipSleep* System elevated itself from underneath the table. It was an elegantly designed cuboid, about thirty centimetres in height and fifteen in width, crafted together with strong, silver Tuloian steel. Its mechanical voice soothed Ajay, anticipating his imminent refreshment. *Ajay, how many hours' worth of SkipSleep would you like this evening?* He was given the options from 1 to 4 hours. He probably didn't need as much as usual, given his dangerous slumber the night before. Then again, if the system allowed him the maximum dose, then he'd be an idiot not to take it. Ajay selected 4 on his Watch and placed his forearm comfortably onto the black cushion inside the box. Above his arm hung the syringe needle, which glinted slightly in the reflection of the City's lights from outside. The system detected his arm was in position, and released its metal straps around his wrist and top of his forearm to tie him down. The coolness of its metal was always a welcome touch in the desert's heat. Ajay could feel the tingle of technology running up his arms as the moderation scan began; it creeped across his chest and into his brain to determine whether his body's chemical levels were stable. *Moderation Scan Complete. Dosage level accepted.* The needle began its work, lowering itself smoothly towards Ajay's arm, much like a snake would hang from a tree and inspect its dinner. *SkipSleep in progress.* Ajay didn't even wince as the injection went deep through his skin and he watched the red progress bar creep closer to 100%. Proteins, iron, multivitamins, creatine, Fo Doktrin and other natural herbs were being slowly absorbed by his body. Fo Doktrin was a plant that grew wildly in Tulo country and infected most of the Side. It brutally destroyed most other plant populations in the desert, but when cut, boiled and prepared, its vitamins and health benefits were anything but brutal. Their effects would be obvious within an hour or so, and Ajay looked forward to it. That fresh wave of energy without the need for sleep.

The progress bar continued forward. Ajay thought back to today's promo video, the shots of the old city, which was now the Side. His Grandmother used to tell him stories about people who lived out on the Side. It was in moments like these, when he was quiet, waiting, that he missed the concept of a bedtime. Waking up, watching the day pan out, and returning to the same springy mattress, ready for his grandma and her bedtime story. She would sit on the small stool by his bed, probably wearing some plain coloured floor-length dress, and would look at him fondly over her bent, narrowly framed glasses. Having her there was comforting. It meant every day always ended on a high, and he never had a bad night's sleep. It was different to this life, when in the rare, quiet moments, he felt her absence strongly, or just the absence of anyone at all.

Ajay sat up as he heard the satisfying ping. He lifted his arm out from the cushion, ignoring the message that it was his last boost for 8 hours. He turned to his wrist as the system lowered itself silently back into the table. Mindlessly, he started scrolling through *Personi*, to find anything to take his mind away from her. He didn't want to think about her, it only made him sad. It worked, briefly. Ajay repeatedly swiped his finger past people's updates: Davi had bought his own driverless car; some girl he'd met at networking posed in front of the Glorified Gate; Pearl had started a new campaign with a nutrition brand; and his colleague, Matu, had written some boring, political monologue about Command's Clean Streets plan. There was a load of other guff too. Adverts, 'motivational' videos and images, most of which were posted by people he didn't even know or cared about. He really needed to do a clean out of his profile, he thought. Get rid of the dead weight. Then again, he never knew what connections might be useful for merit someday. Without conscious thought, his finger kept scrolling. Then it stopped. On a picture.

It was one of Genni's family friends and her husband. He looked good. She looked awful. Pale, red eyes sat heavy beneath a flock of sweaty, tied back, blond hair, though her smile almost concealed all of that. It was astronomical. Ajay actually wondered if her jaw ached afterwards. It was one of those wide, teeth revealing and completely contagious grins. The baby in her arms was wrapped delicately in a white, cotton blanket, and despite its face being shrivelled up into the resemblance of a prune, Ajay could understand that it was cute. Until it screams death through the night and splatters poo all over their best rug, he thought. He read the caption: *It's been a long night. We would like to introduce you all to Tiel Ruana, born 7lb 4ounces at 3.20 this morning. She came out alive and kicking, already ready to earn some merit we think [laughing emoji]. We want to say a special thank you to our midwife. Gyna* . . . Darn, Ajay thought. He was supposed to be getting her out of his head. Here she was again, sitting on that stool, telling him a story of Marlena, or was it Marlina? A midwife who worked on the Side.

Ajay flicked away his Watch. Stop thinking about it, he told himself. *Do something useful. The news, have a look at the news.* He returned to his wrist again. Anything interesting? Not particularly. He wasn't much bothered about the latest break-up on *The Glorified House*, or a rise in *SkipSleep* overdoses, or the current heatwave that was drying up everyone's garden plants. You've got to be kidding me, Ajay thought. There's the story again. He remembered it vividly. The way he and his grandma had laughed. She was telling him the story of the midwife and how she would take home women's placentas to feed her plants. "It makes them bloom like nothing else." Grandma had said it so matter of fact, but Ajay, as an eight-year- old kid, or a *human* in fact, thought it was disgusting. He'd shown it, scrunching up his face and sticking out his tongue. "Yuk," he would have said. Ajay noticed he was pulling the same face too and he smiled to himself softly. It *was* funny. The two of them had always had times like that. Wow, he really did miss her. He still went to see her every month, if time allowed it, but it wasn't the same since she'd taken ill. He felt the guilt again. That pain in his chest, urging him to go and see her more, while he still could.

Ajay shuffled again on the sofa and willed himself to dismiss his thoughts. What educational movie should he watch? He whizzed through the streaming menu on his floating Watch screen, but nothing really took his fancy. In the end, he settled for *The Financial History of Tulo.* Despite having seen this movie a few times, the merit was still adequate. Apparently finding out about the past inspired citizens to become their most effective selves, and the fact he worked in the financial district was just an added bonus. He flicked with his fingers and synced his Watch with the projection port on the table. A much larger screen appeared, running the opening sequence to the movie. Ajay sat down and lay his head on the back of the black sofa, his hair camouflaging into the material. His eyes felt fresh again, and he reckoned he'd stay awake all night; he even considered going to the office after the film to squeeze in some overtime. If he got there before Hollday, he'd then see him at his desk as he walked to his office. That'll be good, Ajay decided. He had told Genni he'd help her shopping, but he could bail on that if he was on a roll.

"She must have got lots of merit for that." His eight-year-old voice popped back into his head. Ajay closed his eyes slowly in frustration as he thought over the stupid midwife story again.

"Stop it," he whispered to himself. His mind was racing back to Marlena, Marlina, or actually, was it Madelia? She had been caught in a wildfire drift following a storm, and had helped people evacuate their houses, assisted the medical services, and delivered a baby, all in one night. Yet when Ajay had suggested about her obviously large merit count, his grandma had said words along the lines of, "It doesn't quite work like that." Ajay remembered being bewildered that night. It was the only night that his grandma's story had actually disturbed his sleep. He soon discovered that people who choose to live like those on the Side, following what they called The Guiding Light, would only ever reach M-200, unless they then applied for Command's Purification process. Ajay thought back to the conversation in the bar; he wasn't so attuned to the humour the others found in Genni's father's servant requesting a reference. He still didn't really understand why City folk *hated* the Side so much. It was like the discrimination was so deep-rooted that they themselves didn't even know.

Chapter Eleven

Genni looked even worse in the morning. Her brown, usually wavy hair looked as if it hadn't been washed. It was tied up and smoothed over with something that Ajay could only describe as sweaty grease. She was walking quickly towards him, wearing loose hanging blue trousers and a frilly white top that revealed just the bottom of her torso. If it wasn't for the hair, the excessive make-up, and the red flushed complexion in her face, she would appear just as beautiful as always. Ajay had been waiting for at least five minutes. He did notice that she didn't bother letting him know that she'd be late, but he let it go. It had been okay, just Watch scrolling in the sea of disinterested people that swarmed the shopping centre. He had read an email from Hollday saying he'd like his input during the next executive meeting. Ajay knew getting into the office early was the right call. He was there at 4am, an hour before Hollday himself. So when Genni called to confirm their plans, he figured he could sacrifice a little time after being so impressive.

"Sorry, sorry, sorry," Genni said, rising on her tiptoes to give him a kiss. Her lips felt dry to him, and she smelled musty, as if her clothes had laid stagnant following a wash. "I got caught up at work." She smiled and tried to subtly lick away the dryness of those small lips.

"It's fine. You okay? You look . . ." Ajay hesitated. Genni looked at him, her eyes tired and distressed, eyebrows tense and stiff, in a way that stopped him from asking her. She probably didn't want to talk about it. If she did, she would have already, right? He convinced himself that she was just stressed. The new project was probably taking its toll, and he shouldn't add to the pressure by pointing out her greasy locks. It wasn't anything a few boosts wouldn't sort out. So he just said, "You look nice."

"Thanks." Genni eyes were questioning for a moment before softening again. "Fancy a drink first?"

"Sure. How about this place?"

Ajay had been waiting in a pop-up kiosk set in the walkway of the gloriously white centre, between a store that sold office wear and another selling high-end suits and dresses. The exteriors of the shops were white and clinical, exaggerated by the way the sunlight beamed through the entirely glass roof. Ajay knew that this place wouldn't last forever. Shops seemed to be closing daily as drone deliveries increasingly became a lifestyle, but not for people like him. He opted for the old-fashioned way. Though, he did notice that people still enjoyed coming in, so they could make an hour or two or it, for some sort of momentary release from their merit-making lives. Genni swooped past him and found a table next to one of the encasing walls of the circular cafe. It was right next to the entrance of *Dress,* which not surprisingly displayed vibrant dresses of every colour in its window. Genni looked at it too.

"I'll need to get my dress for Liberation Day soon," she said as she scanned the menu code on the table and started flipping through the options on her wrist.

"Sure. What are you thinking?" Ajay asked. Last year Genni wore this mind-blowingly hot red dress covered in splatters of glitter that showed off her curves. Plus, the cut was really low, proudly boasting her chest. Ajay felt like a boss with her on his arm, and despite it angering him that other guys were looking at her, it felt insanely good that she was his.

"Maybe a short one with a high-neckline. I went for boobs rather than legs last year, so might go for the opposite."

Disappointment. Of course, he knew that was the right approach, but it didn't stop him hoping. At least it might calm down the prying eyes of others. He looked at his wrist and ordered a spinach smoothie with extra vitamin boost. He briefly looked back at the dress store. From what he could see, between the motion of scurrying people, every dress seemed to have a high neckline. Darn, he thought. *That must be the trend.*

Soon a drone arrived with his smoothie and Genni's iced coffee. Ajay lifted his wrist and paid against the drone's side. *Thank you for your custom,* it said as Ajay immediately took a sip of his smoothie. As soon as the liquid hit his tongue he wanted to gag, but he ended up spluttering in a pathetic cough.

"Alright over there?" Genni asked, slurping at her coffee.

"Yeah." He coughed again and lowered his voice. "I just always forget how foul these are."

"I know. It's alright when you get used to it."

"Yeah."

She was right. He'd soon be able to tolerate the complete lack of any milk or sugar. He glanced over Genni's shoulder and saw an older man with no hair indulging in a slice of cake that was covered in, he guessed, vanilla cream icing and multi-coloured sprinkles. It looked amazing. He couldn't wait until he was old, retired, maybe living in the Quarters, and had so much merit that those small deductions for bad eating wouldn't matter. Genni had obviously noticed his drooling.

"Put your tongue away," she demanded with a smile.

"It was the cake, not the old man," he said. They both laughed. "Shall we drink while we shop? Conscious of time."

"Sure."

They left the table and walked hand in hand past the shops. Ajay noticed the sweatiness of Genni's palms. He sympathised with the iced coffee in her other hand; it must have been melting unnaturally fast with the heat that seemed to be seeping through her skin. They walked at their usual pace, quickly but not so fast that they'd get a stitch. It was in keeping with everyone else's coming and going. Ajay knew it was an art to walk in this place without getting pushed flat on your back by a person dashing to get their stuff and go. Shopping wasn't so much a leisure activity but a sport. Who can be the quickest to get their new suit, Watch screen replaced, and then get back to the office? The only exception was the food outlets, where people did seem to stop for a breather and a bland lunch. Ajay mindlessly looked at the stores they were quickly passing: *Suits For Men, Look Your Best, Active You* – that was Ace's favourite. He was always in there, allowing the digital assistants to advise him on the best trainers or running shorts for his physique. Ajay wondered if Ace fancied them, he was there so much. The voice of technology filled every store, every changing pod, and hid behind every mirror. There was something fun about trying clothes on. One time, in the early days, he and Ace had been messing about, ordering the changing pod to show them wearing every description of dress and female lingerie. Ajay scowled at the memory of briefly seeing a digital representation of Ace in a thong. It was a mistake, and Ace had quickly flicked the 'No' button and the augmented reality had faded. That didn't mean it wasn't forever etched in Ajay's brain. So disturbing. Talk to Genni, he thought, *get your mind off that monstrosity.*

"So, what strap are you wanting?" he asked, briefly looking down at his reflection in the white tiled floor.

"I'm not sure. They've just brought out a new gradient style. I might have a look at how many credits that is."

"Nice."

"Why don't you have a look at one? You must be bored with yours."

Ajay took another sip of his smoothie. It was tolerable, finally. He was *beyond* bored with his plain black Watch strap, same as the day he got it on his eighteenth birthday. Strap Personalisation modified the casing of the entire Watch, around the screen and the strap. Each time he saw someone of higher merit whom he respected with an edgy or inspiring Watch strap, the jealousy was unreal. To personalise it a little bit would be nice. He'd once seen a guy with a case patterned with green-fonted code. That hurt the geek inside him. Not to mention the way personalising straps was becoming the norm, and therefore anyone like him with the Command branded strap was seen as cheap. Painfully, it wasn't an option for him. He'd seen them take the Watches away to alter the mechanical strap into the customer's pattern of choice. They put them through a machine he was unfamiliar with. Who knows what they do with it? It wasn't worth the risk, but boy, did he want it.

"I'm okay. I like the simplicity of it. Plus, it saves credit," Ajay lied. He let go of Genni's hand to look at the underside of his own wrist; the Command sign was imprinted stylishly against a black background. Five dashed circles, all different sizes, all dropped inside each other with small specks of a royal purple colour layered through it. It reminded Ajay of the cross-section of a tree trunk, which he'd seen as a kid, though it was actually the bird's eye view of the City from above. The outer rings to the inner rings, each separated by a river, all of it running towards the bullseye of the walled Glorified Quarters. He stroked his fingers over the logo softly. Maybe one day I'll change it, he thought.

It suddenly occurred to him that he'd stopped walking, which was dangerous to do, as people traffic wasn't always kind. Genni was a few steps in front of him, walking into *Watch, by Command*, which was obviously the largest store in the centre. The symbol on his wrist was in front of him in full glory, hanging over the store's entrance.

"What are you doing? Come on," Genni demanded impatiently. He understood; they needed to get on with it, so he joined her and walked into the store.

* * *

"No, thank you. Just the one pattern please," Genni said as the sales assistant tried to persuade her to spend more credit. Ajay sat next to Genni impatiently, barely listening to a word her or the sales assistant were saying. He was passing the time by looking aimlessly around the store.

Watch, by Command was an entire store suffocating in Command white walls, consultation tables and shelves, with sensitive splashes of royal purple in its branding. It was the only store in Tulo that offered Watch maintenance and upgrade services, so it was hectic and busy. Ajay watched as a man struggled with a toddler having an absolute fit by the 'New Releases' section. He felt sorry for the poor sucker. The man, not the kid. He was wearing a white t-shirt completely covered in what Ajay assumed could only be his son's lunch. The man looked on the edge of desperation, pleading for his son to calm down, and scanning his purple-marked eyes around the store in utter embarrassment. Despite the indirect merit Ajay could earn from raising successful children, little irritants like that one put him off having them. It was wailing incessantly. The promo video behind the kid then caught Ajay's attention; it was for the newly released 'Double Strap' – allowing a Watch to have a different pattern on its strap to the casing surrounding its screen. Not revolutionary, Ajay thought, but the credit-making scheme seemed to be working. He could see many consultations happening across the store, digital prototypes floating in front of the lustful eyes of ready customers.

It was also the only store that had any people working in it. They were all so used to the digital changing pods or order screens spitting out products that it made Ajay almost uneasy to be greeted by an actual person. This assistant was a piece of work, though. She was clearly following the corporate script perfectly. Every time Genni wanted to close the deal, she suggested another feature or hardware upgrade. A tinted screen? A double strap? Deluxe screen protector? *No, for Tulo's sake. Just give the girl what she came for.* Ajay was resisting the urge not to smirk every time Genni rejected the offer.

"Very well then. I'll get your request set up." The assistant began tapping furiously on the table. She was wearing a white Command jumpsuit with the symbol just above her right breast. Her red hair was tied back neatly into a tight bun and matched the colour of her bright lipstick. Her voice was pitch perfect, as if it were controlled by an auto-tuner. Ajay suspected that the Command training must be ruthless; there's no other way they could've gotten every one of them looking and sounding the same. The assistant flicked her fingers from the screen on the table into the air; a working prototype of a Watch floated in front of them. It boasted a gradient patterned case and strap; blues, pinks and purples. Ajay saw Genni's eyes light up, joy still distinguishable under their increasing redness. He didn't like the strap.

"Oh, I love it!" Genni said, her voice coming out whiny. "I'll take it."

"Very good," the assistant said, whilst lifting a black cushion from underneath the table, willing Genni to place her Watch on top of it.

Ajay watched as Genni disconnected her Watch, currently encased in a pattern of golden stars. The strap retreated itself back into its sides to leave only the casing and the screen behind.

Genni placed it on the cushion and the assistant disappeared with it.

"Always feels strange not having it on," Genni said as she cupped her wrist with her other hand.

"Yeah," Ajay said. "I love the feeling of the strap though."

"Oh yeah, the tickle," Genni said.

It was a tickle, Ajay thought. Whenever he placed the screen on his wrist, the mechanics of the strap would run across his skin, like a crawling insect, until it met its other side and merged together in sweet, smooth unity. The first time Ajay wore a Watch, it wasn't even his. He just couldn't wait until he was eighteen to at least try it. It had massively improved since then; its model was more streamlined, flatter on the wrist, waterproof and so lightweight that no one even noticed it was there. It was easy to sleep and shower in. The current model was the best yet, so much so that Command hadn't changed the core hardware for years – everything about it was almost perfect.

"Okay, here we are." The assistant was back in next to no time, holding Genni's Watch on the cushion, encased in its new attire. Genni placed the screen back on her wrist, and the newly painted Watch crawled around it. She looked at

Ajay with a small smile. The tickle, he thought. She then looked at her wrist and revalidated her fingerprint. As she was doing so, the assistant addressed Ajay with her ruby-red lips.

"Can I help you with anything? I can see you haven't yet opted for personalisation."

She was staring at Ajay's Watch. He smiled at her, wishing he were wearing long sleeves so he could cover it up. Nosy camel, he thought. Thankfully, Genni spoke so he didn't have to.

"I wouldn't bother, I've tried. He's more of a simple soul." Genni giggled and faintly patted Ajay on the shoulder. He looked at her disapprovingly, but hoped it had come off in a jokey way.

Whilst he was grateful to Genni for deferring the assistant's question for him, he didn't find her using humour at his expense funny. At least his hair looked like it had been washed in the last week, he grunted to himself.

"Well, if you ever need any help with it, we can sort you out." The assistant's tone felt deliberately patronising. It was clear she was judging him for his lack of crowd compliance. He was tempted to put her in her place; he knew more about the Watch than her, and all her bland Command buddies put together.

Chapter Twelve

After a few hours had passed, Genni was sat on a bench outside the library, turning her wrist back and forth and admiring her new Watch strap.

Get back inside, she thought. She knew she needed to. Though the outside air was hot and clammy, it was just fresh enough to ease the headache. She held her head in her hands to at least try and lessen the pounding. The library was always rammed on a Saturday, even when the sun was setting. She hated the place for everything but the immediate merit. Exhaling deeply, she looked up and noticed a woman from across the square. She was beautiful. Genni couldn't make out all her features as different people wandered across the line between them, but she noticed the way her long brown hair flowed gorgeously down her back. She wasn't doing anything special. Just standing in the sun, looking at her screen, in a loose red dress that was drifting in the slight breeze. Genni closed her eyes and placed the girl next to a waterfall.

The brightness of her dress contrasted with the greens and blues of nature. She considered going home to paint or beginning a sketch in her notebook. Yet when she opened her eyes again, her model was gone, disbanded into the life of the City. Get back inside, she told herself.

Genni rose from the bench, her mind still partially fixated with the girl and the ideas she could inspire, when she felt the deep soak of sweat on her back. Feeling around her, she realised she had drenched her blouse and her headache continued to press hard. Making it to the bathroom, she stared into the mirror. A red circle appeared, accompanied by the voice of technology. *Your skin is presenting only a 30% moistu-* Genni slammed her hand at the mirror's controls. It was silenced. She tried to conceal the redness around her eyes, noting that her skin was almost as bright as that girl's dress. Was she just tired? Stressed? What was happening to her? *I was M- 500 by the time I was your age.* Her father's words were back. She threw off her blouse and put it in her bag. After adjusting her bra straps beneath her vest, she breathed deeply and staggered back out into the library.

She walked back through the building, but all she could detect were blurred figures and strange shapes as her vision began to suffer. Genni wandered past many desks, screens and distracted eyes, all learning more contributory skills. As she struggled to walk in a straight lane, drones dodged her as they served people with requested files, drinks, food or anything else they fancied. She'd spent too much of her life in this place, she thought, as a dull ache crept into her chest. It was depressing how many nights she'd worked through on *SkipSleep,* either here, at home or at the office. Sometimes in her slippers, just so she was comfortable in some way.

Right now, she was anything but comfortable. Genni's vision was suffering more. As she arrived back at her desk, she managed to shake off the distortion, turning a page on the screen and downloading information about the Cleaner Tulo Initiative. Reading but not absorbing, her eyes went from sentence to paragraph as the dull ache in her chest became a sharp pain. Her legs and arms began to tingle, and she quietly yelped as her left foot began to spasm. She scrambled back to the bathroom, whacked open the cubicle door, braced herself against it and realised she couldn't actually breathe.

Chapter Thirteen

Ajay was pleased that he'd managed to get another hour in at the office before heading out for volunteering. He had been slightly irritable with Genni when they'd left the shopping centre. It had taken half an hour longer than he expected to change her strap. It wasn't even worth it, he didn't think. Why didn't she go for something more sophisticated? Though the colours did suit her.

The sky train was always busier on a Saturday afternoon; weekends tended to be when people moved about the most: from offices, to the Sports Tower, to volunteering and community services, networking events, and – if there was time – social gatherings. Today, after he'd left Genni, the carriage was so full that Ajay ended up being pressed against the window, in the lovely resting place of an older man's armpit. The man was wearing a sleeveless black vest and training shorts. Obviously off to use the little energy he has left, Ajay thought. Ajay's mouth wasn't far from the sprouting hairs of his armpit as the man reached up to hold onto the pole above him. To Ajay's relief, the man departed at the next stop. The upgrade to the sky train's schedule couldn't come quick enough; Ajay assumed extra services would reduce the congested and hairy travelling conditions.

As the train whizzed closer to The Glorified Gate, more Tuloians disembarked, allowing the remaining passengers to breathe again. Ajay managed to grab a seat and look at the latest news articles. He sat back and positioned the screen straight in front of his eyes, giving himself the reassurance that no one could see his face. He wasn't in the mood to be watched. Words blurred to him as he scrolled through several articles celebrating new business ventures, one about rising stormy weather, and some about population decreases and the forming of anti-Command groups. Then, a live news programme appeared at the bottom of the screen. Ajay tapped to listen whilst simultaneously reaching for his earphones from his suit trouser pocket.

A news reporter's voice filled his ears.

". . . will meet tomorrow to begin the debate. It is an unprecedented question, and this is the first time Purification has been reviewed since the merit system was first introduced." A man in his mid-thirties, with a shaven head and a dimpled chin, spoke with clarity. He was standing on the high street of the Side, as indicated by the text that ran beneath his name. *Stevin Jenk.* Behind him was a huge sand hill, towering over rows of grey-boxed houses and pothole heavy roads, which allowed the desert sand to resurface. It was sometimes so easy for Ajay to forget he was living in the desert. The City was so chaotic and marvellous in its development that the only real reminders were the heat and the view from the tallest buildings. Though it wasn't easy for anyone to forget the Side. It always came back, on the news or in conversation. He concentrated again on the reporter's words.

"It is expected that the clause to have the acceptance age lowered to 20 years old rather than 25 will be rejected. However, an alternative has been proposed. Command Officials are now also to discuss the possibility that members of the Side community will only have to undergo one year of Glorified service, instead of two following a valid reference." Stevin Jenk paused, clearly listening to the person in his ear. "The Hevas family have yet to make a comment, but we do have a few City citizens online to offer their view. First, let's go to Jessa from the Inner-Ring."

The camera switched to a young girl with blond shoulder-length hair and a slim jawline. Ajay thought her small, finger-size hoop earrings were a nice touch to her already attractive face. "I personally don't think anything should change. I don't see how we can be confident that their indoctrination has been fully reversed after just one year in the City. Command is always saying that we need to protect the merit system as it's got us where we are, and I think this could become detrimental to that protection." Ajay continued to listen as he was presented with Vick from the Inner-Outer-Ring.

"Hi. Thanks . . . erm . . ." Vick clearly wasn't as prepared to make his argument as Jessa. He was dressed nicely in a light blue shirt, but one side of his collar was pointing up. "I wonder whether at the age of 20, you know with them being younger and that they might be more, you know, easily released from the brainwashing that the Side has done. Then again, Jessi is right." *Jessa.* Ajay shook his head. *He's got his collar turned up, used the wrong name, and clearly has no experience of public speaking. Where did they get this guy?* Ajay briefly wondered whether Vick could be a Purified citizen, but realised that he couldn't be, he was too young.

"Command needs to think . . . errr . . . a lot about . . ." Vick looked down at the floor, thinking for words. "How . . . erm . . . you know, progress is strength." Ajay felt like laughing out loud, but he didn't want to bring attention to himself. He briefly looked to the window; the grey blurs of skyscrapers flitted past as the train neared closer to his stop. He liked

Vick. Throwing in Command's signatory line was a good save. People will no doubt agree with him and admire his patriotism, rather than judging his foolish incompetence.

Ajay had had enough of this. He swiped further down his screen to find some more drivel about the illegal administration of *SkipSleep* to people who wanted extra. Ajay dismissed his screen back into his wrist. *Didn't people know what too many boosts do to the body? There are warning adverts everywhere and they limit it for a reason.* He sighed over people's stupidity.

Everyone left on the train was dressed beautifully and held their heads high. Ajay was suddenly conscious he might have been the only non-Glorified left. He straightened his tie and sat up, his thoughts turning back to the debate. He never really spoke about constitution politics, mostly just keeping quiet whenever the topic came up, which, with the likes of Genni and Ace, was a lot. They'd grown up around it, with people from the Side cooking their dinners and ironing their clothes. Ajay imagined that they had never spoken to them, or if they did, it would only have been with a functional or derogatory comment. He had occasionally laughed at Ace's mocking of the Unworthies, but he mostly found it cheap. He sympathised with them. Why couldn't they have the chance to make their contribution like everyone else? It seemed inordinately harsh for them to be limited to M-200, just because of the family they were born into. He thought of Genni. She was always saying how she wanted to be cut off from her parents, from their ruthless pressure for her to get back in the Quarters. So, Ajay often questioned, why didn't she see that those from the Side wanted the same? They were just escaping from a different kind of prison. Ajay knew this view was controversial, so he stayed quiet. It was easier that way.

We are now approaching The Glorified Gate.
His journey's end distracted him from his thoughts. As the train smoothly stopped, he stood by the door, impatient for them to open. Once they did, Ajay bounced off the carriage and walked determinedly towards the Gate. He hadn't noticed his complete disregard for his surroundings until he collided with her: the small woman wore a large beige hat with a tasteful brown ribbon around its centre, and a golden necklace sat simply on her chest. She was clearly Glorified, and he'd knocked her to the ground.

"Maam, I'm so sorry," Ajay cried out politely, offering his hands to her for support. She didn't take them but lifted her head slowly; not enough so that Ajay could see her features, but enough for him to notice a poorly concealed mark that fell over her slender neck. It must have been a sort of maroon colour, though it was clearly distorted by a level of make-up above it. Something was fairly familiar about it. Something Ajay couldn't quite capture. He bent lower to see more of her, but she got up too quickly and sprinted on her heels towards the station's exit. Ajay caught a whiff of cheap camel meat. It smelt like the Outer-Ring streets but it must have been from someone else. It can't have been her. He started to wonder if she'd even looked at him.

Hopefully not. Then she wouldn't remember the face of the man who knocked her down, and she wouldn't tell all her Glorified friends about him.

Ajay's Watch vibrated. He was late. Dashing down the steps from the station, he felt relief as he saw the Glorified patrol guards weren't there. There'd be no interrogation today. Ajay removed a tissue from his pocket and wiped the sweat drips from his forehead, leaving a greased shine to his tanned skin tone. Ajay's manager was waiting for him outside the Gate.

"Hi," he said and climbed into the car. She told the car to go and then immediately started talking. Ajay was thankful. It stopped the possibility for him to apologise for his lack of punctuality, though she never had anything interesting to say.

"We're expecting a few new recruits in the coming weeks. I think Command's campaign towards promoting Community Spirit is really working," she said, looking at Ajay over her red-rimmed glasses. She was good at her job, M-520ish Ajay would guess, but quite soft. He didn't always trust her. No one is that nice just because they are.

"That's great news," Ajay said, smiling at her.

The car glided forwards and Ajay looked up through the its panoramic roof to see 'Progress is Strength' engraved in gold and displayed proudly across the Gate's decadent archway. He never got tired of The Glorified Quarters. It was like being transported to another world engineered by the same craftsman. It still had the usual sights of drones flocking to different jobs, and flurries of people. Though rather than walking through the streets, most were carried by hover vehicles with black-tinted windows. The rows of neon advertisements had been replaced by immaculate walkways, tastefully planted trees, and flamboyant flowers that shrouded the entrances to pavement cafes. The air felt cleaner, the only smell being from the flowers or freshly baked goods. Spidering off from the main streets were numerous gates that opened onto residents' long driveways, some of which wound up into the desert's mountainside, giving them the highest levels of privacy.

The car hovered left and headed towards a large set of gates behind which stood The Old Golden's infamous sculptured fountain; a group of older people were carved into a golden material, with detailed facial expressions of joy and delight, surrounded by jets of water. Around the fountain's base was a greyed bricked wall covered with letters in a curled typography that read 'Caring for the Best'.

Upon getting in and putting on his blue care uniform, Ajay set off on his list of jobs for the morning, with his Watch listening and recording. He spruced up Mr Moren's front garden with some new lavenders and perfected the edges of Mrs Delwenny's high ceilings and covings with a paint called 'Shining Sunrise'. Next, he walked over to the Village Hall and up the gleaming steps to take Mrs Laptoff her pills. Ajay walked into the hall, which was ladened with hanging baskets of yellow and golden flowers that gave the room a constantly fresh and floral smell. It was almost overpowering, hitting him instantly as he made his way over towards a group of older women, sitting in exuberantly patterned armchairs. He always felt jealous of these people, coming in here to sit, chat, sip on drinks, and look over the splendour of The Old Golden's garden, its greenery so pleasant in the white natural light.

"Another one's here," Mrs Laptoff said and snarled to her friends as Ajay approached. "Why don't they just use drones for these things?"

Ajay widened his eyes as he opened a bottle of water for her and greeted the group. Mrs Laptoff didn't look at him but gazed out of the wall-to-ceiling windows at an old couple sitting on one of the many garden benches. Ajay wondered what he had done to offend her, and how he might rectify it.

"She doesn't mean that. She's lost the plot in her old age." Miss Genard was sitting across from Mrs Laptoff, wearing a mint green golfing outfit.

"No problem," he said in response. "You look lovely in green."

"Oh, stop it," Miss Genard giggled. She paused, looking again at Mrs Laptoff. "You know, back when Julie was working, she was a big advocate for gaining merit through community work. Do you remember girls?" She looked around at her fellow loungers. "Even set up protests against using drones for simple jobs." Miss Genard jumped up triumphantly in impersonation, her arms high. "LONG LIVE VOLUNTEERS," she roared before lowering herself back into her seat as the other ladies found the nostalgia amusing.

Ajay smiled. A fake smile, of course. He just wanted to do his job, as much as he wanted their respect. He gave Mrs Laptoff her first pill, which was quickly swiped from his hand. She looked disgusted as he held her chin to guide the water from the bottle into her mouth. *What was this snotty woman's problem?* He was helping her.

"Those were the good old days," Mrs Lockgean said. Ajay didn't look at her, but continued to eavesdrop. "I don't know why these young people think they have it so hard. We didn't have the technology they have now. No *SkipSleep* or talking wardrobes." Ajay felt as if he should defend himself as one of 'these young people', but he didn't have much to say.

"It has come a long way in the last twenty years, because of our lot's contribution." Miss Genard turned to the other lady beside her. "Hey, Dess. How's Mindy getting on with her little one?"

"Oh he is just adorable," Mrs Trenmill said, and she rose from her seat to walk over to Miss Genard. "Let me show you a video," she said as she tapped at her Watch. Over the next few minutes, all the women – apart from Mrs Laptoff, who was still glaring suspiciously at Ajay – gathered around the screen giggling. Ajay found the persistent laughter annoying, but he kept his eyes sharp and looked out the window in between shoving pills down the old woman's throat.

"Just splendid," Miss Genard said. "You've got another, haven't you? I've forgotten his name. David?"

"Daved . . . yes . . ." Mrs Trenmill closed her screen and tucked her Watch away underneath the sleeve of her pink silk blouse. "He's doing okay, thank you. Still low on merit, but okay."

"Oh I'm sorry to hear that," Miss Genard said, ordering a drink from the drone that was flying past.

"Don't be. He'll get there," Mrs Trenmill continued. "Just needs to work harder to be like his sister. Her contribution has certainly got me a nice bit of indirect merit."

Miss Genard interjected. "Oh yes, it's so nice to be rewarded when your child makes something of themselves." She took a sip of her bubbly that had arrived on the table beside her. Ajay was thankful that the conversation seemed to be ending, and that he only had one more pill to go.

He gently placed the remaining pill in the old lady's hand, but Mrs Laptoff turned in a flippant motion to look Ajay straight in the eyes. Ajay felt the sting as she slapped his hand away, spitting at him in anger.

"You know, it's disgusting they let you in here," she barked, her tanned skin reddening and her body rising with rage. Ajay froze. She was insane. Completely lost it. He wasn't sure what to do so he just stood his ground, water bottle still in hand.

"Julie, calm down," Miss Genard said, jumping up and holding Mrs Laptoff's hand. "This young man is just here from the outside the walls to help, and to raise his merit. For a greater Tulo, remember?" Miss Genard was gently stroking along the hand of her friend, who seemed to fall into a frenzy.

"No . . . NO!" she shouted as she flailed her arms out, trying to push Ajay away and knocking over drinks and the furniture around her. Blimey, Ajay thought. Maybe he'd delivered her pills too late. As more care assistants were rushing towards them, Ajay decided as he had completed his task, he better leave *Mrs Mental* to get sorted out. He walked away, quickly.

Then, a sudden crash caused him to turn back. Mrs Laptoff was on the floor, having taken Miss Genard down with her. *What a show.* Mrs Laptoff soon had scurrying care workers lifting her from the ground, but her burning eyes were only looking at Ajay. She screamed at him. "THEY'LL FIND YOU."

Chapter Fourteen

A few hours later, Ajay was still thinking about Mrs Laptoff when his door chime rang loudly, causing him to jump up and spill his coffee across the desk. "Crap," he groaned. The chime rang again.

"I'm coming," he shouted, as if whoever was at the building's entrance could hear him. If it was Genni or Ace, he'd have to let them in. They couldn't see this, he thought, as he looked down at his desk and across his computer screens. The chime sounded again. He quickly yanked the electrical cable out from his Watch and held the device above his wrist, letting its strap dance around his skin. He dismissed the screens and swooped into the kitchen for a cloth. Back at his desk, he hurried to wipe up the coffee. The ringing of the chime yet again filled the apartment.

Crap, crap, crap. He stood back. Everything looked normal, until he noticed a tiny bit of the cable peeping out from its hiding place underneath his desk. As the chime sounded once more, Ajay dashed forward to ensure the cable couldn't be seen. Satisfied, and running over to the intercom by the apartment door, he spoke clearly into it.

"Hello." There was no response. "Hello? Who's there?" Nothing. Ajay assumed it was some stuck-up kids, messing about and wasting themselves. Shrugging it off, ready to ignore them, Ajay turned away, but then the intercom erupted into a deafening continuous noise as they held their finger down on the button. Frustrated then, Ajay was back at its mouthpiece - "HELLO?!" No response. His wrist dinged at the elevation of his heart rate. *I'll go tell them to do one,* Ajay decided, swiping himself out of the apartment and heading for the elevator.

As he walked down the nicely lit corridor, the lights tastefully cased in light blue shades, Ajay couldn't help but think about Mrs Laptoff again. He'd headed straight home after her outburst. He was constantly convincing himself that he had nothing to worry about. She was a deteriorating old woman with a crazy talking tongue. There was one question Ajay couldn't dismiss just yet, however – how did she know him, and his secret? The elevator arrived at the ground floor, its doors gilding open. Even if she did know, it didn't look like she'd done anything more than give him a bad report, meaning he earnt a little less merit for today's shift than usual. That ticked him off. He'd done his usual trick, which he had tried to stop doing all together, but sometimes, like today, injustice meant he needed to. Before he turned the corner to reach his apartment building's front door, another thought occurred to him. He could be walking straight into a trap. It could be an Unworthy wanting to take everything he owned, or a Command Official there to finally arrest him, or the button could just be broken, or someone rang his place by mistake, or this was where he died. Ajay almost laughed. The rate at which his mind raced around was, even to him, unbelievable. He walked forward confidently, but still had his fists clenched in case they were needed.

Arriving at the door, his muscles relaxed and he sighed. It was Genni. He could see the top of her head, through the door's glass window, from where she sat on the front step. Ajay waved his wrist to open the door. It slid away.

"Getting happy with the intercom, are we?" Ajay spoke with a sarcastic tone, but as he stepped closer to her, he had no more jokes. "Genni?" He demanded a response. She was hunched up, leaning against the wall, barely moving. Ajay stood, stunned, still expecting her to move or speak. Nothing happened. He couldn't even see the rise and fall of her chest. Realising what that meant, he promptly crouched towards her and pulled up her head. He felt slightly nauseous. Blue-green veins were angrily pulsating across her face and around her eyes. Ajay's insides suddenly felt severed, like there was something breaking him. How could she be lying here motionless? He began to shake violently, wailing and sweating in desperation. "Genni? Genni?" he cried again and started to shake her. She still didn't respond. His hands were unsteady, but Ajay managed to sweep her up in his arms and flew them both upstairs.

The smell of vomit from her clothes was sharp. Ajay moved faster. A loud, fast beeping proceeded from Genni's Watch. Ajay looked down - *an increased heart rate and lowered oxygen levels.* Ajay experienced a desperate relief that she was even still breathing. He moved quicker, scanning his wrist to the wall and flying through the gliding door. He lay her down gently on his bed, the veins on her face looking more irritated and her skin feeling volcanic on his hands. He rushed to the windows, opening each one. Then, flinging open a kitchen cupboard, he found the first aid box and ripped open the packet that contained the at-home cannula kit. Running back to Genni's side, he was thankful for the merit-making first aid course he'd never thought he'd have to use. Ajay exhaled loudly to steady his nerves. Despite his hands shaking wildly, he managed to get the needle into a vein in Genni's right arm to restore some deficient fluid. He stroked her forehead as a tear fell from his eye onto her face and became stagnant on her skin.

He synced Genni's Watch to the screen port by the bed so he could monitor her stats. She seemed to be stabilising. Stumbling onto his feet, Ajay looked over her veins again and knew they weren't normal. Suspecting what it might be, he spoke into his Watch.

"Show me the side-effects of *SkipSleep* overdose."

His stomach churned. Sick and distorted faces that resembled Genni flickered across his screen. He felt numb with guilt. How had he not noticed? She could look after herself, but he'd failed to protect her. Ajay sat himself down on the trunk at the end of the makeshift hospital scene, looked out of his windows and saw a few humid clouds gathering together in the twilight. He put his head in his hands, in an attempt to stop the pounding.

He looked back at Genni and whispered, "What have you done?"

Chapter Fifteen

Still sat on the brown antique trunk at the end of the bed, Ajay's hands were clasped together, arms braced on his thighs. He watched Ace as he threw his top layer t-shirt over the sofa and stood panting in a white vest. His muscles were bulging. Ajay assumed that he'd run to the flat after Ajay's call. Despite the trauma, Ajay still managed to feel jealous glancing over his own bicep, pathetic in comparison.

"I need her to wake up . . ." he said.

"Of course you do, mate." Ace caught his breath, walking over to Genni and placing the back of his hand on her forehead, stroking her affectionately. He then looked to the screen monitoring her heart and fluid levels. "When is the medical service getting here?"

Ajay fell silent, staring down at his black ankle boots, perfect for wading through the deepest plains of sand, even in a storm.

"Jay? They've been notified, haven't they?" Ace said, with a tone of demanding urgency.

"I stopped her Watch from sending the alert," Ajay mumbled. He knew Ace would kick off about this. He didn't care. She was *his* girlfriend. He needed to be in control, though he hoped Ace would understand and not judge him for it. Before Ace could vent his anger, Ajay spoke loudly. "She's the daughter of the biggest businessman in the City, her face would be plastered on every news headline. People would see her differently." He shook his head. "I can't let that happen. It's not what she'd want."

"Are you completely mad? She could die, Ajay!" Ace immediately sprang from his feet towards Ajay to stand right in front of him, breathing hard. Ajay could smell the remnants of Kale Chips on his breath. "I'm calling them," Ace said defiantly, lifting his wrist.

Ajay stood, grabbed Ace quickly and said calmly, "Don't. Please. You can see her stats are good, just give her a few more hours and . . ." Ajay paused. "If she's still not awake, we'll call them. Okay?" Ajay looked at Ace with pleading eyes. He knew he looked weak, and it hurt.

"Okay," Ace said. "Okay." Ajay, relieved, collapsed back onto the trunk. Ace came with him and patted Ajay's shoulder reassuringly.

Ace sighed and stroked the top of his recently shaved head. It was a growing trend. Ajay's mirror had suggested it yesterday; there was a limit to how much he listened to technology. He instinctively tucked his own hair behind his ears and watched as Ace chewed his tongue. He did that when he was thinking. Then he stopped and turned to Ajay with narrowed eyes. "How did you stop her alert? She must have been past the optional limit."

Ajay didn't panic. He'd expected the question. It had taken him minutes to get inside Genni's Watch using his hacking equipment, normalise her vital signs to reverse the alert and call the medical service off. "I selected *no* just before she went over."

Ace seemed to accept this. Ajay looked at his friend with tired eyes and then tapped at his wrist. "When she wakes up, she'll be pretty exhausted, and I imagine she will need some time to recover. Would you mind helping me care for her? I can't miss any more work."

At this request, Ace puffed out some air as, Ajay assumed, he considered the potential merit sacrifice of this agreement. After a few seconds, Ace agreed.

"Thank you. I'll keep her here, so here's access . . ." Ajay lifted his Watch to meet Ace's. A dinging sound vibrated into the momentary silence between them as the access key was copied and transferred.

As Ace confirmed everything on his own Watch, he looked over at Ajay empathetically. "You look dead, mate. Have you had any boosts at all?"

Ajay laughed solemnly and shook his head. He couldn't bear the thought of touching *SkipSleep*; he'd just settle for whatever natural sleep he'd get that night.

"I just can't stop thinking . . . She did that . . . I didn't stop it . . . and . . ." Ajay paused. His words fell over one another and he screamed out, yelling with frustration that flew around the white-walled room. "Command, as well. How can they even let it happen? With everything they have to stop it." Ajay's veins were pumping as he finally expressed his frustrations out loud. They'd been simmering underneath all the adrenaline ever since Genni had turned up on his doorstep.

Ace twirled his lip in consideration, before jumping to Command's defence like a puppet.

"But they are trying to crack down on it. I heard they caught two admins just last week." Ace's words grinded on Ajay. He felt angry at him. At everything. He closed his eyes as Ace continued to speak. "Look, Genni made a bad decision and now she'll lose at least two days when she could have been making merit. It was stupid, but you love her."

He was right. She was stupid. And he did love her. Though there were moments where he wished he didn't. It would be easier. Simpler. That's the problem with relationships: sacrificing precious time to invest in someone else's problems. Maybe that wasn't fair. He didn't really know.

"You're lucky you've found her, and she's *right* for you," Ace mumbled. Ajay sat up. He knew there was something more behind Ace's comment. Ajay had never known Ace to say anything so cliché or romantic. The guy didn't have it in him. So he meant something else. Wanting a distraction from his own depression about Genni, Ajay decided to push for what it was.

"What do you mean?"

"Can I have a boost?"

Ajay wasn't surprised by Ace's dismissal of the question. He calmly raised his arm towards the activation pad on the coffee table to welcome Ace to his *SkipSleep*. Ace swiped in. As the beeps and bleeps of the analysis sounded, Ajay looked over at the bed where he could detect Genni's light, delicate breathing beneath the very thin white sheet. He then turned back to Ace, who was staring forward blankly as the progress bar reached 60%.

"Ace? What's going on?" There was a gravity in Ace's eyes that Ajay had rarely seen, so he pushed further. "You can tell me."

Sighing and deflating his shoulders, Ace removed his arm from the system and fell backwards on the sofa, groaning. Ajay watched as his friend shifted his body uncomfortably, his head in his hands. He was mumbling to himself words like 'embarrassing' and 'pathetic'. Ajay had never seen Ace like this. It actually disturbed him. He felt too uncomfortable to let this linger so he clenched his fist and gave Ace a dead arm. Ace moaned at the slight discomfort.

"Tell me!" Ajay demanded.

Ace puffed out some air again. "Okay. So I haven't mentioned this to anyone, and I swear mate, if you do, I'll kill you." Ace smirked, but his sincerity did not go unnoticed, so Ajay agreed. "So there's this girl. I met her on the sky train a few months back. She's gorgeous." He laughed.

"Seriously hot. I was amazed she was even vaguely attracted to me. We've been on dates, you know, but the thing is, this isn't like with a girl from work. You know, a short fling and that's it. I think this is the real deal. I've seriously fallen for her."

"Ace, that's awesome. What's the problem?" Ajay was confused, and almost happy for him that he'd finally found someone he could actually commit to. Ace's body language changed; he shuffled on the sofa, the leather making a sucking sound beneath his legs.

"She's M-290," Ace said.

They were both silent then. Did Ace think Ajay would judge him? Well, he did. A little. M-290 was low. Embarrassingly so. Deep down, Ajay knew it shouldn't matter, but the relationships they had mattered; they were fundamental to individual status, how people respected each other, and the merit opportunities offered. It was much more respectable to be single than go out with someone below your ranks. Ajay didn't know what to say. His throat felt dry. So in the end, he said next to nothing.

"That's tough, mate." Placing his hand on Ace's shoulder, he could feel the hard surface of refined muscles beneath his fingers. He felt new respect for Ace; he never knew he could be vulnerable like this. In fact, vulnerability was not something he ever saw in anyone.

"Why don't you help her increase her merit?" Ajay suggested, knowing it was futile.

Ace shook his head. "I think I'm coming to terms with the fact that our relationship would be too much of a risk. It's been killing me though." Ace stood up and walked over to the kitchen, probably to avoid Ajay seeing any emotion in his expression, but it was all in his voice. Caught in his throat.

"I'm sorry mate," Ajay called out in consolation.

Ace shrugged his shoulders as he started tapping at his Watch. "It's okay. Just a girl, right?"

Yeah, I guess it is, Ajay thought. He looked out the window as a drone flew past. There was a low, hoarse moan. Turning around, he could see that Genni was waking up.

Chapter Sixteen

Opening her eyes, everything felt fuzzy. Strange images; memories of market stalls, drones, and flickering light bulbs. A feeling of floating or being carried. More peculiar colours and shifting shapes. Her mind felt like the canvas of a cryptic painting, splattered and chaotic. A fast, black box hurtling towards her.

Genni moved her neck, her muscles sore and protesting. She willed her eyes to open further, but they kept drooping closed again, as if a magnet on her bottom eyelid was forcing them shut. Squinting, she could make out the white walls and a screen covered in coloured lines. She could hear a faint, consistent beeping. Not highly pitched, but soft and non-bothersome. Where was she? The hospital? Was this a dream? She heard herself groan as she tried to stretch her body out. It felt numb. She couldn't move. Her arms felt flaccid at her sides. The thought came that maybe they'd been tied to the bed she was lying in, that she'd been abducted, but as her fingers twitched and she started to regain feeling, she realised it was just a dead cold weakness in her limbs. What had happened to her? Everything felt bleak. Her eyes started to release, and finally graced her with sight. His face was there. Ajay. She relaxed, instantly knowing she was safe.

"How are you feeling?" Ajay said, wiping her eyes with a wet cloth. The cool touch of the water refreshed her senses and brightened her clouded vision further. She began to see clearer: the bed, the lines in her arms, Ajay, Ace, and the brightness of the sun through the windows.

She responded with a dark croak in her voice. "Not great."

"Not surprised. You gave us quite a scare there, girl," Ace said. He was standing behind Ajay, wearing a vest and training shorts. All his hair had been cut off. Genni noted how it made him look older. She didn't like it. She felt something cool crawling around her fingers then. She knew it was Ajay's hand. Ignoring Ace, she looked at Ajay as he perched on the side of the bed. He looked exhausted. His wavy hair was uncombed and only tucked behind his left ear rather than both. The purple marks around his eyes intensified their confused stare, both sympathetic yet disappointed.

"What . . . what happened?" Genni asked.

"You'll have to tell us that, Gen," Ajay said monotonically.

"What do you mean?" She remembered the library, and that she went back Downtown to get help, but everything else was blank.

"You turned up here last night, half-dead on the doorstep."

"What?" Genni said. How had she gotten here from Downtown? Her body then alerted her to a deeply dry throat, as if she was a plant out in the desert, holding out for the rainfall of a storm. "Can I have some water?"

"I'll get it." Ace disappeared to the kitchen.

"So you don't remember anything?" Ajay asked, still gripping tightly to her hand.

"No . . . I . . ." Genni wondered if Ajay knew about the *SkipSleep*. He might have figured it out. Please no, she thought. She hoped he didn't know, and she decided to hold onto that. "I was at the library, and I went to the bathroom . . ." She paused, looking forwards rather than at Ajay. "I got . . . a bit breathless . . . then, maybe I fainted?" She scrunched up her face like she was trying to remember something; it added to her performance of this half-truth. Her face relaxed. "And I can't remember anything after that.

I was just at the doorstep?" That question was real. She really didn't know how she'd got here. Ace returned with a glass of water and offered it to her. So thirsty, she let go of Ajay's hand and raised up her right arm without hesitation.

Pain. Sudden and agonising. It ricocheted along the entirety of her right shoulder. Genni hissed aggressively, feeling the little saliva left in her mouth dribble onto her chin.

"What's wrong?" Ajay quickly said, stroking her right arm tenderly. He took the water from Ace, setting it on the side.

Genni could hardly speak, the throbbing crippling her ability to even think. She loosely pointed to her shoulder with her left hand. Tears trickled down her cheeks and snot fell from her nose. She was a mess. She knew that. Ajay got closer to her shoulder. Genni bit her lip in anticipation of more suffering. He was gentle though, and lightly lifted the top of her t-shirt away from her skin.

He gasped. "Wow, Gen. That's broken."

She managed to control her breathing and bend her chin so she could see her shoulder. There was a giant lump there, a bruised rainbow of colour: yellows, browns, and purples. It resembled the miserable tones of some of her more sinister paintings. They were stashed in a cupboard in this apartment, unbeknownst to Ajay. He never was very observant.

She didn't understand. When or how had she been in a situation to break a bone? She went Downtown as soon as she caught her breath in the bathroom. That's what they'd said to do if she had any side effects from the enhanced *SkipSleep* they'd given her, to go back to them. She'd assumed they could help her, give her something else to settle things down. Though, when she'd got there, she remembered, her usual administrator wasn't there. It occurred to her then that she didn't even know his name.

The first time she had been very nervous, so didn't want to make conversation. She was terrified that anyone might see her, and she felt shameful that she couldn't make enough merit with the normal, Command-accredited doses. After a while, the shame subsided and she didn't feel anything towards it at all, other than she needed to do it. She went in, got the injection and got out. Ultimately, this meant his name was never important, but this time, he definitely wasn't there. There was another guy. Attractive, young, and . . . that was it. That was all she could remember.

"It's definitely broken. We need help," Ajay said, lazily swiping on his Watch to call the medical services, Genni assumed. He knows, she thought. There was no doubt. He knew what she'd been doing. That's the only reason he wouldn't have already sent her to hospital. To protect her, so the media couldn't latch on to the fact that Boris Mansald's daughter was a failure. An addict who breaks the rules. She almost opened her mouth to thank him when she stopped. Ajay held her gaze for a moment, a ring of bitter agitation crawling its way across his eyes, nose and lips. He threw his arms up in the air with exasperation and placed them tightly around the back of his head. He looked at Genni again. Not with love, compassion or even with anger, but as if he had nothing to say to her at all. He turned away, walking solemnly across the room and falling out of sight. Ace said nothing either but looked down at the floor, following Ajay and leaving Genni alone. The pain in her shoulder was nothing compared to that. Tears began to stream down her face, which she did not yet know was completely bruised, and she felt utterly and completely Unworthy.

Chapter Seventeen

Developments in Tulo medicine allow a broken clavicle to be restored quickly and non-invasively. Microscopic, wormlike robots burrow their way, by programmed direction, under the skin either side of the broken bone. Using light, their telescopic capabilities and suction, they slither around and dissipate blood clots, and then delicately weave together cloths of artificial cartilage – tightly and comfortably, like a baby in its swaddle. Their work done, they return to the surface, leaving not even a hint of a scar in their wake.

Sat on his sofa, Ajay returned the medical explanation document to his Watch. "The innovation is incredible," he said to Mila as he walked over to the bed, where Mila sat holding Genni's hand. He sat in the blue swede armchair by the bed, looking over to Genni who was sleeping, a thing she liked to do excessively since her surgery.

"It is great," Mila said. "The team had been working on that particular op for a while. It just shows what a little patience and hard work can result in." She smiled at Ajay, letting go of Genni's hand to tuck her own short blonde hair behind her small, delicate ears. She had brown eyes but Ajay had preferred the blue. Their colour jarred with the black makeup she'd laden around them. Petite and with a soft demeanour, Ajay always thought Mila had a simplistic beauty. Not quite as obviously pretty as Genni, but still attractive. He couldn't understand why she was changing that. He didn't understand the rising trend in the changing eye colour thing in general.

"Why didn't we see it, Ajay?" Her voice was sincere as she looked sadly over Genni's bare, partially-healed face.

"I don't know." He felt as if she was taking a stab at him. Mila wasn't around much with her job. He was with Genni all the time. So really, her question was: *why didn't you see it?* Yet perhaps she did feel some responsibility herself. Maybe it wasn't all on him. Though, every time he felt guilty, he came back to Genni and how it was her choice to overdose. Her choice to miss all her medical check-ups, although Ajay did wonder why Command never picked up on that. It could have been because they're testing those new androids Mila was involved in. Maybe they didn't notice. Still, it was Genni's mistake.

Mila sighed. With the movement of her breathing, Ajay noticed how her green wide-fronted dress sagged over her skinny chest.

"So, how's work?" Ajay asked, needing to distract himself from Genni, his thoughts, everything. He did find the medical profession interesting, though. Mila worked closely with Robotics, helping those who programmed the androids. Her job was to give them situational tactics and the medical knowledge needed for the robots to give the highest standards of care.

"A bit tough recently. Really, if I'm being honest . . ." Mila paused and looked at Ajay with trust in her synthetic eyes. "I want to see patients, not screens. There's this other job going, where the merit and credit aren't as good, but it's on the trauma wards. Androids aren't sophisticated enough for the spontaneity of emergencies." Mila stopped talking as if she wanted to control her passion. She couldn't take that job. Ajay knew it. He knew she knew it.

Ajay nodded. He glanced out the window and saw a man stretching in the apartment building opposite. A screen floated above him, merit-tracking and displaying workout instructions.

"You think I should stay where I am?" Mila said as she looked at her hand in Genni's. Ajay wondered whether she too had noticed the chip in her own nail varnish against Genni's newly polished fingers. Pearl had been around to paint them, because apparently, she should still look good even when she's sick.

"Is it worth the merit loss? That's probably the question you need to ask first," Ajay responded, honestly.

"I suppose. I do need to get higher, and I'm currently closer to the ones whose opinions matter than I would be on the wards. It's just that ..." Mila paused again and didn't look up from Genni's hand. "No, you're right. I've got to keep looking up."

Without his permission, Ajay felt a heaviness fall over him, like a blanket of bricks that wouldn't keep him warm. He saw in Mila what he had missed in Genni. A false happiness governed only by a number, people's opinions and unrealistic expectations. Was that in him, too? Was he right alongside them? It was like their whole world was a wheel; day by day they ran, furiously pressing for progress, for the greater score that their contribution had promised. Genni fell off that wheel and Ajay must be the one to pick her up again, though he didn't really want to, only felt he had to because of love and commitment. Who would help Mila up if she also fell? Surely, that wasn't his problem too.

"Okay. I'll get out of your way. It's already been 10 minutes out of our days," Mila said, rising from her seat after giving Genni a kiss on the forehead. Ajay stood up with her.

"You're doing a great job looking after her Ajay," Mila threw her shoulder bag on and moved closer towards him.

"A really great job." She touched his arm before wandering towards the apartment door. "By the way, where's your house drone? I've never known anyone above M-400 not to have one."

Ajay grunted with laughter. She had to be so observant. "Maybe I'm more of a simple soul than you thought." Mila responded with a small nod and a charming smile as she walked away, the door sliding shut behind her.

* * *

About a week later, Ajay stood on the roof of his building, observing a flock of drones fly towards the Outer Rings where smoke from the Side train puffed into the night sky. Ajay had his hands nestled in the pocket of a hoodie, away from the unusually cool air. He closed his eyes for a moment and took in some calming breaths. It was hard to ignore the presence of others on the roof. There were oohs and aahs as they watched the billboards, but Ajay wasn't so impressed with the deals tonight. He looked up higher, hoping to see the shimmer of the night stars, but still they were overshadowed by the sparkles of the artificial. A great big billboard was the biggest disruption. Ajay initially scoffed at its headline – *Help you and your future family be their most effective selves* – but what captivated him really was the image. A young Tuloian couple were in a lush apartment, full of green plants and expensive-looking furniture. They were laughing and holding onto one another whilst cradling a delightful giggling child between them. The girl was wearing bright coloured tights and her hair was tied up in pigtails. It hit Ajay right in the chest. Tara, his sister, used to wear tights like that. He missed her, like he missed his grandma. They were a family, a family like this one, a family like the one he could create with Genni. The one he wanted to create with Genni. He raised his arm to scan the button – *Book Couples Counselling Session* – but he hesitated. No, it's just marketing. That's not his future, that family didn't exist. It wasn't as simple as cuddling in front of the sofa. For one thing, he probably wouldn't have it with Genni. Not the way things were going.

The two of them had spent the time since her operation in a painful roundabout of disappointment, short-lived reconciliations, falling merit and unspoken misery. Occasionally, they rowed about Genni's bad choices. Other times, they spoke practically and rationally about how Genni's merit had continued to decline. She was struggling at work; her energy was sapped, so volunteering or personal merit-making were tough too. She needed to pull herself together, as Ajay had repeatedly told her. Most recently, they had been talking normally, but there was an invisible fence between them that was slowly growing higher. For Ajay, the distance would make it easier when her merit fell so low that it could affect his own.

As Ajay looked over the picture of the sparkling family, that distance felt even greater. He couldn't see Genni's face in place of this blonde woman with fantastical teeth. He was starting to feel the pain Ace felt after ditching his M-290 lover. Surely this would be worse. It wasn't just a fling. It was three years down the line and was supposed to be *it*. *What do you do when the one you love is no longer Worthy of you?*

As he could feel his emotions building, he turned away from the perfect, pretend couple. Ajay felt numb with confusion. He hated himself for getting so attached. It was never his intention when he created this life. He needed to walk, clear his head.

Down and out on the street, he turned left towards the Inner-Inner-Ring, strolling along at pace. It was around eight in the evening, the main commuter time. He was pleased. Watching commuters was a novel pastime to drown out his own problems. He spotted a few school kids marching earnestly towards their destination, gripping cautiously to books. Others stared zombie-like up at the adverts whilst others scrolled through websites or *Personi* profiles on floating screens. He never cared much for social merit. Never needed it. Though Genni had gotten into it since her accident; she was on the phone to Pearl every other minute for hints and tips.

It was exhausting listening to them and having to take part in it. He thought back to the week before.

"Just a quick picture," Genni said. She had been sitting on the bed, holding her Watch in front of her, and had demanded Ajay to put his head on her shoulder. They had both smiled and the camera had snapped. Genni had then tapped and typed at her Watch whilst asking, "Have you spoken to Pearl yet?" Ajay, who had walked away towards the kitchen, shook his head and had groaned at the question he'd heard four times that week.

"Please just call her? She won't stop asking, you know what she's like." Genni had been wearing green sweatpants and a baggy top, almost giving the illusion that she was relaxed and comfortable. She had now surrounded herself with a large screen, displaying volunteering opportunities and an article titled 'Top ten tips for gaining merit through Personal Development'.

"What makes her think her channel will improve with me on it?" Ajay had said quietly, a note of tension running through his voice.

"That's a question you can ask Pearl. She just wants to chat about how you can help each other. If for nothing at

all, do it for me." Genni had continued to scroll her finger down the screen whilst reading. Ajay had felt as if Genni had just crunched him up like a tin can. Did she not realise how much he'd already done? He'd lost merit with how much time he'd dedicated to her recovery. He had breathed slowly to prevent himself from erupting, resulting in an unheard mumble from his mouth, "Yeah, that and saving your life."

"What was that?" Genni had asked vulnerably. Ajay had dismissed this and fell silent. He had opened the fridge and hidden his face behind its silver, mirrored door. As he had looked over the lack of produce inside it, he'd heard the swooshing of the sliding door. With a bottle of water in hand and the fridge closed, he stood static and gazed over the empty space on the bed where Genni had just been sitting. A notification had pinged from Ajay's Watch, and he had swiped for the screen to appear. There he was. His beaming, smiling face resting on Genni's shoulder. He had read the caption: "I've got myself a man who supports me no matter what. Don't stop trying to find yours."

He'd been mad about the picture. She hadn't even shown it to him for his approval. It was awful. He stopped walking then, and leaned against a wall to look at the photo again. In hindsight, he thought he should have changed his clothes. He looked scruffy in an unironed t-shirt. His hair was also uncombed and not tucked behind his ears, which gave it this wild sex hair look. He then noticed a slight stain on his t-shirt. Just above his right nipple. If someone were to zoom in, they could see it clearly. She should have checked with him. Tulo was able to see him, sloppy and unprofessional.

Looking towards the glowing lights from the nearby Glorified Quarters, he considered messaging Genni to get her to delete the photo. He stopped when he saw the engagement. Over 150 loves. So people liked it. Okay, he thought, I'll let her off.

Ajay flicked off his Watch and continued walking. As he was approaching a sky train bridge down an unlit alley, he stopped.

Something was moving beneath it.

He was standing twenty metres away from it. Whatever it was looked misshapen, like a large overfilled bin bag, shuffling slowly towards him and weakly dragging itself along the ground. The black was impenetrable. Ajay couldn't see anything further. What was he thinking, walking down a dark alley at night? He considered running, but something willed him to stay. He planted his feet on the concrete but then decided that he should turn back. It could be a wild animal that had migrated from the Country, prowling and preparing itself to rip into his flesh, but he still stayed. As the creature moved closer, a sky train roared over the bridge above. Its flickering lights revealed that the beast was really a man.

"Please . . ." His voice was dry and coarse with a hint of desperation. "Help me . . ." Ajay was close but the train was gone and so was the light. The image of the man had just flickered momentarily to the point where Ajay questioned if any of it was even real. He lifted his wrist, turned on the torch from his Watch, and could then see the man in full colour. Part of him was relieved he wasn't going to be attacked, the other part was disgusted by what he saw.

The man's grey beard was dressed in sweat, and his face was layered with dirt. Bruises colonised over his face and there were cuts along his dried lips. His black t-shirt was ripped around the neckline, revealing a tuft of presumably unwashed hair. Unworthy. Ajay was sure of it. No one else in the City looked like this. Ajay didn't blame them. *Why self-care when you have no merit to live for?* Following the man's body, Ajay saw a small tattoo on the underside of his right wrist; an imprint of the three-layered flame he knew well. It was only then, under the limited light of his Watch's torchlight, did Ajay see the real problem.

Chapter Eighteen

A few inches below the man's right knee, trailing down his leg and stopping just above his ankle, was a nasty, open gash. It was a straight cut, yet the way his flesh fell open around it made it look like he'd been mutilated. The man was pressing a blood covered jacket into the wound. It was bad. He'd probably lost a decent amount of blood, Ajay thought. *He might already be a goner, especially if that gets infected.* There was no benefit to Ajay helping him. In fact, there was more to lose than gain. If anyone were to see him assisting an Unworthy, what would they think of him? Plus, this Unworthy didn't deserve his help. They don't contribute; they're lazy and selfish, and quite frankly, disgusting. Look at this guy, he told himself. He was drenched in every imaginable detestable substance: blood, sweat, saliva. Not to mention the hole in his leg meant that Ajay would likely have to carry him. Ajay felt a little queasy looking over the man again. It wasn't his problem. He put his right foot forward, ready to cross over to the other side of the road, but something dragged him back. A sort of compassion was resurfacing that he hadn't felt for a long time. He groaned internally. It was Genni's fault, he decided. Her issues had turned him soft and more susceptible to helping other people. It was a curse that he was born into and had managed to repress in recent years. He knew he shouldn't give into it – he can't sacrifice too much, he had worked too hard – but the guy could die. No one was around. It wouldn't be seen. So, Ajay placed his foot back on the pavement and turned back to the man.

As he got closer, the man began to wail. "Oh thank you, thank you," he said. Ajay wanted him to be quiet, but he didn't have to tell him. The man fell silent and stumbled in exhaustion. Ajay ran and caught him, preventing his head from smashing the concrete.

"Okay. It's okay," Ajay said as he held him up, trying to ignore the stench. It was unbelievable. Ajay needed to cough, or heave, he wasn't sure which. "How long have you been here like this?"

The man took a big breath and Ajay heard the whistle in his chest, confirming to him that the guy wasn't well in general. "About twenty minutes." He paused, whimpering. "Two other Unworthy sods saw me lying here. Neither helped." He lifted a bruised hand to wipe his battered face, which reminded Ajay of Genni's shoulder. The way her olive skin had been disguised by the colours of purple and yellow to form a dull pattern along her collar bone. With this man, it was all around his eyes.

"Do you mind?" Ajay said pointing to the man's leg. The man shook his head. Ajay gently lifted the limb closer to the flashlight on his Watch, listening to the man's hisses of pain. "It doesn't look critical, nothing a few Stitch Bots won't fix. I can pay for a hover cab to the hospital for-"

"No. No hospital," he pleaded, and yelped again as his panicked movement agitated his leg.

"Why not? You need stitches," Ajay said insistently. He was desperate to get away, or at least cover his nose with his hand.

"Why can't you do them manually?" the man asked almost confidently. Ajay was aghast, silent for a moment. He gazed over the man's face, his eyes speaking of his vulnerable defiance. He'd never met an Unworthy who would expect such a request to be granted. The audacity of it. The situation was surely a mistake, Ajay thought, as he began to slowly shake his head, standing over the man. He purposefully didn't express any empathy and the man looked terrified, but something pulled Ajay's thoughts back again. He needed his help. Everything within him wanted to walk away, but he just couldn't. Upon the realisation that the stinking idiot would have to come to his apartment, Ajay closed his eyes and took a steady, deep breath.

He sighed. "Okay. I'll do them manually." The man started to spit out his thanks, but Ajay interrupted and raised his hand. "Only if you answer two questions." The man deflated again.

"Why no hospital?" Ajay asked sternly.

The man turned his face away. Ajay could hear him whispering to himself. Was he really about to take this psycho to his apartment?

"I'm . . . on the run." The man spoke quietly and Ajay raised his eyebrows. Brilliant, he thought. *A criminal. An Unworthy – filthy, injured, crazy criminal.* He knew how to pick them.

"Well, not quite. I'm a street seller, but some of my products aren't exactly acquired in the most legal way. No hospital because the TPD will find me."

Okay, not a criminal. A petty criminal.

"That's how I bust my leg, you should probably know. I was running from a swarm and managed to lose them by canning it over a wall. It was covered in that historical bird wiring and I caught my leg. Ripped right through me as I fell." The man shrugged his shoulders at the misfortune.

"That is unlucky. Hardly any of that around now since the drones frightened the birds away," Ajay responded.

The man made a murmur in agreement. Ajay hesitantly placed his hand on the man's shoulder. He could sanitise when he got back, and he was doing well to breathe through his mouth to save himself from the sewer of a man he was touching.

"Look, if they really wanted you, they'd have overridden the VPG privacy on your Watch." Ajay was very familiar with how to disable his location on the Virtual Positioning Guide. The man looked up at Ajay and smiled. Not a sweet smile, but also not sinister. Something in between. Ajay wasn't sure what to make of him. He was vile, that was for sure, but there was also something genuine buried beneath the dirt.

"You had a second question?"

"Yes, what's your name?"

"Saman," he said. "But please, call me Sam."

* * *

Back at his apartment, Ajay rolled his eyes as Sam's bristly voice barked loud in his ears.

"Steady on, man . . . steady!"

Lowering him onto his bed, Ajay was sweating. The guy was heavy. Too many stolen fatty foods, Ajay assumed. It certainly didn't look like he had a particularly nutritious diet; the skin of his face was cracked and his belly ballooned over his waistline. The walk back had been anything but pleasant. Ajay had needed to support Sam all the way, while he hopped about pathetically on one leg. It probably didn't help that Ajay insisted they go the long way round, and he'd pulled them into side alleys each time someone appeared on the street. Ajay had taken the opportunity every time Sam yelped in pain to threaten taking away his aid; it kept him quiet. At least, until they got back and Sam started shrieking like a traumatised fox and Ajay fancied pressing on his wound as a discipline method. Or he could just leave him out on the street again. Of course, he opted for neither.

"I've got to nip and get some supplies for the stitches. I'll give you some fluids and painkillers now, so that will see you through until I get back."

He went about preparing things, all the while feeling Sam watching him with sceptical eyes. What does he think he's looking at? Without another word, Ajay turned on his heels and headed out into the night again.

Dashing out onto the street, into the light moving crowd, Ajay felt like running away. What was he doing? It was crazy. Completely and utterly mad. An Unworthy was in his bed, on drugs, in dirty, stinking clothes. Ajay started to walk quicker, swerving in between people and drones, the noise of the City feeling louder than usual. The social discreditation could be catastrophic.

Helping an Unworthy was down there with becoming one. It was seen as shameful to waste time on those who have already wasted themselves. If word got out, he could be excluded from his networks, and then lose the merit opportunities that tidily came with them. Ajay stopped walking then, causing a woman behind him to walk into his back.

"Oi, watch it," she said as she moved around his body. She was small, and her hair was tied nicely into two sweet buns, but the scowl she gave him was anything but.

Seriously, what am I doing? Ajay thought as he wiped the sweat from his face. He walked himself out from the crowd to lean against a wall. Just breathe, he told himself.

His thoughts started to darken. He wondered whether he could just leave Sam there. He could stay at Genni's, or Ace's. Let the guy starve or bleed out. Then when Ajay had been gone long enough, he could just dispose of the body somehow, and no one would ever miss him. It was unlikely he had a family, or even if he did, he probably wasn't any more useful to them alive than dead. Ajay felt his wrist vibrate. He swiped at it and Ace's face appeared.

"Jay!" Ace paused and looked at the camera. He was at the office, still wearing his tie with the top button done up. Hollday must still be at work, Ajay thought. *He* should be at work. "Where are you?" The backdrop of an outdoor wall wasn't Ajay's usual setting.

"Just out. Getting some stuff from the shop. I missed the drone cut-off."

"Ah, I hate that. When are the suckers going to be 24/7?"

"Who knows." Ajay told himself to relax, not wanting Ace to catch on to his panicked, heavy breathing.

"Anyway, you coming back in?"

"No. Not tonight."

"Fancy a drink?"

"I've got some work at home."

"Okay, just I know things aren't great with Gen right now. Wondered if you wanted a distraction."

Had Genni been talking to Ace? Ajay wondered. *Stop it.* He couldn't let his brain get angry about that; there was already too much going on in there. Like the Unworthy in his bed, the one he was considering starving to death.

"I'm good. Thanks."

"Alright, well, let's have a match tomorrow instead?"

"Sure. Sounds good."

"See ya later." Ace disappeared.

Ajay breathed a sigh of relief, not that he knew what he was relieved about. Ace was never going to suspect what was happening. Ajay still had a big problem. He wanted to curse at himself out loud. Why did he get himself into this situation? He could have just walked away, but no, he went through the trouble of carrying the stench into his apartment, and then was on his way to get him medical supplies. Maybe he could help him, no one would find out, and he could get back to his life. Then again, how long would that take?

Ajay then realised that he had left a thief in his apartment. A thief. Ajay felt like punching the wall behind him. He could return to an empty apartment, all his possessions sold for credit to spend on fatty foods. As his mind moved towards hysteria, Ajay reminded himself that the flesh of Sam's leg was hanging off – he couldn't even carry a glass. However, Ajay needed a plan. So what was it? Help him, leave him to die, or get rid of him quickly? He hadn't the first clue of how to get rid of a body. On that thought, he felt sick at himself. He was so twisted.

The last time he felt like this was before, when he'd considered cutting off a dead man's finger. That was equally as disturbing as mulling over the disposal of a body. Memories flickered through Ajay's mind. There was also a Command guard there, downstairs, whilst Ajay scrambled and hurried to warm up the dead man's hands. It was stressful, and a close call. Ajay ended up lying underneath the bed of the dead guy, holding his breath whilst Command dealt with the body. He'd been successful, though. Ajay smiled; it was quite a moment. He wouldn't be where he was without it. Would he really risk it all for an Unworthy? The question remained: did he need to kill Sam?

Chapter Nineteen

Your skin's moisture levels have improved by 10% since this time last week.

Genni looked at herself in the mirror as it spoke, the screen displaying its analysis. It was suggesting a soft brown, neutral blend for her eyeshadow, after she had told it she was going to work. It would be the first time she'd put on a full face of make-up since the overdose and having surgery. Working from home had been painfully lonely and Genni thought she might be ready to get back, even though in reality she didn't know how she felt. It was as if she had been put through a fire, and she wasn't sure how to soothe the burns. She could hide them. Cover them over, like the foundation and concealer that masked her freckles. Or she could display her trauma openly, and not be ashamed of what she'd gone through. Yet would anyone listen? Accept it? The only way she'd known people react to *SkipSleep* addicts, or those who overdosed, was with scorn. They were seen as failures or cheaters of the system, meaning she could never be open about her struggle.

No, she'd hide behind the lie about food poisoning her father had told, though the freedom it gave her only trapped her more. The withdrawal made it worse too. She'd had on and off fevers, vomited occasionally, but above all, it was the muscle aches that crippled her. When they came on, it was like her body was a heavy loaded hover car that she had to push up a hill. The lack of energy was depressing, and she'd only coped because of her regimented sleep schedule. Genni had to make peace with that. She couldn't paint. Her active time had to be for merit, without which she would lose everything. She couldn't bear the thought of not having Ajay. She knew in her heart that he wouldn't stay if the merit went low enough. She wouldn't blame him. She'd wish she'd never met him, but she wouldn't blame him. It was moments like that when she wondered what kind of world she lived in. A world where she couldn't do what she loved, or even be with who she loved if she really let her score drop.

Everything reminded Genni of painting. Even as she patted the brush into the brown eyeshadow palette, she thought of a fresh, blank canvas and the potential of what she could create. She'd always painted best when she had feelings to express. The brush tickled her eyelid as she followed the indication line on her mirror. Her thoughts returned back to Ajay. Despite the intensity of her recovery, she couldn't help but worry about him. The trauma probably sparked repressed emotions; a reminder of the loss he'd suffered when his parents died. He said that his childhood was better than some, being raised by his grandma, who sounded amazing. Genni had longed to meet her, and Ajay had assured her that she would soon. Maybe she never would. But on those rare occasions when they spoke about his childhood, Genni had always noticed the sadness in his eyes. Perhaps it had all been too much, that he'd almost lost her too over something so superficial, so reckless on her part. She knew she hadn't explained herself well to him. It didn't help that she still couldn't remember what happened. The broken collarbone was still a mystery, though she still had the same flashes of memory: the market stalls, Downtown, and the movement of something large coming towards her. She just couldn't distinguish what it was.

She'd accepted by that point that she wouldn't remember, and actually, it didn't matter. She had to move forward. There was no point dwelling on her mistakes. Work hard, control the merit, no *SkipSleep* for a while, and just hope that Ajay would be there to help her.

She blinked a few times and beheld herself again in the mirror, eyelids shimmering with glitter. Her full, blue eyes spoke to her. *You can do this.*

Chapter Twenty

Despite trying to convince himself otherwise, Ajay felt that Sam was surely too young to die. He guessed around the mid-forties. Even though he was pretty sure that the world wouldn't miss the Unworthy, Ajay wasn't the one to make that decision. The decision he *had* made was to bring him back to his apartment to help him. He had to commit to that. Ajay had resisted the darkness within himself and made it home with the supplies.

He was welcomed by a disturbing snore, which was something he didn't often hear. He'd only ever seen people sleeping this deeply at the retirement village. That was fair enough; they'd already experienced the necessary lifetime of sleepless activity. So to observe a middle-aged man in a tranquil rhythm of snorting and sniffling was slightly disconcerting. Although, knowing he was still there and not having stolen anything was a relief. Ajay walked towards the bed to find Sam's gaping mouth sending trickles of dribble down his t-shirt and onto the bed linen.

Repulsive. He walked closer and closed his nostrils again to the smell. Maybe he should have given him the shower first. Pulling up a chair, he also spotted yellow stains of what might be sweat or grease that had seeped onto the bed. Vile. He told himself to get over it. *Sort Sam out, then kick him out.* Ajay reached out his hand slowly and lightly prodded Sam's shoulder. Rolling his eyes at Sam's lack of response, Ajay tried again with more force.

Sam shuffled in bed and groaned, his eyes flickering as they lazily adjusted to the light. Ajay met his eyes and watched as Sam began pulling himself up to sit straight. As Ajay watched him rub his eyes, he was reminded of the way Genni looked after she slept naturally. It was rare, but he liked it. She would rub her eyes like Sam, but not in his brutish way, in a more endearing way as if she were relaxed and peaceful. Though that was a facade. She was never relaxed and peaceful. None of them were. Ajay noticed the tattoo on Sam's wrist again, very curiously.

Sam spoke. "You got the stuff then?" The guy was so demanding and outspoken, Ajay thought. If Ajay were in his position, he certainly wouldn't talk to a M-460 in that way.

"Yeah. I'm going to do your stitches now."

Noticing Sam's look of anxiety, Ajay wondered if he was afraid of needles. He lowered the anaesthetic needle to the skin of Sam's leg, the bed covers ruffling suddenly as Sam moaned and clenched his fists around the bed frame. After a few insertions, Ajay got to work fabricating the stitches. Having moved a screen port over to the end of the bed, Ajay ordered the screen to display a very outdated instructional video for manual stitches. He muted it. Knowing that Sam was watching him closely, Ajay looked back to the real mess of a leg.

"You're going to need at least six here." Turning to the video for guidance, and after checking the anaesthetic was doing its job, Ajay began. He had avoided asking Sam any personal questions. He didn't want to get involved or attached. He'd once had a habit of doing that and had worked hard to wean himself away from people not worthy of him. But he couldn't pull his thoughts away from Sam's tattoo; the small three-layered flame sitting there on the underside of his wrist. Ajay didn't think it would be rude to ask. After all, he was helping him, in *his* apartment, and he was M-460 and Sam was Unworthy. Even if it was rude, could Sam do anything about it?

Ajay posed the question bluntly. "So, what's your story?"

"What?" Sam responded. "What do you mean? I've told you, I'm a street sell-" Ajay interrupted.

"No. How did you fall out of merit?" When Ajay asked this, Sam instantly looked both confused and amazed.

"Your tattoo." Ajay gestured towards Sam's right wrist where the small flame sat black and blue on his skin. "I've never seen someone born Unworthy sporting the Prosper branding. So, did you work there?"

"Yeah," Sam said quietly. "The tattoos were a stupid thing we did one Liberation Day."

Heartache seemed to paint itself across the canvas of Sam's face. Ajay didn't feel sorry for him. Unworthies in the City weren't there by chance, they'd often committed crimes or missed work deadlines, leading to lost jobs and falling merit. It was a destiny of their own making. Something didn't quite add up about Sam though. If he contributed enough to get in at Prosper, Ajay couldn't understand why he'd become a petty thief, or ended up this low.

"What happened?" Ajay asked whilst finishing off the first stitch.

"I guess . . . it was my kids really," Sam said sorely. "They live with their mother, in the Glorified Quarters."

"You lived in the *Quarters*?" Ajay paused, disbelieving, with the thread held high in line with the bottom of his chin. A thought passed through his mind that terrified him. Something he had always known, but never let surface. *If a Glorified could fall, surely anyone could.* He'd never heard of it before though. It wasn't something they ever advertised or talked about the news, which made him wonder if it happened a lot more than Command cared to let on.

"I was born there," Sam continued. Ajay felt his eyes widen. He was born there? He had been raised in the Quarters? Ajay couldn't understand it, and Sam clearly noticed.

"I know. How could a lad with a top education, Glorified parents, a financial district job, end up like me?"

Ajay didn't say anything.

"I told too many lies," Sam mumbled, took a breath, and looked uneasy. *Lies.* The word almost took Ajay's breath. He was suddenly very uncomfortable with the conversation, almost as if he didn't want to hear any more. If lies ruined Sam, they could ruin him too, but he continued to listen as Sam opened up.

"My wife and I were part of a very well-to-do community. You know, the most exclusive venues. I was happy. Gaining reputation, merit and credit. And I was good at it," Sam paused. "Really good. People respected me." Sam paused again. Ajay could see water in Sam's eyes as he looked out to the glow of the lights through the window. He was tempted to tell him he didn't have to carry on, but before he could even convince himself not to, Sam spoke again.

"Then I had kids, and priorities shifted slightly. Suddenly our goal in life was to fabric together their lives, to shelter and guide them; just to make sure *they* gained reputation, merit and credit. In everything they did."

Ajay spotted Sam following the movements of his hands, going up and down with each weave. "But Cynthia got obsessive about it. She made them stay in the Education Centre after hours, restricted them from seeing friends, doing creative things, leisure activities – all so they could concentrate on personal development or volunteering at every opportunity." Sam shook his head and adjusted the bed sheet to cover more of his torso. To be fair to Cynthia, Ajay thought, it didn't sound a bad parenting strategy. It only seemed right to make sure children had the best shot at a merit-filled life.

"She was suffocating them. The relentless focus on merit was making them miserable."

Ajay stopped for a second. Suffocation. The word suspended in his mind, dancing around his brain cells. Genni had said that yesterday, when she'd shown him her paintings.

"He's suffocating me. Like he has my whole life," Genni had exclaimed as she was pacing across the black furred rug in front of Ajay's sofa in bare feet. She had received a message from her father, detailing his disappointment. Apparently, he'd had a lot of press enquiries about his 'poorly' daughter.

"He said I should be grateful he's covered it up with some sob story about food poisoning. Grateful? He's part of the problem." Ajay thought she should be grateful. Her father's influence had saved her from discreditation by her colleagues and the media. Saved her from being reported. That would have been a hefty merit fine.

"So he's pushed you. Can you really blame him? He wants you to do well." Ajay had responded with frustration as he watched her walk back and forth.

"Yeah, so he can blow his own trumpet. Look at me, I'm Boris Mansald, look at what I created." She'd thrown her hands up and paused in discomfort, bending her shoulders backwards. Ajay was a bit sick of her whining, and she still hadn't told him why she did what she did. The overdose. Her trips to Downtown.

"Why did you do it, Gen? Really? It can't just have been for your father's approval."

There was silence then. Ajay had watched as Genni had wandered over to the windows with her arms crossed. Ajay repositioned himself on the sofa, whilst feeling his sweaty legs beneath his shorts jar uncomfortably with the leather upholstery. He'd waited. What was she thinking? Coming up with a new lie? Eventually, she'd darted quickly towards the closet room at the back of Ajay's apartment. He hadn't moved but only heard bangs of things falling over as she rustled about in the cupboard. It was his apartment. What had she hidden there? Soon she'd appeared again holding three cardboard tubes.

"What are those?"

"They're why I did it." She placed the tubes down on the rug in front of them. Getting down on her knees, she'd softly tied her hair up into a messy bun and popped open one of the tubes. She pulled out a large piece of card or paper, laying it out and weighing the edges down with empty glasses. It was a painting. Alive with colour. Blues, pinks, purples, yellows, and greens. He'd gazed over the detail; the intricacies of water falling down a rocky hill, and splashing beside deep green leaves and trees. It was a place he'd never seen but would love to exist. And it was one of the first images he'd seen in years without the gloss of a screen. It was beautiful. Genni did this? He'd felt love and hatred all at the same time. Love for her undeniable beauty and talent. Hatred for the fact he didn't know. She'd never told him. Or did he never let her?

"You painted this?" He'd asked, as she lay out another that was an unfinished sketch of people walking. They all looked sinister. Miserable.

"Yeah. It's what I do when I want to escape, and relax, and stuff . . ." She had spoken rather timidly.

"How did this make you overdose?" he'd asked.

"I wanted to do my art. But it's meritless. So I got it into my head that if I had more boosts, I would have time to do it alongside everything else." Genni had stroked the painting of the waterfall as if it were a living baby. She was clearly proud of it. Ajay was impressed but knew she shouldn't be proud. She'd almost killed herself for painting?

"And for a while it worked." Genni had shuffled her body so she sat upright, tense and tight. "At first, it was just like normal. You know, the gradual tingle or shake you get from a 4-hour boost. Then after a few sessions, it became something quite different." Ajay had watched as Genni stood up, and began walking slowly in graceful circles, making sure to avoid stepping on the drawings. "I felt like I was floating, elevated within my own little world. I was productive and invincible; I gained 1 merit in a week whilst painting that waterfall. I didn't sleep at all." Ajay bowed his head. A waterfall. How did she draw one? Had she seen it in a film? He hadn't even noticed her peak in merit either or even congratulated her. "I liked the way it made me believe I was Worthy. That everyone cherished and adored me, and I could still do the thing I love." Genni had looked longingly over the pages on the floor whilst exhaling heavily. "I was so anxious about being Unworthy and in the end, I went too far. It becomes a sick, twisted fantasy I suppose."

"But you were no way near Unworthy!" Ajay had exclaimed. The outburst had been as much a surprise to him as it had to Genni. He'd had enough of it. She was stupid. Pathetic for risking everything for a few splatters of paint on a page. She had no idea what it was like to be Unworthy.

"I know Ajay!" Genni had shouted hysterically. "But you, Pearl, my father, Rod, Ace — you high-flyers made me feel as if I was! And that this . . ." She pointed again at her art. ". . . was insignificant. That it would never be worth my time, even though it makes me feel great." Ajay had paused and looked into her teary eyes. She was blaming him? Others?

He hadn't felt angry. He'd felt done. She was too much. He didn't care at that moment. He didn't care about his feelings for her. He didn't care about the insanely awesome things she could clearly do with a pencil and paintbrush. He didn't care that it gave her joy. If he wasn't careful, she would pull him down with her. He'd sacrificed and risked too much. Ajay had said nothing, but just grabbed his hoodie and left.

Genni had called after him. "AJAY!" He'd marched down the hallway, deaf to her calls. It hurt him to walk away but he just did.

That was the last time they'd spoken. Ajay snapped out of his trance when his wrist vibrated. He looked down, setting down the stitching needle. *Hi Ajay, just a reminder that no merit points have been added to your merit score in 5 hours, 17 minutes and 56 seconds. Is it time to do something of worth?* He paused, feeling slightly disoriented. Even though he knew he shouldn't, he dismissed the message and felt a weight of anxiety in his stomach.

"Did I lose you there, mate?" Sam's voice was a slight surprise, as Ajay was head deep in so many things. Ajay nodded, looking back blankly at his Watch.

"I wouldn't worry about the alert. One time won't kill you. I don't get them anymore. They stop bothering after a while." Sam waved his Watch at Ajay; it was dusty and covered in a dried yoghurt-like substance. It confirmed Ajay's suspicion. There was nothing this man had that wasn't dirty. Ajay tried to hide his grimace. Despite the clock ticking, and how he wanted this Unworthy out of his place, he couldn't help it. He needed to know more of Sam's story. What if Genni could end up like him?

Chapter Twenty-One

"What did you do with your kids? To make them feel less suffocated?" Ajay asked and gathered himself. He picked up the needle and thread and set back to stitching.

"I offered to start picking them up from The Education Centre for my wife. She could then take more time for her own merit-making. Well, that's how I played it. I said I'd take them to extracurriculars, ensure they were learning the Tulo values, everything they needed for 'adult life' . . ." He gestured in quotation marks. ". . . that they didn't cover in the Centre. I'd actually take them for full fat ice cream and chocolate and let them watch those old movies with no educational merit. Occasionally, I even took them over to the Side. They have playgrounds there with no drone surveillance. They loved it." Sam smiled as he spoke, shrugging his shoulders. "I just wanted them to be kids."

Ajay thought of Genni and her father. Did she really face such hardship? Something hit him like a machete slicing through wood. Was she ever a kid? Like he was? Did she ever have anything like a grandmother tucking her into bed at night, and telling her a story, or playing stupid games with her friends? Anything?

"So, what happened then?" he asked as he prepared the final stitch.

"Well my wife found out." Sam spoke calmly. "To cut a very long story short, she blocked me out. From my kids, our networks, my colleagues. It started with my socials, especially on *Personi*. No-one engaged with me or liked my content so naturally my sphere of influence diminished. That wasn't too critical merit-wise." Sam started to sniffle slightly, clearly coughing to hold back tears. "Losing my kids completely floored me. At first, I saw them on weekends. But as they grew, they didn't want to spend time with me. So, I struggled to get to work on time, meet deadlines, have any physical or mental motivation to do personal development or community work. I lost the job. Then, someone reported me for what I did with my kids."

"Do you think it was your wife?" Ajay asked.

"I don't know. I hope not. Though I suppose it doesn't matter much anymore. I fell under M-200. And then below M-100." Sam stopped talking and smiled, which Ajay could tell was forced. "Just the way it went for me in the end."

Ajay set down his instruments and struggled to find the words to say next. He felt nervous to feel sympathy for Sam. It was his own fault. He chose his kids' short-term happiness over their long-term success and well-being. It was right he was punished for that, but it just didn't sit well with him. Ajay tried to ensure his facial expression didn't change, he didn't want Sam to sense any of his care towards him. It seemed that he failed.

"It is what it is," Sam said, shrugging his wide shoulders. "Eh, maybe I'll be the first Unworthy below M-100 to make it back to Glorified." Ajay didn't bother laughing, knowing that Sam wasn't expecting it with no smile on his face and his irrational positivity hanging toxic in the air. Sam sighed. "I have wondered about moving out to the Country, like those crazy folk they rave about downtown. One woman apparently-"

The ping of the door chime cut through the moment.

"Are you expecting someone?" Sam asked anxiously, eyes widened.

"No, I'm not." Ajay shot up and swiftly made his way to the intercom. He swiped his Watch and greeted his guest. There was no answer. He tried again. No response. Standing back, he was reminded of the night Genni fell ill. Had she hurt herself again? Would it be worse? Had he lost her forever? Ajay looked at Sam.

"It's the TPD, isn't it? They found me!" Sam flattened his hands over his greying hair in panic. Ajay wondered then if he was right. He started to think about the best place to hide an Unworthy. They'd have no time; whoever it was surely had already made their way up, having forced their way in. A persistent knock started on the door. Sam yelped, but Ajay relaxed.

"Ajay!" The familiar voice travelled through the concrete. Ajay breathed again. "Ajay, darling!" The voice continued. It wasn't often that Blake called.

"For goodness sake, Blake, you scared me to death," Ajay said through the door and, out of habit, lifted his Watch to open it.

"Wait!" Sam said with his arm up, sitting closer to the end of the bed with his leg raised. "They can't see I'm here, they'll report me!"

Ajay knew it was true. He considered how Sam probably should be reported. Then again, people would question the stitches; they would know he'd helped an Unworthy. His reputation was too important. He couldn't risk it.

Thinking fast, Ajay whizzed to grab his screen port and flung it down on the trunk at the end of the bed. Sam looked completely startled by Ajay's speed.

"Now move back and don't make a sound," Ajay said. Sam nodded and touched a finger delicately to his lips.

Ajay tapped furiously at his Watch as he heard Blake's voice penetrate through the door once more. The screen projected itself and broadcasted a documentary show about *CityShimmer,* an up and coming rock band. Its volume roared around the apartment, causing Ajay to wince and Sam to slap his hands to his ears. Ajay turned it down slightly and stood back to ensure the screen covered the bed and its occupant. It would have to do. Blake was knocking harder at the door.

Ajay rushed over, took a deep breath, and opened it.

He was forced to step back as he welcomed a Blake he didn't even recognise. Wearing a discreet navy-blue suit with smart brogue shoes, Blake strutted smoothly into the apartment. His reinstated short, natural brown hair looked fantastically suave in the solar-powered light.

"Sorry, I was just finishing a boost," Ajay said convincingly. "Blake, how did you get in the building?"

"Someone opened the downstairs door and I just sneaked in," Blake said as he snarled at the rock music. Blake was never good at keeping his opinions about something to himself; his face always gave him away. He walked further into the apartment to take a seat on the sofa and Ajay hurriedly walked with him, setting himself at specific angles so Blake couldn't see beyond the screen. Before sitting down, Blake stopped at the sofa and gazed at the screen, as the music subsided and a young Tuloian started talking about the intricacies of stringed guitars.

"Are you watching this through the back of your head?" Blake asked, amusingly looking at Ajay, then at the screen and then back at the sofa.

Ajay laughed confidently. Lying was easy for him. "I just had it on in the background."

Blake seemed satisfied with this. He took a seat, the usual squeak of leather sounding as his body made contact. "How are you then, Ajay?" Blake asked. Ajay joined him on the sofa and his right eye twitched in the direction of the screen. Ajay imagined the lying figure of Sam behind it, just stiffly existing.

"I'm fine, Blake. How are you? How's the dancing going?"

"Well, that's what I came to talk to you about. I've given that up."

"You're joking? But you love it!"

Blake put his arms up and defended himself. "I wasn't getting enough merit. I didn't want to end up on a downward spiral towards Unworthiness. After all, soon life wouldn't be as glittery without being able to hang out with my beautiful friends," he said as he beamed, his white teeth shining. Ajay actually wondered if he'd had some treatment on them; they'd done almost too good a job if so, they could have camouflaged with the immaculate white wall behind him.

"We'd still hang out with you!" Ajay said this and thought of Genni, of Ace's lover, of Sam. They quickly reminded him how unlikely that was and how Blake's sarcastic cackle in response was completely appropriate.

"I do love your optimism, Ajay. Can you imagine an Unworthy hanging out with Glorified folk?"

Blake continued with his laughter, but it jarred with the sadness in his eyes. "So I've got an apprenticeship in Transport Engineering. I've been there a week, *and* I'm close to the apartment I wanted because of it. I'm definitely around the *right* people." Blake said as he patted his head to flatten a small lock of hair that was out of place. He clearly then caught Ajay looking at his hair.

"I know, I miss the pink too, but it was too out there. I wouldn't have got my job with a head the same colour as candy floss." Blake laughed with a nervous undertone. He then turned his head and squinted inquisitively at the screen as if he heard something or even as if he was trying to see through it.

"So you're not dancing at all?" Ajay asked. His words felt as if they rushed out his mouth sickeningly like projectile vomit. It worked. Blake looked back into Ajay's eyes.

"Now and again when I've got time. It's not bad merit-wise doing it for leisure, and the girl I met online enjoys it, so I'll go occasionally with her. Maybe I'll go full-time when I retire." Blake flapped his right hand loosely and his nervous laugh was even more obvious this time. Ajay speculated as he watched Blake rise from the sofa with the energy of a man decades older. Blake's face held a smile, but again it gave him away. His eyebrows were tense and there were dark lines beneath his eyes. Ajay could almost feel the grey fog of disappointment that Blake held inside. Is that what Genni felt every time she couldn't paint? Every time she enjoyed sketching and then beat herself up for time wasting? Maybe he'd misjudged her. Maybe he was wrong. It felt painful to even admit that to himself. He decided to never say it out loud.

"Well, now I've informed you of my life improvements, I best be off." They both wandered to the door, rock music still vibrating in the background. Blake turned and offered Ajay a strange, professional handshake rather than their usual teddy bear hug that Ajay hated. Though in that moment, when it wasn't there, he missed it.

"Bye, Ajay." The door slid closed behind him.

Ajay dashed over to his bed whilst simultaneously shutting down the documentary from his Watch. On his way over, he heard a release of pain from Sam.

"You okay?" he asked as he reached him. Sam was shuffling slowly with his mouth open and his tongue falling flaccidly over his straggled, grey beard. *Disgusting.* He was still disgusting. Then he nodded in response to Ajay, who started to pack away the stitching kit.

The momentary quiet between them was severed by Sam's gruff voice. "That's a shame, that."

Ajay paused, staring down at the shrivelled offcuts of thread that lay side by side.

"The kid's dancing." He was getting frustrated with Sam's audacity by this point. He didn't know Blake, who was way above his score, so he wasn't in a position to offer him sympathy. Ajay decided to take the comment as genuine.

"Yeah, it is. But it will be better for him in the long run, I guess." Ajay did believe that. Like it would be better for Genni to do less painting. And like it would have been better for Sam to have not taken his kids where he did. It was just the harsh reality they lived in.

"It will be. If you can't beat the system, join it. It's my biggest regret." Sam looked lifelessly down to his leg, looking tired again, the purple tinge around his eyes even darker than before. Ajay decided to let him rest there until morning.

* * *

It wasn't long until morning came, with the white sun sneaking over the horizon. Ajay had been busying himself to make provisions for Sam – who he needed to get out. This had been a one-off. He needed to get back to his life. The sun was barely shining when Sam awoke and Ajay ushered him to move himself quicker. Ajay found some crutches in the back closet from when he twisted his ankle; he gave Sam some fresh clothes, allowed him to use the shower, and packed up some food in a satchel that Sam could carry easily around his shoulder. He'd also managed to gift himself with the merit he could have earnt during the past 12 hours. It was only right, he thought.

"Okay. That's everything I can give you now," Ajay said eagerly, as he steadied Sam over towards the apartment door. It was a relief that his nasty stench had gone.

"Thanks pal," Sam said, stood in the open doorway. He turned to depart, but then stopped, looking back at Ajay. "Why did you help me?"

They stood for a few moments, considering each other. Ajay was still truly repulsed by him. Most of him hoped that he would never see him again, while the rest of him felt glad they'd met. Their encounter had somehow helped him, had given him something familiar. At that moment, some words ran around his head in his grandmother's voice; ones he was taught yet would never say out loud.

Ajay just shrugged his shoulders. "Somebody had to."

Sam grunted. "No they didn't." He didn't look at Ajay again, just hobbled down the corridor.

When Sam was out of sight, and Ajay had ensured no one had seen him leave, he ordered his Watch to call Genni. He wanted to make it right. Genni knew she'd made mistakes, and he couldn't let her end up like Sam – asking someone why they had helped them. She was Worthy.

Genni's face appeared, still looking angry with him. Ajay spoke to her in a caring, regretful voice. "Hi, I love you. And I'll ring Pearl tomorrow, *for you.*" Genni didn't smile or even say anything, but she did agree to meet him for breakfast.

Chapter Twenty-Two

It was Saturday. The skies were hot, as usual, but there was a restlessness in the air. The City's streets were packed; Liberation Day shopping was in full swing. Ajay thought about how he didn't know what to get Genni this year, as he observed her standing before her green wardrobe mirror fastening up the brass buttons of her suit jacket. She had an interview to volunteer for the summer camps. Big merit. Big opportunity.

"What time will you finish at the village today?" Genni asked. "About midday."

"Okay, great. I'm meeting Pearl around then." Pearl had agreed to start helping Genni with her social merit. She had worked really hard these last couple of months, at both her recovery and maintaining her score. It had taught Ajay not to underestimate her. In fact, he was even starting to think about their future, what they might plan once they get into the Quarters.

As Genni took another look in the mirror, Ajay stood up and crawled his arms around her belly, resting his head on her shoulder. Things felt good again. "You're gonna be great," he said, kissing her on the cheek. Genni released herself from his grasp and Ajay watched as she walked towards the door.

"Let's not work too late tonight. I got a weather alert, there's a storm due," she said, excited. "Shall we watch from the roof? The view might finally be good enough to paint."

He nodded and watched her go. Despite not agreeing with Genni's decision to continue painting, it was nice to watch her enjoy it. Now she was doing it so openly: she had learnt to multi-task, usually sprawling her papers and paints out whilst watching an educational film. Her Watch saw the film, not the drawings.

Anyway, it was time to get on, he thought. Ajay turned to his wardrobe and selected the ripped, grey denim jacket that he hid behind his suits. His wardrobe mirror turned to a red mist. *Not on trend.* It was always difficult for Ajay to resist the urge to change, but he reminded himself where he was going. He shut the wardrobe door, grabbed his hat, and quickly left the apartment.

Once outside, Ajay welded the hat to his head as a slight breeze attempted to whisk it away; he craned his neck and mused over the small puff of clouds meeting above the concrete trees. His flat, black hat always worked well for hiding his face as he bent down into the taxi, the sky train being too risky for this particular trip. The car drove him around the City as ladies were brunching and couples walked undersized foxes, all of it filtering past the car's windows.

Soon the buildings became smaller; the houses were less developed, and the pavements were untreated by litter picking drones. The nearing storm was swooping packets and bags up in the air and the car swung round in front of a rusted arch that led onto a dirty and rusting rail platform. Ajay swiped his Watch onto the car's monitor and made his way out. As the tip of his shoes reached the platform's yellow line, he could see the carriage approaching. It was an agonising wait from the first sighting to its arrival at the terminal. Ajay almost missed the need to brace himself as the sky train usually hurtled towards him. Instead, this train slouched to a stop. Ajay boarded, the only passenger at the station, before the train chugged and jerked slowly away.

* * *

As Ajay walked through the familiar streets, deep in the pool of his thoughts, a vibration disturbed him. He looked to his Watch to see Ace cuddling and smiling with a pretty girl who was kissing him lightly on the cheek. Ajay looked closer and recognised her as Mr Bancorp's niece, a Glorified born and bred. How the heck did he meet *her?* Ajay was secretly envious. He glanced over the caption. *"Are you the one I've been looking for?"* Ajay felt so sick at the cringe that he literally stuck his tongue out. Yet he was still jealous – it had got a lot of loves. Good for Ace with his biceps and trendy shaved head, Ajay thought. They hadn't seen much of each other recently. Ajay had been too busy, though he was looking forward to seeing him on Liberation Day. He considered dropping him a message but thought against it. There was nothing funny or rude he could think to say, and as that was how their conversations started, a serious message would be an easy way for Ace to ridicule him. Though, they did have that one heart to heart about Ace's relationship with an M-290. It was true that Bancorp's niece was a better fit, if it was actually anything real, which Ajay suspected it wasn't.

His thoughts turned to his grandma and how she might be when he arrived. The last time he'd seen her had been months ago. She had been rather chirpy for a dying woman, a fact that Ajay often ignored. To him, she wasn't dying, just going through a tough spell. Soon, she'd bounce back to how she was. Ajay shunned himself for his optimism. He, more than most, knew that nothing could ever be how it was back then.

He turned the corner onto the main high street; various shades of blue and green bunting hung above the uninspiring rows of shops and terraced houses. A large red flag hung off the outside of the central mail office, warning the residents of the coming storm. Ajay continued walking beneath the flag and the rim of his jacket blew in the strong gale. He scanned his feet, and then quickly moved them away from a Fo Doktrin leaf. It wouldn't hurt him, just stain his white branded trainers with its permanent orange mark, damning evidence of where he'd been. It was the unwanted weed which scattered itself along these streets where the pace of life was much slower. Ajay spotted a lady he recognised from childhood; she had the same leisurely wobble as she walked and wore the same bright purple sandals that matched the colour of her reusable shopping bags. People stopped to chat to one another, but Ajay continued walking. He was startled by a playful scream from the far end of the street but relaxed once he saw it was just a child falling from the monkey bars on the playground. With a squint, he could see that adults were running to her aid next to the slanted merry-go-round. He remembered how he had spent hours spinning Tara round and round on that thing.

A crisp packet flew across Ajay's feet and he smelled the sweet aroma of fresh bread wafting over from the bakery. It was soon masked by the stench of the week-full bins standing outside houses. Ajay kept his eyes low under his hat and hurried towards the third cul-de-sac off the main street. He was greeted by the semi-detached house that sat on top of the street's curve, and he approached the slightly musty green door, turned the brass handle and let himself inside.

The halls of the house were still burdened with the faded wallpaper – flowers of the forest in greens, blues and yellows. Ajay watched as his mother walked delicately across the doorway of the kitchen into the dining area. She was still petite and wore the same pink dress she had for years. Ajay couldn't remember a time where there wasn't an apron tied around her waist or her hair wasn't tied in a messy ponytail, though now it looked greyer. He smelt bread. They must have done well on the recent ration, as he remembered that flour was popular. Maybe times had moved on, he wondered. He never brought them anything from the City – they shouldn't expect him to – though for some reason this time, he felt guilty. He had enough credit to redecorate this whole place, which was so uninspiring, just like all houses on the Side.

Chapter Twenty Three

Ajay Ambers had created a space in his brain that would home his childhood and it would only ever be thought about when he allowed it. That was his plan. The entirety of events that led up to his City life were unknown to everyone but himself. He was originally Karle Blythefen; son of Joon and Keli Blythefen, grandson to Karlane Devlop and brother to Tara Blythefen. The five of them lived, all cooped up together, in a small home on the west part of the Side.

Karle was an inquisitive child and growing up on the Side invited a lot of questions. He wanted to know everything: about the Revolution, the drones, the food rations, the old City, merit, and the Watch. "All in good time," his grandma would say at bedtime, when she told Karle stories of their past. He would always ask for more. She would often remind him that they were the lucky ones. The development of drones and robotics had led to the redundancy of many in the Side, who had travelled into the City for what they called 'pre-redundant' jobs. There were even cuts on the Camel farms, and occasionally he and Tara would go down to a neighbouring farm together. Tara went to feed the camels; Karle went to be fascinated by the robotic machines at work. He only ever saw the milking process, but he would have loved to have watched the technology that processed the meat or that pulled a new calf into the world. Fortunately, Karle's father managed to keep his job as a maintenance worker for the railways. This didn't mean Karle wasn't made aware of how many Side families didn't earn enough credit to even eat. "It's our job to help them," his mother would say over his apprehension to share *their* crops from *their* garden. It was part of their culture to share. Every Monday, Karle would have to assist his mother in washing and chopping homegrown potatoes and cucumbers to then divide them into separate baskets, ready for Tara and Grandma to deliver them to their neighbours. Karle made sure never to share the 'good' stuff, like candy or tinned goods from the small convenience shops on the high street. All food was rationed, because the City never quite sent enough and the desert's heat meant not all crops survived, so when Karle got his hands on *that* stuff, it was all for him. Eating food with actual flavour was a luxury he wanted to enjoy alone.

Sometimes he would share it with Tara. Other than his grandma, his little sister was the only person he'd ended up caring about. The others all became irrelevant collateral once he'd left. Tara was also the only one who, in his teenage years, managed to get him to come out of his dust encrusted bedroom. It would be to teach her how to play cards, or they would run across the sanded streets to the playground and he would spin her on the faulty merry-go-round. "Karle, it's playtime!" she would say as she bounced outside his bedroom door in her rainbow-striped thin tights, her black hair tied up in adorable pigtails. If Karle ever refused by shutting the door in her face or by telling her to get lost, she would weasel her way back into the room and jump on him, squishing the insides of his stomach. That would lead to Karle grabbing her playfully and tickling her until she squealed for mercy. Even as she got older, her little, immature giggle stayed, and it still somehow had an effect on Karle. More often than not, he would play with her. When he agreed to play, she would often run rapidly down the stairs with her blue pinafore slightly dishevelled around her waist. She would erratically run to the tall oak cupboard that leant, with a slight wonkiness, against the back wall of the dining area. She once pulled at the box on the highest shelf, going as high as her tiptoed feet would lift her. Karle walked into the room and watched most of the contents from the top shelf fall and plummet to the ground. It just missed Tara's head, causing her to topple backwards and be caught by a chair behind her.

Karle never thought to stop Tara from doing things too hard for her. It just became something they did, laughing and clearing up after her clumsiness. If it wasn't the cupboard, it was the dropping of a cup, or the bad scraping of her knee by running into something at the playground. She was the type of person that if Karle met her in the City, he would want to throttle her. That type of incompetence would need to be monitored and hidden. Not on the Side. People were much more accepting of imperfections; they didn't seem to bother trying to better themselves. Everything seemed to stay the same, which, as he grew, aggravated Karle. The more he learnt about the City, the more the Side felt backwards to him.

It started when he'd go to the sand hill, a huge mound that overlooks the Side. "Can I come with you to the hill?" Tara would ask, but her cute eyes and charming laugh never worked for that.

The hill was Karle's place. It was said to have formed by a drone dump of sand over old government buildings. Karle had never really cared how it had gotten there. He used to sit and dream about the City he could see but never touch. He would watch as, over time, the silhouette of the skyline became even more dense. Skyscrapers would appear as if overnight, and when the white sun hit the City in the right way, it would glitter and sparkle from across the desert. The hill was where he began to imagine the life of a City kid. He reckoned they had everything they could ever need. Their food wouldn't be rationed, their meals would taste divine; their lights wouldn't flicker, their work would be rewarded; their wallpaper wouldn't be mouldy and they'd go into shopping malls, theatres, sports centres and three-hundred-storey buildings. They would have access to all the latest gadgets and games; he'd always wanted to play in the virtual reality of *TuloCombat* or *DroneDefenders*. Karle would read about them whenever he stole his father's Watch. He would get into the news updates and read up on the latest releases.

His father never liked him taking it. "Karle, have you got my Watch?" The soft yet authoritative tones of Karle's father would echo up and bounce off the walls of the staircase. Karle would jump and quickly turn down the screen of the Watch, hiding whatever it was he was reading. "Karle?" His father would stand in the doorway and immediately point at his Watch, whether it was resting on Karle's desk, bed, or just in his hands. His father always looked disappointed, but never surprised. That's why Karle never bothered hiding it. His father knew that he took it, and in a way, he let him. "Just because I take it off now and again, it doesn't mean it's easily replaceable. I'd prefer you not to take it." His father had said one time. Karle had translated his father's word choice to mean 'I don't want you to take it, but it's okay if you do.' So Karle took that liberty. His father's Watch became his personal fix to feed a growing City obsession. He delved deep into everything he could: books on initiations, Watch updates and personalisation, the development of energy boosters, and videos of Glorified celebrities. There were materials on fitness, home life, Education Centres, eating out, and looking after pets. He would watch the Liberation Day promo on repeat and then indulge in the highlights of their annual celebrations. Life had so many layers out there, while Karle felt pointless in his plain existence.

Then there were the billboards, which in the City were as common as people. He learnt that over there, they advertised everything: nutritional drinks, educational movies, beauty products, and even dull stuff like insurance. But there, on the Side, they only ever promoted one thing. *Purification.* It was a word that literally hung over their community, on the side of buildings and within the adults' Watches. The adverts often featured a message like *'Become your most effective self'* or *'Don't let your ancestors down'*, or sometimes they'd show an interview with a successful 'Purified'. The most prominent one in Karle's memory was the girl with long, red hair from down the road. She would often walk past Tara and him on the playground, and she would always wear a light blue anorak with its hood up. Karle never took notice of her, other than the fact that she was older and seemed kind of strange. She did it, though. She applied for Purification and, five years later, she was almost M-400. Karle remembers seeing her face on the billboards. *Be like Charlen,* they would say. In the shots they used, her hair held more volume and she wore a pretty, yellow summer dress that complimented nicely with her dark skin tone. "It was the best decision I ever made," she would say. Karle agreed with her. She hadn't looked so strange anymore, she had looked happy. The first time he saw her story was when he was twelve, and he went home to his grandma and asked the question.

"How does Purification work?" Karle had bounded in, sweating in a black t-shirt and shorts. Grandma was sitting at the kitchen table, sewing up the holes in his father's shirts. She paused, looked up at him and smiled sweetly. She pulled out the chair next to her, which squeaked unpleasantly across the concrete floor. She patted its seat, inviting Karle to sit down. He sat, staring at her with questioning brown eyes.

"Why do you ask that, love?"

"I see it everywhere. It's how people like us get to the City, right?"

"Right. It's a process Command introduced alongside the merit system. After the Revolution."

"You've never told me about it." With everything Grandma had taught him about Command and other historical matters, it had seemed bizarre to Karle that this had never come up.

"I . . ." Grandma had hesitated, sighed and set down her sewing. "I wanted to wait until you were ready to hear it." She stood, walked into the open-plan kitchen, and turned on the fan that sat on its worktop. As it began its rotation, her short, greying hair blew and banished the beads of sweat on her forehead. She removed the blue cardigan to reveal more of her floor length, brown polyester dress. Then, she sat back down.

"As you know, Command believes our lifestyle encourages the ideals of the old government-"

Karle interrupted, "But they didn't teach anything. Wasn't that the point? They just took everything from those who worked hard. We don't do that."

"No. We don't, but we don't strive for what Command calls 'progress' either, which is classed as anti- constitutional. So, when you reach 25, you can go and serve The Glorified. Those above M- 500."

"Wow. Really?"

"Yes." Grandma gave a slow nod. "You could go there as their butler or chef or cleaner. Whatever they decide. Then, after two years, you can be submitted for Purification. That's where the court decides whether you have been 'Purified' from your upbringing under The Guiding Light."

"And then you can become . . ."

"An accredited City citizen, yes," Grandma finished.

Karle had thought for a moment, trying to take it all in. He imagined himself walking the City streets that he had only ever seen on video. He would wear a dark, sophisticated suit and expensive, polished business shoes. People would admire him, reaching out to shake his hand. He would tuck his well-brushed black hair behind his ears and snap up the latest gadgets from the boards. There would also be a drop-dead beautiful girl on his arm. Until that moment, Karle hadn't understood that it was possible, that he could be a City kid.

"When can I apply?" Karle had asked fleetingly. His grandma had returned to her sewing, but abruptly stopped again, looking a bit blindsided.

"Apply for what?" she asked.

"Purification." Karle had stood from his chair. The same squeak against concrete. "I want to go." A short pause.

"Okay well. All in good time, love." His grandma had stroked his arm. He'd wondered whether she could feel his goosebumps. "We'll talk about it when you're older."

Though as he did get *older,* his desire for the City began to fuel a burning resentment for everything about the Side, especially the teachings of The Guiding Light. It was that which held him back from the dream of a beautiful girl and expensive, polished business shoes. Soon everyone who believed in The Guiding Light became foolish to him. Karle struggled to build a healthy relationship with anyone near him, especially his Father.

Karle began to see him as a sad excuse for a man. He would roll his eyes at the way his father would bounce into a room with joy, gazing at everyone behind his crooked glasses. Karle wished others saw him for what he really was: a waste. The only similarities Karle saw between himself and his father were: A, that they were both – annoyingly, for Karle – skinny and lanky, and B, they were both inexplicably clever. It was no surprise that Karle had excelled at school and ended up working at Prosper when his father could hold intellectual conversations about how they could improve drones and railways. One time, his father singlehandedly repaired a hover bus that came as scrap from the City. He'd even overridden the driverless function so some lowlife could drive it. It was then used to help old people get to the shops, or the kids rode it to school when there was a storm. If anyone in the neighbourhood had a computer or even a Watch problem, they would come to his father for help. So, Karle found it extremely irritating that his father had never once shown a desire to be Purified. He had more ability than most people to make a better life for himself and for them as a family. Instead, Karle actually felt like his father spent more time with other people. Always visiting their houses if someone had died or was having a hard time. It was like he had no time for them, so Karle decided he would have no time for him either.

He began to steal his Watch even more. Not just for research, but also as a way to anger him. Unfortunately, it didn't upset him quite as much as Karle had hoped, but then Karle learnt the one thing that really bothered his father. It was his refusal to go to the meetings. So, naturally, Karle refused a lot.

Chapter Twenty-Four

"I'm not going," Karle shouted as he darted up the wooden staircase. He deliberately made a point of smacking his feet down. His father was running after him, anger pulsing over his olive face underneath his smeared glasses. Karle knew that most middle-aged men in Tulo had done away with manual spectacles, but the Blythefens didn't qualify for, nor could they afford, digital counterparts. They weren't Worthy enough.

"You've got to go. People are expecting you." His father grabbed the underside of his arm before he made it to his lockable bedroom. His grip had been tight, but not so much that it caused pain. Karle struggled before releasing himself free. He didn't retreat, but stood breathless, staring up at his father who sighed and spoke with a calm yet still agitated tone.

"Look, son. You're coming. That's the last I want to hear of it. These meetings are important for your mother and I, and the rest of our community. You need to show your support."

Supporting something would mean agreeing with it, Karle had thought. Though as a kid he'd enjoyed the times they'd spent with neighbours, squished around their inadequately sized dining table, listening to The Guiding Light. It told marvellous stories. Karle's particular favourite had been the one about the lost worker in the storm, and he'd always relished the chance of wafting his small fingers through its dancing figure of light. His mother would always pull him back and tut. It was a device that was once beautiful to him, oblong like a fresh loaf of bread and a flat top surface from which the mesmerising hologram would appear, connected together through veins of sparkles. It looked like a man or even a woman, but it didn't have a face – only a strong, joyful, storytelling voice. That was when he was a kid.

Later, as he stared at his Father, he thought about how the meetings were dull enough to make him want to eat sand for dinner. He'd heard everything before and had no interest in listening to what the others believed it meant for their plain, empty, starving lives. His time, and their time for that matter, was much better spent marvelling over the City and preparing himself for when he would get there. There was nothing glamorous The Guiding Light or those meetings could offer him that the City couldn't surpass. Plus, not going to the meetings got his Father looking as irritated as he did in that moment, his thick eyebrows turned down behind his glasses, lip twitching in agitation. Karle looked right through him to see threadbare patches in the beige carpet and the mould crawling up the maroon painted wall. The place he would have in the City was going to be stylish and plush. Now sixteen, he'd only ever expressed his Purification dream to his grandma. In that moment, as his father looked into his eyes, Karle decided it was time he knew, and never once had he regretted what he said next.

"I'm not coming because I want no part in this community. You stifle progress. You're lazy. You believe in something you can't fully explain. You get nothing for the hard work you do." His eyes flicked back to the mould up the wall. "Well, not me. I won't be like you, Dad. I'm applying for Purification as soon as I turn eighteen."

His defiance and aggression had flattened the air and made it feel toxic; it was like his Father couldn't catch his breath enough to think before he spoke.

He'd roared at Karle with a volume that rarely passed from his lips. "HOW DARE YOU? YOU ARE KIDDING YOURSELF IF YOU THINK YOU CAN SURVIVE THERE. YOU WILL NEVER BE CROWNED WORTHY IN THEIR EYES."

Immediately Karle saw his father's eyes soften with regret and remorse, but he himself had been incensed. He'd spun on his heel, slammed the door in his father's face and bolted the lock with such force that it nearly fell off. On his bed, he bundled himself into a ball and groaned loudly into the mattress.

An hour or so passed and still Karle had heard nothing from outside his room. He just lay there, awaiting his father's apology. Soon he heard his parents talking and slithered along the length of his bed to listen in. The gaps between their bedroom doors were so significant that Karle was even able to see his mother's earnest yet compassionate expression.

"You might need to do something differently. Take some time and ask our Friend what you should do." She'd stroked her husband's arm and he'd pulled her closer to himself. Karle watched as his father's lips settled on his mother's forehead and he'd wondered if his father's silence was a plea to hold back tears. They'd then disappeared into different rooms.

It wasn't long until Karle heard the pitter-patter of a knock on the rotting wood of the door. He unbolted the fragile lock and was greeted by his father carrying a huge plastic sack. Karle had immediately tried to see its contents, but his father moved it behind his back.

"I'll get to that in a minute. Sit down, son." Karle sat on his bed, feeling the springs spiking his backside. His father sat beside him and the two of them dipped closer to the floor. They spent a moment in silence. Karle wondered if his father was expecting him to speak first. He absolutely wasn't going to; he had the right to do what he wanted, and he wasn't going to apologise for voicing the truth of that. To his relief, his father spoke.

"I am sincerely sorry for the way I spoke to you. I was wrong to do that." His father hadn't kept his eyes off Karle's empty, rotting desk at the back of the room. It seemed as if he didn't have the decency to look Karle in the eyes when he apologised. Typical, Karle had thought. "And I'm sorry we've not always got along. We're very similar in many ways and sometimes that means we clash. It's my fault. I've been believing I should deal with that by resistance and that was a mistake." Yes, it was, Karle thought, though he was slightly surprised to hear him admit it. His father took a long, loud, deep breath. At first, Karle had thought he was struggling to breathe or something, but in the end, his father looked to be processing something. Like the next words he would say had to be chosen carefully.

"I've now come to accept that you don't feel you belong here. You want to be out there." That's when his father stopped staring at the desk, instead looking out the small, square window by Karle's bed where the outline of the City's skyline could just be seen.

"And I believed in The Guiding Light when he just told me: I have to let you go." His father stroked the bristles on his chin and slowly lifted his glasses closer to his sincere eyes. "So . . ." His father rose as he moved the plastic sack in front of the bed and finally displayed its contents.

"This is for you."

Karle stood up then, open-mouthed and amazed. He'd ignored his father's gaze that was on him and jumped forward to pull the entirety of the black bag away, revealing every inch of an outdated computer set. It wasn't much to look at. It had a clunky transparent screen and stand, and the keyboard came as a separate entity, but Karle didn't care. It belonged to him, and he could do what he liked with it. His father's voice was muffled alongside his excitability.

"I figured if you're going to go for it, you better brush up on your tech skills. Now I know it's not what they have over there, but it's what they were rationing down-" His father's speech had been broken by Karle's rush. He was completely animated, hurrying to snap up the set and place it onto his desk, which wobbled with the new burden.

"Okay, well, I'll leave you to it," his father choked through his words. Karle hadn't turned back to watch his father leave. He was beaming, and kind of wished he'd said thank you at the time. He was just so caught up with it. Finally, freedom would be his. With his father's approval. Not that he'd need it anyway, but it did feel nice to have it. The sun filtered behind some clouds and the silhouette of the City glistened. Karle looked towards it with a new hope. He'd shifted the computer further back on his desk, knowing this was how he would prepare himself for a top engineering job in the Inner-Ring.

That was the original plan, but things changed not long before Karle turned seventeen. He did something terrible, meaning he no longer wanted to be Purified.

Chapter Twenty-Five

"Karle, we can't be here. We have to leave now." Callum had run to catch up with Karle as they walked through the shopping mall. His soft brown hair bounced around his baby face, splattered in freckles. Karle had often thought his best friend was too soft, worrying about every little thing, though he would soon learn that Callum had been right. They shouldn't have been there.

"Just a little longer. Don't you feel free by just being here?" Karle hadn't been able to help his enthusiasm. They were inside an M-350+ venue. It was a cathedral of luxury and possibility, wealth and popularity. Groups of well-dressed people filtered in and out of digitally operated stores. He was mesmerised. At the time, he saw it as a good decision, slipping onto the train and heading into the City just for a taste of it. In his ignorance, he never anticipated anything bad would happen.

"Come on, let's just try one suit on." Karle, empowered and negligent, headed into *Deluxe Suits for Men*. Callum, with a worried expression, followed on. Karle whipped open the curtain of one of the many changing pods that filled the entire store and, ignoring Callum's whimpering, he closed himself inside the pod.

Welcome to Deluxe Suits for Men. I'm Carla, your personal stylist, the voice boomed from the full-length digital scene, its camera acting as a mirror. *First, let's find your style. Please select your preferences from the following options.* Karle proceeded to select his favourite colours and styles that appeared on screen. In a startling transformation, the mirror showed Karle wearing the sharpest suit he'd ever seen. He had never looked like this – rich, smart, prosperous. He imagined himself wearing this suit to a classy bar and setting his charm on a beautiful woman who actually wanted to speak to him. It was dark green suede and it shimmered as he twisted and turned in a glorious moment of augmented reality.

Are you happy with your new look? I think you look amazing. Would you like to proceed to payment? Karle, of course, didn't have the credit, but in his delusion, he tapped 'proceed'.

Okay, fabulous! First, we need to take your delivery address and an ID scan for merit validation. Only the Worthy can look this good. The disappointment was painful. Idiot, he cursed himself. What did he expect? Through gritted teeth, he cancelled the transaction. He looked at himself once more in his suit, which then faded back to his grey shirt and brown speckled trousers.

"Who says I can never have it?" he whispered to himself. On flicking back the curtain, he was welcomed by a sweating Callum.

"Karle, I cannot stay here any longer, we're going to get caught. I should never have sneaked past those guards with you."

"Calm down, we can do anything we want to do. Let's check out the food court."

Karle had set off at pace. Callum ran after him, tugging on his arm and begging him to turn round as they narrowly missed barging other people in the crowd. As they headed past more white-fronted shops, Karle noticed the huge billboard that hung over the central aisle. It was advertising some new energy-boosting product called *SkipSleep*. An alluring lady with flowing brown hair and shining white teeth smiled down at him, with the words *"Have more time for you and your merit"* sprawled closely to her bewitching eyes. It felt almost magical, but he pulled himself away when they arrived at the food court, which was even more like a fantasy. Even Callum stopped moaning, for a moment.

Never had the boys seen so much food. Life on rations had willed both their mouths to drop open at the spectacle before them. There were beautifully presented delicacies of every description. There were fat iced cakes, fresh cuts of meat; glazed breads, nicely cut vegetables; gluttonously stuffed pies, and fruits crafted into the shapes of flowers and birds. Trying to compose themselves, they walked slowly past the stalls.

"Watch it!" Karle said as he grabbed Callum's shoulder and forced him to duck away from a soaring drone carrying two pink milkshakes.

"I didn't even see it!" Callum exclaimed, whilst laughing nervously.

"They're everywhere here. It's incredible." Karle had gazed over the drone as it arrived at a table and served the drinks to young, giggling girls. He noticed them looking at him, obviously finding the near collision amusing. Karle smiled back at them in a charming way. They giggled again, looking at one another with blushed cheeks. Karle couldn't believe the reaction; he'd flirted with City girls and they'd liked him. Then, a sharp tugging had started on his sleeve. Callum had started up again.

"No, no, no . . . We have to go, we're getting noticed." He pulled on Karle's arm once more, whispering into his ear. Karle felt Callum's hot saliva spitting out onto his cheek. Gross, he thought.

"Have you seen this? We're not going anywhere. Look at the way that chef is preparing that, what even is it?" Callum followed Karle's pointing finger to see men dicing and frying at speed, as if there were a million things to do within the same minute. Karle also marvelled at the machine next to them. Drinks glided from it with such precision and quality that to do it by hand would have taken hours. Drones then proceeded to take the drinks over to tables, seconds after they had been ordered.

"Karle, we really have to go now." Callum's words seemed to splutter from his mouth, tugging again at Karle's arm but this time, more forcefully. Karle had had enough of it. He shoved Callum on his arm.

"Stop your fussing. Let's try and sneak some of that, it looks so fresh." Karle began an advance forward, the glazed lemon loaf in his sights. Callum grabbed him, the slap of his hand on Karle's forearm making a loud clap.

"Karle, just look!" Callum moaned, tears in his eyes and shakes in his fingers.

Karle followed Callum's finger to see a man in a lightweight dark suit rising from the comfort of his nicely padded seat. He had abandoned his iced coffee on the table and was walking towards them with piercing, angered eyes, and Karle then saw the security drone that was accompanying him. Karle suddenly understood Callum's alarm, but to him, it didn't mean they knew who they were. Yes, their appearance was slightly dishevelled, but that didn't mean they weren't entitled to be there. Their parents could be M-300 and off buying some clothes.

They were fine.

"It's okay. We should just stay calm. We can say our parents are here." Karle shrugged his shoulders and felt confident that they could get out of it easily with some overcooked and exaggerated lie. "Okay Callum? Callum . . . ?"

On his friend's silence, Karle turned quickly and saw Callum sprinting towards the mall's exit. Karle's heart rate rocketed, especially when he then heard the revving of the drone's acceleration, and even more so when he saw there was a whole swarm of security drones in on the hunt. This wasn't what Karle had imagined on his first real visit to the City; an eruption into unanticipated chaos.

Karle knew nothing more to do than to run and join his friend in escaping. He was faster than Callum and managed to catch up with him whilst trying to block out gasps and insulting shouts from the crowds.

"Come on, this way!" Karle screamed. They dashed down some stairs through a restricted exit door into a new store that was being refurbished. They slammed the door shut but knew that was unlikely to stop an army of drones.

"What do we do? WHAT DO WE DO?" Callum was inconsolable. Karle took stock and tried to see beyond the white painting sheets on the walls and tubs of open paint left sporadically across the floor. It felt as if there was no way out, but in that moment, he'd heard the calming yet dangerous sound of moving water. He scanned the store again and saw it: a door labelled 'balcony'.

"The river, come on!" he roared.

"The river, are you joking?" shrieked Callum, pale as anything.

"We just need to get up on the balcony. Come on!"

At that moment, the door to the store exploded open and the drones swirled in like a fierce swarm of bees, covering all directions. Karle sprinted forward again, ushering Callum to join him. He approached the balcony door, delighted to see just a low railing between them and the moving current below. The hairs on his neck stood up when he heard Callum's terrified voice call his name.

That's when he witnessed his friend being tasered and restrained by three or four drones, his body bouncing in electrified spasms until it stopped. Callum's right cheek was pressed hard to the ground, his mouth slightly agape and expressing anger, pain and vulnerability, all rolling together to display uncontrollable and paralytic fear. Before Karle abandoned him, the quivering mouth had echoed his name once more.

Karle had no other choice but to mount the railing and jump hopelessly into the moving river below.

Deafened by the roar of the water that was rushing around him furiously, he couldn't move against the strength of the artificial current. His mind was caught on the depth of the darkness beneath him, home to the whirring machines that gave the river movement. He thought of what it would be like to drown or get caught in their spinning blades. His family would be devastated; he knew they wouldn't stop looking for him. A painful lump in his throat had brought a sudden calm. He managed to stretch out and battle the weight of his waterlogged clothes to force his body to desperately splash above the surface for air. The drones were still flying above him as the river moved between two long blocks of buildings and Karle, acting only on instinct, dived low into the water. He resented his parents for many things, but as he ducked himself lower, he was thankful for his father's swimming lessons, despite the griminess of the Side's badly maintained swimming pool. He resurfaced by a wall not far from where he'd disappeared beneath the current. He kept his head low in the water and watched in relief as the drones flew straight past him and advanced further down the river. He knew he needed to move, suspecting that they'd surely be back to search the perimeter.

Karle scrambled up the nearest ladder and came out on a residential street, just down from the shopping mall.

It looked no different than any other street, covered in advertisements and excitingly busy. Before he was able to gather his thoughts, he heard a soft but stern voice from behind him.

"Pssttt, boy." Karle turned. "Psssst, get in here." A small woman was leaning out of her front door, ushering Karle to come in. "Quickly, they'll be coming back in no time."

He hesitated. How did he know she wasn't just turning him in for a hefty chunk of credit? However, he didn't have any other choice. He looked around and then ran through the steel door that slid shut behind him.

Karle had never been into someone's house in the City. He suddenly felt self-conscious as his soaking clothes dripped onto the floor, though as he looked around, he decided not to be so bothered about his appearance. The house was nothing like the glamorous life he'd expected. It was big, no doubt, and the open-plan style and high ceilings had real potential. Unfortunately, that could only be seen if one imagined that the piles of clothing, empty food carriers, overloaded worktops and slightly musty smell weren't there. The colour scheme of a dark maroon and cream also didn't complement any other feature in the room. It only made it feel smaller. Karle had stared for a minute, standing still, trying to take it all in.

"Alright, boy. I know it's a little messy, but it's a busy life. Don't go judging me."

How did she know what he was thinking? Karle became very aware of his facial expressions. She shuffled past him into the kitchen with a certain bullish grace. Her long, patterned tunic was painted in vibrant colours – a big contrast to the current black and white trend Karle had read about. Looking at her from the back, Karle wouldn't have been surprised if she was an Unworthy. Her mousy brown hair was unkempt, straggly with split ends sprawling down the length of her back. Karle moved himself into the large living space where the sofa and armchairs were covered in pieces of clothing and books. He then noticed a wall in front of them. It was completely littered with child's paintings and sketches of locations in the City – the river, the Glorified Gate, the Quarters, the Command building, and the Retail and Financial Districts – all places Karle had only ever dreamed of visiting.

He was quickly taken away from the art gallery by a growl and sudden force on his body. A strawberry red fox had playfully jumped up to lick his face. Karle, slightly surprised and hesitant, stroked the fox as it fussed over him with adoration.

"Alpha, get down!" the woman shouted from the kitchen as she marched over to control her pet and stood squarely in front of Karle. That was the moment when he had seen her face clearly for the first time. Her skin was almost impossibly pale for Tulo's climate, and if put against Karle's skin would resemble the complexion of camel's milk. But that wasn't her distinctive feature. She carried some sort of sore on the right side of her neck and chin. Was it a rash or a skin deformity? Karle had never seen anything like it. It was like a stark red, rough textured pond that lay stagnant across her face.

Karle pulled his eyes away from it quickly and spoke timidly. "Thank you. For letting me in."

The lady flapped her hand as if to say 'no problem'. "So what are you doing so far from home?"

"I just . . ." Karle gulped with fear over the implication that she knew. ". . . came to explore."

"Hmmmm. Risky thing. Just explore outside, don't be going to venues where you're not accepted. Getting caught for trespassing can lead to some complications." Back in the kitchen and with the fox sniffing at her feet, she swiped the only empty black worktop to activate the electric hobs.

"You're blessed you don't have your Watch yet, they'd be on your VPG, no problem."

"You can disable that," Karle spoke too quickly. He was tempted to throw his wet hands over his flippant mouth. She was a City woman. He shouldn't sound so arrogant.

"Well, yes. But there's not always time for that." She started cooking, steam evaporating instantly into the air.

"Are . . ." Karle hesitated but then continued. ". . . your children home?"

"Children?" she asked, still preparing food. Karle felt her eyes on him as he gazed further over her drawings. "You're nosey, aren't you?" She gave Karle a stern look, forcing him to look down at his squelching shoes vulnerably. "If you must know, I'm a teacher in the walled part of the City." Karle was surprised and he didn't contain himself in showing it.

"You work for a Glorified school?"

"That shocking to you, boy?" she asked. Her voice was condescending, but then she shrugged her shoulders and spoke softly as if it was a perfectly reasonable question for Karle to ask.

Karle wondered then if she was a little unwired. "I teach language and communications."

She then plunged a knife into an onion and started frying camel burgers on a pan. The aroma tantalised Karle's taste buds, a sudden hunger manifesting itself as a growling goblin in his stomach ready to devour some meat.

"So . . . what's your name?" Karle asked.

"Come on, boy!" she roared as she slammed a plate down from the cupboard. "Just mind your own business."

"Sorry." Karle smiled in a plea for her to like him. She simply smiled back with an eye-roll, tied up her straggly long hair, and pushed the juicy burger, plated up, across the worktop in Karle's direction.

"You like onions on top, yes?" She asked as she hovered a spoon of onions over the top of the burger.

"Wow. Thank you. I . . . Yes, how did you know that?" Karle took the burger and went to sit on the torn sofa. He stopped. There was no way he could sit on her furniture while dripping wet, even if the cushions were repulsive. So he just stood and ate.

"I just had a feeling," she said as she began washing up. "Now eat that up. And go home. They'll have lost you by now."

Karle didn't respond, as he was enjoying the heavenly taste of the meat between the bun. He had never before tasted meat of this quality. He didn't answer her, consumed with pure gluttony, wondering if she'd make him another if he asked.

"What about the boy you were with then?" the lady asked, before taking Karle's plate the instant he took his last bite.

Shocked by both this flippancy and her question, Karle found it difficult to swallow. "Callum?" But how did you-?"

She interrupted him. "It doesn't matter. What matters is, how do you plan on helping him?"

"What do you mean? I'm just a kid. A kid from the Side. There's nothing I can do. They'll just send him back, right?"

"Not automatically. You need to go home and tell his parents what happened. They'll be able to apply for his release."

"But won't they come after me?" Karle was scared, but he tried not to let her see it.

"I doubt it. The TPD don't tend to waste time on Side kids if they don't catch them the first time. I guess it's the assumption that once you're 18, your Watch will do the job for them. And if it doesn't, they have means of dealing with you." She walked towards Karle then and placed her greasy hands on his shoulders. Karle felt a pinch as she ever so slightly gripped his skin. Is this where she kills him? He supposed it would be fitting. Karle had never realised how people like him were treated in the City. The discrimination and the shame. He was utterly confused and had never felt so lost. Would he experience this feeling even after he'd been Purified? These thoughts all ran through his mind as he stared at the unfortunate monstrosity on the woman's face, which he would later learn was a birthmark. She spoke again with fire in her eyes.

"You've done a bad thing. And there will be consequences. The way you're going, you're set for a very unpleasant end. Now leave my home." She lifted her grip from his shoulders and paused. "Please."

Timidly, Karle turned away from her and her strange house, giving one last look at the drawings on the wall. The door opened and his host had the last word.

"Boy! Don't go right at the end of the road. You'll end up Downtown. Dodgy stuff happens there. Go the long way back."

So Karle did. He went home, the long way back, without Callum.

Chapter Twenty-Six

That day had ended with Karle sitting on the hill, staring down into the sand, his brown tattered sandals merging with the grains. The sensation of it felt scratchy and abrasive. Tears had rolled down his teenage cheeks in a way they never had before. The sun was setting over the City, its perfect outline resting against the lilac sky. Soon his Grandma joined him, panting as she reached the top.

"Oh love, you had to choose the tallest hill, didn't you?" His grandma put her hands to her knees and let out a few sharp breaths. Karle said nothing, his eyes bloodshot and hair greasy with sweat. He continued hugging his knees and hid his face in them, the smell of sweat strong on his trousers. Grandma sat down next to him and they sat in silence for a few minutes until Karle finally spluttered out words.

"Why did that have to happen? Why didn't Callum run faster?" His fists were full of sand and he beat them onto the ground, the sand escaping through the edges of his fingers. He felt the tight squeeze of Grandma's arms around him. His instinct told him to shove her off, but he didn't.

"You were told you should never go to the City, you're not accepted everywhere there."

"But the City kids have no Watch or merit until they're eighteen either. Yet they get to go to the shopping malls, the best games arcades and buy the best stuff!"

By this point, Karle had learnt so much about the City that he probably knew more than those who lived there.

Yet there were a few questions he hadn't yet found answers to. Why did he have to wait? Why was Callum taken? Why were they so shut out? Of course, he had read through the political reasons. The lifestyle The Guide taught was based on rest and taking things slower than Command required; that sort of idleness and selfishness had led to Tulo's poverty stricken past. Command couldn't risk that ideology, as they called it, infecting their City and reversing everything they had all worked hard for. But Karle never understood the injustice, that those born here, those who had never been given the choice, were also shut out. Marginalised. As his Grandma started to speak, Karle could feel the irritable itch in his mouth intensifying, and he felt as if his limbs were about to start shaking. He closed his eyes and breathed, calming himself down, but nothing could truly suppress his anger at the world.

"That's not how we live, Karle. It's not what The Guide says is . . ." His grandma attempted to appease him, but Karle burst out in frustration.

"I hate The Guiding Light, it stops me from doing anything I want to do, you and Mum and Dad stop me from doing what I want to do because of it." He shrugged off her arms and threw sand out into the humid air, which just fell to the ground in the absence of any breeze.

In that moment, Karle told himself that the next time he saw its shimmering hardware or talking man of light, he'd throw it straight into the nearest wall. Karle had heard that its name originated from when construction workers had gotten stuck in dark tunnels and used the shine of its hologram to guide their way to safety. Well, it could never offer him sanctuary, he thought. He felt so angry; it wasn't the joyful storyteller he remembered from childhood, but the reason he wasn't accepted. It must be some sort of hypnosis, he decided, convincing people that they couldn't live without it, like a psychological crutch for the hardship they face. Yet that was a hardship they chose; the City would accept them if they were Purified, but its teachings held so much sway over many members of the community. He didn't understand it, but he knew that he wanted nothing more to do with it. His grandma had then given him some version of the usual guff.

"The City isn't built on a sure foundation. It's as unstable as the moving sand between our toes. People are taught to strive for more, towards selfish merit-making for their own vanity, and eventually they crack. They drive themselves into oblivion for a futile and ungrounded 'worthiness' determined by other people. But those who build their life like The Guide teaches, they have a rock-solid foundation. It allows you to rest and take the time to become the person you're destined to be. You're defined by that and not a number on your wrist." Karle felt his grandma's arm move around him again. "That's why we stay here and contribute what we believe we should be contributing. We don't always get it right, but we're seeking to live by a different standard to the City's."

Karle said nothing in response. He'd heard it all before. His grandma didn't move, only sighed as they both looked towards floating scaffolding surrounding a newly constructed Prosper building. With tears rolling down his cheeks again, Karle asked his grandma a final question.

"Grandma, do you think I'll ever see Callum again?"

"I don't know, love." She was stroking his arm for comfort. "Let's just have faith he'll come home."

Faith in what? Karle asked himself as his heart hopelessly dropped in his chest. He looked down to see his Grandma holding his hand, and that was the moment when Karle

Blythefen had decided he wouldn't wait for Purification. He didn't want the stigma of his Side upbringing hanging over him for his whole life. He'd have to find a way to become someone other than himself.

Chapter Twenty-Seven

His opportunity came on a restless and stormy evening, when Theo Badds died. For months, Karle had spent sleepless nights analysing the software of his father's Watch using the old computer, but he'd hit a dead end. To test the concept of changing a Watch's identity would mean turning his father into someone else. He couldn't imagine his father being very impressed, or not the least bit suspicious, if his Watch started telling him he was Didi Traves. That was the lady who worked in the shop, whom Karle thought was mind-numbingly boring. She wore the same grey short-sleeved dress with the same deeper grey apron over the top, which always had the same greasy stain across her saggy aging breasts. He'd never noticed it as a kid, but as he got older, he noticed more of his neighbours' disgusting appearances. So whenever Karle thought about changing his father's name, Didi always came to mind, because as a seventeen year old that was the height of humour. Unfortunately, though, being serious about his plan, which had to remain a secret, his father's Watch wasn't an option.

Then, just when Karle thought his luck was out, his father's friend died. Theo Badds was a mentor to his father and a very close companion. When he finally breathed his last, the entire family was invited round to their house to bless his passing.

The five of them shuffled single file down the narrow, enclosing walls of the Badds' hallway. Their house had a familiar smell. It wasn't unpleasant; it was like dying flowers, not quite fresh but not quite rotten. Karle had realised that this was the smell of Theo himself, it used to walk around with him and would remain in their house for at least a couple of hours after he'd gone. They made their way through a left-hand doorway, which opened up into the living room. It was similar to their own; slightly dated, with chipped red paint covering the walls. Admittedly, though, Karle didn't notice this much on that particular day due to the presence of Theo's corpse displayed across a table in the middle of the room. He had been given a bunch of bedraggled flowers to hold.

Karle had never seen one before. A dead body was no way near as gruesome as he'd imagined. Theo could have been sleeping; the only difference was that his tanned skin looked lighter. Karle's thoughts were interrupted by the touch of his little sister's hand slipping into his as they gathered around the table. He held it tightly.

"Thank you so much for coming," Glenda said as she immediately gave Karle's father a hug. The poor woman looked as if she could be on the table herself. Her eyes were puffy, her grey hair was dishevelled and the skin under her neck sagged like the fat you cut off a camel. Karle avoided looking at her. Instead, he saw *it*.

Just behind his father, to his right, stood a small raised table. Lying on top of it was Theo's redundant Watch. Karle's pupils widened and his heart skipped as he contemplated the magnitude of this opportunity. If he could use that Watch, he could see deeper inside. Stupidly, he had wondered whether he could ask to borrow it, but his only real option was to steal it. He had made a promise with himself to never invite questions from anyone.

"Shall we bow our heads?" his father said through his continuing tears. Karle took a chance. Everyone bowed their heads, closing their reddened eyes, but Karle transferred

Tara's hand from his own to his grandma's and walked towards his father. He carefully positioned himself in front of the table and, in a false act of comfort, put one arm over his grieving father's shoulder. He needed to be sure everyone's eyes were shut. They were. He used his remaining hand to slip the Watch into the gaping pocket of his tattered trousers. Once this was done, he bowed his head as if he always had.

* * *

Karle had only had the Watch in his possession for less than twenty-four hours before it had been deactivated. It hadn't given him loads of time.

For the first four hours, he'd tapped at his keyboard, mind and eyes focussed.

Initially he had attempted to send random requests to the Watch. Fortunately, Karle had developed a lot of ingenuity over the last few months. He had delved into every device he could get his hands on. The alarm clock had been his first victim, slowly followed by a broken screen projector, Tara's only interactive doll, a malfunctioning drone he found on the street, and even The Guiding Light. Even though Karle had played around with his father's Watch, as he was getting deeper into this one's interface he realised he had never seen software as advanced as this before.

It was going to be challenging, but Karle didn't let that scare him. It pushed him on. He had begun sending messages from his computer to the Watch, just trying to get an idea of what the API looked like. He analysed network calls, searched for unencrypted files, even profiled the hardware performance metrics. He then started to piece together the snippets of information he'd gathered to find the Watch's weak spot. Using the command line, he tried injecting code into its graphical user interface, with the help of some automated scripts he'd written. Then, it happened.

"Yes!" he said, but not too loudly. His rotting bedroom door certainly wasn't soundproof, and given his grumpy behaviour recently, his family would ask questions if they'd heard him sounding happy. But he was happy. He'd found that weak spot: a network request made from a server to the Watch, which he could intercept and manipulate.

Karle's excitement mounted. He rattled his fingers across the keyboard, his fingers bouncing off it. He began changing the details of Theo Badds, as if to erase his existence altogether. "Come on, come on . . ." he murmured. The code flicked about on the screen. Until it stopped. The test was successful. "No way," Karle said beneath his breath. He had been fidgeting in his chair like a fox preparing for a walk. He handled Theo's Watch, lifting it up to his eyes almost in disbelief, to see his own name displayed on it. Karle Blythefen, M-310.

* * *

Karle had then spent the next hour back at Theo and Glenda's house. His return there was necessary. Theo's Watch had become inactive. At first, Karle didn't understand it, and was worried that Command had deactivated it sooner than he had expected. He realised then he was being stupid. Of course it wouldn't work after a few hours of Theo not touching it. Karle had read all about its security features, and there'd been many times his Father's Watch had stopped working after he'd 'borrowed' it.

In order to test the legitimacy of Theo's identity change, Karle needed to wake the Watch up. To do that, he needed Theo's finger. So, after stealing his father's keys, he ended up on the Badd's front step in the hot, post-storm air. Gasping but not relenting, Karle fumbled into his pocket and rattled through the bunch of keys to find one that fit the lock. Failed. He tried another. Failed. He tried once more and scrunched his eyes with hopeful anticipation. Success. The key turned a full 360 degrees. Karle was thankful his father was so good with people. Trustworthy enough to have a key for most homes in the neighbourhood. Karle slowly opened the door and sneaked inside.

He stood once again in the incredibly narrow hallway. Frozen. He hadn't considered this far into his plan. What would he say to Glenda? How was he going to get Theo's fingerprint? All sorts of sickening plans of action had come to Karle at that point. He couldn't quite believe he was considering carrying a dead man's severed finger in his pocket, though he had been more disgusted when he found Glenda sleeping inelegantly over a mouldy floral armchair, mouth wide open and saliva dripping down her wobbly chin. He had also been disappointed to see that Theo's body had gone. No longer on the table but replaced with an empty vase. At that point, Karle's instinct was to give up, but as he got back to the front door, something forced him to go upstairs. Before long, he found himself in a bedroom, staring down at Theo's body.

Karle thought again of how peaceful Theo looked. So at rest. He smiled, but felt suddenly uncomfortable. It felt wrong and sinister, smiling over the dead. What did he expect? He went there for a dead man's fingerprint, not to sit and have a chocolate biscuit with his feet up. There was a job to be done. No matter how sick and twisted it might be.

He grabbed Theo's Watch from his pocket so quickly he'd almost dropped it. Kneeling by the bed and throwing back the floral duvet to expose Theo's right hand, he nervously grabbed Theo's forefinger and swiped it across the screen. *Access denied.* After a few failed attempts, Karle had thrown Theo's hand back down in frustration and had rubbed his own hands together after feeling the icy touch of death. He's too cold, Karle thought. Back at work, Karle had rubbed Theo's fingers between his own as if he was spinning a stick to start a fire. He added a few sharp blows from his warm breath into the mix and repeated these two motions intensely. He paused. The unexpected slam of the front door. The voice of a man. Beeps of a drone downstairs.

"Ma'am. Wake up ma'am," the man said loudly. Karle was still. He couldn't move. He'd then faintly heard Glenda greeting the man. "We're here from Command for the body."

With adrenaline pumping, Karle had recklessly continued his warming routine over Theo's fingers. He'd tried his luck and swiped the screen once more. *Access denied.* Karle had screamed inside and heard Glenda invite the man upstairs, along with the vibrations of footsteps on the staircase. Karle was red in the face, his hands clamming up as he gave everything he had. One last chance. Karle frantically dived down under the bed as the door behind him had swung open.

The room filled with Glenda's sniffles as she blew her nose into a tissue. "We won't be a minute," the man said. Karle had seen his black boots walk clockwise around the bed. Despite the fragility of the situation, and all it would take was one shuffle or sneeze for him to get caught, he couldn't stop himself from smiling cheek to cheek at the active Watch he held in his hand.

* * *

The next two hours Karle had spent in the City. On the journey there, after having sneaked onto the train, he breathed heavily, trying to recover from the stress of the previous hour. Not only was he slightly nauseous remembering the cold feeling of the dead man's hands between his own, but his hands were still shaking after hiding from Command. Karle told himself it didn't matter. Yes, it was a close one, but he had succeeded. The Watch was active and it was time to test it.

Karle had looked out the window to the open stretch of desert between the City and the Side. For miles to the east and west, the orange sand didn't seem to end. Its colour was particularly stark against the reflection of the yellow post-storm horizon. The Side was the only surviving area of the old city, left out on the edge when the new Tulo moved further south. Demolished buildings were left to be buried, but this didn't mean all things were hidden. For years to come, even after becoming Ajay, Karle would ponder over the huge slabs of stone sprouting out from the sand like unwanted weeds. There were also torn pieces of old curtains or sheets, shattered glass panes, broken doors and concrete bricks; all just left to the elements. He would wonder why Command left them there. As a reminder of what went before? He would also question the resources railway line that went out to the West, and still when they were replaced by hover planes the same question would remain. Where do they go? Karle had always imagined there were more people out there. A world apart from his own little one. He would miss the wild liberty of his childhood brain. He'd still seen it in Tara; the freedom of imagination. He would always miss her too.

Once the train squeaked to a deafening halt, Karle had jumped off it quickly. He knew he didn't need to go far; he just needed a shop that sold an *M-300 or above* product to test the M-310 version of Theo. Street after street, Karle just found more slightly run down flats and apartments, but no shops or bars. After the fifth or sixth turn, Karle could see the onset of the next ring of the City, the balcony to its river, and the construction of a new sky train line becoming clearer to him with each step. He had considered turning back when a flash of colour caught his eye.

There was a small convenience store emblazoned in bright purple. It displayed a dozen digital news headlines across its front window. Karle skipped across the road, barely missing a parked hover car with his right leg. Outside the shop, Karle clipped Theo's watch around his wrist. Straightening his jacket and brushing down his sweat-ridden trousers, he went inside.

He was startled slightly by the loud twinkle chime that greeted him as the door automatically slid open. Despite being a small, probably insignificant store, it was a spectacle to Karle. It was a myriad of glistening colours as each aisle presented itself with a floating digital sign aglow with the words of its respective product lines. Rows of indulgence were replicated brilliantly across the store. News headlines circled on an LED display in blue letters, and Karle spun around keenly to follow them on their axis. Not that he was reading them, there was too much information to process all around him. So much stuff. He felt the same elation from when he and Callum salivated over the food court. His mind turned back to Callum. Lost. Never returned. It was painful to think about, so Karle would eventually repress it completely. He dismissed his thoughts and looked around for something to buy. The purple twinkling sign over one aisle instantly caught his eye. *Candy.*

He'd made his way over to the aisle and found an unbelievable array of Tulo chocolates, sweets, pop drinks, and basically any other merit-deducting confectionary product that existed. Ignoring the Chocos, Drone Drops and Tulo Caramels, Karle selected what he was looking for: *Merit Millions*. Karle read the small print description. They were small roundel shaped chocolates, made with the highest quality ingredients and low-fat dairy, and excluded any artificial sugars. Then Karle read the red messaging encased in a call-out bubble on its shimmering, silver packaging. *M-300 or Above. Less Merit Deducted.* Perfect. It was just what Karle had needed.

Without wasting any more time, Karle paced over to the checkout. There, a man stood in a very bold green suit, clearly expensive and clearly tailored. His hair was dark and mid-length, waxed perfectly. He was shouting something at the checkout assistant.

"...much longer. They'll have you replaced by a drone in no time, Side scum." He was very aggressive, to the extent that Karle had felt vulnerable, and wondered about walking around the shop again to avoid any potential interaction with him.

"22.95 credits please," the checkout girl said timidly, without looking up.

"More than you'll ever get," he snarled, scanned his Watch to pay and didn't bother looking at her again before quickly leaving the store. Karle slowly took his place and put the *Merit Millions* down on the till. The man was right. Karle knew it. She wouldn't keep that job. He'd read about drone developments and how they planned to shut down even these Outer-Ring stores. Karle thought that the girl had blonde hair, though it was difficult to tell with all the grease and sand in it. Karle couldn't even see her face because her fringe covered her eyes. She wasn't really helping herself, he thought. The girl scanned the candy and mumbled, "2 credits please."

Karle had been so distracted by her and the man in the green suit that he had forgotten that this was it. The moment that would define his future. He'd paused considerably longer than he should have done. The girl even had the nerve to cough impatiently. He lifted Theo's Watch up to the scanner. The connection was made and his stomach flipped. A rejection sound.

The girl didn't look up but spoke quietly. "I'm sorry, but it's rejecting your identification." It was only then that she looked up and her slender fingers moved her hair from her face. Karle winced inside as he saw the recognition in her green eyes. They were surprisingly beautiful, and he knew them. They often passed each other on the high street; she always gave him a sweet smile and he ignored her. She was usually leading big groups of children, either taking them to school in the morning or for after-school activities on the sands, so he assumed she was involved with child caring services. She always had her hair tied back and looked annoyingly happy. But right then, there was no smile on her face.

Seconds ticked by in silence. Karle wondered whether she was battling with herself over what to do: report him or let him go. They stood staring at each other in a sort of standoff moment as the system repeated the rejection sound.

"Oi, I hate to split you lovebirds up, but I've got somewhere to be?" A woman in a jumpsuit and sunglasses stood to the right of Karle with milk and bread in her hands. Karle quickly looked back to his accomplice for guidance and started to edge away. He saw her hand drift towards the screen on the desk, ready to betray one of her own. His heart was racing. Brain throbbing.

Then he saw her mouth something to him. He made it out to be *go.*

* * *

After that, Theo's Watch had died. Cut from the system. Karle, though, was both ecstatic and frustrated. Ecstatic because he knew what he had overlooked. Frustrated because he didn't know if he could change it. It was simple, really. Karle had cursed himself for not realising sooner. He had given Theo's Watch the identity of himself. Of course the transaction couldn't be authenticated. The data sent from the Watch mismatched with Theo's identity that Command stored within its database. It was so obvious that Karle felt like smacking himself between the eyes, not just because he'd been so wrapped in it that he'd overlooked the most important detail, but also, if he were to start a City life, he would need to get into Command. Surely, that was impossible, wasn't it?

Karle was determined to try, and he soon had an inkling about where he could start.

Chapter Twenty-Eight

For the week that followed, Karle didn't stop thinking about 'Downtown'. The mysterious place he had never heard about. Yet it was where that strange woman, with the stain on her face and drawings on her wall, had warned him about. *Dodgy stuff happens down there. Don't go right.* Those were her words. If he were to 'go right' from her house, he would end up somewhere dodgy. He'd come to the conclusion that hacking and identity fraud probably fell into the 'dodgy' category, so he took a chance.

Karle felt nervous as he stood breathing heavily across from her house. It was unchanged since the day he lost Callum. It had come out earlier that week that Command had released Callum a day or so after he was arrested, but he never came home. His parents feared the worst and had frantically tried to appeal for missing person alerts to be issued. Karle heard his own parents talking about it. It seemed Command wouldn't approve it. Of course they wouldn't. Karle agreed it was totally unconstitutional to have Worthy people spending their time looking for an Unworthy. What progress would that give them? By that point, Karle had decided it would do him no good to bother about Callum, a friend he believed would want him to move forward. So, Karle forgot him and continued walking down the street.

It was much like any other street; the hustle and bustle of evening commuters and low swooping drones. There were more of them since the last time he was there.

Karle was wearing a tight white t-shirt and black trousers. He'd tucked one side of his t-shirt in to cover up a gaping rip at its bottom. Slipping through the crowds unnoticed, he crossed a bridge. He looked down to the flowing river. Beneath the current, he imagined what he must have looked like when he'd jumped in. Stop thinking about that day, he told himself.

Karle was nervous, walking into the unknown. He needed to act casual and work hard to avoid anyone getting suspicious. He decided to put his hands in his pockets – that would look cool and relaxed. A pretty girl walked past him wearing a dark mini skirt and carrying designer shopping bags. He stared at her, maybe a little too intensely, so he moved his eyes upwards at the surrounding architecture, but he looked at her again when he realised, she was smiling sweetly at him. He smiled back and his eyes followed her as she disappeared out of view. Was she flirting with him? She'd probably feel embarrassed if she knew where he was from. That was the first time Karle fully realised the power of deception, that he was capable of making this work. He could control how people saw him, and that excited him more than anything else.

The evening darkness had begun to surround the City. Karle could see the reflection of the yellow moon in the river and soon he wandered upon a line of market stalls in a large alley between two buildings. Neon coloured lights flickered, and electronic lanterns glittered. He slowed down. There was loud, intrusive music, accompanied by the shouts of salesmen. Karle had read about night markets. They had a miniature version in the Side occasionally, when the ration had been kind and people made homemade cakes to sell, but this felt very different. Karle then saw a group standing at the top of the market. They were City folk. All well-dressed, clean and presentable but smoking nicotine. Karle had never smelt it before. He inhaled the smoke as he walked by. It tickled his throat, so he forced his mouth shut to avoid coughing. Why would they smoke? The e-books clearly stated that merit would be deducted for stuff like that, including what another man was eating. Karle watched as the man indulged noisily and impolitely into a sauce-slathered hot dog. The sauce dripped and oozed down the man's sweat-blanched white vest. He could be an Unworthy, Karle thought. He corrected himself when he saw the man's shoes, which were clearly authentic camel skin. This wasn't an ordinary night market.

Karle edged forwards and overheard some of the exchanges happening. His attention was caught by a woman wearing orange-tinted sunglasses, who was trading what looked like an expensive blender for a bag of Tulo Caramels. Looking around him, Karle saw this behaviour mirrored down the entire strip of street; a high-end TV for a bottle of stronger ethanol, a silent hair-dryer for a pack of cigarettes, and a ton of fresh, quality meat for litres of fizzy pop. Every Worthy-looking customer wore either a low hat or sunglasses, and other than the group at the front, they never stuck around to mooch or chat.

"What you want, son?" A man with greying red hair and wearing a black vest that just covered his balloon belly appeared in Karle's path. He was holding three bottles of clear liquid in each hand. "I've got 35%, 50% . . ." He leaned closer and quieted his voice from the rest of the market. "Even 75%, but keep that one between us, huh?" He winked and stood back, waiting for Karle's response.

Karle hesitated. He didn't even know 75% ethanol existed. The thought of being offered it was alien to him. He'd never tried it, nor would he want to. He fumbled over his words. "I don't ... I can't ... not ... erm ..." Karle looked behind him. He wanted to escape, but people had flooded the road between the stalls, blocking his exit.

"Look if you ain't got anything to trade, I'm happy to take an *I owe you*. I got your face, I'll let the merit police know you got the ethanol if you don't come back." He was still waving the bottles in his face, and Karle could smell the strength of the drink and the man's sweat.

"I don't want it, thank you," Karle said politely.

The man stood back and shrugged his shoulders. "I don't get why you young lads won't take the drink when it's no merit lost." The man began to saunter off in pursuit of a willing punter.

"Wait," Karle touched the back of his shoulder and felt the coarseness of the man's skin. The man turned back to see him, the small amount of red hair he had left mirroring the orange lantern above him. "I didn't come for a drink. I'm looking for someone who could help me with ..." Karle looked round, moved closer to the man and whispered. "... Identity fraud." Karle gulped.

That was brave. He'd almost congratulated himself and tried to ignore the jellylike feeling in his legs.

"Yeah I know someone that can help with that," the man replied casually, not a tiny bit fazed by Karle's request. "But you gotta give me something. What you got?"

Karle reached into his pocket and pulled out a round silver object. He willingly handed it over. "This is all I can offer," Karle said. The man snatched the device from him swiftly.

"This is one of those Guiding Light junks," the man said curiously. "How did you get it?" Karle opened his mouth to answer, but the sweaty man had stopped him. "It don't matter. It'll do. The scrap materials will go for something."

Karle smiled, possibly too intensely, as the man gave him a curious look. "This way," he said, flurrying his arm in the direction he began to walk. Karle followed him further down the street where the trading continued. As they got deeper into the market, Karle started to smell more cheap meat; he spotted burgers grilling to his right, the grease dripped into a tray beneath. Karle stopped to look. His mouth salivated.

"Oi, over here!" The man had moved quickly. Karle hurried over to him, where he stood in front of a group of smokers under a flickering purple light. The man tapped the shoulder of a lady in a cream trench coat.

"I've got some business for ya," he said. The woman snarled over her shoulder and stepped lightly in Karle's direction. The man grunted at Karle as he brushed past him out of sight.

"So, what you want, kid?"

Her friends disbanded and she stood before Karle with a cigarette smoking in her left hand. He needed to cough again. Her brown hair was tied in a braid that fell over her right shoulder; she wore a cap on her head and her coat was secured with a few buttons over what could have been her bare chest. She was stylish, on-trend, and beautifully mysterious and fascinating. Karle had lost his words at first.

"I'm looking for a . . ." he whispered again. ". . . A new identity."

She took a drag. Karle felt startled by her violence as she threw the cigarette down to the floor and crushed it under her black ankle boots, all the while looking at Karle with sinister eyes.

Karle's heart was pumping, and he covered his wrist as she looked down at it, clearly noticing the absence of a Watch. He didn't know what to do or say. He'd looked at this incredibly mystifying woman, waiting for her to give him hope.

"Come with me," she said.

Karle felt strangely relieved they were going somewhere. It didn't at that moment occur to him that it probably wasn't the wisest idea to go into a room with a stranger. They walked through a pink curtain, entering a small room, and Karle felt the grease on it as he drew the curtain back behind her.

The light was dim, only provided by an industrial cage lamp made from copper that sat on the wall. It was a tiny room. It housed an off-colour plastic table that Karle guessed used to be white and two matching chairs. On the table was a very fancy looking coffee machine that the lady demanded a coffee from as she walked in.

"Want one?" she asked as she sat down on the chair furthest from the door.

"No, I'm good," he said nervously. The unbearable mugginess outside was intensified in such a small space. It had then occurred to him how odd it was that she was wearing a coat. It was a lightweight one, but no storms were forecast, and it was insufferably hot. That was the moment when it first occurred to Karle that this woman could be mad. He had willingly found himself alone, in a dodgy place, with a mad woman.

"Well, have a seat." She pointed to the vacant chair.

Karle hesitated, his feet only slightly shuffling as he looked back to the closed pink curtain – the only thing between them and prying ears.

"No one is listening, kid. Go ahead. How can I help you?"

Karle sat and, to both his and his listener's surprise, his previous hesitation evaporated to join the humidity. Words began pouring out of him like a violent waterfall.

"I'm from the Side. I'm seventeen and due to get my Watch in just over a month. I can't stay there. I want to live here. Not here, here. But in the City. At first I was going to be Purified, but I changed my mind." Karle paused slightly for breath. "Anyway, I had figured out a way, using a dead guy's Watch. Well, he wasn't just a guy but my father's friend. So I used his Watch and I got into it. I created a new identity – me. But I used it to buy some Merit Millions on the Outer-Ring road. Didn't work. Luckily got away with it. A woman who recognised me helped . . ." Karle paused again. ". . . That doesn't matter. It didn't work."

"Sure it didn't," she interrupted him and smiled sardonically. Karle stopped talking, almost panting at the speed of his dialogue and desperate for some water.

"That's pretty obvious, kid. You need someone on the inside, but first you need to chill out," she swiftly said. Karle hadn't felt any more relaxed, wiping his sweaty hands on his knees.

He nodded, his eyes fixed hard on hers in hope and anticipation. She sat back on her chair, the plastic creaking as she did so. She threw her feet up on the table and the force of her ankles hitting it startled Karle. She casually lit another cigarette, gave a few short puffs, and smirked at him. It wasn't a friendly smile, but cunning and mischievous. It made Karle imagine that she would soon order two brutish men to rip through the curtain and take him away to a Command torture chamber, if they even existed.

But instead, she just spoke.

"I can do it. I work in Command Security. It would be a simple operation." She lobbed the cigarette onto the table, its black ash flicking across it. Karle hadn't actually believed what he'd heard. She could do it? As easy as that? He didn't know how to respond. This woman was clearly hard, and it would look too needy to drown her in his gratitude. He'd wondered if he should just nod graciously, but as she took her coffee from its machine and slurped loudly, she spoke abrasively again.

"So, what you offering me?"

Darn, Karle had thought. Not as easy as that. He looked down at his clammy fingers that protruded from his Watch-less wrist.

"Nothing."

"What's that now?" she barked as she flung her feet down to the ground. "You want me to do this for nothing?"

"I don't have anything to give you," Karle said quietly and honestly. He looked up so she could see the sincerity in his eyes. She laughed then, a dark and unnerving sound. Yep, he'd thought. She surely believed he was a City kissing, Side born imbecile, and she would probably kill him. Karle wanted to shut off his erratic mind.

When she'd stopped laughing, her body language changed, and Karle watched her as she began pacing the small width of the room. Back and forth, back and forth. Some time passed. Maybe she was deciding *how* she would kill him, or whether it would be easier to just report him for some credit or merit. Perhaps his grandma, or The Guiding Light, was right. The path of the City really does lead to destruction; he'd hardly started walking it and he already felt the pang of vulnerability as this peculiar and potentially malicious stranger, who wears a coat at the hottest time of year and knew everything about him, was mulling over his fate. How could he have been so stupid?

Finally, she stopped pacing and smashed her fist down on the dirty surface of the table. The cigarette ash scattered across her fingers. With her other hand, she'd pointed fiercely at him. "You said you were from the Side, right?"

Karle was surprised by her sudden movement and confused by why his origin mattered. "Right?" she snapped again.

"Yeah," he said as he cleared his throat. "The west side." Karle recoiled in his seat as he responded, terrified over the uncertainty of what was coming next.

"Alright. I'll do it for you," she said with a smirk on her face. She sat down and put her legs up on the table once again and returned the cigarette to her mouth. "This is what you do for me." She looked at him sternly. "You know the plant, Fo Doktrin? The one with the lethal leaves?"

"Yeah I know it," Karle responded.

"Hmmm." She nodded and smiled again. "That stuff goes for quite a credit round here. Some lads want it for some off-the-market *SkipSleep*." Karle was reminded of the advert he'd seen at the shopping centre.

Taking off her cap and pointing to the space between Karle's eyes, she demanded, "You bring me five kilos of that each week until your Watch day, and you've got a deal." She sat back again.

At first, Karle had questioned internally. Why didn't she just go and get it herself? But he'd reminded himself of what he already knew. City citizens had merit deducted for travelling back to the Side without a legitimate contributory reason, which was non-existent because the Side was deemed fundamentally unproductive towards society. And he knew it would be easy enough to collect enough Fo Doktrin to satisfy his new accomplice.

"Okay, I'll get it for you," Karle agreed. He stood up, ready to leave the insufferable cave of heat. She rose too and stuck out her hand, which held a small rusting key. He hadn't thought anyone used keys in the City anymore.

"Just leave it in the hatch there."

Karle looked to where she was pointing. In the corner of the room, behind where she'd been sitting, lay a bolted wooden hatch over the concrete floor. He was instantly thankful that he hadn't seen it before. That definitely would have sent him into a frenzy believing she was a murderer and that's where she'd keep his body. He'd immediately placed the key in his trouser pocket.

"But kid, don't get caught. They'll hang us both."

Karle actually thought he saw fear in her face. Only for a moment, before she spoke again.

"I'll get you your identity. We got a deal?"

Karle hesitated, the blatant suggestion of a governmental death sentence paralysing him for a moment. He'd be brave. He'd come too far. They wouldn't catch him if he was careful.

"But when and where will you give it to me?" he asked.

"Your Watch day. I'll be by the Glorified Gate. Leave the details to me. M-350 a good starting point?" she asked as she lifted her still-burning cigarette from the table to her mouth, squinting her eyes over Karle with conviction.

"That works." Karle nodded as she let the rolled tube of nicotine hang between her lips, and they sealed the deal with a very sweaty handshake. *There's no backing out now.*

Chapter Twenty-Nine

For the month that followed, Karle was focused on only one thing. Fo Doktrin. Every morning, Karle rose early.

"Why are you up at this hour?" his grandma had asked the first time, as she was quickly chopping shoots off old potatoes.

"Starting a new fitness cycle," Karle had lied. It had worked perfectly. No questions asked. Only praise from his grandma when he returned all sweaty and worn out. Of course, this was from all the exhilaration of being out in the desert, under the beating sun, chopping up Doktrin and then hiding it in bags. He'd gotten away with it every time. Even when he'd offered to help his mother in the garden, which he rarely did willingly. He would help prune the vegetable patches and pocket any Doktrin that had weeded its way in. Their total lack of suspicion made Karle realise they were even more naive than he'd originally thought. Absolutely oblivious to everything around them. Although, it was surprising that his grandma didn't wince at his change in behaviour, as she was usually very inquisitive. Maybe she knew and was keeping quiet. It didn't matter to Karle if she did or not. He just got on with it: wake early, get the Doktrin; avoid its leaves staining his shorts, pack it up; hide the bag, go to the City; drop it in the hatch and repeat.

It was, in some ways, a little too easy. He'd even begun to hope that something would go wrong, just to prove it all wasn't too good to be true. That one day he might whip back that pink curtain, and the mysterious woman whose name he'd realised he didn't even know, would be there, finally ready to take his head. Or some Command Guards or TPD drones would arrest him like they did Callum.

Yet there was never anyone there. It was all so unbelievably straightforward. Though there was one day that stood out, easily distinguished from the others.

Karle's fingers were clamming up, the day's heat scorching his skin. He'd exhaled deeply in an attempt to ignore his increasing dehydration. He flipped his cap around so that the pointed edge protected his neck from the white demon in the sky. Beginning to feel numb, he'd shifted his position from squatting deeply to standing, the electronic scissors still in his right hand. He watched as his six-foot shadow blanketed itself over the Fo Doktrin plant he was disturbing. The orange-dusted leaves were wide with a surface area similar to an ordinary dining plate and its millimetre thin, grey stems just sprouted up from the sand, almost as if there were no roots beneath. But evidence showed that this plant spawned many children, it burying its foundations deep under the Tulo sand. Karle had looked up and could just see the huge central tree of the forest within the heat wave, where he used to imagine Country folk gathered around campfires, dancing or telling one another spooky stories. Its branches spread far across the horizon as if it had arms open wide to embrace another tree in a hug.

Karle had exhaled and squatted again. He placed the scissors under the stems and pressed the 'on' button, which illuminated green. It set to work, chipping and chopping away at the stems without Karle having to do anything but direct and hold its end. Karle gathered the offcuts in bundles and shoved them into his black holdall. "Damn it," Karle had mumbled as he saw some plant powder had drifted onto his trousers during the cutting. He had rubbed at it with force, but this only made the orange mark darken. He had stood and wiped his sweaty face with the bottom of his t-shirt. He looked at his analogue watch. Time was running out to drop his cargo off for the day, so he picked up his stuff and headed out towards the City.

Yet when gathering his things, something to the East had caught his eye. Through the floating heat waves and sporadic wafts of orange-red sand in the air, Karle had squinted and could make out some moving black figures. They were moving slowly in a group, not far from the hugging tree. The strength of the heat wave created an illusion that they were much shorter than in reality. They were definitely human; their silhouettes plodded across the desert land. It wasn't mindless plodding. They almost marched. Soon they disappeared, fading between the spindles of the trees to leave only a confused teenager wondering who they were and where they were going.

These mysterious forest figures ran across Karle's mind as he stood impatiently on the platform. He was thankful to be distracted by the memory, not that he cared who they were. What he was most anxious about was how Command would react to his hand-me-down suit. Its cuffs were frayed and trousers a little too short, like scrap material compared to the clothes he'd seen people wear in the City. If only there was something more distinguished he could have worn for arguably the most important day of his life. His eighteenth birthday, the day of his initiation, the day he would get his Watch. The start of a new life, one where his suits would be tailored. He looked down at the empty platform, pleased that he was the first one here, which wasn't surprising as he'd arrived two hours early, much to the confusion of his family.

"You're going now?" his grandma had cried out as she put down a cup of tea to tighten the belt of her dressing gown.

"You'll get too hot just waiting at the platform," his mother had said. Her and Tara had been coming down the stairs, both still wearing their pyjamas.

"That's okay." Karle had opened the door and sprinted through it before any family member could even say 'Happy Birthday'. He hadn't noticed the splendidly coloured, handmade card that Tara held in her hands.

Soon, along with six other Side kids, Karle arrived at The Glorified Quarters on a hover bus. Lucie, the City official who had ushered the group from the train, stood up as the vehicle came to a smooth gliding halt.

"We'll be walking from this point."

Karle was already bored of her robotic voice, and looking at her, he couldn't quite believe that someone who worked for Command was so plain and simple. She was wearing a plain white vest and trousers which weren't uniform, because Karle noticed no Command logo on her breast. Her face was also just as bland. He couldn't help but feel slightly disappointed. Surely Command should advise officials to make a big deal out of initiation day, he'd thought, the day when citizens could start making their contribution, but Karle had reminded himself then: he and the other kids there weren't considered citizens.

Regardless of that, though, Karle felt his breathing quicken as they walked down the gleaming white walkways of The Quarters. He had been looking forward to it for so long. Just to get a glimpse of how The Glorified lived. There were so many fancy gates, some gold and some black, but they all guarded a winding driveway that disappeared into the mountains. He'd wanted to stop and just think about what the houses up there must be like. Secluded and paradisal. All those families could surely never want for anything. It did surprise Karle how small the crowds were. He'd almost expected the Glorified to be constantly out and about in their glad rags nattering to one another about their latest accomplishments, but there was no one around, other than the occasional hover car with blacked out windows. Perhaps that's what luxury is like, he'd thought.

It wasn't long until the group were at Command. Karle felt his heart rate accelerate as he goggled at the rectangular building, encased wall to wall with transparent glass and boasting three white pillars at its front. They walked closer. The driveway was dressed in purple flags on lampposts, all featuring Command's logo. Karle had read all about it. It was a bird's eye view of the City map. Circles within one another representing the rings and their rivers, all coming to the bullseye of the walled Glorified Quarters. Personally, Karle thought it looked like the cross-section of a tree trunk, and he always would.

Karle felt terrifyingly small as he walked through the gigantic pillars and then the glass doors. Inside was almost blindingly bright. Everything was white, with small tasteful purple details such as the cushions on seats and linings on Command workers' suits. They walked around regally, greeting one another as they disappeared and appeared through doors. Karle was transfixed mostly by what stood in the open foyer. Straight in front of him were big three-dimensional blocks of letters, arranged centrally across the floor to read: PROGRESS IS STRENGTH.

Karle's curiosity controlled him. He moved closer to the letters, blazoned white yet with tiny multi-coloured specks across their surface. Karle could then see that these specks were, in fact, handwriting. Peoples of all ages and abilities had all scrawled the same thing in varying colours of ink: *For a Greater Tulo*. Karle felt himself go soft. There was such a sweetness in a community, from the young to the old, standing together for something better.

"Blythefen!"

The sharp, coarse voice had startled Karle. He'd turned around to find Lucie standing with one hand on her hip at an open doorway. He was actually pleased that her voice suddenly had some character to it. "This way!"

Karle moved quickly, conscious that the rest of the group had disappeared. He followed Lucie through the doorway, down some concrete steps and into a basement room.

"Take a seat," Lucie said. They entered a box room littered with small wooden desks, not far removed from Karle's desk at home. He chose a seat at the back of the room and grimaced at the screech the chair made across the concrete floor. He felt so claustrophobic, like he was in a tin can. What kind of reception was this? He was pretty sure that City kids weren't thrown down in the basement at their initiation. They were probably pampered and treated to a five-course dinner. He felt himself getting agitated, but he calmed himself down, knowing he wouldn't have to deal with this for much longer.

"Welcome everyone to Tulo Command — the centre of governmental operations for Tulo." Lucie had turned robotic again. Karle dropped his shoulders. Get on with it, he thought.

"To begin your initiation, please turn your attention to the screen. We will show you an introductory video before then taking you through for Watch Administration." She gestured to the screen that ever so slightly wobbled with the floating motion of the powering drone behind it.

A narrated, subtitled video sprang into life and bounced off the four white walls, reflected in the skin and clothing of its bright-eyed young audience. Karle read along with the subtitles, but not without appreciating the authoritative, booming voice emanating from the speakers.

Welcome to Tulo Command.

Before the Revolution, Tulo was run by selfish and greedy dictators who contributed little to the progress of society, leaving the majority of citizens enslaved and insignificant.

But now Tulo is different. Tulo is greater. We are now a society based on the equal contribution of its skilful and ambitious citizens. And to ensure that those who contribute to our positive growth are rewarded with a life they deserve, we instigated the Merit System.

Karle stopped himself from audibly sighing. He'd looked around him. The other kids there looked much more engaged, all eyes staring at the screen and watching words and images fly over each other.

Merit Scores indicate the extent to which an individual has used their time and skills to contribute towards the welfare of all of Tulo. Merit can be earned directly under three main categories: Technological and Societal Advancement, Personal Development, and Community Spirit. Merit can also be earnt indirectly if an individual keeps themselves healthy enough to contribute and encourages others in their contributions.

Did they not all already know this stuff? Karle felt like laughing out loud at the girl sitting next to him. He'd thought he'd heard her gasp at this apparently new information.

Deduction in merit occurs under the following circumstances: when an individual attends a venue or area of Tulo that is deemed unproductive or anti-constitutional; an individuals' Watch detects they haven't earned merit for a week; when an individual purchases foods containing high sugars, high saturated fats or high levels of ethanol; or when another citizen reports the individual for proved unproductive behaviour or discouragement of others to contribute. For more specific details about merit gains and deduction, please refer to the constitutional handbook which can be found from your Watch's user interface.

The girl did look a bit naive. Her hair was tied back in a bun, and from her baby-faced complexion and puppy dog blue eyes, Karle could have sworn she was about twelve, not eighteen.

We are glad to welcome you from the Side to Tulo Command on this occasion. We hope you will have been made aware of your position. Whilst we never wanted any citizen to be restricted in their contributory ability, past events have meant we have had to put the necessary measures in place to avoid any anti-constitutional ideology infiltrating the values of Tulo City. We hope to welcome you into the City following your Purification in a few years' time. Enjoy your initiation and remember that Progress is Strength.

The light and backing music subsided. Everyone but Karle shuffled restlessly in their seats. Had none of them read up on any of this? Did they just live with their family and accept that's all there was? Absolute fools, Karle thought. Of course, this was all conjecture. Karle knew he was being kind of an obnoxious asshole, but with every moment he had gotten closer to City life, the more he'd stopped caring. Soon these people would be nothing to him but a fading, Unworthy memory.

Lucie appeared again through a door on the left-hand side of the room. "This way, please."

Karle grimaced again at the simultaneous screeches of the chairs as they all stood to leave the room. He was relieved when he saw the next room was much more spacious. The walls were white again, with beautifully blooming plants dotted around in corners. A long, white desk stretched the entirety of the room, forming a barrier between the group and the other side.

Several Command officials dressed in remarkably white suits and dresses sat behind the desk, each one wearing a beaming smile. Karle smiled back.

"Tantley!" shouted the official at the very far left of the room. The group simultaneously turned their heads to see the official gesturing towards the empty white chair that sat in front of him. A young girl with a pixie haircut, dressed with a quaint blue bow, moved from the centre of the group by tapping on others' shoulders to let her through.

"Slinson!" the next official called, and the boy standing next to Karle made his way across the room, but not before turning to Karle and whispering, "The Guiding Light bless you." Shut up, Karle thought.

"Blythefen!" The name echoed and bounced off the walls, hanging in the air. This was it. He'd tightened his tie and stood in front of the seat belonging to a blonde-haired man with unbelievably smooth skin and shining teeth.

"Please have a seat, Karle." He'd pointed to the chair and Karle appreciated that this one made no sound when he moved it.

"My name's Quain and I'll be your Watch Administrator. Any questions you have along the way, just let me know." Quain spoke with a confusing tone, both patronising and welcoming.

"Great," Karle said in anticipation.

"Okay then." Quain tapped in a furious motion onto the desk that had become a giant keypad. Karle looked around to see clones of Quain's movement in the other Command officials. "First things first, we need to do your fingerprint scans. Please place both hands down as indicated," Quain instructed.

Karle looked down at his side of the desk, where two hand outlines appeared. He'd placed them down and was surprised by the coolness of the desk at his touch. There was a slight tickle and vibration as the scan was completed.

"Thank you, Karle." Quain swiped his hand across the desk. "The fingerprint is how you gain access to your Watch and there are also intermittent scans whenever you're using it. Just a security protocol." Karle nodded, even though he already understood. He probably knew more about Watches than anyone else in that room.

"Okay, any second now . . ." Quain said as a drone swooped down to Quain's left-hand side. "Perfect." The side of the drone opened and he pulled the contents out. Karle felt his heart rate increase and his legs start to fidget. There it was. *His* Watch. "Are you left handed?" Quain asked.

"Right, actually," Karle responded.

"Oh, I've got a rightie. Amazing, you're only my second one this year," Quain giggled. Karle smiled, but he didn't find it funny. In the hope that Quain would move forward quicker, he'd offered him his left wrist.

Quain lowered the Watch over his wrist and placed it carefully onto Karle's skin. Immediately metal crawled from either side of the Watch and scurried across his wrist until each side of the strap found one another. It tickled and then made a satisfying clicking sound. Karle looked over it closely, moving his wrist back and forth. Its model was very sleek and slimline; it had a black casing with a rectangular screen that covered the width of his wrist.

"Beautiful," Karle said to himself, before Quain rudely interrupted.

"So, let me just run through the basics. It's waterproof, obviously. The controls are pretty simple, and the majority of commands are produced in a pop out screen. Oh, there you go . . ." Quain sounded surprised as Karle had fashioned a screen displaying his health stats. He started flicking through different screens at speed, his eyes dancing as they followed the movement of the screen's contents. He had yet to find any user differences from this model to the one Mr Badds had, which had been reassuring. Karle then almost tipped off his chair as a hand flew through his screen and almost touched his face. "Okay. You're obviously a natural, but there's still a few things to run through." Quain was frustrated. Karle found it amusing but made sure not to show it. He turned the screen off.

"So on a privacy level, no one other than those directly in front of your screen can see its contents. Additionally, the Watch does not record your every move. Tulo Command takes their citizens' privacy very seriously. For merit-making, there is the option for conversation and activity recording, but your Watch will ..."

"Always ask for your permission?" Karle asked, knowing he was correct.

"Yes . . . exactly." Quain was surprised again. Hadn't he learnt by now? Karle knew what he was doing. Quain then fumbled around on his desk a little to find his next topic to tick off the list. "Yes, so . . . just to reassure you, you can absolutely take the Watch off. But it is needed as identification when necessary." Quain said. "I personally never take mine off, you never know when your next merit opportunity will come along." Quain smiled and sat back slightly in his seat. "I think that's everything, Karle. Do you have any questions?"

Karle didn't hesitate. "No, I think I've got everything I need."

* * *

Where was she?

She'd said she'd come. She said she'd be in the Quarters on his Watch day. That was their arrangement. The deal.

Yet as Karle desperately willed her to appear from around a corner, she was nowhere to be seen. Karle could feel his rage and frustration rising the closer they came to boarding the hover bus for the return to the Side. He no longer gazed at the opulent gates or cared much for the tantalising smells coming down from the mountains. Before he even began to wonder what was being cooked up there, he'd felt sick enough for his rations to reappear. For a whole month he had laboured and risked everything to lug that Fo Doktrin around. And for what? So she could just break their deal? In some ways, Karle wasn't surprised. He was stupid enough to trust someone he didn't know. In that moment, he'd felt so angry that he even considered tracking *her* down and killing *her.* Maybe he'd been the murderous stranger all along.

He could see the black bus ready for the group to board. *No, no. Come on. Where are you?* Karle was beside himself, and struggled not to voice or show his desperation.

Then, he saw her. Though he still felt nauseous, she was there, leaning against a lamppost not far from the Glorified Gate. Her head was down and her brown hair was tied in that same braid that fell over her right shoulder. She wore baggy trousers and that cream coat. She was then stark and obvious as Karle got closer, standing out in front of the golden walls. She looked up, and their eyes met. Those menacing, evil eyes and that sardonic smile. She started walking towards the group, but no longer looked at Karle, as if to act like a passer-by. Karle's heart was pumping hard. His wrist vibrated. He'd heard the notification sound of a raised heart rate for the first time. She got closer, until she was right there. Next to him and whispering in his ear.

"You did good, kid."

Karle felt the soft tickle of her fingers drop something into his trouser pocket. They both continued walking, not stopping to look at each other again. Karle believed that was the last time he would ever see her. He'd felt pleased about that. She was hardly someone he wanted to be friends with. She would become another part of the life he wanted to forget. The life of Karle Blythefen from the Side.

Once he got settled on the bus, only then did he pull the note from his pocket. It was a dirty and slightly ripped piece of lined parchment folded two ways. He opened it, and there he found the identification details for Ajay Ambers.

Chapter Thirty

Ajay, of course, had never let anything slip. Genni, Ace, nor anyone else had even a suspicion about who he really was. When he first arrived in the City, he'd slipped in unnoticed, renting a M-300 apartment and getting an assistant computing job. No one ever questioned his fabricated life story. Why would they? He was a well-presented keen socialite with a healthy score of M-350. It had all worked flawlessly, and never once had he regretted it. Of course, there were sticky moments. He'd have heart palpitations every time he heard rumours over new Watch models or security features, which would be inevitable. But Ajay had learnt to have confidence in himself. He would find a way. Karle Blythefen was dead, and Ajay Ambers lived on.

Except *she* kept him hanging on to the past he longed to forget.

Grandma was the person he'd trusted more than anyone. On the day he left, he'd cried only because he couldn't take her with him. He'd even suggested it, but he knew he could never persuade her. "I am who I was made to be," she had said on his last night as they'd sipped their hot drinks before bed. Their late-night chats became the new bedtime story, and Ajay missed it desperately when he often returned to his apartment alone.

Nowadays, every other month or so, he'd come back to see her because he'd promised. It wasn't for anyone else. Not for his mother, who hadn't noticed him standing by the front door. She walked past through the kitchen again, clunking pots and cutlery together as she was setting the dinner table. It baffled Ajay how everything could be so unchanged. The walls, the carpets, and they still hadn't painted over the childhood graffiti that travelled up the walls. Coming back was the only time he allowed himself to think too much about those memories. He had to stay grounded. Perhaps he should slip upstairs without saying hello to his mother, he thought. That would be nice and discreet, and would completely avoid any awkwardness, and he'd probably escape quicker.

Rustles and bangs came from the front room, and its door swung open. Ajay's father stood before him, with a faint smile on his face.

They looked at each other in silence. Ajay laughed internally. It wasn't just the house that never changed. His father's checked shirt pocket had lost its stitching and his dusty glasses were still bent across his face. His hair was slightly thinner than the last time he saw him. Ajay thought he looked even more dishevelled with that bald patch extending across his head.

"Nice to see you, Son," he said calmly.

"Hi."

"Are you okay?"

"Yeah. Yeah, doing good."

"Good."

This is awkward, Ajay told himself. He never understood why his father bothered with the small talk. The day before he'd left, they had shaken hands in the kitchen, sort of like a parting gesture. Why couldn't he just leave it at that and ignore him when he turned up? It wasn't like Ajay ever stuck around long enough to warrant any actual conversation.

"Fancy a drink?" his father asked. "Your mother's through here."

Really? Ajay couldn't be bothered to refuse. With everything that had happened the last few months with Genni, he'd used up all his confrontational energy. He hesitantly followed his father into the kitchen, with one eye on the time on his wrist. He'll get the drink then dart upstairs.

Quick in and out.

His mother was slicing into a slightly stale-looking loaf of bread. Ajay met her eyes and she beamed, instantly setting down the knife and rushing towards him.

"Sweetie, lovely to see you." The squeeze on his arms felt compassionate, followed by the firmness of a motherly kiss on his cheek. He hated the way it made him feel warm. He hated any feeling of attachment he had towards her. She'd always looked after him, doing everything a mother should do, but they'd never had much of a connection. It was as if they'd just been necessities in each other's lives and that was all.

"A drink then? There's also bread. The ration was generous today." She grabbed the bread knife again and started sawing into the loaf, the wisps of crumbs flaking onto the breadboard.

"Just some water's fine." Ajay paused. "Thanks."

His mother stopped again and moved towards a cupboard above her. Ajay watched as his father graciously stopped her.

"I'll get it, love," he said over the creaking of the cupboard door. Ajay noticed that they'd never replaced the glasses as his father chose the one with the small chip on its rim and headed to the sink. Take your sweet time, Ajay thought with sarcasm.

As the sound of running water filled the silence between them, Ajay fleetingly scanned the dining room. The table had changed, no longer the wobbly wooden one he'd sat round for many dinners, countless board games; to write innumerable answers to innumerable homework questions; and for unproductive hours listening to The Guiding Light. He actually thought the one they'd replaced it with was in a worse condition. It was a white hard plastic, covered in black scratches, and its wooden legs had chunks missing. Strange choice for an upgrade. Tara wasn't sitting there again. For the first few years when Ajay visited, she would sit at the table, just reading or writing whilst their mother cooked. She didn't speak to him much, but it had been months, maybe even over a year since she'd last been here. Ajay assumed she was out at a neighbour's or working at the school. His grandma had told him she'd been training as a teacher. She never said anything more and Ajay didn't ask. It had been six years too long for him to start getting too invested in their lives again.

"She's been a bit hit and miss lately. So don't worry if she's not her usual self." His father placed the chipped glass, full, down onto the cruddy table. Ajay picked it up immediately, expecting it to cool down his sweaty palms. He'd forgotten. The water wasn't chilled from the tap out here. These little reminders of their chosen poverty were welcome to him. It was nice to know how right he'd been. He sipped and swallowed the lukewarm water silently.

"I'll just . . ." Ajay paused. His father looked at him as if he expected Ajay to say something else. What did he want from him? He'd left. To him, he wasn't even his son anymore. Maybe he needed to make it clearer to him, perhaps by shouting him into the ground until he got the message. Ajay wanted nothing from him, but as always, he opted to say nothing, brushing past his father and heading towards the stairs. He needed to get on with keeping his promise to Grandma; come now and again for a catch up, and then he could get out.

He took the stairs two at a time and darted straight towards his grandma's closed bedroom door. He hesitated. Stop it, he thought. He couldn't help himself, he always had to look into his bedroom. He peeked through the ajar door, which welcomed visitors with red peeling stickers that spelt 'Karle' on its outer side. Seriously? They still hadn't changed it? It was as if they expected Karle, that lanky skinny kid, to walk through the front door and just slip back into his old life. His bed still wore the same bedclothes since the day he'd left. The posters of City video games hung creased on the wall, and his old computer was practically grey now, cuddled up in its dust blanket. Every time it was the same. Ajay didn't know why he expected anything different. Maybe he thought they might have some sense and use the room for something useful. With that idea, he let out a small sarcastic laugh; he was kidding himself. This room would be as it was for the rest of their lives, and maybe even the rest of his life. He decided to let them stew in their false hope and closed the door. His grandma had heard him.

"Ajay, is that you?"

Her voice was deep but faint. Ajay was surprised he heard her through the woodwork. He reached for the door, the brass doorknob feeling cool on his skin. He twisted it and pushed open the door to find his grandma sat up in bed. No matter how much he tried to convince himself otherwise, this was his best friend. His energetic, spritely elder who raced him up hills, taught him how to treat a wound, and played hours of cards until he was good enough to beat her. The lady who plaited Tara's hair, who told him all those marvellous stories, who supported him unconditionally. This wasn't her. Or, it was her, imprisoned in some worn, deteriorating shell of a body. He'd seen her just a month ago and she hadn't looked this bad. She looked years older; her wrinkles resembled the deep gorges of a canyon, the skin under her eyes had yellowed and thinned, the moisture of her lips was non-existent, and the deep, strained croak of her voice had no similarity to the vibrancy it carried before. Ajay gulped hard and tried to remain dry eyed. As little attachment as possible, he thought. Make it quick and get back home.

"How are you, Grandma?"

As Ajay walked towards her, he noticed the window was slightly open and there was an orange splatter of sand on the windowsill. The wind was rising outside with the coming storm and wafting sand in. He reached over and pulled the rotten wooden frame towards him, closing them in.

"Oh, you know." Grandma coughed as if her insides were ready to project from her mouth. "Dying," she laughed muskily.

She looked at Ajay with tired yet intent eyes, smiling sweetly like she used to. Ajay went soft. That smile. Why was it always so good at comforting him? Even with the dryness of her mouth and the wobbly skin surrounding it, that smile was still his weakness.

"What's been happening around here then?" Ajay knew this question would please her, even if his interest in the neighbourhood was a lie.

"Well," Grandma had a solemn look on her face and said bluntly, "Doreena from down the lane has disappeared."

"Which one was Doreena?"

"You know, Doreena Laptoff? The one with all the foxes?"

"I'm not sure I remember her."

"Oh come on, love," Grandma wheezed. It sounded painful, yet still she was able to talk. "Her sister was the one who went for Purification?"

Ajay remembered. He knew exactly who she meant. She used to walk her foxes at least five times a day and would let Tara and himself pet them on the street. *Laptoff. Doreena Laptoff.* As in, related to Mrs Laptoff from the village?

"Do you know if her sister did well in the City?" Ajay questioned.

Grandma nodded. "Oh yes, she was Glorified."

Ajay shuffled uncomfortably on the wicker stool, his bum already going numb. So, that's how she knew about him. He recalled her face against the ground and the words that she spoke: "They'll find you." Ajay felt his fingers tingle and a small pain travel across his chest. He breathed hard and, of course, Grandma noticed. She was looking at him with a stare of interrogation, like she was telepathic. How did she do that? Looking so deep into him, he knew the very question she was asking.

"I met her. She's in the retirement village I work at."

"Oh, well maybe you could ask about Doreena."

"Yeah. She's a bit past conversation." That's when he remembered how ill Mrs Laptoff was. Everyone in the village thought she was mental. Anything she said was dismissed as delusion, so he should be safe.

"She recognised you, didn't she?" Grandma was always able to read his face. It was annoying. Ajay kind of wished that in her deterioration the ability might have subsided, but no, he still couldn't hide most things from her.

"Yeah, but she's perceived as a bit deranged. I'll be fine."

"Not forever you won't be."

Ajay decided to ignore the comment. "So when did Doreena disappear?"

"A couple of weeks back. Her neighbour said he'd seen her walking towards the allotments on a morning, as she always does. Then, she never came back. Now the whole community has become a bit engrossed in finding good homes for the hundreds of foxes. Fortunately, with my condition, your parents got out of that extra responsibility." They laughed briefly together. It was familiar and Ajay enjoyed it.

"So where did she go?" Ajay then asked, as he took a sip of water. Warm and gross.

"Well, apparently her VPG confirmed the City." Grandma heaved herself upwards to sit straighter.

"Well there you go. She's probably followed her sister and is serving the Glorified," Ajay said.

"That, or *your* thing," she coughed through her words and spluttered some green looking substance into a tissue. The condition of her lungs must be toxic, Ajay thought, saddened.

"No offence to Doreena, but she never looked like someone who could hack her way in." Ajay raised an eyebrow, and then appreciated that Grandma found the thought amusing.

"No, that's very true. She'd get caught immediately. But she's like the third one this month who's gone. The others I suppose I can believe, but Doreena was just as committed to The Guiding Light as I am. And why would she go now, in her old age? I just don't believe it." The saggy skin beneath her neck wobbled as she shook her head.

"Well," Ajay paused. He was about to say something about people coming to their senses, but he decided against it. She was dying and he knew that comments like that upset her. It wasn't worth it. If she was well and active, it'd be different. He'd defend a City-goer to the end.

"So how's that girlfriend of yours? Will you let me meet her before I die?"

She spoke about death so matter of fact, as if it was as simple and ordinary as having dinner. She wasn't afraid, though Ajay remembered she never was. Even when he left, with all the danger he was putting himself in, his grandma never once looked worried for him. He sometimes wondered if it was because she knew he'd pull it off, but that didn't quite sit right. It was most likely her unfounded expectation that The Guiding Light would protect him. Her faith in it was strong, to Ajay's despair. He let it go, let her continue believing a fallacy. It made her happy, that was something at least.

"She's fine. And probably not, Grandma." He was honest. Genni would never go there.

"Right." Grandma yawned, opening her mouth so Ajay could see the blackened crevasses of her back teeth. When did she get so old? He stopped himself from thinking about it. If he started down that road, he'd start to regret missing more of her life. *Change the subject.* Or maybe it was time to go. His chin started to move and a yawn was coming his way, too. He let it out.

"Sorry, love. They're so contagious." She smiled as her breathing grew heavier. She slowly wiped the small blots of sweat off the brow of her greyed hair. "Ajay, love? Could you rearrange my pillows for me?"

Ajay rose instantly from the stool, took his arms behind her and straightened the pillows so they were more supportive of her back.

"It's okay if you need to rest, Grandma." Ajay lightly tapped her wrinkled fingers, feeling the scrape of her slim rings on his hand. "I need to go anyway."

"No, love. Stay a while longer."

"Okay." Ajay couldn't resist the eyes that told of unrelenting love. It was almost desperate, like she *needed* him to stay. He kept hold of her hand, enjoying her warmth despite the increased humidity that accompanied a Tulo storm. Gazing at the window, Ajay saw how the skyline looked like a child's drawing they weren't happy with, scribbled over and barely recognisable as the sand was carried higher and faster. Bits of trees, plants and rubbish were joining the picture, floating erratically in the angered wind. It was getting darker too, as the rare troops of clouds marched over the defence of the white sun. Maybe he should go, he thought. He didn't want to be out in that, but Grandma was still staring at him in that way. He decided to wait until she was asleep and slip out then.

"I've been having lots of dreams, Ajay." Grandma spoke as if she was drunk, slurring her words as her eyes started to close.

"Yeah?"

"Yeah."

"What about?"

"Last night I got stuck in the loft."

Ajay laughed. She was so random.

"What were you doing in the loft?"

"Just going up there. I got locked in."

"That's traumatic."

"Not really. Some people would think I was trapped . . ." She yawned. "But I was nice and warm."

There was something so peaceful about watching her fall to sleep. But Ajay's heart broke at that moment, because she reminded him of Theo Badds. Content and restful, yet she was alive. Very much alive. Still telling him stories, even if her material was now the crazy dreams of a dying woman.

He rested his eyes then, trying to change his thought pattern.

Ajay needed to stop thinking about losing her, despite the fact he'd already lost her when he left. That was the decision he'd made. He listened to the moving rhythm of his grandma's breathing and the inconsistent tap of flying branches hitting the window.

His eyes must thank him for this. They rarely closed. *SkipSleep* changed people's lives; the ability to make merit almost twenty-four hours a day was revolutionary. Yet there was nothing like natural sleep. It was a lust everyone carried but no one spoke about. Only dipping in and out of it, never over-indulging. He needed to open his eyes. Sleep was dangerous. He needed to go. *Ajay, don't!* He lazily lifted his eyes and gazed over the desk beside him. He could rest his head there, just for a minute. Next to that small picture. It was of Tara with her black pigtails and rainbow tights. He assumed, anyway. She was hard to make out as his vision went fuzzy and he placed his head on his arms. Stop, he thought, get up. Then his brain went black, and he drifted off into a deep sleep.

Chapter Thirty-One

Genni was sitting on a high stool upholstered in royal blue fabric with light oak legs. Pearl was pacing around the thirteenth-floor meeting room, tastefully illuminated by stylish low-hanging ceiling lights. She was harking demands at the walls. Genni felt sorry for the willing soul at the other end of Pearl's headset. She watched as Pearl stopped at the refreshment station and started to inspect each individual apple from a bowl, continuing to talk loudly. Genni slipped off her stool and stood by the window to mindlessly watch the weekend crowds.

The interview for the summer camp had gone well, better than she ever expected. She'd almost sobbed all over the interview table when the organiser had said, "We'd love to have you on board." It was a profound moment for her. A realisation that her recovery might not actually be a recovery anymore, that she had, perhaps, maybe, recovered? She'd been tempted to ring her father and boast about how she wasn't a complete screw up. She decided to save her pride. The summer volunteering would give her a merit boost that would speak for itself. She'd have to get fitter, though, and better at teaching. She wasn't sure her body was quite ready for all the activities she'd have to lead. He'd mentioned teaching them military-style circuit training. Genni had nodded along, pretending that she did that often, when the truth was, she'd done it once with Ace and had sworn to herself — never again. So that would be fun, she thought, as she looked down over The Social Sphere.

This place would make a beautiful painting, she considered. It wouldn't quite be her style, but it would have so many layers. Genni mused at the countless buildings that formed a 'social' circle, each one connected to the other via spherical bridges encased in reflectively clean transparent glass. Genni saw people rushing along them, all wearing various colours, not stopping to greet one another on passing. The picture's main feature would be the Content Bank that Genni pondered over; it was a grey elliptical building rising high up into the sky and could be seen from most places in the City. There were people streaming in and out of its entrance below; social nuts and influencers accessing its trending content library. Genni looked over the televised sphere that sat on its top. She recognised the ginger woman on the display. She wore bright red lipstick and long fabric earrings that resembled fancy curtains. The text beneath her ran around the sphere's circumference; she'd just been voted off The Glorified House and was explaining her experience in the house as 'life-changing'. Genni's upper lip tightened. She despised all that reality TV stuff, despite how it was meant to teach you the best ways to live a merit efficient life. She'd had enough of her reality, let alone any celebrities' dramas. The colours of the neon social icons travelling around that sphere would pop from a painting's canvas with vibrancy. What a picture.

As Genni followed the rotating purple *Personi* icon, she felt dizzy again. It was fine. Normal. She anticipated what always came next. The vision or the flashback. She wasn't sure what to call it. Maybe she was remembering what happened that night; the visions would flutter in her mind like dark, broken-winged butterflies, fully formed yet distorted. Here we go again, she thought, as she steadied herself against the window and tried to remember.

It was really wet, the rain trickled down in the black night. He was there. Quite young, but relatively good looking. He was there instead of her usual administrator. Her memory was fuzzy, but he definitely had big biceps and wore a khaki green vest jacket with dark blue jeans – or maybe they were black. He was talking to Genni and his jet-black spiky hair was tinted with the light of a purple lantern behind him. She was still Downtown. She'd felt numb. She'd felt sick. The image was confused again, rattling through her brain. She almost felt the moisture of the water that had fallen on her face as she'd been carried by . . . someone. Genni scrunched up her face and squeezed hard in a plea for her mind to recall it. The water dropped – tap, tap, tap. Genni opened her eyes, the sound of Pearl's heels reconnecting her to reality.

"Sorry, Gen." Pearl's words danced as she strode determinedly across the room, her long legs emphasised in tight black trousers and a flowy grey blouse. "I was instructing Jove to sign a deal with a property brand, he was being difficult. Anyway, shall we have a look?" Pearl beamed.

She did have the tendencies of a self-involved tyrant, whining and fighting until she got her way, but she was loyal. Genni knew if anyone ever said or did anything to her in front of Pearl, she'd have them running. And most of the time, she wanted to help. Even more so if whatever Genni needed presented a merit-making opportunity for her.

Pearl strutted over to sit at the table and commanded a screen to hover over it. She swiped down with her fingers and found Genni's *Personi* profile. *Pearl, would you like to record this conversation?* Her and Genni touched Watches.

Genni slid onto the stool beside her, feeling both anxious and keen to learn. Genni's filtered face appeared within a small, privately enclosed square at the top of her profile. Pearl scrolled down past Genni's 'About' section, past her merit score, family credentials and relationship network, which had an impressive average. Then, she paused at her latest post – a tasteful shot of a kale smoothie in her hand with the City's buildings rising in the background. She'd picked that up on the way to work. She'd felt particularly stressed that day, as she had been engrossed in a new painting and lost track of time. Ajay thought she should give it up, especially after what happened, but Genni was determined to find that balance. As she'd rushed to work, she knew she needed to post something quick for the merit and the smoothie bar was right there. In the caption, she wrote: *'Relaxing with my delicious green friend.'* Genni remembered how it made her heave on the first sip and she was bitterly discouraged when it was all for nothing and the post only got two stinking loves. Pearl was squinting as she browsed through Genni's latest updates, videos and blogs, mainly about what she'd eaten or a picture of her and Ajay. Genni held her breath for the ridicule and humiliation.

"Oh honey . . ." Pearl said sympathetically.

"I told you," Genni laughed falsely, actively trying to suppress her embarrassment. "I need help!"

"Well," Pearl leant back, but still smirked over the screen. "This all depends on how much you are committed to gaining significant merit from this. The greater the engagement, the greater the merit you earn."

Genni was slightly taken aback at Pearl's basic start. Everyone knew that correlation, but of course, it wasn't surprising at all, Genni realised: the Watches were listening. Pearl continued.

"So if you decide this will be a key personal merit-maker for you, then take the time to provide better content. If you're not going to commit, you're better off not even trying."

"So what exactly is wrong with my profile now?" Genni asked the question tentatively, despite already having a pretty good idea of the answer. She was beyond boring.

"If I'm brutally honest, no one cares about your early-morning selfie. If you were wearing a new trending foundation, then maybe." Pearl sat up, poised herself and pursed her lips. "It's got to be stuff that inspires people, encouraging them to be greater than themselves; they want you to give them tips about feeling more confident, or snippets of what a high-quality life looks like, or suggestions of brands that offer better personal efficiency. They won't engage otherwise, nor will you ever go to the big screens."

Go 'big screens'. Genni hated the concept of it; she didn't like how people's private lives ended up on the billboards once they'd had above average engagement. Then millions connected their Watch to the board as they fluttered and flowed through life, hitting love or even endorsing the poster as an effective motivator towards individual progress. The day that Pearl's endorsements finally got brands interested in her was painful, Genni remembered. She was happy that Pearl's merit-making hobby had become a credit-making career, but she had felt a little resentful that she suddenly had more merit and credit than her, mainly just for posing in a certain brand of swimwear. Genni hadn't the first clue of how to get to that level.

"What if I have nothing like *that*?" Genni asked timidly with eyes low, watching the swing of her every day, uninspiring black ballet pumps beneath the stool.

"Oh, you will. And if not, stretch the truth a little." Pearl leant forward and tucked Genni's brown curls behind her ear gently. "Let's think. You're a great baker! You could do a video series about new and trending recipes. Then people will be inspired to use them to bake for community events or Glorified parties. You could do health cakes – low-fat and sugar-free!"

Genni was surprised at how animated Pearl was getting. Her eyes glinted with excitement as she began to type at the desk, her ideas collating as a list on the screen. Genni wondered if she should tell her to add painting or drawing to the list. Would people care? Would it inspire them? Maybe it would, Genni thought.

"Have a baby! Family stuff is so hot right now!" Pearl was giddy from across the table. Is she joking? Genni hoped she was.

"Oh yeah, great idea," Genni laughed, but Pearl clearly didn't appreciate the sarcasm as she looked less glittery and inspired. "You were serious? Pearl, I've only just got back on my feet."

Despite what seemed like an insane suggestion, Genni often wondered about herself as a mother. She'd love her children endlessly, almost enough not to push them into a life like the one she was living. This life had no loopholes or brake pedal and even when you fell, you'd be straight back up, running shoulder to shoulder with everyone else but always pressing to have just one toe ahead. Maybe she would teach her child a different way, where the number on your wrist didn't matter. Genni stopped thinking, realising the poison that was invading her mind. The City was the only world she knew or wanted to know. No, a child would not be 'greater' for her. Pearl was still tapping at the desk. Tap, tap, tap – like the water drops on her forehead as she was carried that night, fire in her shoulder.

The moment was broken. The double jiggle of a breaking news alert cut through, and both her and Pearl looked to their wrists.

Weather Update. The coming storm is expected to reach speeds of 50 rings per hour and the electrical activity will likely cause wildfires in the Country. Citizens might experience a slight disturbance when travelling around the City, but this is no cause for concern.

Pearl quickly dismissed her Watch and got back to their growing list of Genni content. It was set to be a good storm, Genni thought, which would mean a great view from the roof. Genni loved watching them with Ajay; hopefully tonight she'd get to paint something.

"I'm just going to ring Ajay to see if we can travel back together before watching the storm. He's just in the Quarters." Genni tapped at her Watch.

"Ask him when he's getting back to me about our collaboration while you're at it."

Genni wanted to scoff out loud. Pearl wouldn't stop nagging her about that. It wouldn't even work – Ajay wouldn't do it. She probably should have told Pearl that already, but why not save herself the grief and say nothing? Her Watch started dialling and its noise persisted for more rings than Genni would have liked or expected. He usually took her calls instantly, even when he was volunteering. Still, the ring continued. Pearl shuffled on her stool, clearly agitated by the incessant noise resulting from Ajay's lack of response. Genni felt embarrassment tingle on her toes; it rose up her legs in motion with the ring's continuing repetition. Genni fiddled on her Watch to mute the call. She transferred it to her headset to relieve Pearl from the annoyance.

"Sorry," she said feebly. "Maybe his Watch is off."

Pearl shrugged her shoulders. "Why would his Watch be off? Just find him on the map."

Pearl's comment made Genni wonder whether Pearl ever looked at where she was on the map when Genni missed her calls. It felt a bit intrusive, but then if someone's location is on, she supposed it was good enough permission to spy. She tapped around at her wrist and opened the map on her screen. She found him.

What? She didn't understand, refreshing the map repeatedly. "I think it might be broken," she said.

"Broken? Why?" Pearl asked.

"It says he's . . ." Genni paused. After the third time refreshing, it still told her the same thing. The same unbelievable thing. "It says he's in the Side."

As Pearl raised her eyebrows with the same confusion Genni was feeling, Ajay's voice boomed through her earphones.

"Genni, hi, hi, hey . . ." He sounded alarmed and unbalanced, as if he'd woken up from a dark and twisted dream.

Chapter Thirty-Two

His head was fuzzy. His vision was blurry. Lights were flashing. Genni's voice was loud and piercing.

"Ajay! What . . . ? Are you?" Genni wasn't speaking sentences, flapping through her words like they were tasering her tongue.

Ajay sought clarity in his surroundings; he saw his grandma sleeping, her peaceful face wrinkled, swollen and dry, but she only came in flashes as lightning cracked outside. He looked to the window, drenched in the clear blood of the sky.

"Ajay . . . The map is saying you're out in . . ."

Ajay interrupted Genni hurriedly, immediately condemning himself for not turning off his VPG. "I'm fine, Gen. I'll be back real soon." He spoke calmly and confidently.

Having no way to explain this one off the cuff, he hung up almost instantly. Panting heavily, still sitting on the wicker stool, he looked over the sweat patch on the desk by the bed where his sleeping head had lain. Beside it was the photo of Tara. It was the way he remembered her – wearing bright flamboyant tights with her hair in pigtails. He knew he had to move. How could he have fallen asleep? What was he thinking? Getting back as soon as possible would lessen Genni's intuition to go snooping for answers. He was distracted again, glued down by the weight of his grandma's condition. Just looking at her again welcomed tears to sit on his bottom eyelids. No. He couldn't let himself do this. Other things were more important. Stopping himself from looking at her, he released his legs from the wicker stool. He instinctively grabbed the picture of Tara, shoved it in his pocket and headed for the door, which swung suddenly open.

"Oh, you're still here?" His mother carried a tray of food, looking startled as Ajay nearly flattened her in his rush. He didn't even know how long he'd been asleep.

Get. Out.

"Yes. I've got . . ." He paused. His mother looked distressed as she looked at his grandma.

"It's coming soon . . ." she said quietly before asking bluntly, "Will you still come home after she's gone, Karle?"

Ajay didn't answer. Genni and Ace were probably already hunting down clues in his apartment. He knew he was being irrational, but he couldn't help it.

Get. Out.

He whipped round his mother and bolted towards the landing. The noise of his quick feet plummeting down the stairs made the whole house shake. He could hear his mother following him, yelling.

"Karle . . . Ajay, the storm. You'll get soaked . . ."

But before she could finish, Ajay had battled with the stiffness of the door handle, swung the door open with force, and set off as fast as his legs would take him.

The air was lava, and the rain was like hot, mushy sweat plummeting against Ajay's head. He ran through the violence of it. Hard drops of water were lashing the ground. A cry of thunder wailed through the clouds. The hot-tempered wind was rough enough to knock Ajay's long legs off course, wafting him into a zigzagging run to the train. On his approach, a zap and crack of lightning beat the dormant telephone wires that hung above the streets. Awestruck, Ajay watched and ran in parallel with the galloping electric sparks as they raced and cantered along the line, hastening towards ground. Ajay felt the heaviness of vulnerability accompany the whacking of the rain over his head, shoulders and back. He couldn't think of anything else but to get out. If there was a train. What if there wasn't a train?

He hurtled himself onto the platform and could barely see through the rainfall, but he heard the sharp blow of a whistle and a howl from a man hanging from the sitting train, ushering Ajay to board. Relief.

He jumped on and planted his feet hard. The door closed behind him and the train pulled away as the rain continued to pour, and the wind threw sand at the window with hard persistent slaps. Ajay rested his head on the door window, observing the sheer magnificence of a Tulo storm.

He'd never been out in the thick of one before, though he and Genni often watched from the roof. The lightning didn't relent, and the intense glow of a furnace erupted as the Country forests began to burn wildly behind the Side. Ajay bowed his head, ashamed and guilty over his sudden abandonment of his dying grandmother. It was necessary. Priorities. As he travelled back towards the City, he contemplated the lies he would need to tell. He felt confused by his emotions, ready to defend his identity yet still clutching tightly to the photo of his sister in his pocket.

Chapter Thirty-Three

"What the hell were you doing?"

Ajay felt the hard battering against his chest as Genni hit into him with rage and tears in her eyes. It was like she was possessed. He didn't anticipate this reaction. Not sure what to do with it, he pulled her closer to him. It seemed to work as she settled down and sobbed into his chest, not the least bit bothered that Ajay was dripping wet. They stood there for a moment in his open doorway.

"I was worried sick about you. Why did you go there? You could have been killed," Genni whimpered.

"I'm sorry," Ajay said. Could have been killed? Really? He looked over at Ace, with eyes that questioned what was wrong with her. It wasn't received well. Ace stood in a long-sleeved navy top, arms crossed with a scowl on his face. It reminded Ajay that he was in trouble.

"Well?" Ace demanded, standing by Ajay's breakfast bar. "Your VPG confirmed you were in the Side?"

Ajay had mulled it over the entire journey back; how could he have left his VPG on? How could he have been so careless as to fall asleep? What would he say to them? How could he have been so selfish as to sprint away from his dying grandma as if he'd just see her again tomorrow? He didn't have a choice, he knew, but everything was so confused.

Genni let him go and wiped her eyes. They both watched him. A weight was pressing down on him, the heaviness of incomprehension and fear crushing his nerves. It was killing all sensation in his feet and legs, driving tingles down his arms and across his chest. His head was burning. He imagined one day that his secret might be threatened but he never imagined it would feel like this.

"I need a drink," Ajay breathed strongly as he spoke. Inhale, 1, 2, 3, 4 . . . Exhale, 1, 2, 3, 4. His throat was dry and sore. He thought he was in control, but maybe he wasn't.

"No. Don't get a drink. You're going to sit there and explain to us why you'd do something so stupid!" Genni was crying again and pointing to a spot on the sofa. Ajay wanted to tell her he was on the brink of a panic attack. His legs felt like they might drop from his body. "Ace will get you water." She calmed down a little and looked to Ace, who nodded and made his way to the fridge.

Ajay walked slowly, his wet boots squelching on the concrete floor. He felt like someone with broken limbs but was conscious that he needed to look natural. So, he threw himself down on the sofa the way he usually would, slouching backwards in a relaxed manner. As soon as Ace placed the water beside Ajay, he sprang back up to immediately quench his thirst. He gasped. It was so beautifully cold, refreshingly soothing as it slipped down his throat.

Ace and Genni stood in front of him again, waiting expectantly.

Ajay had conjured up a weak unbelievable excuse, but there was no other reason a M-460 high-flyer would ever cross the desert. He took a deep breath. Here it goes, he thought. *Act confident. They won't suspect anything. They won't.*

"Okay, so lately I've been having more boosts at night for personal development. Mainly educational documentaries." Ajay's voice came out assertively, but internally he was shaking his head and whispering 'pathetic' in his own ear. Despite this, he expected them to believe him.

Lying had become easy.

"One of which has been . . . what to do in the situation of a wildfire. So, when I was finished with volunteering early, I decided I'd go out there to help shield the fires from the Unworthy houses. You know, for a little merit." Ajay said nothing more but just relaxed again, the wetness of his clothes seeping through to his skin and presumably his sofa. He needed to change, but he didn't think walking out on two angered people was the best strategy.

There was silence as both Genni and Ace stared at him, inspiring repeated pangs of anxiety in his stomach as if it were a trampoline being used by an erratic child. Finally, Ace spoke.

"Mate, do you realise how crazy that is?" he said, scratching his shaved head. "The fire service would have gotten there quicker. It wouldn't have been worth the merit. Helping the Side earns next to nothing."

"I know. I just . . ." Ajay sighed. ". . . had the time. It was a stupid idea."

Ajay looked at them both again. He was starting to wish he could reach out, tell them everything and let them into his real world. Like many times before, though, the temptation was axed by the swing of their ancestry. Both Glorified. Both ruthlessly pressured by their parents and undeniably loyal to the system. He could never tell them. In that split second, Ajay spotted Genni's clenched fists, the changing colour of her skin, and the fury rising again in her eyes.

She erupted at him, shouting forcefully and leaving both Ajay and Ace wide-eyed.

"You're such a dick! Just for a little merit, you'd risk your life? What about me? About us?" She gestured to both her and Ace. "Liberation time would have been very joyful without you, thank you very much." Ajay couldn't keep up with her. She was speaking so quickly. He wanted to tell her to calm down and take a breath, but he let her run away with it. "And the Side?! Why would you help those ineffectual, unproductive nutcases anyway? People are starting to go missing there daily, never mind the wildfires, one of them could have taken you!"

Ace interrupted then. He too clearly wanted her to stop screaming. "Those people have just moved to the City, Gen."

"Shut up Ace! This isn't about them. It's about him." She pointed violently at Ajay. "And how . . . how . . . he . . . " Her speech slurred, her body wobbled, and her hand lifted weakly to her head. Now what was happening? Ajay thought she might have had a relapse. His heart broke. The colour drained from her face the way it had that night. He stood up and grabbed her before she fainted.

Chapter Thirty-Four

Genni remembered.

His handsomeness was marred by the way he'd looked at her; a stare that sucked everything good away, making Genni feel like a blank piece of paper – empty and lifeless.

"Where is he?" Genni had asked him again, her head rocking on her neck as she felt the nausea spew up inside her again. She'd fallen forwards, vomiting over the concrete floor, just missing the tips of his dark, black booted feet. He jumped from his seat, kicking the plastic chair backwards into the middle of the small, airless room. Dragging her eyes open, she'd lolled her head up to look at him – this new, unfamiliar man. He said nothing, but looked down on her with the same evil gaze. She tried to speak again. "He said . . . my administrator . . . that if I ever had problems with it, to come back and . . ." Genni heaved again through the unsettling in her stomach.

"He's not here today. You've got me," he'd said sinisterly. "Now where were we? You were born Glorified, and what Education Centre did you go to?"

"What . . . why?" Genni had looked around the room she'd sat in too many times. There were no needles or vials out ready for administration; the table where they usually sat had been upturned and was on the other side of the room, like it had been thrown in a rage. And this guy was strange, asking her the most random questions and talking about some club he'd joined who lived out in the Country. It was bizarre and something felt off. It didn't feel right. She shook

her head slowly, trying to shake off the haze. "I'm going to go . . ." She tried, struggling to her feet.

The man looked over, his face gaunt and ghoulish in the clinical strip lighting above them. "You stay right there!" he'd snapped, striding over and knocking her back down to the floor, his biceps bulging with a strong grip on her shoulders.

"Get . . . off . . . me . . ." she had demanded. He'd tried to restrain her arms as she'd struggled to escape, screaming out for rescue as everything spun around her. As soon as his grip had momentarily loosened, she pulled herself up again and lurched forwards, throwing herself through the door to the street. Genni hadn't looked back, she'd just ran. Until there it was, bright and shining in front of her. The lights of a hover vehicle, pressing closer and closer for the inevitable to happen. As it hit her, she was thrown skyward towards the circumference of the yellow moon and gravity pulled her back, smashing her into the ground, bruising her body and snapping her collarbone brutally and swiftly. She lay there, her head pounding and body hurting.

That's when she turned up. At first, Genni thought she was a ghost, but then she spoke to her softly. She'd carried her through the night under the artificial stars and dropped her blue-veined on Ajay's doorstep.

Genni felt a sensation on her right arm, a constant tugging.

"Genni, are you alright?" Ajay was tugging persistently at the sleeve of her Tulo branded t-shirt. He and Ace were staring at her. They looked concerned. She must have blacked out for a moment. Again. It was probably the time to tell them about this.

"I'm having visions, flashbacks of that night," she said quietly. She didn't want to explain everything, not when Ajay had sent her into a mad frenzy. She felt a bit embarrassed. A tantrum wasn't how she thought she would react. Then again, she never expected to find her boyfriend taking a trip to the Side. And the memory of that disgusting man grabbing her so violently had left her constantly unsettled. Who was he and what did he want with her? It was becoming too much to handle.

"I can't talk about it now," she said, "but I'm still mad at you. I know I'm overreacting, but I was scared." She tapped him lightly on the shoulder as he knelt in front of her. She felt the water drip into the skin of her fingers as she ran them through his black hair. She was unbearably in love with him. Yet why was there something not quite right anymore? She couldn't shake the feeling that he was hiding something. Let's not pry, she thought. She knew it was stupid, but if he was lying, she didn't want to know. That would break her for good.

Chapter Thirty-Five

Ajay felt the movement of the sky train as he rested his head against the glass, staring emptily at the trickles of raindrops that slivered slowly down the window. They resembled the motion of tears he wanted to cry. He felt senseless. Genni was distant. He'd expected more questions from her, but she'd just asked him to give her space. It was a relief but also slightly worrying. That moment when she'd fainted and he thought she'd relapsed, he'd felt as numb as he had when he saw his grandma decrepit. He didn't know if Grandma was dead or alive. For all he knew, she could've died when he ran out on her. She'd looked so feeble. He still had Tara's picture and he wasn't sure why. He wondered whether he could tell Genni. She probably deserved to know, but he wasn't sure how she'd cope with it. It wasn't just a little lie. It was a big, stinking, life-crippling lie.

The train stopped at *Liberty, Outer-Ring*. Ajay felt his legs carry him from his seat and out into the evening chill. Citizens were wearing fleece coats to protect themselves against the sudden drop in temperature that came after a storm. Ajay walked past several people who had loaned blankets from a bar, locking their bodies in warmth as they marched forward past him. He considered getting one, but it wasn't the air that made him feel cold. Two girls posed in front of a Watch in their new cashmere robes, smiling and cuddling to then turn their backs on one another, stuck in the translucent glow of their wrists. They were both gorgeous. Long flowing hair and full faces of makeup. Ajay wondered what those girls were really like. Were they just the posey faces that would be seen on *Personi* in a matter of moments, or were there actual personalities there? Were they bubbly or shy? Reckless or sensible? More people filtered past him. More people with stories he'd never know. Yet out on the Side, his parents knew everyone on their street, in their neighbourhood. They knew each other's birthdays, likes, dislikes, and habits. Here, Ajay had nothing like that. The City had always been about him. Genni and Ace were exceptions to an unwritten rule of selfish ambition.

He looked up, standing in the street. Where were these feelings coming from? Everything he saw above him was full of colour, enlightening the darkness in his mind. As he walked, he spotted advertisements for automatic dishwashers, ring jewellers, Liberation Day and short breaks. Without realising, he soon found himself in a night market. He thought the stalls looked suffocated by their fairy light coverings. He continued walking, enticed by the smell from the meat that drones were spinning over hot plates. Even more colour took his attention; the confectionary he'd once longed for so freely available to him. Sweet necklaces, toffee apples; bon-bons, lollipops and candyfloss. All artificial and merit-deducting, yet completely delicious. Karle inside him was tempted but Ajay walked away.

Coming out from the market, Ajay thought again of the photo in his pocket. He didn't even know if it was still there. Quickly, he stuck his hand in his pocket and could immediately feel the sharp edges of the curled photographic paper. There was a brisk breeze. He wrapped his suit jacket around himself before seeing him. What was he doing here? He couldn't believe it, he didn't want to tolerate him in that moment, but of course, he accepted the handshake offered by Genni's prick of a brother.

"Rod! Nice to see you," Ajay said. He felt the tension in his voice, trying to mask the rotten depression feasting away inside.

"Got caught in the chill, did we? Fancy a drink to warm up?" Rod asked, his smile curling across his face like a snake slithering down a sidewalk.

Ajay hated the suggestion, but he considered how nothing in the whole of Tulo could make him feel any worse, not even Roderick Mansald.

"What are you doing in these parts?" Ajay asked. Once he made Glorified, he certainly wouldn't be coming to the Outer-Ring to get some air.

"Just seeing some friends." Rod pointed down the street in a generalised fashion. "Shall we?"

Rod looked towards a bar on their left, The Fox & The Camel, the sign of which was swinging in the temporary icy air. The windows were rife with condensation. Ajay was surprised that Rod would even consider going into such a venue. He followed him through the slow sliding door.

Once they got inside, Ajay wished he'd said no. It was rammed full of giggling, drunken people body bouncing off each other and the tables. The music was painfully loud. Ajay joined Rod at the only free table and could feel the resistance of his shoes as he walked, clinging to the sticky ground beneath him.

"You can tell this is for the M-300s, can't you?" Rod said as he looked with disgust at the cup rings and crumbs on the table. He ordered a drone to come and sanitise it. Another brought them two Tulo Ales. Ajay lifted his arm to pay but Rod intervened and paid it for him.

"Thanks," Ajay shouted over the music as he took a sullen swig.

"So mate, you've been with my sister three years and I don't know much about you. Whereabouts in the City did you grow up?"

"The west side. Not far from where I live now. Wasn't all bad, but nothing compared to The Glorified from what Genni tells me."

"It was pretty sweet. Still is." Rod looked around and gave a dirty look to a group of men joking with each other a few tables down. He looked at Ajay and nodded his head in their direction. "I can see why they're allowed in here." Ajay nodded. He did agree with him. They were badly dressed and one of them had a black eye. Hardly top-standard citizens.

"So, does Liberation Day planning make a full-time job?" Ajay asked.

Rod shook his head after filling his mouth with ale. "I have four months off afterwards. I tend to holiday or do community work."

"Must be intense right now, though," Ajay said.

"Yeah, with two weeks to go, it's no joke. I'm currently finalising the entertainment side of things, met with The Tulip Twins today to plan their set."

Ajay laughed; he knew Genni would be pleased about this. Too many times had he asked her to turn that rubbish off when she was getting ready or, more recently, when she painted.

"Don't tell anyone, though, their attendance is on the down low for now." Rod sniffed politely. "So, what about your parents?"

Ajay was momentarily speechless. He'd never had anyone ask such a question so sharply, in a way that suggested they were seeking information. Rod had always been a strange one, but it felt too much of a coincidence for Rod to demand talking about his parents after Genni's outburst about the Side. She must have tipped him off about something and so the prying sod was on Ajay's back. That didn't make much sense, as Rod and Genni hardly ever spoke. Why would she go to him? It could be a normal question to ask, Ajay thought. It was the way in which he asked it. Flippant. Hard. He felt his fingers clamming again. He wiped them on his trousers as he became aware of his thumping heart. Calm down, he told himself. There was no way he could suspect the truth. They hardly knew each other. It was just his darkened emotions making him paranoid. Ajay had his cover story, and he was reminded that he'd told it too many times for it to suddenly sound disingenuous.

"Dad worked in Genetics, and Mum was a teacher at the school down on Tibble Street." Ajay paused and took another sip. "They . . . died, actually. In a hover vehicle accident when they first became driverless. A faulty prototype."

"Wow. Sorry mate. Genni never mentioned." Rod looked at Ajay with his green, piercing eyes. Just when Ajay felt like his soul was being cross-examined, a news update vibrated on his wrist. *Calvin Traines was captured on the south side of the City attempting to gain admittance to a health gym. He has been wanted by the TPD following several criminal offenses and suspected anti-Command activity. Further investigations are . . .*

"So how'd you get into Prosper . . . ?" Rod hadn't stopped looking at Ajay.

He noticed how the surface of Rod's skin was tight, tense, and smooth around his chiseled jawline. Ajay lifted his tongue to answer, but then a shrieking volume erupted from the bar's speakers and the disco lights turned to black. Everyone on the tables and on the dance floor ducked and held their ears for protection. The high-pitch vibrations lasted a few seconds but were enough to make ears ring. When the lights returned to their former glory, an announcement was made: *We apologise for that minor technical glitch.*

In the sudden moment of darkness, Ajay had been terrorised by uncontrollable fright and agitation. He'd sprang from his stool, which clattered to the ground, ready to fight off invaders or Command guards. But when the lights lifted, in a soothed and easy motion, Ajay felt only embarrassment. Rod and a few other spectators were scowling at him as he stood with his fists up high.

"What are you doing?" Rod asked bluntly, a small smirk on his face. Ajay sighed discreetly. He lectured himself; there was no need to be so uneasy. Ace and Genni may be suspicious but they weren't sending an army for his head. He was being ridiculous. As he wiped the sweat from his brow and gathered himself, fear returned in larger magnitudes. It wrapped around him so tightly he felt like he was being strangled – unable to move or even breathe. Ajay watched as life seemed to move in slow motion, his vision blurry and the music muffled. Rod was reaching for a rectangular piece of paper, probably stuck with grease to the bar floor. Ajay flippantly reached into his pocket. Tara was gone. No longer there, but in the Glorified grasp of Rod's large hands, being examined by the serpent-like eyes.

"Who's this?" Rod asked and Ajay's normal senses returned, the music feeling louder and stronger than before. His mouth was dry and his body felt unsteady, but his mind remained sharp.

"My niece," he said as he calmly picked up his stool from the ground.

"You have a sibling?" Rod asked, still holding on to Tara despite Ajay reaching out his hand in a plea to give her back. He left his hand floating there.

Give. Her. Back. He thought with anger.

"A sister. She's a hairdresser in the Outer-Ring, a few circles from here. I don't see them much. Didn't quite walk in our parent's merit footsteps like myself." Ajay tried to discreetly force his hand closer to Rod, but still he clutched on, peering down and narrowing his eyes with observation. Ajay hoped his explanation would deter Rod's questions about the picture's surroundings, and Tara's dishevelled appearance and poor-quality wardrobe. He felt anger rise in a violent somersault in his belly, a longing to force himself on Rod and get his sister back. It was as if someone had heard him. Rod was thrown slightly forward by a keen socialite colliding with him and throwing some of his ale down his back. Ajay wasn't surprised by Rod's aggressive reaction towards the man, who threw his arms up in surrender with fearful quivering eyes.

Rod turned back to Ajay and said bluffly, "I've had enough of this place." Rod hadn't drunk half of his ale. "It . . . was nice to see you, Ajay. Let's do it again sometime and you can tell me more about your . . . *niece*."

Rod gave him a wink, threw Tara thoughtlessly across the table, donned his suit jacket and left the bar. Ajay sat alone and didn't move for a few minutes, letting the pounding music fall over him. He quickly returned Tara to the safe place of his pocket and replayed the last few moments over in his mind. Rod's questions. His huge fingers around the photo. The wink.

Did Rod know? He couldn't. There was no way. Ajay couldn't cope with this paranoia. His feelings were beginning to cripple him, so he decided he needed another drink.

Chapter Thirty-Six

Two weeks later, it was Liberation Day and Ajay was running around his apartment, shirt unbuttoned and only wearing one sock. He frantically pulled the other onto his left foot. He was late. Very late. Genni would be here any second. The intercom buzzed. Darn. She's going to be mad, he thought. As he scooted over towards the door, he caught a glimpse of himself in the dressing table mirror. His black hair was standing on end, natural and uncombed; his skin was dry and the purple markings around his eyes seemed to have gotten worse overnight. She's not just going to be mad, Ajay decided. She was going to kill him. Genni had deliberately said to be ready when she arrived so they could get ahead of the crowds. Yet somehow, he'd managed to do the exact opposite of what she wanted. Nice one, mate.

"Come on up," Ajay spoke into the intercom and swiped his Watch to let her in.

He probably had about a minute before she made it upstairs. Get ready in a minute. He was back at the dressing table. His hair was wild. He'd had over two hours sleep last night and clearly slept on it in a creative way. Pulling the comb through it, he soon managed to tame it. He stuck his fingers into his hair wax, its texture squishy and cold. Good as new, he thought as he ran his gloppy fingers along his head.

"Ajay?" Genni shouted through the apartment door.

You're joking? That wasn't a minute. The girl moves fast. Ajay looked at himself, all he needed was to button up his shirt and put a tie on. So he was practically ready. Though he was sweaty and felt like he needed another shower. He walked towards the door whilst simultaneously buttoning his shirt over the uneven patches of his chest hair.

"Hi," he said to Genni as he let her in.

"Are you not ready?" Genni demanded. She stepped into the apartment wearing a short teal blue dress with sequins around the halter neckline. Her hair was curled and fell beautifully just above her shoulders. Ajay paused. He'd have preferred the red dress she'd tried on the week before, but she still looked hot enough to make him completely forget what he was doing. Tie. He needed a tie.

"You look stunning," he said, running towards his wardrobe.

"Thanks," he heard her say timidly.

"Just getting a tie," he called out from behind his wardrobe door. He began hunting through his drawers and up on the hangers for his ties. Where was it? In frustration, he started throwing clothes out onto his bed. Genni came through from the kitchen.

"What are you doing?"

"I can't find my ties."

"Ajay, stop it. You're making a mess and we're already late. Just ask your wardrobe and I'll put stuff back."

He moved to his wardrobe mirror, Genni moving clothes back into the drawers behind him. Tapping at his screen, he was then shown a clip of himself moving his ties from the wardrobe to his chest of drawers beside it. What did his past self do that for? What a waste of time.

He'd been wasting too much time recently. Sleeping, reading irrelevant news updates, or eating. He blamed it on the phase of depression sparked by seeing Grandma, whose dying body kept appearing in his head, but he couldn't bring himself to ring the Side, just in case. His paranoia about Genni and Ace's suspicion had consumed him for the best part of a week. Every time they were together, he was trying to think of ways he could prove to them that he really had gone there because of an educational movie. So he kept dropping lines from a few to show it was a merit pastime he was invested in. It was completely stupid. He knew he didn't need to do that; it'd blown over so quickly. It had become one of Ace's new running jokes that Ajay was an Unworthy lover. Whilst it was painfully close to the truth, Ajay was satisfied with it, and had started to move on. Yet he was still being ridiculously inefficient, like with this tie thing – and he didn't even want to think about the Prosper networking day from the day before. It was nothing short of a disaster. Ace, of course, had breezed through, lapping up merit through conversations like a drone taking orders in a heaving restaurant. Ajay, on the other hand, was completely distracted and only educated one person with a feeble explanation of his meal planning. He did well to avoid any questions about how much merit he'd earnt whilst Ace had boasted about his success. Hopefully, he could forget the whole thing.

Ajay wrapped a tie around his neck. *A red tie would be a better choice for the current season,* his wardrobe spoke. For Tulo's sake. He could feel Genni getting agitated behind him. She was doing that thing where she lightly tapped her toes on the ground. Like she's being casually patient, but really, it's a stab at him to shift himself. He threw the blue tie on the ground and she picked it up again. Ajay quickly perfected the knot on his red one.

"Okay, ready."

"Your jacket?"

"Right. My jacket is . . ." Ajay paused. Where was his jacket? "Hanging up by the door. Let's go."

"Shoes?" Genni laughed sweetly then, but he couldn't ignore the patronising tone she was carrying.

"Sorry," Ajay sighed and sat at the end of the bed, pulling his smartly polished shoes on.

"Why are you so late?" Genni asked.

"Just got caught up with work," he responded quickly. That was a lie. Well, a half-lie, he justified himself. He was working until he got a communication piece through from volunteering. Mrs Laptoff had died. It was a peaceful moment. Ajay didn't feel the slightest bit of sadness, only relief. The only person in the City who clearly knew his secret was dead. Plus, he'd no longer have to feed pills to the demented crone. A great Liberation Day present, he'd thought. That's when he realised, he hadn't got Genni anything and did a panicky online search to find anything that would do. He'd settled for a silver bracelet with a charm in the shape of a paintbrush. She'd think it was thoughtful, but really it was a luck of the moment thing when a charm bracelet advert had appeared on his feed. A drone delivered it straight away. It was fine. It wasn't the present he wanted to give her. He wasn't too keen on encouraging this painting thing, despite how much social merit it'd gotten her since she came out as an artist. He'd told her that it was a bad idea, but she'd completely proved him wrong, which was annoying. They were together when she did it the first time.

"I just wonder whether the inspiration I feel when painting could be felt by others if they saw them," Genni had said, grabbing a sandwich from the fridge and plonking it into her handbag.

"Hmmm. It's just a big risk, Gen. Eyes are on you after what happened and I'm not sure if people would respond in the way you want them to." Ajay had thought about how her work was beautiful as he had readied himself for a boost on the sofa. But he knew this world. It wasn't

always kind towards openness. Genni had nodded, leaning on the breakfast bar. Ajay had watched her. She was clearly thinking it over. The right side of her lip curled in its characteristic way. Ajay had noticed that her freckles were particularly stark in the morning light. Her yellow skirt also clashed miserably with her pale green blouse. He'd wondered whether he should advise her to check the wardrobe again. He didn't, distracted by Genni dropping her handbag to the floor and dashing to the apartment cupboard. Watching as she had pulled out her paintings' tubes, he felt nervous for her, knowing what she was doing.

He had stood from the sofa, ignoring the SkipSleep asking for his arm. "Gen, are you sure?"

"Don't talk. You'll convince me not to do it." She had spoken with a power in her voice.

Flattening out her landscape of the waterfall across the black rug on Ajay's floor, she sat back for a moment to admire it. Flicking her fingers and angling her Watch, her camera took artistic, close-up shots of the waterfall. She started tapping at her wrist. Ajay had wondered what the caption would be. Would it be a heartfelt story about her journey as an artist? A twisted tale about it not being her work? He wasn't sure. This Genni was slightly new to him. She wasn't usually this impulsive, this brave. Then, in a small whisper to herself as if Ajay wouldn't hear – although he did – she said, "This is for me."

He had been wrong about the caption. She'd gone much simpler, with very Command-worthy prose. Something about finding a life more beautiful than the one you have and reaching for something better. She may as well have written Progress is Strength. To Ajay's surprise, the loves came flooding in. Genni had been erratic in excitement. Pearl rang within minutes. There were of course a few comments about her being a timewaster and a good-for-nothing, mostly by The Glorified, the likes of her father's friends and Rod's colleagues. She'd somehow managed to filter that out. Ajay was impressed. He'd never been able to ignore the opinions of The Glorified.

"Are you ready now?" Genni said as Ajay finished tying his small, thin laces and the memory faded.

"Yes, ma'am." Yes ma'am? He'd never said that before. Genni looked at him strangely.

"Are you alright? You seem jittery."

"Yeah, yeah. Just tired after yesterday. They do say too much talking sends you mad."

Genni laughed that sweet little laugh as the sun from the apartment window fell over her face and exaggerated her natural beauty, despite the heaviness of her make-up. Ajay's Watch vibrated. He drew his eyes away from Genni and looked down. He'd been awarded a Liberation Day Bonus. Nice one. As soon as the thought passed his mind, a small speck of shame crept in and settled on his chest like an irritable itch. Why did he feel guilty all of a sudden? He'd been hacking his Watch on ad hoc occasions for years. He never felt like this. He'd normally feel a little bit naughty, like when watching a dirty movie or when he stole his father's Watch as a kid, but never would he feel remorse. It was just a nice coincidence that he'd boosted his score on a City holiday after wasting time looking for Genni's precious bracelet. His feelings were probably an aftermath of everything. Genni overdosing. His grandma. The paranoia. But he decided that from now on, he would be all good. Ajay discreetly put his sleeve over his wrist and walked towards Genni with an open arm. She embraced him as they left the apartment together.

* * *

The metal of the pole squeaked between Ajay's fingers. Gripping tightly to it as the sky train stopped, he planted his feet firmly to the ground to balance himself. He hated standing on the train and having to cuddle a bright yellow pole that thousands of others had touched. When it was this busy, he sometimes felt trapped, like he was never going to enjoy solitude again. Genni was needing to lean against the glass of the door beside him. He could feel the heat of her body against his, as well as the heat of the hairy man next to him. This happened to him too often. Maybe if he wasn't so late, this could have been avoided. Genni was right.

Even his people-watching habit was a no go in these crowds; everyone being so close to one another, he couldn't pick out enough detail about them. He looked down and wondered if he could decide what people were like by their shoes. No luck. All the same. Smart, polished lace ups like his own, or strappy sparkling heels like Genni's. The train stopped again. No one got off, as they were all heading for the same place, but there was a stream of people wanting to board, all standing eagerly on the platform. You've got to be joking, Ajay thought. There was no way they're getting them all on here. Yet by some miracle, people jumped on, including Ace, Pearl, Mila, Jaxson, and Blake.

"Hey!" Ace shouted as he squeezed through the crowds and stood straight in front of Ajay, so close that Ajay could smell his fresh, minty breath. "We're practically kissing, mate."

"You'd be so lucky."

"Fighting talk." Ace smiled as his body tilted with the movement of the train.

Pearl was in front of Genni, wearing a tight, long black cocktail dress that tastefully covered her breasts and blended with her hair that carried a natural wave. She always looked so good, Ajay thought. He knew it annoyed Genni incessantly how Pearl could look glamorous even in sweatpants, yet Ajay always reminded her how he preferred Genni's more natural beauty. That was the truth. He didn't know how much she believed him, though. Ajay gave Pearl a greeting nod, to which he only received a faint effort at a smile. Oh, this must be it, he thought. Genni often mentioned Pearl's incredible ability to belittle people who didn't do what she wanted. She was clearly distant due to Ajay's avoidance of their social 'collaboration'. He'd pretty much downright refused. He did not want his face plastered all over the socials; what a way that would be to fuel his paranoia, having the public interested in him and making enquiries about his past or his parents. The amount Genni knew about some influencers was frightening, like how they liked their meals prepared or what brand of perfume they used. He was probably thinking of himself too highly. The public surely wouldn't care about the intricate details of a Prosper engineer's life. He wasn't going to take the risk, though, so he'd just have to deal with Pearl's aloofness.

That's when Ajay saw a large hand rise up over Ace's head.

"Ajay, hi!" said a voice from behind him. It was Jaxson.

"Hey!" Ajay reached up and tapped his own hand to Jaxson's, scraping the side of Ace's face with his arm.

"Eh, eh!" Ace said. "Can we save the meet and greet until after we're out of the sweat box?" He had a point.

Ajay could see Jaxson's face. He was laughing at Ace. Ajay always thought Jaxson found Ace a little bit too funny. Like the way Jaxson would suck up to Rod every time he was around. Ajay noticed he too, like Ace, had shaved his head. That trend was growing. Ajay didn't get it. For one thing, Jaxson having a fringe did him many more favours; his lack of hair made his chin look about three sizes bigger.

The train stopped again and Ajay braced himself as everyone's bodies shuffled and changed position. He was pleased then to find Mila next to him. It had been a while, and unlike most City-goers, she was interesting to talk to.

Ajay decided to give her a sideways hug. A stupid decision. The squash of people shifted again, and his left arm became stuck around her back. Perfect, he thought. He lifted his fingers away from her so his hand ended up hovering. It was highly awkward, but Mila laughed so Ajay relaxed his hand.

"Did you go for the higher job?" he asked.

"Yes. I got it!" Mila gave a half-smile. "Thank you for asking. You're looking very sharp!"

"Why thank you. And you look great," Ajay said with a beaming smile as he noticed the sequins that covered the entirety of her gold cocktail dress. "So, how is the job?"

Mila sighed. "Oh, I don't know. I'm happy, the merit is good, so I shouldn't complain."

Ajay noticed how she flicked her sparkling eyes from side to side, as if she were conscious of people listening. It was impossible for people not to hear their conversation. This was getting ridiculous. Ajay's knees were knocking against Ace's. Very, very uncomfortable. Even more people were boarding now. Really? At least this was the last stop before the Quarters and they'd all flood out from this torture carriage. Mila ended up even closer to Ajay then, and she immediately whispered into his ear, her breath warm on his skin.

"I just want to do patient care. The technology will only take us so far."

Ajay didn't respond. Why did she tell him that? She'd just accepted a job developing medical technology and would be practicing next to no patient care. That was the right decision for both merit and credit. She looked at him with an innocent sincerity, almost like a vulnerability. Ajay felt uneasy; he didn't know what she expected him to say. He could hardly tell her that her ambition was not compatible with making it to M-500. Silent seconds ticked by and he knew he needed to speak. He didn't want Mila to feel stupid for confiding in him, but he couldn't find any words. To his relief, Genni spoke.

"So what are you guys talking about?" Genni had managed to swivel herself around to face him on his right. He then managed to untangle his arm from around Mila's back. Not that Genni would care, but just in case she had a random emotional episode, it would be much easier for him if she didn't see that.

"Oh, just work," Mila answered. "Gen, tell me more about this Fat Reduction thing. I'd be interested in signing up for the testing stages?"

Ajay blocked out Genni's response, confused at Mila's question as he observed the slenderness of her body under the shimmer of sequins. Was she mad?

As their chattering continued, the train rolled into the Glorified Gate, whistles and shouts erupting as the entire population of the carriage fell out. Ajay could breathe again as he stepped out into the open air. Only for a moment, though. The crowds soon swept him up and he was ushered down the platform. He supposed he had better prepare himself for all the forced jollification. It was Liberation Day, after all. It had already been a welcome distraction from his grandma: since leaving the apartment, he hadn't once thought about her or about how his parents might be organising a memorial. Yet there he was, surrounded by many women wearing varying colours of dress – sequins, glitter, frills, and tassels all widely featured. Under all that though, every dress was the same: all long and tightly fitted around the backside and V-necked above the chest. He thought back to Grandma, thinking he should maybe feel disrespectful for not even bothering to ring, to know if she'd made it through the last few weeks. But he supposed after years of distancing himself that he had become numb to family and that the depressive episode from the other week was just a one off . . . or was it? He guessed one thing was for sure: he had no idea how he felt. His runaway thoughts were interrupted.

"Ajay! How are you?" Blake said, walking beside Ajay. He wasn't as colourful as Ajay would have liked or expected. Despite their talk at his apartment the other month, he thought Blake would have at least picked something vibrant for Liberation Day. Instead, the navy suit had made another appearance and this time, even his bow tie was a dull yet tasteful plum.

"Blake, I'm great!" Ajay went to hug him, but Blake held out his hand for a formal handshake. Ajay appreciated he was maybe too informal. Perhaps Blake expected Ajay to be more respectful now his merit was climbing.

"How's the apprenticeship going?" Ajay asked. They started walking slower as the crowds got stopped at the Gate.

"Oh, splendid. Yes. Working on such an exciting project right now." Blake did seem enthralled and passionate. "It's basically a new idea to help ease the demand on the sky train. It'll be underground and the carriage will be private pods that are shot at speed through air-tight tubes. It'll be so fast to get around!"

"That sounds awesome. But how will that work, we're just walking on concrete above sand, aren't we?" Ajay asked.

"Yes. That's our first hurdle. The safety and stability issue." Blake spoke professionally. "But think how good it

will be. Of course, the pods will be plush and glamourous –
for the Glorified and friends."

"Right. So how long?" Ajay kept looking forward as they
moved painfully slowly. Thousands of heads bounced
beneath The Glorified Gate. They'd be there soon. The
festival of compulsory fun.

"Oh, it'll be awhile. But I think Command is hoping that
the time earnt through its velocity will mean more of our
generation will have the time for children," Blake said.

"Cool. The population decrease has been a news
headline for too long. It's about time they replace it." Ajay
laughed and then asked Blake, "So will you be sambaing
with me tonight?"

As they moved forward once more, Ajay attempted to
demonstrate some of the moves Blake had once taught
him. He tried to be discreet in case others saw how poor a
dancer he was.

Blake giggled joyfully in his usual way. "Yes, I'll be
dancing. But maybe not samba tonight, something less
flamboyant might be more . . . acceptable." Whilst Ajay was
disappointed that Blake was neglecting his favourite dance,
he was pleased he was laughing as himself and not with a
nervous undertone. He'd surely made the right choice, Ajay
thought. The job over the dancing.

His subtle and unexpected questioning over Blake's
career decisions faded as they approached the Gate,
finally at the front of the queue. Ajay took a deep breath,
preparing himself for the entry scan. Despite still feeling
low, he was excited for the distractions that lay beyond
those walls.

Chapter Thirty-Seven

Pulling his sleeve away from his wrist, Ajay admired Blake's new blue strap engraved stylishly with his initials. He glanced at his own Command-branded wrist before turning his attention to the identification scan beneath the decadent archway. Its digital sign read: *Entry: M-300 and above. Internal venues: M-400 and above. Progress is Strength. Remember to still have a merit-making day.*

Even after all this time, Ajay still felt slightly apprehensive when approaching an ID scan. There was always a niggly feeling that perhaps the system had been updated and he had missed something, and that this would be the moment when everything good would dissipate into nothing. He felt his heart beating against his chest; he held his arm out to the scanner as Genni was being checked to the right of him. The drone began its scan. *Scanning,* it said. *Scanning,* it repeated. *Scanning,* it repeated again. Ajay held his breath. He looked beyond the drone to see that everyone else in the group was already through, and were looking back, waiting. *Scanning,* the drone said for the fourth time. Ajay closed his eyes, but they were soon forced open by the sound of a positive ping and the green light shining from the drone onto his wrist. *Entry accepted,* the drone murmured, and Ajay walked through.

He felt his legs move quicker to catch up with the group and Genni opened her arm to him. They all walked together down the main streets, whose planted trees and flamboyant flowers had been replaced with bunting, balloons and banners. It looked similar to last year, Ajay thought. He thought they were going bigger than ever. The smell of freshly baked goods as usual accompanied the aroma of weak ethanol and cooked meat from the gourmet burger and healthy salad stands. Music played loud from the drones hovering overhead.

"Hey Gen, you reckon you'd get a discount on pedicures at the pop-up spa?" Pearl shouted across the crowds of happy and fully contented attendees.

"For sure. We could get one now before the gig later?" Genni asked. "I'll come too." Mila hooked her arm around Genni's.

"Me too, I fancy a swim," Blake said.

"See you in a bit then guys," Genni said, her voice disappearing as the four of them scurried away towards the spa, leaving the remaining three men alone by a hot dog stand. That was a bit flippant, Ajay thought. They'd not even asked what he, Ace and Jaxson wanted to do.

"So . . . dodgems?" Ace suggested.

Suddenly, Ajay didn't care about the others ditching them; he'd forgotten about the dodgems. They were hilarious. Last year, he and Ace had managed to get Pearl stuck in a corner and she couldn't figure out how to reverse so just sat in her cart whimpering. It would probably be considered bullying by some people, but Pearl held her own. She put salt in Ace's drinks for the rest of the night.

As the three of them got deeper into the Quarters, Ajay saw what Command had meant by 'bigger than ever'. The *Challenges* section was an absolute marvel. Ajay felt nauseous at the explosion of colour. There were red and yellow striped stands and others with exteriors of pink and purple polka dots. Multi-coloured balloons were taking off through the blue sky and towards the bright white shining sun. Along with the polished colours of ladies' dresses, the whole thing reminded Ajay of a packet of candy. Every colour of the flipping rainbow. It was enough vibrancy to make anyone miserable physically sick, but no one here seemed to be complaining. Looking around, Ajay saw so much laughter, as well as some occasional aggression from those playing at one of the many competitive VR stands: there was laser shooting, basketball, boxing, dancing, and driving challenges.

"Wow, they've seriously gone for it this year," Jaxson said. "Ace, you should have a go at that." Both Ace and Ajay looked over to where Jaxson was pointing. It was a challenge called *Revolution Combat* and in front of the stand, a willing subject wore VR slimline glasses and was holding a computerised laser gun. The man was ducking, kicking, jumping, and shooting as spectators watched on the observer screen within the stand. There were groups of armed men coming straight for him, all donning old city uniforms. Intense music and battle sounds accompanied the virtual construction.

"He's doing pretty good. Go on mate, get em!" Ace roared as the three of them joined the group gathered around the agile player. The game was over very quickly. A man could be seen on the screen charging towards the camera. He jumped with all his computerised weight, which physically threw the player backwards onto the ground who, without time to get back up, got shot by another computerised official. The small crowd sighed and cheered in sympathy. *12 minutes played. Credit of 3 earned,* the stand's drone bleeped. How humiliating, Ajay thought.

"Only 3?!" the player moaned as he pressed his Watch to the drone, gathered himself up, returned the VR glasses and then laughed with his friends. They headed back into the crowd in pursuit of their next game.

"You have a go then, Ace?" Jaxson asked, as he loosened the collar of his high-quality shirt.

"I think I'm alright for now, mate. Maybe after the dodgems. You can though?" Ace responded confidently, with a tone to inspire Jaxson to get involved.

"No. That's fine," Jaxson said timidly. "I'd just look stupid, I'm not very nimble." Jaxson gave both Ace and Ajay a self-deprecating smile as another willing subject had gone forward to don the slimline glasses, this time a lady in a shockingly see-through green dress.

"Let's go for the dodgems then." Ace led them as they joined the moving magnitude once again, and soon they'd reached their destination. Slickly designed hover carts with bright patterned exteriors whizzed around in a metal cage with sparkling lights and flashing colour; the momentous noise of them banging and bashing into each other injected some violence into the otherwise dazzling scene.

"Psssst guys. Look," Jaxson said as they joined the line, distracting Ace and Ajay who were enjoying watching a man get targeted by a group of three women ramming his hover cart into one corner of the cage. Ajay turned around and saw two particularly well dressed, slightly older men join the line a few people behind them.

"They're from Command. Obviously come to join the party and give themselves a break too." Jaxson looked at them adoringly, as if they deserved higher praise than anyone else.

"How do you know they're Commanders?" Ajay asked, as he saw no clear indication of their employment.

"The one on the right gave me my Watch." Jaxson shook his wrist at Ajay, who responded with a nod. A mighty noise boomed from the cage to indicate this round of cart bashing was ending and a digital countdown began at 10 seconds in the centre of the cage. This only encouraged the women to continue ramming their male subject faster, who was crying out in jovial desperation.

"Poor sucker's got himself in knots there." Ace was clearly amused by the situation. The operating drone then announced it was time to switch drivers.

"What are we saying, then? A point for every bash when it's your turn?" Jaxson asked the other two, who immediately agreed with his suggestion.

"So, Ajay, are you ready for another trashing?" Ace playfully punched Ajay on the arm, to which Ajay rolled up the sleeves of his jacket, squared his friend sternly in the eyes, and walked backwards slowly towards the cage gate.

"You . . . just . . . wait." Ajay let the words fall gradually from his lips. Ace and Jaxson laughed and the three of them went up the small concrete steps to find their hover carts. It felt good to let his guard down a bit, and it occurred to Ajay that he hadn't felt this relaxed in weeks.

Walking past the floating drone on his left, who was robotically calling out safety instructions, Ajay stepped into the cage and chose the number seven cart. It had a purple glitter exterior, slightly ruined by the layers of 'bumping' rubber that covered most of its bottom half.

These were an upgrade from last year. Much more advanced, and the paintwork had a better polish. The cart hovered slightly lower to the ground as Ajay gave it his weight. He sat uncomfortably in the plush seat and observed the dazzling mechanics of twinkling decorative lights that covered unusable buttons. The steering wheel was still slightly warm from its last driver.

"Wouldn't mind one of these to cruise around in, eh?" Ace tapped Ajay on his left shoulder from his blue cart.

"I know. Not bad are they?" Ajay strapped in his waist belt.

"So Jax, you wanna form an alliance?" Ajay heard Ace mumble to Jaxson on the other side of him in cart number five.

"I don't think so, mate. You'll just stab me in the back. You fight this fight alone." Jaxson then slowly put on his reflective sunglasses and sat poised and ready in his cart.

"Yeah we fight this fight alone." Ajay raised his eyebrows playfully at Ace.

"So be it," Ace said, just as the buzzer for the start of the ten-second countdown began.

Ajay then looked to his right and spotted the two Commanders in carts ten and eleven. He instantly felt threatened. Stop it, he thought. This was the first time he'd felt happy in weeks and he wouldn't let them ruin it. He'd come this far. People walked past him every day and never suspected anything. It was like he was above the system. Invincible. He'd even got caught in the Side and gotten away with it. A quick round of hover dodgems with Commanders wasn't going to be his downfall.

Three, two, one.

The buzzer sounded and the carts all took off at once, except Ajay, who was caught internalising and ended up with a false start. He quickly repositioned his feet and floored the accelerator, sending him hovering rapidly into the mix of carts bouncing in every direction. Upon reaching the far edge of the cage, Ajay turned to his right, just missing a bash from one of the Command men. As he scooped around the circumference of the cage, he spotted a person watching the mechanical chaos with a hooded green coat that just covered their eyes.

"Ramming speed!" He heard Jaxson's timid voice explode into an eruption of sound as he plummeted into Ajay's cart, sending it hovering it to the side of the cage. His cart vibrated and an LED display of electric sparks ran up and down the outside rubber. Jaxson rejoiced as he'd won his first point. He then scooted around to find Ace.

Ajay turned again into the centre of the cage, narrowly missing colliding with another driver. As his head went side to side and he felt a slight muggy breeze on his cheeks, he saw Jaxson coming for him again but amazingly, he just dodged him and Jaxson rocketed into another driver and into the right hand wall. Ajay turned as he could hear Ace wildly laughing where he was driving. When Ajay looked to find him, he saw Ace look up at the clock, and his facial expression change. It was Ace's turn.

Ace spotted him and gave him a predatory look. Continuing to drive and skilfully dodging others, Ace was coming for Ajay – fast. Kill me now, Ajay thought. He let out a girlish squeak and hovered quickly in the opposite direction. He put his foot down to gather more speed.

"Ha ha, there's no getting me Acey boy!" he screamed and turned to see Ace cornering Jaxson and repeatedly ramming at his cart; its lights reflecting up the metal of the cage. Ajay smiled and looked to the clock. His turn. He took the corner at speed, causing his cart to hover at a perpendicular angle up the sidewall. Ace was still ramming Jaxson, clearly unaware of his impending fate, but Jaxson, the good guy that he was, indicated to Ace that he had a killer on his back.

Ace screamed with a certain hilarity as he left Jaxson beside himself in laughter. Ace and Ajay found themselves in a showdown where Ajay did not waver his focus from the back of Ace's blue cart; he was determined to win. He edged ever closer. Ace let out another whimsical cry of distress. Ajay then felt someone close to him. He looked behind him to see one of the Command men was pursuing him for a bashing. Ajay panicked: a bump from him would set him off course to catch Ace. The drama intensified when the ten-second countdown boomed from the central speakers of the cage. Ace was heading round the left edge of the cage and Ajay had about eight seconds to make his move. He swung his cart out wide from behind Ace and floored his accelerator so they were side-by-side. *Five . . .* boomed the speakers. Ajay then turned sharply, causing the front of his cart to spin rapidly, but he simultaneously floored it again, thrusting his spinning vehicle forward.

He bashed Ace at serious velocity, hurtling them both into the side of the metal cage. The merging lights of their rubber was almost blinding. Further vibrations rippled through Ajay's cart when his pursuer, the Commander, consequently plummeted into his cart from behind, forcing him forwards just as the *game over* buzzer sounded.

"Oh!" Ace cried from his cart. "You got me good mate, but you get what you give. He just burned you!"

Ace threw a wink at the Commander, who responded with a faint-hearted laugh, driving his cart back to the starting line. Ajay didn't respond but only felt disgruntled that his victory had been downplayed.

As they walked away from the cage, Ajay noticed them again. It was a man, or maybe even a woman – it was hard to tell. They were wearing a long, green cloak with their hood so low that Ajay couldn't see a face. Just a still, unmoving mouth. He'd seen them watching the dodgems, they'd been standing at the edge of the cage. Ajay felt anxious by their presence. They were standing still, facing his direction. Like they were there for him.

"Had a go at the dodgems, then?" Genni was back, flashing the golden sparkles of her newly manicured nails in his face. He gently grabbed her hands and looked at them. Tasteful, he thought.

"They look great," he said. This seemed to please Genni, who was smiling incessantly. He put his arm around her and then looked back for the hooded stranger. They were gone. The space where they'd been standing now occupied by other happy, colourful people. Forget it, he told himself. It's probably nothing.

Chapter Thirty-Eight

"Anyone fancy a drink?" Blake straightened his new square-shaped spectacles as the group walked around, trying to decide what to do next.

Pearl gasped and spoke hyperbolically, letting the word fall slowly from her lips. "Please!"

"Wait. Everyone stop." Ace stretched his arms across the group. Ajay felt its force across his chest. They all stopped, and looked at Ace, confused.

"What?" Genni asked.

"Did Pearl just say please?" Ace laughed, and everyone else sighed.

They started moving again, and Ajay noticed that Pearl gave Ace the 'grow up' eyes.

It was the consensus that the group would go and get a drink, and perhaps meet a few strangers to network and merit-make with, before heading over for *The Tulip Twins* concert. Ajay hated their music. It was just generic pop that carried no substance. No individuality or meaning. Just the same old dribble churned out in a slightly new way. He tolerated it, though, because it was popular, and he could sing along to the blandness of it along with everyone else.

He and Genni walked under an arc made from tree stumps and a wooden sign engraved with 'Drinks & Networking'. The area they entered was laid out in a square, formed from numerous wooden chalets that resembled architecture Ajay had seen in films set in much colder climates. They were serving weak ethanol spirits, soft drinks, iced water on tap and some slightly stronger stuff. He wondered whether Ace would indulge as much as last year. He'd gotten so blindingly drunk that he was deducted almost a whole merit point the next week. Ajay doubted that would ever happen again. Not when Ace was so close to being back in the Quarters. He watched as Ace scurried forward to save a plastic table that had just become available. People around him carrying drinks looked annoyed that he'd stolen it.

"What do you want darlings?" Blake waved to them from the nearest chalet to the entrance.

"Hey, Jun!" Genni shouted towards the crowd of talking people. She ran away from Ajay, leaving his arm back by his side. He followed her and watched her embrace a man wearing an entirely white suit. The stubble on his face must have scratched the side of Genni's cheek; their faces were so close. Ajay wanted to march over and grab Genni back to himself, though that wouldn't look right. He'd need to be polite, so he casually wandered over as if it didn't concern him that Genni was still holding onto this stranger. When he reached them, he deliberately slipped his arm back around her waist, the small gems on her dress stretching his skin.

"Jun, this is my boyfriend Ajay." Genni was smiling brightly and pressed her hand into Ajay's chest. "Jun and I work together. He's the marketing lead for the project."

"Ah, awesome. Great to meet you Jun," Ajay said as he allowed Jun to shake his right hand.

"Hey, you're a rightie too!" Jun said as he pointed to Ajay's Watch on his left wrist. Ajay laughed his greatest fake laugh and nodded.

"I'm going to sort our drinks. Why don't you two chat?" Genni said sweetly. She kissed Ajay on the cheek and ran over to Blake at the chalet bar. Ajay watched her go, her dress slightly rising as she moved.

"Well, I guess we're supposed to talk," Jun said as he stroked his partially shaved head. Yet another one following the trend. "So where do you work, Ajay?"

"I'm at Prosper actually," Ajay answered. "I work in transactional technology."

"No way. That's a great gig. How did you land that job?" Jun asked, before looking embarrassed. "Sorry, I didn't mean it like that. I just mean getting in at Prosper . . . That's good going for even the most skilled person." Ajay felt pleased with the way Jun was suddenly flapping around his words. The Prosper privilege; it demanded people's respect.

"I guess they saw something in me," Ajay coughed. "How is the project going? From what I've heard from Genni, it could be quite effective for people's well-being and merit scores."

"Yeah, it should be good. Despite my reservations, you know, encouraging people to be thinner, its testing has had amazing results, and if people can be healthier because of it, everyone in society will be better off." Jun took small delicate sips of his iced water. "I've got a bold strategy, but I think our targeting is really refined due to more sophisticated online trackers that have been introduced this year. So the likelihood is that we'll reach the right people, really fast."

"Right, that sounds interesting. I can't say I have much to do with marketing. But I bet there's some social influencers that would be good ambassadors for the project," Ajay added.

"Oh, for sure. We're already pursuing some people, but that's a secret that'll die with me." Jun tapped his nose twice and leaned closer towards Ajay. He expected Jun to smell overwhelmingly of mediocre aftershave, but there was no smell at all.

"So, what marketing happens at Prosper?" Jun paused. Ajay couldn't help himself. He screwed up his face. He had very little interest in this conversation, as he knew exactly where Jun was trying to take it.

"Given by the look on your face, it seems you need some education," Jun laughed. "I can share some stuff if you like?" Jun waved his left wrist again.

There it was. The merit-making grab. Ajay couldn't think of anything worse. Why should he bore himself to let this almost bald, girlfriend-hugging M-400 get merit from it? He turned around.

Genni and Blake were still giggling together at the bar. He decided to comply. Mainly because Genni would probably find out he'd said no and grill him for being rude, and because he had nothing better to do at that moment.

"Yeah, why not!" Ajay acted as if this was totally welcome and he was even excited by it. Jun started tapping at his Watch to set up the interaction. But then, he stopped.

The atmosphere changed. The air had become irritable. The music of joyful chatter turned into something else. What was that? A scream? Gunfire?

As this happened, Ajay was watching Jun. Watching as his fingers stopped moving. Ajay could then clearly distinguish a piercing scream of a woman from across the square. More screams then accompanied hers. The ground rumbled beneath him. Jun's eyes widened, his pupils conveying a meshed story of fear and pain. Bright, red blood trickled down Jun's forehead and out from his nose, the blood seeping through the fabric of his pristine white shirt. Before Ajay could even think, Jun's body fell forwards towards him. He took his weight and they both plummeted fast to the ground.

Chapter Thirty-Nine

His back was on fire, pain throbbing all along it from the way he'd smacked the hard concrete. He scraped his fingers along the ground, feeling tiny specks of gravel lodge themselves beneath his fingernails. At first, for a moment, Ajay had forgotten what he'd just seen. When he opened his eyes, it was impossible to forget. It was staring straight at him. Jun's silent, static face layered with blood fresh enough that Ajay could smell its iron. Disorientated, Ajay didn't know how long he had been lying there, but the raw wet redness of Jun's skin confirmed it couldn't be long. He couldn't look at him, so he turned his head in the hope to get away, but all he saw were blurred bodies falling to the floor. Lasers tore through the air, birthed from guns held by people in green-hooded cloaks, just like the illusive figure Ajay saw by the dodgems. He looked to the sky, almost frozen with fear but shielded by the dead.

The screams and the blasts were unbearable; Ajay had never experienced fear that sliced through every bone, nerve, and muscle. Considering everything he'd gone through, he couldn't quite fathom that this would be how he would die: by the hand of some unknown lunatics probably not even Worthy enough for the Side. Who were they? What did they want? Why were they doing this? Ajay felt as if he could weep, but as he caught the silence of Jun's wide lifeless eyes, he thought back to Theo Badds who was silent and cold, but restful. This dead body was different. Horrific and premature. Ajay could feel Jun's escaping warmth against his skin, and the eyes spoke of the anguish it was to be cut down in your prime. Ajay knew he needed to stay, protected by Jun, so he wouldn't be handed the same fate.

Then Ajay's thoughts turned to her. Genni. Where was she? Was she dead? Did her eyes carry the same suffering as those that looked at him now? He couldn't be a coward for her; he needed to survive, find her and get them both out of this battleground. Struggling some more, he managed to lift his arms out from underneath Jun's torso. He wanted to lift Jun's body slowly out of respect, set him down and cover him over, but there wasn't time for that. The sound of this nightmare continued. He steadied his hands against Jun's sides, feeling the squelch of his blood on the once clean suit. He pushed and threw Jun's body off himself, grunting as he did so. Jun's landing gave a small thud as he hit the tarmac beside them. Ajay jumped up; a relief that he could still walk past quickly. He saw Jun's killer standing with his back to him, still shooting into the crowds. Ajay looked around frantically at bodies: the injured were crying out for help, some of them screaming in agony. Ajay fumbled over bodies, feeling inhumane and sick by leaving them all behind, but he just had to find her and get out. He made his way over to the still-standing chalet where he'd last seen them. *Ace*, he thought. Where was Ace? Ajay moaned out loud, limping towards the chalet, his back and legs starting to feel bruised. Scanning the area, he could see smashed glass scattered like celebratory confetti cursing the spot where they all once stood. None of them were on the ground, which Ajay took as a good thing, but still he didn't know where they were. He moved closer and then he saw him. Ace.

He didn't look like him. Ajay had never seen his face expressing such emotions. Distressed. Traumatised. His eyebrows were bent down at an unfamiliar angle. Ace had squeezed himself in between the opening of one chalet and the next. With little movement, Ace waved Ajay over, fear in his eyes.

"Genni?" Ajay mouthed to Ace as he continued to rush towards him. Ace nodded, turned his head and mumbled something to someone behind him. Due to the tight space, Genni obviously couldn't lift her head up, but she slipped her hand underneath Ace's armpit and waved, ushering Ajay to come to them for safety. Ajay could see the golden shimmer of her fingernails. Relief flooded every part of him. He picked up the pace and started to run towards the opening. Almost there, he staggered between the dead, trying to respectfully kick off the injured who grabbed at his legs when a hot, burning pain ricocheted across his right arm. He felt his body flop forward and settle into what he assumed were Ace's arms. He looked up and saw he was right: though obscured, he could see Ace's brilliant eyes looking down at him. His right arm was on fire, as if boiling water had drenched his skin until it ate right through to the bone. He yelped out in pain and he heard Genni squeal in desperation.

He'd been shot. Ajay's breathing lost its balance. He'd been shot. Shot. With a gun. So he was going to die here? Looking down at his arm and breathing heavy, he saw the wound: sore, red and gushing fluid, but not that deep. Ajay settled his breath. This wasn't going to kill him, but something else today might.

"Ajay. Ajay, you okay?" Ace's voice was like a high-pitched whistle, his words hard to distinguish.

"Ye-yeah . . ." Ajay said. He lifted his left hand and ripped the right arm of his shirt and jacket to fully reveal the throbbing burn beneath. "Just scratched me . . ." Ajay moaned in pain and started to take deep breaths to control it.

"Ajay!" Genni screamed. Ajay could feel Ace's body being forced forwards, meaning that Genni was trying to get to him, but there wasn't space.

"I'm here. Don't move," Ajay said slowly. "Where are the others?"

"We're all here, Ajay!" Blake called out from further down the opening. He couldn't see behind him, but he could imagine them all, Genni, Mila, Blake, Jaxson and Pearl, squished together within this small opening, faces repulsed and fearful yet painted with a hope that they might survive the horrors outside.

The sound came then; the sound of that hope. The sirens of the TPD were clear and Ajay felt his body relax despite still being audience to ongoing destruction. Then he felt wrong.

Something was very, very wrong.

"What is going on?" said Ace, clearly still reeling from Ajay being hit a moment ago. "WHAT IS GOING ON?"

"We need to move," Ajay said instinctively. He didn't know why, or how, but he just couldn't shake the feeling that something was about to happen.

"Are you crazy?" Ace's voice cracked. "Those madmen are still out there."

"We can't stay here," Ajay said. "There's nowhere to run if we stay here." Ajay ripped down his jacket arm further and then proceeded to tie it around his burn tightly. His eyes watered and he winced in pain. He exhaled dramatically. "Okay, everyone needs to follow my lead." He steadied himself to stand, surprised at his sudden bravery. There was a loud whimper from behind him.

"I can't go. We can't go . . . We'll die." Pearl was crying, struggling to get out words.

Ajay knew it in his gut. They needed to move.

"Pearl. If we don't go now, we're stuck in a trap." Ajay spoke loud enough so Pearl could hear him from the back of their single line squash. "Blake's with you. Hold his hand and be brave. We'll all be brave together. Okay?"

Ajay heard nothing for a couple of seconds, but soon Blake responded, "let's go, Ajay," indicating that Pearl had given a silent indication of her unwilling but essential bravery.

Ajay stayed ducked down, in a half squatting position, and started to creep slowly around the front of the chalet and the others followed. He felt slightly faint as his arm began to swell.

Whenever he moved his arm, a fever and nausea would almost overcome him. He used his left arm to clutch his right, stopping it from moving. He reached the edge of the chalet and forced himself to filter out the tormenting screams, the continuing gunfire, and the flurries of panicked people, to get his friends to safety. Looking behind him, he could see them all: Genni and Pearl had blackened eyes, and the bright, glorifying sparkles of their dresses had been marred by dirt and blood. Then he noticed someone was missing.

"Where's Mila?" he screamed down the line.

Sirens muffled his words as TPD drones and planes flew overhead, piercingly loud. The group were frozen as they watched the shooters change their target from people to drone. The laser beams caught a few, like shooting birds from the air, sending them plummeting to the ground; lethal fireballs dressed in deep black smoke. Ajay and the others covered their ears as the blasts penetrated the ground. Luckily for them, the drone swarms were too big for the attackers to hold off; the group watched as the tasers had their effect on the unexpected army. Ajay caught the sight of Jun's killer being held, body squiggling and squirming in every direction until he stopped moving and the hood of his cloak flew off, showing a glimpse of his deep olive skin and attractive facial features.

Genni gasped. Ajay turned back to her; she had grabbed Ace's shoulder.

"I ... It's him ... I ... feel ..." Genni was breathing erratically, and Ace held her up for support. She began to heave and vomited violently onto the ground. Ajay moved behind Ace and grabbed her. He wiped the tears and vomit from her cheek with the cuff of his shirt, his right arm beginning to lose all feeling.

"We've got to go now, Gen," Ajay said compassionately, not quite sure what triggered the vomit nor if he could hold down his own. He helped Genni stand, who was hysterical. With her persistent loud sobs in his ear, Ajay ensured that the others were all ready to go, and with Genni on his arm, they ran. They ran quickly away from the chalet and in the direction of The Glorified Gate. Genni then blubbered something to him. "A-Ajay ... It's ... it's him."

"It's who?" Ajay asked.

He didn't hear her response but only saw her lips move as he felt an almighty blast of hot air hit his body and he was thrown down to the ground again.

Chapter Forty

Ajay squinted, his blurred vision slowly coming into focus as more screams were muffled by the temporary tinnitus. He could feel the hard concrete against his back again, the gravel making its way back under his fingernails. It was like the ultimate deja vu, except this time, he wasn't flattened by a body and the sight of gunfire was replaced with towers of thick, black smoke sailing towards the white sun. They were borne by great flames resembling the fallen drones from moments ago. He sat up, his back feeling like a brick. Trying to make sense of his surroundings again, he looked down at his legs, his trousers completely tattered and his limbs boasting several artificial cuts. Squinting around, he could see that the flames were engulfing the chalets, their structures all but blown apart around him, the opening where they were hiding non-existent. It was a bomb; a second line of attack. Whoever these people were, they hadn't thought this up this morning. This has been meticulously and carefully planned. But why?

"Blake!" Pearl screamed, elongating Blake's name so it cut right to the core of Ajay's soul and made it cripple. He twisted his head to the left, his vision only just readjusting itself.

"Ajay, Ace, help him. Help him!" she bellowed again, this time with anger and desperation as Ajay could see her crouching over Blake's body.

His heart dropped like a rock to his stomach. Then, Ajay heard Blake's wailing, and he experienced the relief he imagined new parents feel as a baby cries for the first time.

Blake was alive, but Ajay knew by the distress in the cry that there was potential he soon wouldn't be. He hobbled to his feet, feeling the weakness of his body and hissing at the forgotten discomfort in his arm. He looked at Pearl, who was crying wildly, make-up running down her face enough to mask her natural complexion. She had a significant gash on her upper lip that was dripping blood down her chin and onto her neckline.

"Jay, Gen . . ." It was comforting for Ajay to hear Ace's voice and feel his hand on his shoulder, and to then feel Genni's hand fall into his own. He looked up and saw her again, her eyes just as fearful and anguished as before. Her lips were quivering as she looked at Blake, struggling and thrashing beneath the great piece of concrete that was crushing his legs. Blood was running out from underneath the rock as they all crouched down to the ground. Ajay looked around for Jaxson whom he found not far from them, standing still with his olive skin turning almost white. He was staring at Blake, who was yelping in agony. Jaxson looked as Ajay felt: shocked, numb and disbelieving. Ajay wanted to concentrate on Blake, to try to find a way to help him. As he met his desperate eyes he started to think, perhaps selfishly, that he needed to survive. There could be a third line of attack. First the guns, then the bombs – what was coming next? They shouldn't stay here to find out, even if it meant leaving Blake behind. The thought cut into Ajay painfully, as if it never should have existed in his head.

"Get . . . it . . . OFF . . ." Blake squawked, his voice cracking harshly with the pain.

"But . . . but won't that make things worse?" Genni asked frantically, looking at Ajay with persistent, pleading eyes. Her hair was frizzing wildly off her head. She wanted him to decide? He had no clue what to do. Blake was losing blood by the second as half the concrete bar from the chalet was probably stealing his ability to ever walk again. Yet she expected him, a lad who sits behind a screen all day, to know whether moving it was the right thing to do? It wasn't just her either, Pearl and Ace looked at him for answers too. He was useless and he didn't like the feeling. He'd gone from the saviour, leading them all out of that opening, to the let down in a matter of minutes, unable to live up to the role that was apparently expected of him.

"Out of my way!"

A distressed cry came from behind them and Ajay felt his body being pushed back as Mila took his place beside Blake. She was welcome to it. Ajay stood behind her and examined her back; she was covered in blood, but Ajay was pretty sure it wasn't hers. There wasn't a scratch on her. Plus, with the way she had strategically ripped her dress that was once long and golden but now a short, dishevelled party dress with a torn rim, Ajay assumed she had been treating people, using her dress and what she could find to make emergency tourniquets. She was Blake's real saviour, and thank goodness she was there. Ajay felt the pressure taken from him, yet the situation was still pressing hard on his mind.

"Okay, everyone calm down," Mila said as she looked around and retied her brown muddied hair into a messy bun. She bent lower to Blake and Ajay heard her words of assurance. "Blake, you're going to be fine. Just try to breathe. Okay, lovely? Like this." Mila demonstrated how she wanted him to breathe. Slow inhale, slow exhale. Blake began to copy.

"Now, can you feel your legs?" Mila asked.

"Yes I can . . . feel them," Blake shouted out quickly and then struggled to return to his breathing rhythm.

"That's good, Blake. That's a good sign." Mila held his hand. "Okay, so we need to get this off you now. Everything will hurt, Blake. But we're all here with you."

Ajay imagined the medical teams would get there soon, now that the shooters had been contained, but as he looked around, he saw how they would have their work cut out for them when they did get there. It was a sea of bodies, some moving like fish without water, and others just completely still. A massacre. What would this mean for-

"Ajay!" Mila's voice pierced through him. "Come on. It has to be now."

He refocused and saw that Genni, Pearl and Ace had steadied themselves around the slab of invading concrete, ready to lift. He took his place and looked to his arm, doubling in size from the swelling. He didn't know how he was going to lift this.

"Shouldn't we wait until the medical team gets here?" Ajay asked, knowing he had little strength left for his friend.

"No," Mila instructed. "The longer it's on him, the more likely-" Mila couldn't finish her words, but Ajay understood. He nodded, letting her know that he was willing to try.

"One . . . two . . . three . . ." Mila called, and the group grunted and yelped as they mutually gave everything to lift the thing off. Ajay was panting, puffing through the weight of it and the anger of his burn. He couldn't cope. He was too weak. Pearl was also struggling to hold her side. It was lifting, but it wasn't stable. It felt as if it was tipping towards Blake's torso. Ace let out a cry of panic and despair as he too realised the increasing potential of disaster. But then, in that moment, the concrete changed its momentum away from Blake as Jaxson had run in to assist. They all moaned and breathed heavily as they successfully lifted the piece away from its victim and down beside him. Ajay coughed violently with his head down towards the ground.

For those few seconds, as he stared down at his scuffed formal shoes, he knew he would never forget this day. The day he heard cries of distress and anguish vibrate constantly through his ear drums; the day a man he'd just met stared at him with lifeless eyes; the day he was shot and his friend's legs were crushed; the day he felt only a temporary relief when the medical trucks and planes arrived. Somehow, even through all of that, the most pressing thing on his mind was how this happened, and what such a security breach would mean for him and his secret.

* * *

"Pearl, just calm down!" Ajay heard Genni plead with a distressed Pearl from behind the tall plastic cubicle dividers.

He winced as the android wiped a wet, antiseptic cloth over his burn site. A four-hour wait in the Treatment Centre had driven him almost to insanity. The aching discomfort in his arm had been intensifying and he'd been sick at least five times. Only as he rested his head back on the bed did he feel connected back to the world. Even during his treatment, he hadn't had a clue what was going on. He remembered the stinging of the Stitch Bots burrowing their way into his skin to fashion the stitches, and he had a vague recollection of seeing them retreat into a machine like long, metal worms. Now, in aftercare, the android was taking its time to dress the wound to prevent infection.

As the robot was finishing up, Genni demanded that the glass door to the cubicle slide open so she could enter. She was still in her muddy dress, but having managed to clean her face, Ajay was comforted by seeing it.

"Hey," She kissed Ajay on the forehead, and then moved around the bed to have a look at the scar. "It's incredible. You can hardly see it, Ajay."

Ajay was speechless. She was right. He looked down at his arm to see a wound that merely resembled a superficial knife scratch. He lifted his arm to touch Genni. Pain. Hot and fresh.

"Don't." She helped him lower his arm. "It may look good, but it'll still hurt like crazy. Come on, you have to help me. Pearl's driving me mad."

"I can hear you, Genni!" Pearl screamed from the neighbouring cubicle.

Genni raised an eyebrow and widened her eyes, to which Ajay smirked. He shuffled off the beige coloured bed, which started talking to him.

Please confirm this bed is finished with by pressing the 'Available' button at its end. Genni did so and a green light shone from the end of the bed frame. Next minute, a Tuloian nurse rushed in to take the bed away.

With his arm bent across his torso, Ajay steadied himself as he walked with Genni to the next cubicle. Only then did he realise how unbearably loud it was in there. The noise was almighty. There were beeps and bleeps of machines, shouts and screams, Tuloians running up and down the long corridor with beds, equipment and injured patients in their destroyed glad rags. The only ones who were calm were the androids, walking leisurely whilst observing patient stats on floating screens.

"No you cannot help me, robot!" One nurse was howling at the other end of the corridor where Ajay could see patients waiting for beds. "Stop hanging about. There's people dying here!" The nurse rushed off, but Ajay observed as the android stood still – useless without instruction.

He then saw Pearl on the bed, looking deeply into the mirror extension of her Watch and pulling the skin tissue around her lip. Ace was beside her on a leather armchair, absorbed in his own Watch, eyes dilated at whatever he was reading. Genni opened the door and they went inside. Pearl whimpered as they entered. Her hair was tied back flat against her head, her eyes were red, and she was prodding relentlessly at a large, bumped scar above her upper lip. She looked at Ajay, a sweet smile forming on her face.

"Ajay, hi." She sniffled and sat up in bed. "Are you alright?"

Ajay, slightly surprised by her concern, walked over to Ace and patted him on the shoulder. Ace patted Ajay around the back and then returned to what Ajay could see was a news article on his screen. He sighed, looked at Pearl whose eyes had followed him around the bed and responded, "I'm okay. Thank you." He unwrapped the bandage on his arm. "It's healed over pretty well."

Pearl leant forward to observe the slight scar on Ajay's arm and then let out a wail of frustration.

"They can do that when he gets shot!" Pearl cried. "I got a cut on my lip and I'm left with *this* on my face! Is this a sick joke?" She started to bellow and flail her arms about. Genni rushed to her side and told her to calm down. Ajay stared in disbelief at her reaction.

"She's been like this since we came in," Ace said, looking up from his Watch. "You'll get used to it."

Ajay nodded and turned his head to the corridor, where he saw an android pushing a bed trolley slowly. Its occupant seemed to be lifeless. He then saw Mila sprint past the cubicle. She had abandoned her golden dress and donned some medical scrubs.

"I guess it's what to expect after an unanticipated terror attack," Ace said, as if he was quoting a news reporter.

"You don't understand, Gen," Pearl was shouting louder. "With this . . ." She pointed violently to her scar. ". . . on my face, I'll be a laughing stock. No one will want to look at me. No one will give me loves. I'll have no job and no merit."

She was silent then, and Ajay saw Genni take her hand. Pearl breathed heavily as tears oozed down her face. Genni took a tissue to wipe them away. After exhaling deeply, Pearl said, "Now, all people will see of me is an Unworthy ex-socialite." Genni looked at her sympathetically and gave her a sideways hug. Ajay could sense the sheer amounts of pain and disappointment that was contracting off every inch of the building's walls. He thought of Blake, still in surgery, who may never be able to walk or dance again.

He turned to Ace. "Is that what they're calling it? A terror attack?"

He felt Genni and Pearl's eyes look at him, clearly searching for answers too.

"Well, yeah," Ace said as he scrolled further down the article. "What else do they call it? Here, listen." He began to read.

"*Command Officials have confirmed that this was a savage attack believed to be executed by members of a group that call themselves 'The Rogue'. Drone patrols have been deployed across the Country, where it's believed they have congregated. Investigations are well underway to determine how they were granted access to The Quarters at today's Liberation Day celebrations. Security is due to increase to unprecedented levels. We will stop at nothing to ensure Tulo is safe again.*"

Ace fell silent as he closed his Watch.

"How do they know it was these Rogue people though?" Pearl asked as she was composing herself.

"I don't know. I guess it might be an educated assumption in ..." Ace paused, as Genni spoke defiantly.

"It was them." The three of them looked startled and confused. Ajay ushered Genni to explain. How could she possibly know that?

"Ajay, just before the chalet blasts, you remember I said it was *him*?"

Ajay nodded. He remembered that he hadn't cared at the time, he was just trying to get her to run.

"The shooter who got you, who killed Jun . . ." She started to tear up. "I was with him, the night I hurt my shoulder." Her audience of three were silent and stunned. Ace and Ajay stared blankly while Pearl gasped loudly.

"What? Why were you with him, Gen?" Pearl asked, worry on her face.

"He was Downtown, instead of the usual guy who . . ." Genni paused and then walked around the bed, towards Ajay on the other side of the cubicle. He felt the sincerity behind her voice and reached out for her. "I remember him talking about it being nice in the Country, about how he had a group of people out there. And he was beautiful, you all saw him. The most striking features. He grabbed me. And that's when I ran, got hit by the car and that woman helped . . ."

"He grabbed you? What do you mean he grabbed you?" Ajay asked, as suppressed anger rose within him. Not just that another man had touched her, but that she had never bothered to tell him. How long ago had she remembered this?

"He tried to hurt me, but I got out and a woman helped me get back to you. But there he was. With the gun!" Genni put her head on Ajay's chest, crying lightly. Ajay looked down to see her usually delicately washed hair smothered in dried blood, sand and mud. He wasn't sure whether he wanted to hug her. She kept keeping things from him. The painting, and now this. But he was reminded that anything could have happened to her that night and today. He decided to hold her tightly, and really, he never wanted to let her go.

Chapter Forty-One

One month after the attack.

Ajay felt his hands tremble as he tightened his grey and black spotted tie, his mind numb, not thinking of much but his miserable reality. *You need a spot of colour,* Genni's wardrobe beeped, and Ajay snarled. He tapped forcefully at the mirror and hit the right spot to turn the commentary off. Genni walked in from the shower room. She had fallen into a black trousers and t-shirt combination, had little make-up on and tied her hair back simply. She was putting in some golden studded earrings. Ajay knew she was looking at him, but he dismissed it, leaning against the wardrobe and looking down at the wooden floorboards of the circular flat.

"You ready for this, babe?" she asked softly, but Ajay didn't respond. "Babe?" She walked closer.

"You'd think with all this technology, they could update the stupid wardrobes so they know why I'm not wearing any colour!" Ajay said, as he walked to the large bay window that looked out over the dark river and grey architecture of the now-empty shopping mall.

"You don't have to go today, you know. We can even stay here and tune in. Blake would understand." Ajay felt her fingers gripping his shoulder.

"No, I'm going."

Ajay stared blankly out the window. Genni's flat sat above a line of empty buildings, once retail shops before drone deliveries and the shopping mall punched them out of business. She'd recently redecorated, on the advice of Pearl, as apparently refurbishments add up to a whacking amount of social merit if done right. That was before she came out as an artist. Still, she'd gone for a very on-trend historical look: the walls were burdened with a lining of fairy lights and she proudly displayed her paintings. The waterfall hung above the sofa, the only piece of furniture not thrown together with oak wood and wicker. Ajay didn't mind it, but he much preferred being at home. This all felt too close and claustrophobic, like a dull haze hung over him and he couldn't come out for air. He hated that he didn't have a choice; there was food here, and he couldn't risk buying any for himself anymore.

"Shall we go?" Genni said as she wiped her fatigued eyes slowly, reddening their edges and the surrounding skin. She shouldn't rub them, he thought. His Watch vibrated. *Ace calling.*

"Hi mate," Ajay said, as Ace's face sprang up on a floating screen.

"Hi. You heading over soon?"

"Yeah. Almost through the door."

"Alright. See you soon then." Ace disappeared into the Watch. The lack of pep in Ace's demeanour fell over the room as he and Genni stood on opposite sides of it.

Genni walked towards the door. "Okay. Let's go," she said.

*   *   *

The sky train had reopened its route for the first time since the attack. As they approached the pallid platform, dense swarms of TPD drones covered the sky. It was becoming increasingly difficult to see the whiteness of the sun, its canvas even more littered with mechanical black dots. The streets had been sapped of their previous energy – mainly because the usual vibrancy of advertising had been muted black by anti-Rogue propaganda. He and Genni found themselves drooping through the station's entrance. People were slow to get onto the platform. Ajay hadn't realised the reason before she said it.

"Oh, really? They're checking us here too?" Genni was rolling back the cuff of her black bomber jacket to get her Watch ready for authentication.

It had become as common as *SkipSleep* boosts. Ajay had hoped Command might let up once they were relaxed enough to re-open the sky train. That was naive of him. Ajay could see there were at least six Command guards – actual humans dressed head to toe in dull purple military suits. Accompanying them were TPD drones in high numbers, ready to restrain anyone whom the turnstiles rejected.

Dropping Genni's hand and slowly shifting backwards discreetly, Ajay told himself to sound calm. He didn't want her to notice his anxiety.

He relaxed, and asked, "Hey, Gen. Do you fancy walking to Jaxson's?"

Genni stopped and others rudely murmured at the two of them for blocking the entrance. He tried to ignore them. Ajay led Genni back out into the anaemic streets. She was resisting. He felt her hand snap away from his.

"What do you mean? It'll take us at least 10 minutes."

Ajay instinctively held Genni's hand again and calmly sauntered with her along the sidewalk. "I didn't fancy going back into the crowds just yet."

Genni sighed and stroked the inside of Ajay's right arm. "We've got to at some point, Ajay. I can't live in fear forever."

Ajay hurt inside. He always hurt. Any hope of keeping his secret was getting smaller with every rise and fall of the sun, as quickly as Tulo had transformed from a hard worker's paradise to an imprisoned nightmare. He hurt every time he used Genni to hide everything about himself.

Though, if she never found out, it wouldn't hurt her. Surely?

* * *

Ajay had always thought that Jaxson's place was like a blanket copy of Tulo Command. It had floor to ceiling glass windows that fell over the spectacular view of the City's Inner-Ring Park, where fox walkers and small children looked like small pinpoints on a much bigger map. Industrial steel shimmered and sparkled on the worktops, and the ladder that led up to the second-floor platform was decorated in fake green vines. As they were welcomed in, Ajay could see that Jaxson's bed sat on the upper platform and the white bedding was pristine, folded neatly with light-blue pillows placed thoughtfully on top.

"Blake's been anxious to see you all," Jaxson said as he took them through to the living room.

Ajay hadn't managed to make it over yet. He had been so wrapped up in himself, a friend trapped within four walls seemed to fall to the wayside. Those walls were suffocating, too – bleach white and clinical. Ajay imagined Blake felt the absence of colour strongly. The white sofa had been shifted to the side to make way for the borrowed hospital bed that was floating inside the room. Ajay felt his heart heavy in his chest when he saw Blake smile sweetly at him. He looked awful. The purple marks around his eyes tried to shine with a certain graciousness, but really, it was just pain. Mila and Pearl were already there, engaged in muffled conversation.

Ace nudged Ajay with his elbow. He was looking longingly at Mila.

"What d'ya think about Mila?" Ace asked, his voice lowered.

"What about her?" Ajay asked, drawing his eyes away from Blake.

"You know . . . What do you *think* about her?"

"Oh." Ajay paused. Is he joking? After all that's happened, he's still thinking about girls? Ajay was slightly taken aback by Ace's ignorance over the severity of the situation. Everything was about to change.

"She's . . . great."

Despite his short response, Ajay meant it. He thought very highly of Mila; sometimes he thought that out of everyone, she would be the only one who would understand why he'd done what he'd done. She might even help him get out of it.

"Yeah, she is!" Ace agreed. "She was saying how they've sent the androids back for development on her suggestion. The attack showed that they couldn't deal with crisis management and made things worse. I might ask her out. What do you think?"

"Pearl, darling, pass me my glasses." Blake's strained spirited voice vibrated across the walls.

Pearl walked slowly over to the white cabinet opposite the bed and picked up Blake's rounded specs. Blake placed them slowly onto his face. He lifted his arms up as he said, "Ace, Ajay! I can see you more clearly now. Get over here, you beauties."

"I'm coming. I'm coming," Ace insisted and laughed.

Something compassionate came over Ajay. He just did it. He reached out and grabbed Ace's arms and spoke with authority.

"I think you can't force yourself to love someone." That was probably the most truthful thing he'd said for years.

It was the most honest he'd ever been with Ace. It felt strangely nice to be authentic. Ace looked thoughtful and gave a small, resistant nod of the head. Ajay followed him to Blake's bedside.

"You're looking a bit worse for wear, my man," Ace said as he and Blake clapped hands.

"Oh, I'm not too bad, Acey." Blake looked over as rustles and movement came from the door. "Ah thanks, Jaxs, I was getting a little peckish." Blake chuckled as Jaxson placed a few vegetable-fried chips in Blake's hand before placing the bowl on the side. Ajay watched Pearl throw her hand into the bowl immediately.

"So, do you like it here Blake?" Ace asked.

"It's okay," Blake spoke through munching. "Very comfortable and much better than the chaotic sick place I would have been left in if lovely Jaxson hadn't offered to help me out." Ajay, still standing away from the bed, wondered if Blake was stabbing at his inadequacy as a friend compared to Jaxson, who had given up everything to help him. Ajay hadn't even bothered to call.

"Anyway, Ajay, darling. Where have *you* been?" Blake peered over his glasses and Ajay caved into himself, his suspicions confirmed whilst he edged closer to the bed. "Oh, I'm joking. Come here."

Ajay felt the chill of Blake's skin as he grabbed his hand to pull him closer to the side of the bed. Ajay looked over to Genni as she sat next to Pearl, and Jaxson ordered a large screen to spring to life. It spanned almost the entirety of the back wall. Blake's soft voice drew Ajay away.

"I want to thank you." Blake stared deep into Ajay's eyes, who felt saddened at the severity of Blake's facial bruising.

"Thank me?" Ajay questioned, taken aback and intrigued.

"If you hadn't moved us from behind that chalet, we'd all be dead." Blake was still, tears forming in his eyes. "And I have to be thankful for that. You're a leader, Ajay."

Ajay looked around. The room softened, even the white walls felt comforting. The girls were silent, Ace stared down at the ground and Jaxson worked through the silence by crunching on crisps. Ajay didn't know what to say. This man, a lively and passionate friend, was *grateful* to *him,* a liar and a hypocrite. But he'd only been those things because he had to be. To be Worthy. To be their friend in the first place. That was right, wasn't it? He held Blake's hand tightly in gratification for his words.

"Here, Ajay. Have a seat," Jaxson said as the scrapping of an armchair shook the tiles on the ground.

"Beer?" Jaxson said.

"No, I'm fine thanks Jaxs," Ajay said as he took the chair and held Blake's hand again. "So what's next for you, Blake?"

"What do you mean, what's next?" Blake exclaimed. "I'm back at work next week. Having no legs ain't slowing me down, darling." His notorious laugh loudly intruded into the commentary of a news reporter on screen, who was detailing yet more cancelled sporting and musical events. Ajay stared forward, lifeless.

"Don't look so worried, Ajay! I've got some merit compensation for the first few weeks, but it won't be enough," Blake sighed excitedly. "I can always get healthier but once you're Unworthy, that's what you are. You know how it works, Ajay. It's too hard to get back."

"Yeah . . . it is." Ajay looked down. A strange sense of anger rushed through him, but on looking up and seeing Blake thanking Jaxson for the drink he had brought up, laughing openly with him, Ajay convinced himself that maybe his friend would be okay. Maybe the trauma he'd been through would be exactly what he needed. But he was still fearful. Where would all this take him?

"Don't be scared for me, Ajay." Blake turned back to him. "I'll stay Worthy. Nothing a few boosts won't solve."

Blake smiled once more, but with a quiver in his lower lip that was clearly being forced down, unable to burst out in its full expression. Ajay also worked hard to mask his distress and turned to the screen, where a news reporter stood in front of The Glorified Quarters.

He realised this would be the first time anyone would see into The Quarters since that day. Well, other than those who lived or worked there. He'd been pretty annoyed when the new barricades had meant even volunteering was a no go. Did the streets still glisten or would they be forever marred by their troubled past? He assumed not when he finally saw the roof they'd put over the Quarters' walls. They towered behind the young, pretty news reporter wearing a light blue blouse. She was talking, but Ajay wasn't really listening. The walls didn't even look golden anymore; their magnificence was diminished by a domed, black roof. Ajay had read that only drones and authorised signals could travel through it. He didn't understand why Command thought they needed to protect the skies when the murderous sods had walked right through the front door. He felt pain ricochet through his gut at that thought. Command wasn't going to take any risks, and people like him might not have anywhere to hide. Yet not everyone is like him, he convinced himself. He certainly wasn't like Genni's obnoxious mother who complained about the sky going dark one afternoon, and then when the light was artificially restored, being distressed about ash and dust remaining on their balcony.

"They could have chosen a better colour," Blake complained. He clearly shared Ajay's dislike of the ugly roof. He noticed how the others disliked it too: Genni shifted uncomfortably; Pearl looked down at her wrist; Mila observed the sky above the park outside; and Ace and Jaxson kept their eyes focused on the scene as the news reporter announced the memorial service was about to begin.

The shot switched to a drone's camera inside the Quarters. Clearly, they wouldn't even let the press inside. Its main street was lined in its usual floral bloom and not a concrete block or speck of blood remained. The drone camera spiralled to show a floating stage in the front of the Command building and a petite woman standing on it. She was wearing the usual Command white attire – a white suit with a white Command branded shirt with a white tie. Her brown hair was tied back in a slick bun. Pursing her lips and looking up to her audience of millions, she held out her wrist and produced a screen from her Watch. Only when she was fully in focus did Ajay recognise her as Sandria, a presenter who led trivial debates on *YourVids* or the news.

"This is a different gig for her," Ace said to the room. "We're a long way from the Fox & Lynx debate now."

Ajay smirked, but not deliberately. He agreed that all Sandria's work did seem to revolve around insignificant topics such as the reasoning behind why merit deductions should be introduced for poorly manufactured pet foods. *A healthy pet is a healthy you.* That sort of joviality was gone; her tone and language were sombre as she started reading robotically from a script. Respectfully, Ajay noticed how they all stopped talking. He followed suit when they all looked to their wrists. He set his Watch to record. He may as well get the small merit for attendance.

* * *

"Progress is Strength. They will never be forgotten." Ajay and the others had bowed their heads at the closing of Sandria's speech. "And now we will have a two minute silence."

Ajay imagined what it was like outside as silence fell like a sheet over the entire City. The sky train, he assumed, had stopped moving and all drones and vehicles had been ordered to stop. As he thought about this, he also saw the faces of the 102 identified victims rolling one after the other on the screen. Jun's face appeared. The eyes that Ajay saw without any life shone with ambition next to an M-400 score. Ajay heard Genni's tears from across the room and watched as Mila held her hand. Then, as the scores got lower, the images got quicker. It was difficult to even see them as they soon flickered into nothing.

Ajay still saw him, though: the grey, messy beard and the bruised face.

Sam.

Ajay almost mouthed his name with his lips. He felt even more numb than he did before. Sam, the Glorified reject, died. Meritless and without love. Why was he even in the Quarters? Was he part of The Rogue? Trying to get in to sell or steal? As the commentary from the news reporter brought life back into the room, Ajay decided it didn't matter now, and he painfully detached himself from the Unworthy he once knew.

The group slowly came back from their silence and stillness, talking, moving and drinking as if they'd been turned off pause. Ajay was about to get some fresh air when Ace roared and pointed to the screen.

"You've got to be kidding me, it's Arneld Hevas!"

Chapter Forty-Two

Everyone looked back to the screen to see him. He was a man of small stature, wearing a Command white suit with a royal purple trim. Ajay admired how his blonde-tipped hair was puffed up with volume and his skin glowed with moisture. Looking into the camera, he craned his long neck, highlighting the skinny definition of his chin and cheekbones. Beginning his address to the City, his speaking voice sounded out of practice, but his eyes remained strong and focused.

"At Tulo Command, we believe it is imperative that our treasured citizens should be aware of our progress towards making our City safe again." Arneld spoke speedily, making Ajay wonder if his oblong shaped head might explode. "It is at this time that we want you all to know who committed this attack against us. They call themselves The Rogue." Ajay heard Blake's breathing quicken. He gulped down his own saliva. "The majority of their following are individuals who were once accredited citizens, or in some cases, come from the Side. They live by a distorted ideology that requires them to destroy those who are Worthy." Arneld's eyes were still keenly staring into the camera. "We are working endlessly to press down harder on protecting our City. In addition to the security measures already in place, we are now introducing the following laws . . ."

Ajay's wrist beeped loudly as his heart rate shot up. His hands were clammy and he could feel all motion in his legs freezing, so he was thankful he was sitting down. No one seemed to notice his Watch's interruption; all eyes and ears transfixed on the speaker.

"Our guards now have the right to raid anyone's home who is considered suspicious. Arrests will be made and trials conducted if evidence is unsatisfactory. Watch tampering checks will be intensified: they are now in place for all shops, sky train stations and drone transactions. Additionally, anyone suspected of having helped or facilitated unauthorised access into the City will be arrested and tried. If found guilty, you will be stripped of your merit and privileges, and any resistance will be dealt with. It saddens us to introduce such serious precautions, but we hope it will not be forever. We appreciate your support and cooperation at this difficult time." The vibrations of his final words barely reached the broadcast as he was cut off and the screen turned black. It was soon coloured with the news reporter returning, scrambling for what she should say next.

"Did they have to do that just after the remembrance?" Mila said as she picked up the empty crisp bowl and moved quickly to the kitchen.

"Yeah that was a dud time." Ace walked over behind Genni to stand by the window. He raised his chin, and Ajay watched the white sunlight fall over him. "And Arneld Hevas? Nobody's seen him for about a year." Ace crossed his arms and looked straight at Ajay. He shrugged his shoulders. No words came to him. He was going to get caught. All of this would be gone. Genni – he looked at her – would be gone. She didn't look okay.

Her eyes were fixed on the ground, but she was gripping forcefully to the arms of her chair. He could tell she was controlling her breathing with the deep rising and falling of her shoulders. He jumped up to sit next to her. Ajay stroked Genni's arm as both he and Pearl looked at her, concerned.

"Gen, what's up? I know it was a lot but we . . ."

"He's never going to go away, is he?" Genni said defiantly. There was a pause as Pearl and Ajay looked to each other lost as to the answer. Ajay hadn't taken the time to really listen to Genni about her run in with The Rogue the night of her accident. Despite feeling angry that she hadn't told him, he'd decided he didn't want to know about them, and whether Genni's encounter would reveal the true danger Ajay was in.

Genni spoke again. "Just when I think he's out of my head, out of my dreams, something comes up that gets him right back in there again. Today was meant to be about them, about Jun and all the others, but that ending announcement spat on them. It made everything about *him* and his dirty little friends." Genni put her head in her hands and groaned.

"Look, Gen," Pearl said bluntly across Ajay's torso, "we've all been through trauma, it's how we deal with it and help others that matters." She sighed. "At least you don't have a facial deformity that's costing you your job and your merit." Ajay observed the scar that ran from the right side of Pearl's lip to her inner cheek. It was impossible to completely mask with concealer. It was definitely unfortunate.

"You're going to be fine, Pearl," Genni said, sitting up again. Ajay continued holding her hand as the two ladies talked at either side of him.

"Am I?" Pearl asked, getting upset herself. Ajay knew he needed to intervene before the two of them ended up at each other's throats about whose trauma was the most detrimental. He didn't; his thoughts turned frantically back to Arneld's announcement. How can he live without ever scanning his Watch? Maybe he'd get away with it. Maybe The Rogue tampered their Watches differently and

Command wouldn't be looking for what he'd done. Perhaps he was safe.

"If I can't figure out how to stop people judging me for this thing . . ." Pearl pointed to the scarred lump. "Which stops them from listening to or liking my content, my main merit-maker and contribution to society is gone. What do I do then? Get a new job?" She was breathing through her words to hold back the tears. "You watch, people will see me Unworthy before the year is out. And I'll never be able to step foot into the Social Sphere again."

"You could still use your trauma, Pearl." Blake joined the conversation from his bed. Pearl looked at him quizzically, as did Genni. Ajay stared forward blankly; the conversation muffled around him.

"What do you mean?" Pearl said, as she lifted her perfectly manicured fingers to wipe away the small tears nested above her bottom eyelids.

"I just wonder if you could use your experience to create a whole new area of content." Blake went on to explain, "You said it yourself. Why don't you use what you've been through to help others? Help them feel more positive about their own trauma because you, an influencer, have been through a similar thing and are stronger for it."

Ajay turned to his left to see Genni smiling approvingly at Blake. Would she ever look at him like that again once she found out? Which, surely she would the next time Ajay tried to buy a drink or even get into his apartment. Would they initiate checks there too? They could even search his place. They'd find his equipment under his desk. Evidence, plain and simple.

"You mean, I should be honest?" Pearl asked.

"Well, yeah," Blake said.

Ajay squinted at Pearl then. He had never decided what he felt towards her; she was a bad mood swing, compassionate one minute, a liar the next. She perked up and said vibrantly, "That could really work, Blake!" She hopped up from her seat, moved towards Blake and kissed him on the cheek. "You're actually so clever. I could talk about my scar and how that really hurts my image, and oh, I could talk about the nightmares!"

"You've been having nightmares as well?" Genni asked. She'd been dreaming of him and The Rogue. Ajay hadn't asked for details when she'd mentioned it, but Genni was clearly surprised this was the first they'd heard about Pearl having dreams.

"No, but you have!" Pearl exclaimed. She danced around to face Genni. "What are they about, Gen? So I can use it."

Pearl smiled expectantly for Genni's approval. There was silence between them. "Genni?" Pearl questioned.

Genni grabbed her bag, and Ajay felt her angered grip on his hand. She sprang from her seat, taking him with her.

"I think it's time for us to go," she mumbled. They said their goodbyes and left, without another word said.

* * *

The yellow moon swept breathtakingly over the sky as Ajay and Genni walked hand in hand down the Inner-Ring streets away from Jaxson's flat.

"It's been nice to walk everywhere," Genni said lightly. Ajay smiled, but his feelings inside were dark and sombre. He could feel himself on the edge of a panic attack. *We have the right to raid anyone's home.* Arneld Hevas was ringing in his ears. *Arrests will be made.* He was a train heading for a wall. *Watch tempering checks will be intensified.* His life on track towards a solid brick wall. He would be nothing but crumpled steel and fire. *Every measure will be considered.*

There was nothing he could do. He would crash, hard and fast, with no surviving. But a niggling feeling kept him grounded. He'd *always* beat the system. Surely he could do it again?

"What do you think about what Pearl asked me?" Genni's voice penetrated through the chasm of his thoughts. A delivery drone swooped low from above, causing Ajay to duck slightly to avoid its delivery box scrapping his head. It was difficult to see them without the bright lights of many adverts, anti-Rogue messages not sparkling so much.

"What?" Ajay asked. He hadn't heard her.

"The nightmares."

"Oh." Ajay paused. "Were you surprised? She's always making stuff up for the channel." Ajay spotted a billboard above: *Notice anyone suspicious? Report it on your Watch.*

"I suppose." Her voice got louder. "I just don't want to talk about it."

Ajay turned to look at her face – so beautiful, so innocent. *Anyone suspected of having helped unauthorised access into the City.* He'd put her in danger too. He had to protect her by protecting himself. If he could only know more about Command's plans, maybe he could hack himself through.

"I agree the world shouldn't know about the root of your nightmares, but you can tell me," Ajay said bluntly. He was slightly taken aback by his sudden need for information, but as he looked at her, it felt right to know. If her small interaction with The Rogue could give him any sort of head start, he could stay here and look at her forever. Though, he was honest with himself: it wasn't just about Genni, but also everything else.

"What?" Genni looked up at Ajay, concerned and confused.

"I still don't know what really happened. I know he tried to grab you. But what did you talk about? What did he want?"

"Ajay, it's really hard to . . ." Genni said through a small whimper.

"Just try," Ajay said, as he stopped her in the street and held onto her shoulders softly. "Try, for me." Yes, for me, he thought. *So I can stay here, Worthy, with you.* She looked back at him lovingly, nodded her head, and took a deep breath and continued to walk.

"I don't remember everything, as I told you. But we were Downtown." Ajay listened intently. "And the memory is a little fuzzy, but he was talking about the Country. And asking about me."

"What do you mean?" Ajay asked.

"It was . . ." Genni paused. "I think, just stuff about me. Like my merit score and where I worked. He definitely asked me where I was born because I remember the deep, intimidating tone of his laugh when I told him. And I don't remember much more, other than when he grabbed me."

"He was asking about your identification?" Ajay's mouth felt dry.

"Yes, I suppose he was. He was certainly determined to find out everything about me." Ajay felt the physical drop of his heart within his chest. His worst fears confirmed. And what Genni said next would consolidate his theory.

"But Ajay, when he touched me and grabbed me . . ." Genni struggled through her words as tears found themselves dropping off the round edge of her chin. "It wasn't a touch that he was going to rape me, or kiss me, or anything like that." She took another breath. "It was a touch like . . . he was going to *kill me.*"

Ajay stopped walking, closed his eyes and pressed his fingers hard into his forehead. He felt them force themselves into his skin as if a hat were being fitted tighter and tighter around his scalp. He saw the moon across the vast horizon, speaking of the sheer extravagance of nature, and he felt the deep sorrow of his insignificance: everything he had built to be Worthy would soon be a mere news story or case file buried deep into the Command archive. He'd always known it. They'd done the same as him. The Rogue had chosen people to impersonate and presumably, based on what Genni had said, killed them to cover their tracks. Ajay had never asked who Ajay Ambers really was – whether the woman had just made him up or he actually existed somewhere. It had never mattered much to him, and either way, Ajay was safe to assume that Command was hunting for the very tampered code that sat on his own wrist. It was also a fair assumption to believe that if found out, he would instantly be considered as a member of The Rogue.

"What's wrong?" Genni was tugging on his right arm. "You look like a ghost." She was looking towards the moon, where Ajay was staring. "Ajay?"

Ajay felt the wetness of the tears falling down his dark skin, and he imagined that they made his face shine in the moonlight.

"I just . . ." Ajay was speechless, embarrassed to let her see him cry. "I just . . . I'm sorry he made you feel like that."

"Baby, hey. It's okay. I'm okay." Genni didn't hesitate to embrace him as he cried violently into her shoulder. "You're so tired. When was the last time you had a boost?"

Ajay felt the tender stroke of her fingers across his neck. He didn't answer; he clearly couldn't admit to not having had a boost in weeks. They were checking Watches there too. So he was silent, and they stood there; two crying lovers in the moonlight, soon to be broken apart.

Chapter Forty-Three

A week had passed since that night. Ajay had spent the last seven days in a spiral of paranoia. Every intercom chime sent him running for a window. Every noise in the corridor insisted that he spied through the peephole. Every TPD swarm flying past forced him to quickly cover his hacking equipment. Sitting at his desk, he considered the risk he was taking every time he bumped up his merit. But he had no choice.

After the announcement, and the increasing home raids and day-to-day arrests, he knew Command wouldn't stop there. *They'd stop at nothing to make Tulo safe again.* Something else was coming. He'd tried to find out what. Drilling down into news updates and networking with security geeks online had been a dead end. That wasn't the only thing sending him delusional, though, it was the lack of food and *SkipSleep* boosts. He was managing to scrooge food by staying at Genni's or inviting himself to Ace's for dinner.

Staring at his fridge, he couldn't believe he'd managed to keep Genni away from it, knowing she would immediately question its emptiness. He had to stop himself from thinking about how long he could keep this up before he got called out. *Find a solution.*

Ajay wandered sluggishly over to the dispenser, in desperate need of water. He was sweating, yet he couldn't be bothered to change out of his joggers, the hems of which were dragging across the concrete floor. Ajay knew he needed to get back to recognised productivity soon.

A sudden and unusual fall in merit would not be tolerated by anyone, especially not Mr Hollday.

Ajay sat on the sofa and placed his half-empty glass down on the coffee table next to the dormant *SkipSleep* port. He ensured his Watch came nowhere near that activation pad. Not that he hadn't been tempted. The withdrawal had been very real; the sweating and fatigue, the irritability and the nausea, and the headaches, all of which didn't help his anxiety. He'd run scenarios over his head about how he would explain it to Ace, about how he would say goodbye to Genni, and how or where he would end up. He imagined himself in a Command prison cell made mainly of impenetrable glass. He was always kneeling down, crying out in physical and mental agony, the only light he ever saw being a small spotlight of white sun that creeped its way through a slit in the prison roof.

Ajay always stopped thinking at that point. He usually diverted to searching on his Watch for Command updates, but there was never anything. Not a peep. Not since the remembrance. This led Ajay to believe he was safe, that maybe he could slip under the radar. Then, reality would hit him hard in the chest, he would grieve and start the entire thought cycle again. He'd be back in the prison.

But this time, on the sofa and alone in the apartment, the infinite motion of his uneasiness was interrupted by a call on his Watch.

Unknown calling. Ajay knew it was his father or his mother. He'd tapped them in as *Unknown* years ago and they hardly ever rang. They'd been ringing relentlessly since the attack and Ajay never answered. Only now did the thought occur to him that it could be about his grandma.

Maybe she'd died. In fact, she could have died months ago. *I'm such a selfish dick.* He sat up, looked around at the steel apartment door and then swiped to accept the call.

His father's bearded, rounded face sprung up in front of him.

"Son!" his father said with widened eyes. "You're alive!"

Ajay heard the screeches of his mother, who came running into the camera's view. Ajay was surprised to see her hair down. It made her prettier and concealed her developing wrinkles.

"Kar . . . Ajay . . . You're okay?" his mother said emotionally, moving herself as close as she could to the screen.

"Yes," Ajay breathed. "Is Grandma alive?" He just needed this information; he didn't plan to engage in any other conversation.

"Your grandma's doing okay. She was startled that day when she woke up and you were gone. We haven't told her about the attack-" His father was interrupted.

"Why have you been ringing me, then?"

"Well, it was an emergency. We didn't know if you were alive or dead. The attack . . ." his mother said softly.

"You've got news out there. I'm not on the list," Ajay objected. They'd broken their agreement. Don't call unless it's an emergency, and to be honest, his grandma in harm's way was the only thing he'd consider urgent. So, why had they called? It was dangerous for him. He didn't know what calls could be intercepted nowadays. Ajay felt himself getting angry. Already he was emotionally and physically exhausted. It was tipping him over the edge.

"There are still names missing, son. We needed to know you were okay," his father said sternly.

Ajay looked up at the apartment ceiling and through the window as he saw a drone carrying a box potentially double its weight, bobbing up and down slowly in the scorching heat. He reinstated eye contact with his parents.

"Karle." His father paused. "Ajay . . . Don't you think it's time to come home? Command is not going to let anyone slip through. You're in real danger."

His father looked at his mother, who was wiping tears slowly away from the edge of her cheekbones. "Just come home. Reverse whatever you did to your identity. Tell whoever helped you to keep quiet and no one will have to . . ."

Ajay thought of the mysterious woman from Downtown and the deal he'd made with her. He hadn't thought about her since that day in the Quarters when she'd slipped Ajay Ambers into his torn trouser pocket. A collage of memories ran through his head: the small, box room behind the pink curtain, the braid that fell over her right shoulder, her harsh voice and the Fo Doktrin he collected for her.

"How could I possibly come back? They've already cut off the line to the Side. And what would I do? I can't disappear. People will see me; they'll see me Unworthy."

Ajay shook his head and avoided eye contact again. In that moment, Ajay felt a shot of hopelessness drill itself deeply through his body and demonstrate itself physically through a stinging in his gunshot wound for the first time since its healing. As he looked again at his parents, he remembered their sorrow when he left; the image of them standing in the mint green kitchen alive in his mind. They hadn't moved from their spot as he'd opened the front door. His mother was being comforted by his grandma, and Ajay had never erased the memory of Tara with her arms wound tightly around their father's torso, dampening his t-shirt with her uncontrollable tears. In his despair, he no longer cared about distancing his emotions from the details of his family's lives. He briefly looked over to his desk and thought of the photo of Tara stuck to its underside, untouched for weeks.

He glared into his father's eyes and asked determinedly, "Where's Tara?"

His father sighed and his mother disappeared off the screen. "Tara's been gone a while," his father confirmed. "But the most important thing for now is for you to get out of there. However you became someone else, switch it . . ." His father continued blabbering, but Ajay became distracted by the shuffles of movement from the corridor. He jumped up, recognising the lightness of the footstep. He hadn't anticipated Genni's arrival. In his freight, he hung up the Watch without any form of goodbye. Just as he did so, the door slid open and Genni entered wearing a short blue t-shirt dress Ajay had never seen before. It was nice. She looked nice.

"Who were you talking to?" Genni asked.

"Just the office," Ajay thought fast. "I'm going in this afternoon." He walked towards her and kissed her lightly on the cheek before walking to the bedroom to imply he was going to get dressed.

"Oh, okay," Genni said, sounding disappointed. "Have you had a shower? You look a bit . . ." Genni paused. "Never mind. I was going to ask if you wanted to go to the library. Don't worry, I'll see if Pearl can make it." She leant against the kitchen worktop and swiped at her Watch as Ajay disappeared into his bedroom, slightly paranoid she might look in the fridge.

He could hear Pearl's muffled voice through the door as he shut it. With his mind spiralling once more, he walked slowly towards the wardrobe and donned a discreet long-sleeved top. He wasn't going to the office. In the seconds between hanging up the Watch and arriving at his bedroom, he had decided to take action to protect his fate.

Against all odds, his father's words had shown him how –
he needed to find the woman from behind the pink curtain.

* * *

The late afternoon sun was caught behind a small
whispering cloud, allowing for a dark shade to fall over
the Outer-Ring. Ajay felt the air get cooler, refreshing on
his perspiring body. His hair was laden with sweat and he
had patches on his armpits. He had never felt, or looked, so
disgusting. He didn't care – he needed to find her, and he
no longer had time to worry about appearances.

He approached the familiar market stalls as if he had
been there yesterday, yet something was different.
Everything was quiet. The stalls looked as if they'd been
ransacked. There were cardboard boxes upturned and
remains of product packaging strewn across the sidewalks.
A few TPD drones seemed to be patrolling the area. Ajay
walked through and noticed that the once flickering neon
lanterns had been punched out, the glass of their bulbs
on the ground. He looked around longingly whilst keeping
himself away from the TPD.

"You ought to come back tonight, lad."

Ajay twisted himself to his left to see a middle-aged
man wearing cargo shorts and a black t-shirt sitting on a
small plastic chair. He was slimly built, and the long length
of his legs exaggerated the way his hips were squashed
into the tiny width of the chair. Smoking a cigarette and
sitting next to an open packet of Tulo Choco Bites, he
stared at Ajay for a moment. His green eyes sat beneath
bushy unkempt eyebrows.

"I don't want to trade," Ajay said distractedly, as he
looked around for her. He focused on the curtain, which

he could see was tattered and worn. He remembered the table, the coffee machine and the hatch. It was all so vivid in his memory. Yet disappointment punched into his gut. She wasn't here.

The man's sinister laugh filled the air.

"You won't get much down that end, lad." He drew another drag and looked out for any drones before saying his next words. "The lot of them were cleaned out. Command finally got wind of what goes on. We are more discreet now." He stood up and stubbed out his cigarette.

The man walked towards Ajay, his sweaty stench becoming more obvious. He moved his mouth towards Ajay's ear. Ajay just stood still, anticipating something threatening. He clenched his fists, but the man only spoke.

"You look tired and like you need the merit. I can give you a boost, off-the-record." He looked into Ajay's eyes and raised his bushy eyebrows with invitation. Was this the guy, Ajay wondered, who Genni would come to? Who allowed her merit obsession to manifest in ways she never anticipated? Maybe he should get his fix, he thought. It had been so long. He was stronger than Genni, he could handle it. If he moderated it, he could feel alive again. Alive enough to get himself out of this mess. Soon enough the memory of the blue-green veins across Genni's face came back. Who knows what this guy puts in the shot? He had to think straight.

"No. I'm fine."

Ajay's refusal led the man to shrug and walk back to his plastic chair.

"There was a woman . . ." Ajay shouted after him, before lowering his voice and stepping closer. "There was a woman here. Years ago. She worked in security and . . ." Ajay whispered. "I imagine she sold you Fo Doktrin for what you do." The man stepped away from Ajay and nodded his head.

"I know her, yeah," he said as he lit up another cigarette. "But she ain't been around these parts for a long time. Like I say, those lot down there got their asses kicked out right after the attack." He flung his arm up in the direction of the pink curtain.

"Do you know where I might find her?" Ajay asked flippantly.

"I dunno," the man shrugged. "Don't suppose she would have given up that job at Command in a hurry. Unless she got caught, that is." His deep laugh vibrated down the length of the stalls but soon transformed into a solid husky cough that sounded painful.

"Thank you," Ajay said as he walked away, back towards the river and the bridge, wondering why he had just thanked a grimy drug dealer. Regardless, he had to get going. His time was getting shorter. He marched determinedly away from Downtown to begin his long walk across the City, to The Glorified Quarters.

* * *

His feet began to burn with a ferocity that made walking difficult. It was a pain Ajay had never experienced before. He reached the outskirts of the Inner-Ring and had quite a way to go yet. People were, as usual, dashing from one place to another, and his hobbling wasn't inviting the nicest looks. He hated that. He got himself out from the crowd and perched himself up against a wall. Ripping off his right trainer, he winced as his foot throbbed. He threw off his sock to reveal small, fluid-filled bumps colonising across the lining of his toes. Were these blisters?

It was often reported that athletes had blisters, but it wasn't a condition an everyday citizen suffered with.

Ajay knew he had to keep going. He saw an arguably clean tissue on the sidewalk, maybe dropped by someone rushing by. Don't do it, he thought. *Have you really come to this? Picking up litter to treat your wounds?* He swallowed his pride, grabbed it and folded it two ways. Then he lodged it between his foot and his sock. Starting to walk again, the pain didn't stop, but the padding seemed to alleviate it a little.

Ajay stopped again.

It wasn't the pain that made him.

Hevas had said it would happen and there'd been a few reports but he, and apparently everyone else around him who wore the same traumatised look on their faces, didn't truly believe it. The entire activity of the street had frozen in time, all to watch a real house raid happening before their very eyes.

Chapter Forty-Four

Ajay watched the sparks fly and fall beneath the drone as it lasered through the building's door. It was joined by men in their purple Command overalls, carrying guns and barging their way into the house. A man started screaming. A woman swearing. Ajay almost physically jumped as smashes and bangs filled the street. He noticed that those around him had started to move again, but slowly. It was as if they were all trying to ignore it, but it was impossible. There was no way to avoid listening to the trauma as Command pulled the house apart. Ajay stepped forward discreetly. It was probably a good thing to walk slowly anyway, given the exploding blisters over his toes. He decided he would casually walk past the Guard standing at the door, holding his gun as if it was as ordinary as a handbag. Ajay saw the growing black dots come from a distance. They grew into two more TPD drones who flew through the hole in the door. Ajay acted aloof, and soon he was limping beyond the house and onwards through the Inner-Ring. As he was walking away, the man stopped screaming, alongside a gunshot and the woman's shout of anguish.

* * *

It had taken him hours to get there. He'd staggered through the streets, whimpering occasionally from the pain in his feet and stopping now and then to relieve it. Ajay had also slowed himself down by hiding in alleys or doorways whenever he spotted a familiar face in the crowds. Explaining his limp, sweat, and refusal to use public transport would not have been easy. He wouldn't even have the energy to lie. His body felt numb with exhaustion.

Finally outside the Quarters, Ajay slopped himself against a wall a few metres from the Gate. His legs screamed from their aching and his head felt like a heavy-duty weight flopping on his neck. His breathing was heavy. He put his hand to his chest. Should his heart be beating so out of rhythm? It was slightly embarrassing how breathless he was. It was as if he'd never walked before. He reminded himself he hadn't. Not that far, and especially not in destroyed trainers; the left one's sole had ripped half off so it could flap up and down like it had a mouth. The thought occurred to Ajay that if this woman couldn't help him, he couldn't even buy himself a new pair. He'd have to convince Genni to buy them as a gift. That tactic wouldn't work forever, he knew that. Despite his breathing settling, his heartbeat remained fast and frantic.

This had to work. He had to find her. She had to walk out of those gates.

He looked towards the Quarters, which he barely recognised. Before, the golden walls would softly glimmer in the sunlight, and the Glorified Gate would stand strong with magnificence. Ajay couldn't even see the words 'Progress is Strength' on its archway anymore. All its sparkle was masked by the deep dark covering above its walls. It looked grotesque. He watched as two stale-faced Command Guards paced back and forth, cradling guns and accompanied by a drone each. What a demoralising job, Ajay thought, bet this isn't what they signed up for. Apparently, the security dome was only temporary, but as Ajay had thought before, a protective covering wasn't going to stop a group seemingly as determined as The Rogue. There must be a more aesthetically pleasing way to create a false sense of security for the Worthies inside. Ajay didn't know what that could be. Then again, he felt as if he didn't know anything anymore.

Hearing that gunshot silence a man had sent cold shivers up his spine. Command was killing? Maybe they weren't. They could have just knocked him out for being uncooperative. Ajay had battled with this for almost the entirety of the walk. As he leant his head back against the wall, he mulled it over again. They were raiding the house, that woman was swearing her head off, and the man was screaming with a sort of anger rather than pain, and then, bang. He was quiet. Ajay stopped himself from denying it any longer. He was dead. Command killed him. For resisting? For suspicious behaviour? Did they find something that linked them to The Rogue? The answers didn't really matter. Ajay felt the wetness of a small, light tear trickling down his left cheek. He noticed that his hands were shaking. He turned his head to see the guards continuing their patrol. If they were to question him right now, he didn't know if he would even be able to speak. The fear was paralytic. Command was going to kill him.

"Ajay!" The hard voice made Ajay jump and clench his fists.

Looking up, he saw a vehicle hovering in front of him, and the green, piercing eyes glaring at him above the black tinted window. He couldn't believe it. If ever he hadn't had the energy for Roderick Mansald, it was then. All of a sudden, the tear on Ajay's cheek, the sweat patches on his clothes and the brokenness of his shoe were the heaviest weights of all. Rod was an appearance man. It wouldn't go unnoticed. Ajay's desperation for the woman to appear was even stronger. If only she could walk through that

Gate, then he could make some excuse and run away from Rod's prying. Ajay glanced at the Gate. No luck.

"It's been a while." Rod smiled boastfully and waved his hand, ushering Ajay to step closer to the car. Ajay took a deep breath and managed to walk normally despite the still pulsating pain of his feet.

"I trust Genni is well. Haven't seen her at the parents' since just after the attack. She knows blood relatives over M-400 are allowed in, right?" Rod sniggered.

"She does know." Ajay instinctively tried to act casual and began swinging his right leg loosely, scraping the concrete with his foot. He cursed himself. How could he have forgotten about the blisters? He bit his lip to hide the pain.

"Those are a bit scuffed, Jay." Ajay felt vulnerable as Rod looked up and down his body. "What are you doing round here anyway?" Rod raised one of his evenly distributed eyebrows. Here it comes, Ajay thought fearfully. The questions. The prying. *Just breathe. Speak calmly.*

"Errr . . . I was just waiting to see if I could get the Village Manager. Get an update on when volunteering is back on. I just wandered over from work and these shoes are quite old and . . ." Ajay stopped himself from rambling.

"Okay. Well . . . okay." Rod looked around inside his vehicle and back at Ajay. "Things ticking over okay at Prosper, then?"

"Yeah. Yes, I mean a lot of people have struggled since . . ." Ajay was interrupted.

"Well, who hasn't? I've even had counselling," Rod admitted. "It hit me hard. How can that happen at an event I had a big responsibility in organising? What would people think of me? But I've come round to the fact that people don't blame me. I mean, they can't, can they? At least Command is finally putting those sods in their place." Rod smiled and placed his sunglasses back over his eyes. "Well,

I've got some business Downtown, so maybe see you around if I ever get an invite to yours or Genni's for dinner."

Rod didn't laugh or smile, but spoke coldly and told the vehicle to drive. The window faded back to black and it was gone before Ajay managed to conjure up the word goodbye. He just watched it float around the corner at speed and wondered what Rod could possibly have to do Downtown. He was a strange bloke, Ajay thought, but he didn't care enough to waste any more brain cells on him. He turned back to the Gate, leaning back against the wall, waiting for her to appear. Because he had to believe she would soon enough.

* * *

The dull illuminations of the propaganda adverts and the floating streetlights were reflecting off the white surface of the sidewalks. Ajay was slouched on the ground, looking like an Unworthy, after hours of watching people swipe out of the Gate, hopping in hover cars or running for the sky train. Finally, there she was. She came out in a wave of people. Ajay wasn't surprised that he'd managed to spot her. That notorious cream coat gave her nowhere to hide in amongst the greys and whites of others' Command attire. It was odd that only she seemed to break the dress code. Then again, Ajay remembered, she was hardly normal. She looked exactly the same as she did back then. A cold face with her long brown plait flopping over her right shoulder. As she got closer, Ajay could make out the distinctive clopping of her knee-high boots that skimmed the edge of her coat. She walked past him, and Ajay slid discreetly from the wall and followed her. His excitement was mounting. He didn't really know why. She might not have a solution to his impending death or exile, yet it was hope.

As he limped a few paces behind her, he could see wisps of thread sprouting out from the stitches of her coat. It was surely time for a new one, Ajay scoffed. She seemed to slow down and started to turn her head. Ajay acted on impulse. Even though he wanted to talk to her, he felt as if he shouldn't get caught. He jumped into the entrance of a resident building, guarded from the street by its protruding wall. After counting to twenty, Ajay decided he was probably safe and set out again in hot pursuit. Yet a strong force grabbed at his chest and dragged him back into the entrance, whacking his head against the glass sliding door.

"What you want, kid?" With his eyes closed, he could smell her breath. Tulo Ale. Undeniable. Edging open his eyes, he saw her face in detail. The developing wrinkles around her eyes made them look even fiercer, and he could see that grey hair was developing within her plait. Her menacing pupils burrowed into him and caused an immediate headache. The grip she had on his t-shirt and his skin underneath it was starting to sting.

"I . . . I need to talk to you," Ajay breathed heavily through his words. She let him go and Ajay coughed and bent down to get his breath back.

"Alright, but not here. Come on." She pulled on his right arm, causing him to hiss and wail in irritation. She stepped back in surprise.

"What's wrong with ya, kid?" she whispered as she supported Ajay's left side.

"I'v . . . got a healing gunshot wound," Ajay said, inhaling and exhaling slowly. "It's alright."

"The attack?" she asked. Ajay nodded and straightened up, still wincing. She sighed, put her hands into the pockets of her trench coat, slipped out from the entrance of the building and marched off. Ajay assumed that was an invitation to go with her. He staggered on.

A few moments later, she led him down a side alley. It was dark and narrow. Ajay instantly felt vulnerable, listening to the tapping of her heels echoing up the enclosing walls of the alley. He was reminded of how he imagined she might kill him when they were sitting in that Downtown room all those years ago. The pink curtain was his only way of escape. This time, it was the small entrance they'd come through, getting even further away. Like the small room, this alleyway was only lit by one small lantern. Maybe he'd prophesied his brutal murder when he'd first met her, all of it running up to this moment where she was going to turn around and clobber him repeatedly on the head. He wondered whether he should run as the claustrophobia started to grip at his breathing. Yet he reminded himself that the blisters pulsing on his feet would make running difficult, and if he was going to die, why not at the hands of a woman whom he'd never asked the name of?

The heels stopped as she loitered below the flickering light. Ajay's heart quickened. Ready for the first fatal hit. It never came. Ajay noticed that they were standing next to a grey door indented into the wall. The banging of her fist upon it vibrated down the alleyway. It was uncomfortable. He'd committed his fair share of criminal actions, yet it had been a long time since he was so far out of his element. He looked cautiously up and down the alleyway, but there was nothing to see other than the faint movement of people walking on the far away street. A faint grinding of metal seized his attention back to the opening door. He followed her through it.

The two of them entered into a small hallway lit by red neon lighting and dressed in white drapes along the walls. Ajay reached out to touch one of the drapes. Moist. The floor was sticky beneath his feet and there was a stale smell.

What was a place like this doing so near the Quarters? He felt even more anxious. The door shut. His heart thumped and his Watch vibrated. She disappeared down some concrete steps towards an unknown destination. He stepped forward. The red lights made everything even more sinister, like she was leading him to some gruelling torture chamber where she'd pull out his fingernails one by one. As soon as his foot landed on the first step, he heard music, and relaxed. Then the shouts and angered grunts came, and his whole body tensed once more.

"Come on, kid." Her gruff voice travelled up the stairs.

He held his breath with anticipation. The mouldy smell got worse as he moved himself down the stairs and into what was, to his surprise, a bar full of people. They were all squeezed around tables in front of a long bar, everyone looking towards the centralised attraction: a red roped boxing ring where two large men were jabbing at one another, grunting and sweating. Both were shirtless and Ajay noticed how one was wearing one golden hooped earring, adding to his hairy, wild appearance.

Ajay looked up. There were only spotlights and not one drone serving. It looked to have an old-fashioned 'order your drink at the bar' set up. Ajay had never done that before. Anyway, he wasn't thirsty. The hard metal music was giving him a headache. He needed to get out of there as soon as he could, but he still hadn't got what he needed. Information about how to avoid Command.

"Can we talk, then?" he asked her. She was snarling at the boxing ring as the earring brute floored the other man, cheers coming from the other tables.

"I'm gonna get myself a drink first," she shouted over the music at him. "Sit over there."

She grunted and pointed to a booth on the other side of the boxing ring. As she marched off to the bar, Ajay walked over to the table, but not without noticing the row of small locker-type cupboards that were built along the wall beside him. Above it floated a sign that read: *Watch Lockers.*

What was a Watch locker? Curiosity took hold of him. He peered into one of the glass fronted lockers. A Watch floated on what looked like an activation pad. He was startled by a loud dinging sound from behind. He turned to see two new men entering the ring, both bearded and much more muscular than the previous two. Looking towards the bar, he saw a woman with purple hair staring at him whilst rubbing a tea towel around the inside of a glass. He should sit down, he thought. With a glance back at the lockers, he soon found himself at the agreed seat and sat down, the sponge of the ripped upholstery touching his leg.

"Saw you checking out the lockers over there." She arrived, carrying two small glasses full of a clear liquid. Ajay smelt it instantly. Pure ethanol. She hissed as she took a sip.

"What are they?" Ajay asked. "I've never seen them before."

"Just an opportunity not to be judged for every move you make," she said. "And before you say it . . . the privacy setting doesn't always cut it. People who come here have some . . . let's say . . . grievings with the system." She was looking everywhere but at Ajay. She was avoiding the conversation.

She couldn't, Ajay thought. He shook his head; they had done enough procrastinating, so he just said it. "Look, this stuff with The Rogue."

She stayed silent, looking at Ajay, her eyes stern even though she was smirking. It sent Ajay cold inside, yet he continued talking.

"They claimed identities to get through the Gate. Like with my Watch. Swapping Karle for Ajay."

She still said nothing and just slurped another centimetre off her drink.

"I need to know if you can help me," Ajay barked out in frustration. "I can't live anymore. They're checking Watches everywhere. And it's obvious they're not going to stop with house raids. We're both in big trouble." He pointed at her and back at himself. "We're screwed if you don't do something."

She sat back in an overly relaxed manner and began stroking the rim of her glass with her fingers; her many silver rings tinted in the red glow of the bar. She'd grown ugly in her old age, Ajay thought. Exasperated by her demeanour, he shuffled uncomfortably in his seat. He tried to ignore the music and the inconsistent shouts from the boxing crowd. It was difficult. They grinded on him. His headache started to press more. She laughed. It cut through him, making him numb.

"What are you supposing I do, kid?" She leant forward.

"Give me admin access. I can see what I can do in terms of covering our tracks . . ."

"That ain't gonna help you."

Ajay sat back and threw his arms up, infuriated.

"Look, kid. *That* ain't gonna help you. I know it. And you have nothing to offer me now so I wouldn't give it to you anyway."

Ajay felt something rising within him, but he didn't feel angry. Only desperate. Really, really desperate. He spoke, trying to ignore the trembling of his lips.

"If I go down, you go down."

He moved closer, their faces almost touching. He could smell her ethanol coated breath.

"I'm already going down. I was done with this years ago and I have no cell in my body that gives a shit about you either. There is no help for you now, kid. No help." She moved his face away from his.

Ajay was silent for a moment as he watched her finish her drinks. No doubt she would soon be up to get another. Something wasn't right about what she just said. Did she know something he didn't?

"Why are you going down? What do you know? Have Command got a plan?" Ajay was excited by the possibility of information that he forgot to control his tongue. Who cares, he thought. She knows he's in anguish. Yet she still sniggered at him, drunkenly snarling her lip.

"Nah. A load of idiots, anyway. I'm gonna be spending me last days getting pissed up here, maybe I'll even get thumped up there." She flopped her arm towards the boxing ring, where two new contenders were stepping up. Ajay had heard that pure ethanol showed its effects quickly, but he had never expected like this. Tempted to indulge as an act of dismissal over his situation, he was looking at the empty glasses as she ungracefully slipped off her chair to head back to the bar, but she stopped. The sudden grip of her hand over his right ear made him yelp. She was crazy. Ethanol-drinking, wearing a coat in the desert, selling Fo Doktrin crazy. As he felt the warmth of her breath in his ear lobe, he wondered how he could ever have trusted her. Because he was desperate. He'd always been desperate.

"I'd get out of the City, kid. Or steal some fingers."

What in Tulo's sake does that mean? He cursed at her internally. Her laugh was deep, long and undeniably evil. It vibrated through Ajay's eardrums and induced a strong nausea in the pit of his stomach. Then she let go, turned away and, before Ajay could further contemplate the meaning of her words, she had gone. Ajay remained sitting there, staring into his hands, knowing there was little hope left.

Chapter Forty-Five

Ace calling.

Pulling his tired, depressed eyes away from the ceiling, Ajay limply swiped at his wrist and cleared his throat.

"Hello."

"What's this about you being close to death?" Ace's chirpy voice boomed through Ajay's earphones. Ajay drew a circle on his wrist to lower the volume.

"What?" Ajay spoke roughly. He wished that for once, Ace didn't sound so happy. His face was even worse. Beaming, his perfectly straight white teeth grinding on Ajay's misery.

"I can't see you? Turn your video on."

"No, thanks."

"Is it because you look tired? Genni said you haven't had a boost in weeks."

"Oh I just . . ." Ajay paused. "What is it you want? I'm busy," he said, looking around his apartment, littered in clothes and scraps of unappetising cupboard food.

"Doing what? You're not in the office?" Ace snapped. Ajay sensed a rising frustration in Ace's voice.

"I'm at home," Ajay spoke calmly and lied. "I'm working from here."

"Why?"

"Just felt like it."

"Then why is Hollday asking where you are?"

"Ah, he's probably forgotten. I did clear it with him last night."

"Right . . ." Ace paused. Ajay watched as Ace's eyebrows narrowed with suspicion. He knew he wasn't pulling this off. Ace, Genni, probably everyone, knew something was up.

"Ajay, if you're struggling, there's people you can talk to . . ."

"I'm fine."

"I haven't seen you in days, Genni said you've been avoiding her, and I've seen your merits dropping. I'm worried, mate."

Ajay didn't say anything.

"Well," Ace sighed. "You know where I am."

Ace disappeared into Ajay's wrist quickly, though his tone of disappointment still hung in the air. Ajay rubbed his head. Who did Ace think he was? He must have been stalking Ajay online, checking up on his score, which was rapidly falling. He had two days until the missed work penalty kicked in, and that would be it. The start of the end. He wondered what Hollday thought about him. The fact he was asking after him gave Ajay a strange feeling of pride; he'd obviously made enough impact for his boss to miss him, yet he was also miserable. He'd even contemplated the risk of scanning in from home, but he just couldn't do it. Leaning back on the sofa, he thought of the office and how he longed he could be there. It would be less lonely, even though the flurries of people never actually spoke about anything but work. Since leaving that boxing ring bar two days ago, he hadn't seen another person. He felt too fragile. If he were to see Genni, for example, he knew he'd crumble into a pathetic, weeping heap. He'd completely lost the rhythm of life. He didn't even know what day it was. It was like he was just waiting to die.

Ajay looked around at the tatters of his life: clothes were strewn everywhere, dirty pots with the remains of his out-of-date cupboard food sat on the worktops and tables. As he waited for death, or his arrest, he'd become a wild boar. If anyone were to see this, it would be mortifying. Tears started again. That was another thing, he couldn't stop sobbing. Every time he thought about Genni, he cried. Every time he read about increasing house raids and arrests, he shook and wept. He was utterly hopeless. Even Ace was worried about him. Ace, who never seemed to care much about anyone or anything but girls, work and training. Stop it, he thought. *Get a grip.*

He picked himself up off the sofa and marched towards the bathroom. He ran his hands under the tap that glowed blue at his touch and he splashed cold water across his face, allowing it to disguise his tears. Ajay looked up into his reflection and observed the plum rings around his eyes, confirmed to him by the mirror. It told him his skin moisture was below 20% of its optimal level and needed serious attention. His skin was tight across his cheekbones, dry and stretched, ready at any moment to crack. It was as if his body and mind had become a water balloon that had been growing for years – filling up with life and all its joy and aspiration; filling up with love, dedication, pleasure, and hard graft until it was too much. The pressure was mounting, and water was leaking as the balloon stretched and screamed for its skin to burst.

"You have to hold on," Ajay demanded of himself, looking sharply into his own eyes. "She knows something you don't," he whispered.

For the last few days, he had wished he could have recorded their conversation under the red neon lights and in between the sips of her ethanol. She'd said some stuff that Ajay couldn't let go. Firstly, she'd claimed she was already going down. Why? Was she involved? Had she confessed? If Command already knew about her hand in identity theft, she'd already have been arrested. Yet she was going to work and then staggering around in underground bars. Then there was the other thing. That he needed to 'steal some fingers'. After some time to his thoughts, Ajay had realised she was talking about the fingerprint authentication on the Watches, but what did that have to do with anything? He couldn't make sense of it. Then again, his brain was mush. He missed his old self. Intelligent, quick and respected. Now who was he? A hermit hiding in an apartment he'd soon not be Worthy enough for.

As he dragged himself back to the sofa, feeling the sweat of his legs on his joggers, he wondered about how he might find her again. He'd already been through this. Several times. He could go back to the Quarters and find her like before. Plead with her for the information. As soon as he'd imagined himself falling at her feet with desperation, he'd been repulsed by the thought. He didn't know her well, but well enough to know she'd laugh or even spit in his quivering face. He'd also been through the kidnapping scenario. That maybe he could catch her off guard, drag her to his apartment, and pull out every one of her teeth until she spoke. Or rip her greying plaited hair from her head. The more he'd thought about it, the darker it had got. As he stretched himself out over the leather seat, Ajay laughed out loud. Look at yourself, he thought. Covered head to toe in ungroomed hair, sweat and dried snot. He was in no mental position to pull that off. Not without getting caught and adding even more crime to his record.

So he would stay in his apartment and agonise over her words until he figured it out himself. There must be something. There must be.

As he stared back up at the ceiling to think, his wrist vibrated. He lazily lifted his arm before freezing completely for a second. He shook violently as he tapped at his Watch. His heart was beating fast and dropping in his chest.

There she was. On the news. Her cream coat, the greying plait, her menacing eyes, and that sardonic smile. The word WANTED ran beneath the picture. Ajay lost his breathing and panicked. She was on the run. He questioned whether he would soon be joining her.

Command have identified this woman as Lillie Trumin, a high-level Command security executive, proved to be a member of The Rogue and a key instigator in the Liberation Day attack. There is reason to believe she led multiple cases of identification theft that made the attack possible. If anyone has any information about her whereabouts, please contact Command Security. Merit and credit rewarded.

Ajay read the words over and over, trying to process it all detail by detail. Her name was Lillie? That can't have been right. It was too pretty, too precious, too gentle. Nothing like the woman she was. She was from The Rogue? Of course they had someone on the inside. That much had been obvious to him, and Command he supposed, for a while. Yet he'd never suspected her. Why? All the signs were there. She had him trade Fo Doktrin for anti-constitutional drugs, hung out in secret underground bars, and she happily helped a kid from the Side hack his way in.

Lillie hated the system, and hated Command. Ajay had just never seen it. He'd been too absorbed in what she could offer him.

He was damp with sweat, a puddle forming on the sofa. His hair felt wet as he tucked the left side behind his ear. Another thought occurred to him, one that made him desperate for fresh air. If they had *reason to believe* she'd changed people's identity, could they trace her actions back to him? Of course they could. Ajay said it himself to her in the bar.

"If I go down, you go down," he whispered to himself. Both their dirty deeds were interconnected. He was going down. It was over. All of it was over. *She* still could have warned him, the selfish Rogue-following crone. His body screamed inside despite only a small grunt escaping from Ajay's mouth. He wiped the sweat from his brow, knowing he needed air.

Dashing over to the window, he threw it open but the air was warm and muggy. He felt sick. Numb. Inconsolable with the pain of his unworthiness.

Then, as he was about to hurl out his insides, his wrist vibrated again. He didn't even think but just looked down.

Unknown: *I can get you out. Meet me.*

Unknown: *Inner-Ring 0647*

Ajay swallowed his vomit. A tiny essence of hope sneaked itself back in.

Chapter Forty-Six

"Look, I can do you a deal . . ." the street seller said.

"No thank you," Ajay said for the second time as he looked around him anxiously for any sign of Lillie. It was surely her who sent the message. She had changed her mind and was going to help him after all, not that he understood why. He didn't know what he thought, but he did know that this seller deserved a slap. He was relentless. The guy was small and skinny, wearing a dark blue jumpsuit with his product screens flying around his greasy haired head.

"Come on mate, this is a steal," he said, and tapped at one screen to expand the image of a remote-controlled vacuum cleaner.

"I don't want it. Leave me alone," Ajay bit at him. The seller looked insulted. What did he expect? Ajay had been standing here, looking intently into the swarming ebb and flow of the crowds, and the seller had just bombarded him. Very rude. He didn't care about being rude to him, though. He had much more pressing concerns than a robot cleaning his carpets. The seller stared at Ajay with stabbing eyes. Move on mate, Ajay thought. And he did, jumping on a woman in a lynx-skin t-shirt.

Where is she? Where is she? Ajay was incessantly tapping his right foot on the concrete pavement. Getting impatient, he looked back at his wrist.

Inner-Ring 0647

This was the right place. It was a typical Inner-Ring street lined with apartment buildings and new propaganda adverts. Ajay gazed over the one calling for more house raid volunteers. Crap, he thought. They're doing so many raids that they don't even have the resources? Surely drones could do that. Clearly not. Ajay breathed and dug his nails into the palms of his hands, nervous and yearning to see her. And then, he did see her. Just not the *her* who he was expecting to see.

She was standing gracefully across the street, wearing a yellow dress with a tuft of her straggly hair creeping out from under her hat. Their eyes met. She nodded her head. It must be a coincidence, he thought. It can't have been her message. Why would she be involved now? It had to have been Lillie. He would wait here. A moment passed, and he glanced back to where she'd been standing. Gone. Relieved, Ajay settled his shoulders and continued looking for Lillie and his escape route, or even, he wondered, a way to stay. He could still try and get that information from her and . . .

"It's rude to ignore people, boy."

Her voice and the heat of her body beside him made Ajay jump. He almost shouted with fright. She moved her face closer to him, the rough skin of her birthmark almost grazing his chin, unchanged since the day he lost Callum.

"Why are you here?" Ajay asked hesitantly.

"I can get you out," she said in that deep, coarse voice.

No, he thought. It *was* her. She was his only hope? A crazy, deranged woman he met as a child?

"Let's go," she said as she moved quickly back into the street, disappearing into the sea of people.

"Are you following me?" Ajay demanded as he bounded after her, barging into the shoulders of a small girl. He didn't have time to apologise, as who he was following was moving fast. For a moment in the civilian chaos, he couldn't see her, until the hum of a hover taxi swayed to a stop in front of her outstretched hand and Ajay ran towards her.

"Get in, then," she said, huffing through sharp deep breaths and opening the car door with a definitive flick of her wrist against its exterior. Ajay was obedient and slipped into the vehicle, which was completely leather upholstered inside with an activation pad on each of the two armrests. He kept his wrist away.

She joined him. Ajay stared at her. Just as he remembered, the birthmark covered the right side of her chin and neck. He couldn't recall if he'd seen it this close before. The few hard hairs that sprouted from it were repellent. Ajay assumed she still lived alone, and he looked away as the hover taxi set off towards whatever destination she had instructed.

"Hot today," she said with a hint of a smile and lifted her hat off her head to reveal her unbrushed hair. Ajay narrowed his eyebrows at how nonchalant she was being. He was on the brink of losing everything, she'd sent him a mysterious message and she was talking about the weather. He'd forgotten how odd she was. He felt like he did before when she'd cooked him that burger in a graceful, compassionate way, yet acted like he was a sour taste in her mouth.

He wasn't going to be polite. She needed to give him answers.

"Well?" he inquired forcefully.

She sighed and shrugged her shoulders. "I've not been following you. I've been looking out for you. Ever since you left my house that afternoon, Karle."

"Don't call me that. I'm Ajay now."

"Right. Of course," she grunted.

"So what do you want? You said you could help me?"

"I can. I can get you a safe passage back to the Side."

The car sprang into a tunnel. Ajay's eyes adjusted to the semi-darkness. He felt slightly nauseous as the small flickers of daylight through the tunnel's windows turned the car into a flashing disco. He breathed, disappointed. It was stupid of him. Despite the message saying it could get him out, he didn't want to leave, and was still holding on to the possibility to stay without getting arrested or killed.

"I don't think I want to get out," Ajay said quietly.

"I can't help you with that."

"Well what good are you then?" Ajay scoffed at her in frustration.

"I was good that time I hid you from those drones, and that time I helped your girl." The car spat out from the tunnel and as the car flooded with light, Ajay saw her right eyebrow rise suggestively.

"You?" he asked. "You carried Genni to my apartment? Why? Who even are you?"

"I'm a friend," she said simply.

"That's not answering the question."

Only the soft hum of the car filled the momentary silence as they stared at one another.

"Don't you think it's time you go home?" she finally said softly.

Ajay laughed and shook his head. He stared out the window at the City, not wanting to look at her. Why didn't she just tell him who she was? His thoughts turned dark again. There was no one else in this car. He could attack her right here in the back and no one would know. Maybe she'd stop toying with him then. He felt his fists clench.

"Your grandma said you'd be stubborn about it." Ajay relaxed his hands and whipped his head back to look at her. She was very relaxed, with one leg crossed over the other while she looked at her jaggedly cut fingernails as if she were waiting for something.

"You know . . ." Ajay paused.

"Your family? Yes. I know your grandma very well."

"So *they* told you to help me?"

"Of course they did. They're worried for you – you'll be caught. Especially with the next stage."

The next stage? Ajay couldn't allow himself to get angry at his grandma or his parents for employing a crazy woman to spy on him because *she* knew something. Something about Command's plans to protect the City. That's all that mattered to him. There must be a way he can get ahead of the game. Then again, how could he trust her? She was so perplexing. She worked in the Quarters, taught Glorified kids, yet lived further out in the Outer-Ring when she presumably had higher merit to live elsewhere. Ajay remembered her disorganised, repulsive home with a fox and children's drawings as wall art, and a supernatural ability to know things about Ajay without spending any time with him at all. Yet now he knew it wasn't supernatural. It was his grandma, and he did trust her. So perhaps this woman wasn't a psycho and told the truth, and therefore whatever he could get out of her could help him.

"Tell me." He grabbed her arm and could feel her silky, excess skin between his fingers. "It's about the fingerprints, right?" Ajay said defiantly.

"You're right. It is." Her brown eyes stared deeply at him. "Let go of my arm, please."

Ajay complied, but in his mind he was still gripping on tightly, determined to know everything. The car stopped abruptly, sending both their bodies lurching forward. Before Ajay recovered from bracing himself, his accomplice had already gone. He jumped out, taking a step back to avoid being windswept as the car departed. Relief.

She was standing on the sidewalk, waiting for him. Ajay saw the wrinkled texture of the skin on her pale legs, making him wonder how old she really was. Her eyes looked young, but the wrinkles, flappy skin and that repulsive birthmark confused things. Ajay reminded himself that her age was of no importance.

She started walking down the street, which Ajay didn't recognise. They must still be in the Inner-Ring, as the buildings looked clean and attractive. All nicely painted walls in tasteful whites and creams. There were still people coming and going and they all looked high merit. Ajay stopped himself from admiring or judging people's outfits by running after her.

"Hey . . ." He skipped his long legs to catch her, almost grabbing her arm again but opting not to. "Where are you going?"

No answer. She kept walking forwards, as if she were trying to blend in and not bring attention to herself.

"Tell me what you know," Ajay continued to squawk in her ear. "What are Command going to do?"

Nothing. Absolutely nothing. He felt like he was talking to the air. Anger and frustration started to spew up inside him as they walked alongside the Inner-Ring's river, its artificial blueness reflecting off the white buildings. Just as Ajay thought he might spit at her, or worse, hit her hard, they approached a small house on the river's edge.

"In here," she said, holding the creaking door open for him and ushering him in quickly.

The small house was no bigger than an average size bathroom. The walls were empty. Some were still bare brick. There was nothing in there at all. Ajay felt sweat instantly puddle across his back. It was painfully hot and enclosed. She disappeared through a small door. This is ridiculous, he thought. Why was she doing this, leading him around on some strange treasure hunt? Is there some sort of test he's meant to pass and then she'll talk? Ajay considered walking away. He was bigger than her little games, but instinct led him through the door.

"What are we doing here?" Ajay shouted, spittle in between his teeth.

She was bent down, unbolting a padlock with a rusting old key. Ajay noticed an outdated Watch scanner to the right of another door, covered with grime and cobwebs. Yet she battled with the key, totally inconvenient compared with a swipe, Ajay thought. She heaved open the grey industrial door that crunched as its heaviness echoed down the dark steps that Ajay could see behind it.

"Almost there," she laughed slightly. That really sent Ajay over the edge.

"Don't laugh. Where are we? Just tell me what Command are doing!"

"I will. Down here," she said as the sound of her feet vibrated on the steps behind the door.

Ajay breathed heavily. *If she doesn't tell me soon, I'll kill her.* It scared him how much he meant it. He'd been driven into some dark, twisted reality where he'd actually murder someone out of frustration and fear.

He needed to find a way to keep it. The City. Genni. All of it. Yet it had been dead end after dead end, and if this were another, he'd have to kill something. He fell silent as they descended further down the steps, barely lit by repetitive nightlights. He walked under an old arch that read 'River House'.

Suddenly the space opened into a huge room alive with blue light. Ajay was both disturbed and awestruck. He held his breath. What was this? The creaking of the outside walls caused him to look up and find the river was moving above him. No, he thought. They were underwater. He stared at the hard glass above him, the only thing stopping the violent water from flooding in. He looked around: solid steel walls, held together by strong yet rusty looking steel bolts; four booths built into the far wall, each with blue padded benches and a table nailed in its middle; and a small window with blue velvet curtains that looked out to the river. A bar, he thought. It was confirmed to him as he saw the long bar at the end of the room, covered in cardboard boxes. It must have been completely abandoned. He noticed that the walls were littered on every side with photos, drawings, and wall art. When Ajay finally breathed, he coughed at the musty smell.

"What is . . . this place?" he said without knowing where she was standing. He turned around and saw her by some sofas accompanied by a circular rug in the middle of the room. She was looking longingly at some photos on the wall. Ajay stepped closer. All the photos were taken in this room. He briefly scanned the groups of people smiling, laughing, arms around one another.

"It was an underwater bar," she said calmly. "Before the accident – they went out of fashion after that." Ajay had heard talk of a river accident from years ago, but had never paid much attention. "We met here before the attack. We're being more careful now."

Ajay narrowed his eyes. Her dress looked green under the blue tinged light and her birthmark looked less sore.

"Who's we?" he asked.

"Those in the City who follow The Guiding Light."

Ajay didn't say anything. His brain felt as if it had disappeared, unable to process what she said. He must have misheard her.

"What did you say?"

"The Guiding Light. It's here in the City. Look." She pointed behind him.

He turned around. He saw it then. Perhaps his subconscious had filtered it out at first. Just behind the bar, tall shelves once filled with weak liquor had been filled with *them*. Rows and rows of them. The hologram of his childhood.

Ajay didn't understand it. How had they kept them here? Completely out of sight. Hidden.

"How did . . . " He paused. *Stop it*. This isn't the most important question, he reminded himself. *Think about Genni. City. Merit. Everything*. He turned back to her, who was sitting down in a large blue armchair.

"Tell me what you know about Command." Ajay towered over her, and felt himself expand his chest, in a hope to look threatening.

"Sit down, boy."

"No, I'm fine here . . . Tell me."

"Fine. But I really think it's better if you just go home."

"I don't."

"Yes you've made that clear." She paused and looked up at him with authority. "Sit down please."

"Fine." Ajay said as he fell into the chair next to him, the large cushion taking his weight with ease.

"I suspect a new model of Watch."

Finally, he thought. This was it. No more dead ends. He listened to her voice in rhythm with the moving river above them.

"A model that considers the security oversight Command has missed for all these years. Our fingerprints won't just be for device operation but for device activation. The identification on the Watch and the fingerprint must match with their database, so you using Karle's fingerprints with Ajay's identity will be impossible."

"Is that right? You know that for sure?" A few moments passed until she spoke. Ajay felt like throttling her again.

"I believe so, yes."

Ajay spoke impulsively, not having much dignity left to care about. "So they're going to call for upgrades? New initiations? What?"

"That, I don't know."

"But if-" Ajay paused to think but was stopped by her deep voice.

"You can't stop it. You can try, but the path of the City always leads to destruction . . ."

"Don't." Ajay interrupted as he heard the words. This couldn't happen. He didn't want to hear that. Those words, and all the memories behind them only reminded him of the family he'd left. The grandma and sister he'd left. He had to be strong to protect Ajay Ambers. He was smart, charming, M-480 and loved by many. That is who he was. Not Karle Blythefen. Limited, weak, M-nothing and forgettable. Ajay stood up and spoke with defiance.

"I went most of my life with that Guiding Light stuff going in one ear and out the other. It's not for me. It's not Worthy. So if you're meant to protect me, how long until Command brings in the new models? How much time have I got?" Ajay was half-inclined to fall to his knees with every sincere cell in his body and plead with her until she gave him the answer. He didn't. He'd learnt to ignore his Karle impulses.

"There's nothing more I can do for you," she replied calmly. She swirled her hat around in her dry-skinned hands and twisted it in one smooth motion to place it back on her quirky head.

Standing, she wandered over to one of the booths and handled a small silver tin. She opened it and shoved a single plain biscuit in her mouth.

"Want one?"

"No," Ajay said. It was time to go. He hesitated slightly, distracted by the disgusting crunch of her biscuits and then the squeaking of the pressurised walls.

Then something occurred to him and he moved quickly. The chair beneath him nearly toppled with the speed of which he left it. He had a plan to buy him time. He would head home, break open his Watch and attempt to delete its existence. Command wouldn't send a new model or ask him to attend an initiation if they didn't know his device was there. It might not work. It wasn't a complete solution. But it was something.

Ajay ran away without looking back. He hadn't even noticed his sister's beaming, but matured face splattered across the photos that hung on the wall.

Chapter Forty-Seven

Across the City, Genni found herself inside another dream. Not a nightmare or a paradise, but somewhere in between.

She was floating inside a beautiful garden. Green vines ran down both sides; flowers burst with colour, pinks, yellows and reds. The sound of water trickled, and a slight breeze cooled her skin. Genni reached out to touch a rosebud. Before she felt the fragility of its petals, the pink bud arose and sailed towards her hand, deciding to gracefully hover there. Genni brought her hand closer to her nose and smelt its fine fragrance. Strong yet delicate. She went to walk but as she looked down, she realised her feet weren't touching the ground. Floating along, rose in hand, she found a waterfall much like the one in her painting. The water descended down a freestanding rock face. Droplets flicked from the fall and wet the surrounding vines and bushes. Genni felt water spray on her nose. She looked back to her hand. The rose was gone. She looked back to its original bush; buds and petals were now strewn across the path and its bush had been ripped apart. It had turned a solemn grey. The rest of the garden still bloomed with life. A bird tweeted. Trees swayed. All was peaceful and calm, until she felt a rush of movement behind her. She spun around. Nothing there, but another destroyed flowerbed, now also grey. She turned back to the waterfall, where a sudden mesh of lights materialised from its stream. A dancing body of illumination. It was floating to the other side of the garden. Genni walked towards it, now mesmerised and called by its light. It didn't move, but Genni jumped back as a small fox appeared in front of her. A tiny, strawberry red fox. It floated too, with a cunning look in its eyes. Dashing off, it moved in floating somersaults towards some green vines. It ripped them down quickly and ferociously. The green faded from their leaves and became grey. Genni now saw what she missed before. She stepped back, moving away from the body of light, watching as dozens of floating little foxes ran across the garden. Spoiling everything. Until it was all grey.

Genni opened her eyes. She sprung out of bed, never needing much time to ground herself back to reality. That was strange. Little foxes in a beautiful garden and a dancing body of lights? She rubbed her hair with a flat hand to straighten it down, and quickly remastered her make-up in the mirror. The green mist told her that her pores were healthy. As she finished, she realised. That was the first time she'd dreamt where *he* hadn't been there. Ever since the attack, the man she'd met from The Rogue had haunted her from beyond the grave. Well, she hoped it was beyond the grave, that Command had done their job right. Sometimes, the dreams had been a pretty accurate reliving of the attack but instead of him shooting Jun, it was Ajay. Other times, she'd dreamt that he was in her apartment, standing by her bed, his huge muscular frame dark and foreboding in the nightlight. One time, she'd just been falling. Forever falling in some darkness where his face was all she could see.

This dream was different. He wasn't there. She wasn't terrified, and in some ways, she'd slept soundly. Whipping off her grey t-shirt that hung loosely over her knickers, she moved simultaneously to her wardrobe, her mind still fixed on dreams. Even though her sleeping sessions were only ever a maximum of two hours long, her brain still seemed to tell her so much. No one else had dreams. If they did, they never talked about them. There wasn't even much research about them in the library. She once mentioned it to Mila and she claimed to have never had one. Genni quickly threw on a mint green flowy dress, and the wardrobe approved. Just about ready to go, she lobbed her handbag over her shoulder and marched to the kitchen to grab a glass of water; it was refreshing as it flowed down her throat. For a brief moment, she leant against the kitchen worktop and looked over to the sofa and her waterfall painting that hung above it. That came from a dream. It was in *this* dream, too, in that delightful garden.

Genni stood up straight and checked her Watch. A message from Ace. She looked at the clock first. 8.33pm. She had time. Going back to the office an hour later wouldn't matter, as she'd only slept for one. Excited, she dashed to her easel that stood empty by the window. She sat a blank canvas on it. Briefly looking out to the river running beside her flat, the question of the office came back to her. Should she paint now? Work has been going well lately. Despite the attack and Jun's death, Mafi had even started asking for Genni's opinion now. Though, part of her no longer cared. Her previous frustrations about the impact she'd made towards the project or the credit and merit she earnt, or how much she belonged in the beauty industry, no longer seemed to matter. They did matter, she reminded herself, but just, not as much. Especially in that moment – she couldn't pull her thoughts away from the garden and the foxes. She had to paint it.

She wrapped an apron around herself to protect her dress and began sharpening her pencil, her thoughts turning to Ajay. The attack had affected him more than any of them. Of course, they all had their baggage, but he had become completely disjointed. The way he'd sobbed into her shoulder the night of the memorial was bizarre. Genni was pleased he could be so vulnerable with her, but she didn't know what to do with it. He was usually so emotionally closed. She leant forward and softly began to sketch an outline of the first rose bush. As she drew, she thought again of how recently Ajay had been so unfriendly and harsh, speaking to her as if she was an Unworthy. He was clearly irritable, and suggesting behaviours of *SkipSleep* withdrawal, so he probably didn't mean it. She knew that, but it still hurt. Then, every time she was planning to call him out on it, he'd turn up at the door or pop up on her wrist, and they'd have dinner at hers. Serious mood swings. Though, it had been nice to spend more time here. With her paintings now all over the walls, she wondered whether Ajay liked seeing them. Soon, he would be distant again. He'd been off work for a few days, too, which was really out of character.

The message from Ace told her that Ajay sounded off on a call. What was wrong with him? Why wasn't he having boosts? She'd have to go round later, if she had time. Genni yawned, stretched her arms and looked over the first sketch of the rose bud. It was pleasing. Re-sharpening her pencil, she turned her head towards the many paint bottles on the table beside her. She would mix them to make a very deep pink for the roses. Not a baby pink but a very stark, breathtaking pink. The foxes too would carry their crisp red colour. She got back to work on the canvas. Maybe Ajay was jealous about her recovery, Genni thought. She'd always wondered if he resented her for it. When she overdosed, he sacrificed a lot of merit-making time and now she was the one doing better. Especially with the social merit. It was never very much, but she knew her paintings had an audience. This one would be popular with the fox-owners. Perhaps Ajay was distant because of his arrogance to admit that he was wrong about that. Genni sighed; she had no idea. He'd be alright. Though, maybe she should call him.

Before she could action the thought and as a vine was partially stretched, her wrist vibrated.

> **Mafi (Work):** *Genni, are you coming in soon? Last-minute sales meeting. I need your thoughts and input. Starting at 9pm. See you there.*

Her manager needed her 'thoughts and input'. Genni smiled. That was nice, though she was disappointed not to get very far with her painting. She could finish it later, not being at risk of forgetting the details. Setting down her pencil, she lightly stroked the canvas with her hand as if to tell it she'd be back later. Then, jumping up and swiftly grabbing her handbag, the canvas was left, soon to be home to those mischievous foxes and that dancing ball of light.

Chapter Forty-Eight

Ajay rushed through his apartment door, almost colliding with the breakfast table as he lost his footing. Running over to his desk, he fumbled over clothes and packets on the floor. He swung into his chair and tucked his fingers under his desk. Gathering the long, black cable out of its hiding spot, his nails fringed the photo of young Tara, still stuck down with tape. After fiddling to connect the cable to his Watch, he commanded his four screens to appear. Time to get . . .

The sound of the toilet flushing. Movement from the bathroom. *Who. Is. That?* For about half a millisecond, Ajay paused, confused with reality. Was there actually someone in his apartment, or was he just hearing things?

"Ajay?"

Ace's deep voice travelled through the walls. Nope. It was real.

Ajay's hands moved like lightning and his heart rattled around inside him. Panting, he yanked the wire from his Watch and shoved it back beneath the table, but not without sending the Watch spiralling onto the floor. There wasn't time to close the screens, as Ace stood in front of him. Don't close them straight away, he thought, do it casually during the conversation. Despite trying to convince himself that he was in complete control, Ajay felt riddled with panic. Ace's face was inches away from a command window that displayed the internal workings of his Watch. He'd get through it, though, if he just stayed calm. That's if

Ace didn't pick up on the horrendous sweating and deep panting Ajay had going on at that moment. That would be alright if he just breathed deep, and it was always hot, so the sweat shouldn't raise any alarms.

Everything was completely fine.

"Ace . . ." Ajay smiled. "What are you doing here?"

"I came to see if you were . . . alright." Ace frowned, with confusion in his eyes. "What are you doing?"

"Nothing, just work stuff." He tried to disguise his heavy breathing by clearing his throat.

"You've just come in?" Ace said, as he started to walk around the desk towards Ajay and the open code on the screen. *Crap*, Ajay thought. *He's coming. Turn it off.* Ajay leant forward in what he thought to be a relaxed way. He lifted his arm fast, but Ace was quicker. The grasp of Ace's hand around Ajay's wrist was sharp and firm. The screens stayed where they were, and Ace had a full view.

Ajay's heart stopped and clunked down into his stomach like a heavy weight. As Ace spoke, his voice sat on Ajay's eardrums, vibrating pangs of uneasiness through his body. Ajay felt his heart beating fast to the rhythm of his disbelief that Ace was seeing this – that this was actually, really happening.

"Ajay? What is this?"

Ajay didn't say anything. Everything became a glazed and misted vision he wanted to repress. He imagined he'd gone deadly pale with shock.

Then the adrenaline seemed to subside. He looked up at Ace's questioning eyes and observed him properly for the first time since he'd emerged from the bathroom. He was wearing his smart, khaki trousers that made him look suave, and to Ajay's distaste, his head was freshly shaven.

"Here." Ace calmly gave Ajay his Watch back, which, he must have picked up off the floor. Ajay took it and rolled it in his hands, feeling the weight of Ace's presence behind him. "Why was your Watch down there?"

Ajay stayed quiet.

"Ajay? What's going on?" Ace sounded frustrated. Rightly so. If Ajay were in his position, he'd have wanted to hit him for his silence.

"I . . . erm . . . " He stroked his head in his struggle to communicate. "Work asked me to have a look at some . . . erm . . . " He couldn't think. There was no lie good enough. Ace could see it.

"Don't lie to me," Ace insisted. "You've been off the radar for days. Missing work, merit falling, avoiding me and Genni. I was worried and now you show up, sweating, and with some . . . " He peered closer to the screen. "Wait . . . "

Ajay lost his breath, as he knew Ace didn't recognise the code. It wasn't particularly difficult, Command's logo was right there, on the Watch's interface, crafted together in green font.

Ace shook his head. "This ain't to do with work, mate." He held his arms out wide, shrugging his shoulders with body language that was pleading for the truth. Ajay began to lose control, he felt his breathing falter, his fingers tingle and dizziness set in. He began to wobble sideways out of his seat, but Ace was there to catch him.

"Woah," Ace cried out, as Ajay felt the warmth of his arms support his back. "Come on, mate. Sit down." He guided him over to the sofa. "I'll get you a drink."

Ace walked towards the kitchen, but not without looking back confused at Ajay, who could feel all the blood rushing from his face; he must look completely washed out. By the time Ace returned, he had regained the ability to think and could feel the saliva in his mouth regenerating. He took the water from Ace and gulped the pint down almost in one.

"Thanks," he said as he wiped his mouth. This was the moment where he had to tell him, where he had to trust him.

Ace sat next to him. He placed one arm on Ajay's back and tapped it lightly twice. "So, are you going to . . ."

"Tell you the truth?" Ajay asked. "Yeah, I am." He took a deep breath, probably one of the biggest breaths he'd ever taken, hoping that he wasn't wrong about his friend – that he would have his back, Worthy or Unworthy.

"I'm not Ajay Ambers. My real name's Karle Blythefen. And I was born on the Side."

Chapter Forty-Nine

An hour or so passed as Ajay walked with Ace along the high street of his childhood, along the track of his adolescent rebellion, and across the white walkway of his fabricated life in the City. He included everything – his family, Callum, birthmark woman, Lillie, the Fo Doktrin, and where he and Genni fitted in within the timeline of his transformation. Until he came to the end.

". . . and now, I've got to figure out a way to bypass this new model. I don't know for sure that's Command's plan but if my Watch doesn't exist, it'll buy me time."

Ajay was very aware that Ace hadn't spoken for the entirety of his storytelling. Nor had he looked at him. Not once. Ajay thought about how he'd been the perfect companion through this life: popular, funny, and often so chilled out that he rarely noticed anything untoward. He was also remarkably resilient. As was Genni. Anything slightly difficult, they both bounced back stronger than before, ready to take on the world and all its merit-making joyfulness. It was the Glorified upbringing. Ajay knew that. He'd had to train himself not to be vulnerable or show any weakness; Ace had been taught it straight out the womb. Ajay was reminded of when Ace had told him about his M-290 fling. How hard that was for Ace, and even after that day, they never spoke of it again. Perhaps he was embarrassed. It occurred to Ajay how stupid he was. Why would he bother telling Ace all this? He wasn't going to help him. He wouldn't even risk his status for the perfect girl, and he'd been through enough of them to know that she was hard to find. There was no way he'd help protect an Unworthy bypass Command. But Ajay wasn't an Unworthy, he reminded himself.

He was his best friend. That should count for something. Shouldn't it?

At last, Ace spoke in a surprisingly calm and controlled voice as he rubbed his large fingers over his high-arching forehead. "This makes so much sense."

Ace rose from the sofa and walked slowly across the rug, flicking some sand from his boots between its fibres.

"I mean, you've always been nervous about the TPD. I've never understood that, I thought you were just soft." Ace looked around the apartment, chewing his tongue. That's what Ace did when he was thinking. Ajay had never told him how ugly it made him look. "And you never have drones in here. Then, that time you went to the Side and said it was because of the fire? I knew that was off." Ace sat back down on the sofa and stopped chewing.

"This is so mental," he said quietly. "You haven't been eating, have you? You can't buy anything."

Ajay nodded. "I've got what I could through Genni."

There was silence then. Ajay didn't know what Ace was thinking. He was a little unnerved about how calmly Ace had reacted. It was as if someone measured and rational had been transfigured into Ace's body, replacing his reactive and explosive personality. Ajay would do anything to get inside his head. Just to know his next move. Maybe he was conflicted between reporting him, helping him, or staying quiet and letting Ajay crack on. Perhaps it wasn't the worst thing to tell him. To continue in the City, minus the slight complication of the new Watch model, with someone knowing the secret would be liberating.

"Shit." Ace's skin was reddening, and his eyes were building with fury as he looked at Ajay. He almost whispered, as his mouth started to quiver. "They're going to think we were involved."

Ajay's entire body slumped with sadness. A sadness that was always there, because it was always over, the moment he opened his mouth and told his story. Once someone knew the secret, there was no recovery. No forgiveness.

Ace stared right into Ajay's eyes, who felt their power rip through him. His voice grew louder.

"How could you do this to me? To Genni? We're now part of your game. You've put us in danger of fraternising with an illegal Unworthy," Ace said, his voice rippling around the room and piercing Ajay's ears.

"I know. I'm sorry." Ajay stood slowly. "I never expected to be in this deep."

"Well, what did you expect?" Ace threw his arms up defiantly. "That you'd just come here and be a loner, and not fall in love? Not have a best friend? Not have a life? This was always going to get others involved." Ajay didn't know if Ace expected a comeback. He didn't have one. Ace huffed some more and paced furiously towards the windows.

"Why didn't you just wait?" Ace said calmly but with a frustrated tone.

"Wait?" Ajay asked for clarification. He lowered himself slowly to sit back on the sofa.

Ace lifted a finger to his eye; Ajay couldn't confirm if he was crying or had an itch. It was surely an itch. Ace was too strong for tears.

"You could have waited. Served the Glorified and then applied for Purification? Would have been a lot simpler and you wouldn't have broken the law. You wouldn't have violated . . ."

"Would you have wanted to wait?" Ajay asked quickly. "And anyway, it's not like Purification solves the problem, we all know it's nonsense. They're still hated."

"That doesn't matter. That's how things are, but what you did was completely insane."

"To be honest, if it was insane, it was surprisingly easy. It's no wonder what happened on Liberation Day happened. The measures they're putting in now should have been done from the start. It was as if they wanted people to invade. There's so much more going on than Command knows."

Ace stood right in front of the sofa and spoke flippantly. "What does that mean?"

"Nothing," Ajay said, and it was soon clear that Ace was deep in thought about something else.

Ace lowered his arm and had both hands on his hips, his concentration face stronger than ever. "I've got to report you," Ace mumbled through his breath, but loud enough so Ajay could hear. Ace moved swiftly towards the apartment door.

Ajay dashed from the sofa to catch Ace's arm. "What?" Ajay could feel his eyes bursting from his sockets as he gazed over Ace's unwavering face. "You'd do that to me?" he said, anguish moving through his words.

"You said it yourself, you're just like The Rogue. You did what they did. If they think I helped you, they'll strip me of my merit. You've seen what's happening out there." Ace tapped Ajay forcefully in the chest with his finger. He turned back to the door.

Ajay grabbed him again. "With the Watch. I'm like them with the Watch. I didn't go around killing people. I've contributed just as much to this society as any Glorified kid. I'm climbing the ladder. My merit score shows it," he exclaimed.

The apartment echoed with the sound of Ace's cackling laugh. "Your merit score isn't even real," he said.

The two men stood, looking each other in the eyes and witnessing each other's emotions – anger, pain and devastation – until Ace said, "I've got to go. They have to know I had no part in this."

Ajay felt his lower lip tremble and part of him felt as if he could wail with desperation. Instead, he pleaded with his friend. He scrambled after him once more. "Please Ace, I just needed . . . I need . . . people to say I'm Worthy. I've worked for it. I deserve it. Please," Ajay said as he lifted his hands up.

"Look, Ajay . . . Karle . . . urgh, whatever or whoever you are. The point is, you're not Worthy. You're a wannabe, a waste of space that two Light-believing lowlifes puked up on the Side. You don't belong here. You broke the law. I have to report you, I can't lose the merit. It's everything. I'm sorry, I have to." He walked determinedly towards the door without as much as a second glance, but Ajay, now on the surface feeling only anger, stopped him. He jumped ferociously, grabbed Ace around his middle and shoved him backwards back into the apartment. Ace stumbled and was steadied by the rim of the breakfast bar. Ajay spread out his body across the doorway. "I can't let you go. Please just listen, we can figure . . . "

"You're mad. Just get out of my way." Ace stepped forward towards the door and gripped hard onto Ajay's wrists to force his arms away. Ajay squeezed and pushed with everything he had against the doorframe to keep his arms stable, but eventually Ace's strength caused them to buckle. As his arms fell, he swung his left fist to punch Ace hard in the stomach, who let out a yelp in pain and bent over. Ajay stepped back to shield the doorway again. Ace pulled himself up using a breakfast stool.

Ace had even more fury building in his eyes, puffing out his nose as he breathed heavy. He began to resemble a hungry lion ready to pounce.

Ajay held up his hands. "Ace, just listen to me."

His pleading was cut short – Ace moved too quickly and settled a solid punch across the top of Ajay's nose. A ringing began in his ears and a throbbing descended into his head, but his feet stood firm in front of the door. He could taste the iron in his blood as it ran from his nose into his mouth. Ace was pulling him up again; another punch settled across his face. Ajay yelled. He felt Ace get him up again, but this time he dodged the punch and threw one of his own, hitting Ace above his right eye. Ajay grabbed him by the waist and sprinted towards the sofa, throwing them both onto it. Fists started to fly, and blood merged in splatters across the leather.

Ajay knew how ludicrous the situation was; he couldn't fight his fate, Ace was right to report him but he just needed to hang on, he needed him to listen. They could beat the system together.

As the combat continued, Ajay knew he needed Ace to be still. He flung his arms above him to block Ace's hits and bashes, who had clambered on top of him. Just as Ace threw another punch into Ajay's stomach, Ajay spotted the *SkipSleep* port sitting on the coffee table beside them. He had an idea. Ajay took a deep breath and used all his remaining strength; he managed to pull Ace off him and grab his left arm. In a smooth, premeditated, almost impossible motion, he swiped the port with Ace's Watch. Still grabbing tightly onto Ace's arm, who was struggling and moaning for him to get off, the two of them saw the port come up from the table.

"Ajay, what the . . ." Ace was shouting and whining, and Ajay just managed to step on Ace's ankle to stop him moving. He pressed hard to push Ace's arm down into the port.

"STOP IT!" Ace moaned into the air as Ajay succeeded. Ace's arm was in place and the metal straps fastened it down. The moderation scan appeared on the port's small transparent screen. It was soon completed, instructing the needle to spring to life and lower itself towards Ace's skin.

Ajay knew he had about two minutes to convince his friend to save his Worthiness, and he hadn't even considered the spike in energy that Ace would be gifted with after those two minutes were up. He needed to talk quickly and clearly. "AJAY, WHAT ARE YOU . . ." Ace was screaming so hard that his voice cracked. The needle was in, and Ajay watched the progress bar creep up.

"Just listen," Ajay had his hands out wide, moving them in a calming motion. "We can find a way that you are protected, I promise I can find . . ." But Ace wouldn't listen. He began repeatedly shouting profanities and singing in screeches to block out any pleading or explaining Ajay was attempting to do. The heat was bubbling faster and harder inside Ajay's volcanic body cells; he could feel his face reddening and his knuckles clenching. The balls of his feet were pressing hard enough into the ground so that his heels lifted a few inches. As Ace's screeching and shouting continued, Ajay erupted.

"JUST LISTEN!" Ajay roared, as he pulled back his right arm and threw it forward. The noise of the hit to Ace's face resembled that of a hard clap that would leave hands stinging; Ajay felt the bones of his knuckles crack and disperse underneath his skin. The bruising and discomfort of his hand quickly became the least of his concerns. He hit Ace with such momentous force that Ace's body moved violently. He crashed sideways beside the coffee table, pulling his arm and the needle in the same direction. It sliced the skin of Ace's wrist and ricocheted through both his radial and ulnar arteries. Blood squirted furiously and extravagantly across the coffee table, the sofa and onto Ajay's chest.

Ace squalled in pain as he tried to reach for his arm, still held under the straps. His eyes were wide, thunderstruck by the volumes of blood that were flowing from his body. Ace's expression mirrored Ajay's, who felt as if it were all happening in slow motion; he was witness to how uncontrollably Ace was squirming and how lawlessly the blood was spraying. Dizziness began to fall over him as if his own blood was loose to the atmosphere, but after only a few seconds, he flew into motion. He dashed to the kitchen and found a white tea towel from the cupboard. Ajay sprinted back to Ace, who was screaming for help; he hit the cancel button and freed Ace's arm whilst ignoring the erratic beeping sounds coming from both their Watches, informing of dangerous heart rates, blood loss and blood pressure. The medical service would be informed about Ace, but there was no time to try and reverse it.

"It's alright mate," Ajay said feebly to comfort Ace, whose body was beginning to flop. Ajay applied direct and hard pressure to the gash on Ace's arm and launched it into the air for elevation.

"Why . . . didn't you . . . just let me go?" Ace mumbled quietly, as his eyelids drooped.

"I . . . I . . . I'm sorry. I didn't mean . . ." Ajay was speechless, unable to contemplate what he'd done. He cried liberally through a gush of tears and his body was shaking outrageously. He glanced down to see that stains of blood were stark against his pure white t-shirt, and the olive skin of his arms and hands was bright red. He watched his friend's eyes droop quicker and lower and he distressingly begged for him to stay awake. Ajay wailed out into the apartment, still elevating Ace's arm, applying as much pressure as he was physically able. The moment lingered still; Ajay pressed hard and Ace's eyes closed.

Chapter Fifty

Ajay couldn't feel. *This isn't real.* The words were pounding in his head. *This isn't real.*

This.

Isn't.

Real.

Ace's eyes were not motionless. His lips were not parted, with his tongue rolling back into his throat. His shaven skull and face were not covered with blood like raindrops splattered over a window. Because none of it was real.

Any second Ace's eyes would blink into life and he'd ridicule Ajay for a nasty coloured tie or his pathetic excuse for biceps. They would laugh until they thought they might vomit, or until others around them felt jealous over their companionship. Because it was special. It was real, but what was happening wasn't.

Ajay's hands were not resembling red latex gloves. His arms and legs were not burdened with the weight of Ace's unmoving body. It wasn't real. Nothing about it felt real. He looked around his messy, M-420 apartment and everything felt distorted. The coffee table and destroyed *SkipSleep* port looked smaller and far away, but he knew he and Ace were sitting right by them. His ears were blocked, and his eyes stared forward, but it was like he couldn't move them. Move anything. Like he couldn't even cry, speak, or scream. Everything he wanted to do. The shock of the moment had locked his body in a glass cage, and his brain was the only thing trying to get out. Everything else was numb. Because it was all real. He'd just killed his best friend.

His best friend lay dead in his arms. Eyes staring up, lifeless, to the high-rise ceiling. Ajay felt himself breathe again, and control seemed to return to his arms. He took his left hand and stroked it slowly across Ace's cheek. A tear fell down his own face and dropped onto his friend's. What had he done? He wanted to wail out into the apartment but speaking still felt impossible. It meant that Ajay had seen three dead bodies: Theo, Jun, and Ace. Theo had been peaceful, Jun had been scared, but Ace was unreadable. Ajay couldn't imagine from his eyes what Ace had been thinking in those last moments minutes beforehand. Was it fear? Sadness? That this would get Ajay behind bars for sure? Ajay didn't even know why it mattered, other than he wanted to know how Ace felt about him when he died. He stopped himself because he knew it wouldn't be the answer he wanted. Nothing about the last few hours would have convinced Ace to sing his praises.

Ajay looked again into Ace's eyes, their brown beauty and charming sparkle fading away. He considered his question. Why didn't he wait? Ajay knew he would have breezed through Purification in his sleep. But he did not want to wait, it didn't feel fair. Merit was as much his right as anyone's. That had always been his belief. His clarity of the situation blurred further with the tears in his eyes. There must be a way to take it back. To rewind the time. To take back his punch and the needle out from Ace's arm.

Ajay felt toxic to himself, disgusted at the thought of what he'd done. Or was it at who he was? He didn't know, not understanding how he'd lost complete control. How was he ever going to explain this? Genni would leave. There was no going back to Grandma. Two people he'd perhaps never really appreciated like he should have. Ajay casted a brief look at his desk, musing over the picture of Tara beneath it, which brought a worrying notion to him. The thought passed momentarily as he was distracted by his heart wrenching reality.

He heard it. The sound that had been there all the time. A long, high-pitched beep from Ace's wrist, confirming his lack of heartbeat. It had been muted to Ajay before, but it became loud and clear. He thought about the coming knock or barge through the door by the medical service. They would find Ajay there, with the dead man in his arms, guilty as the sun is white. Should he escape? His arms felt limp, no energy left to survive.

Ajay, deadpan, had not stopped looking at Ace, whose eyes were even darker. He was gone. He had been for a while. Ajay was just holding onto that small speckle of life he thought he saw in his eyes. When that was gone, he fully gave in. Ajay fell forwards onto Ace's body, shaking uncontrollably, wailing out loud until his mouth couldn't make sound anymore. His irregular jumps of breath made him feel like his heart might give out. The tears streamed, wetting Ace's t-shirt and merging with his blood.

"I'm sorry..." Ajay caught his breath. "Sorry... I'm..." He sniffed to catch the excrement from his nose. "So... sorry."

In his self-loathing, he held on to his friend and glanced at the Watch around his skinny wrist. His brilliant, technical mind gave him another problem to solve. Collecting crowns of Worthiness had been everything to him. He questioned: was it ever worth it?

END OF BOOK ONE

Ajay's journey has just begun.

The Rogue will emerge from the shadows.

And Genni has more battles to face.

Get ready to re-immerse yourself in the world of Merit-Hunters as the story continues.

Find out more by joining my mailing list - lgjenkins.com/join

Acknowledgements

There are many people in my life who have influenced the contents and writing of this book.

To those all-important proof-readers who took the time to take me seriously: thank you to Ben, and a special thank you to Anika who dedicated many hours to encouraging and challenging me. Also, a shout out to Julian for his technical brain. To all my immediate family and friends who have always been there; a special mention to John and Pauline for being great parents and for always encouraging me.

And to Stephen, my chilled-out, patient, loving and all-around brilliant husband. You have been the real instigator behind this book all along, and without you and God's guidance, I'm not sure I would have persevered. You inspire me every day.

Finally, and above all, thank you to God my Father. This book was never my idea.

'I praise you, for I am fearfully and wonderfully made.
Wonderful are your works; my soul knows it very well.'

Psalm 139:14

'I have been crucified with Christ. It is no longer I who live, but Christ who lives in me. And the life I now live in the flesh I live by faith in the Son of God, who loved me and gave himself for me.'

Galatians 2:20